RUNNING DARK

ALSO BY JAMIE FREVELETTI

Running from the Devil

Jamie Freveletti

RUNNING DARK

W I L L I A M   M O R R O W

An Imprint of HarperCollins*Publishers*

RUNNING DARK. Copyright © 2010 by Jamie Freveletti LLC. All rights reserved. Printed in the United States of America. No part of this book may be used or reproduced in any manner whatsoever without written permission except in the case of brief quotations embodied in critical articles and reviews. For information address HarperCollins Publishers, 10 East 53rd Street, New York, NY 10022.

HarperCollins books may be purchased for educational, business, or sales promotional use. For information please write: Special Markets Department, HarperCollins Publishers, 10 East 53rd Street, New York, NY 10022.

FIRST EDITION

Designed by

Library of Congress Cataloging-in-Publication Data

Freveletti, Jamie.
   Running dark / Jamie Freveletti.—1st ed.
      p.   cm.
   ISBN 978-0-06-168424-1
1. Women biochemists—Fiction.   2. Pirates—Fiction.   I. Title.
   PS3606.R486R84 2010
   813'.6—dc22

2009042579

10 11 12 13 14   OV/RRD   10 9 8 7 6 5 4 3 2 1

For my father,
who says if you're going to dream, dream big.
With love, J

ACKNOWLEDGMENTS

I'd like to thank the readers, whose enthusiasm and friendly e-mails made my debut launch special, and who continue to cheer me throughout the year.

Many thanks to Tavia Kowalchuk, Danielle Bartlett, Shawn Nicholls, Marisa Benedetto, Wendy Lee, and the entire HarperCollins and William Morrow staff, who helped me time and time again during the launch of the first novel and who made a debut author feel great.

I'm indebted to my editor, Lyssa Keusch, who made suggestions that were right on target and remained patient when I went on a tear and revised an entire section. Her keen eye for detail is greatly appreciated.

Barbara Poelle, my literary agent, trusted adviser, and good friend, keeps me balanced and makes me laugh. Working with her is always a joy.

Quite a bit of research went into this novel, and I'm grateful to Paul Salopek, Commodore Ronald Warwick, Samuel Warwick, and Dr. Jennifer E. Purcell, whose contributions are more fully explained in the author's note at the end.

I was unbelievably lucky to receive the support of two of the most talented authors in the writing world. My heartfelt thanks go out to Tess Gerritsen, who went above and beyond the call by not only giving the first novel a blurb, but taking steps to see that it made it to HarperCollins at just the right time, and to Lee Child, who also donated his name to the cause and who continues to answer all my industry questions with good humor and an insight that I find invaluable.

Dana Kaye, friend and now principal of Kaye Publicity, assisted me with local publicity and the myriad of day-to-day details that go into a book launch. I couldn't have kept it all straight without her.

Darwyn Jones is a trusted reader who I can always count on to give me excellent feedback. My thanks to him for his reactions and suggestions on a key scene.

And, finally, to my husband, Klaus, who worked his own business travel schedule around mine. At one point during the tour my flight was late arriving and his was late leaving, and I'll never forget his smile when we bumped into each other at the airport terminal. He suggested lunch, and dining at O'Hare has never been better. Thanks, my love, for the fun.

RUNNING DARK

1

EMMA CALDRIDGE PASSED MILE THIRTY-SIX OF THE FIFTY-FIVE-mile Comrades ultramarathon in South Africa when a roadside car bomb exploded. The force of the explosion blew her out of her shoes and catapulted her into the air ten feet before hammering her into the dirt at the side of the road. The detonated car burned, flames leaping out of the shattered windows. She lay in the clay-colored dust with the hot sun beating down, blinding her. She moaned, turned her head away from the sun's glare, closed her eyes, and lay still, trying to gather her wits about her. A shadow fell over her face. She opened her eyes without moving her head and saw the blurry image of a man's legs from the knees down. The limbs appeared to shimmer in the heat waves thrown by the burning vehicle. He wore running shoes, like everyone else that day. The shoes stopped next to her and rose to their toes as the person crouched down. A silver necklace in the shape of an antelope head swung into her line of vision. The amulet hung on a black rawhide cord. Emma tried to ask for help, but her dry mouth wouldn't form the words.

The man's dark hand came into view, holding a white plastic injector, similar to an EpiPen carried by people with allergies. In the next instant, the hand jammed the tip into Emma's forearm, right above the wrist. She felt the prick of a needle and the rush of medication pulsing into her skin. Before she even had a chance to make a sound, he jerked the point out of her arm. The shoes flattened onto the dust and walked away with a crunching noise.

2

KHALIL IBRAHIM MUNGABE'S NICKNAME WAS "THE BONE PICKER,"
because he began his career stealing the leftover shreds of offal found
on the commercial fishing boats that trawled the seas off the coast of
Somalia. It was said that Mungabe liked nothing and no one, but that
wasn't exactly true. He tolerated his wives well enough, and his children occasionally did something to make him laugh, even if he didn't
know their names and so could not praise them. He called them "that
one" or "this one" and left it there.

He sat in Dubai and shivered in the snow. Dubai's temperature
that day was a blistering thirty degrees Celsius and rising higher,
but inside the mall where he sat, it was snowing fake snow. Mungabe
thought the affectation ridiculous. To him it just highlighted how the
Saudis had bowed their heads to the European oppressors. He sat in
the food court and waited for his contact, fingering the silver ring he
wore in the shape of an antelope head as he did.

Mungabe's power was on the verge of exploding, and he was taking the next logical step to ensure his future in this life and beyond.
The man he was to meet had the power to bridge Mungabe's world
and the European world, and Mungabe planned on exploiting him
and then killing him, in that order.

The man strolled up, tall and thin, like Mungabe himself, but
wearing an expensive suit purchased in London. He had the hard,
pointed face that Mungabe thought was the mark of a European. The
man's nickname was "the Vulture," because he'd risen to power by

driving his rivals into crisis through any means necessary. When the distressed companies began selling their assets one by one in their frantic attempts to save their floundering businesses, the Vulture would swoop down to snatch up the bones.

The Vulture took a seat across from Mungabe, looking unaffected by the freezing air, which Mungabe thought might be real rather than false bravado. Likely he was far more accustomed to such temperatures than Mungabe.

"How do you like the snow? I thought you'd want to experience it," the Vulture said.

Mungabe clamped his teeth together to stop their clattering. He hated the snow, and he suspected that the Vulture knew it. It was all calculated to put him at a disadvantage. Mungabe couldn't wait to complete their joint mission and then finish the man off. He'd do it in Somalia and leave his carcass in the sun to rot. Wonder how he'd feel then? Mungabe thought. He shifted in his seat and got right down to business.

"Tell me what you require. I haven't much time. My ship leaves from the port today. Did my associate in South Africa perform well for you?"

The Vulture raised an eyebrow. "You look cold. Perhaps we take a seat in the restaurant." The Vulture smiled a fake smile and waved Mungabe to the nearby bistro. Once inside, the Vulture crossed his legs and leaned back in the wooden chair. A waiter came by to hand them two menus. Mungabe took one and was somewhat relieved to see pictures next to the names of the dishes offered, which made ordering much easier. The Vulture waited for the server to leave before continuing.

"Your associate worked fine. But I have another request of you. There's a large ship off the coast of Somalia that I want you to intercept."

Mungabe's ears perked up. He excelled at stealing ships. He commanded a large crew of Somali pirates, and in the last years his enterprise had grown exponentially. He'd expanded his fleet and just this quarter had purchased night-vision goggles, GPS radar-scanning equipment, and new weaponry. All so his pirates could troll farther out and net bigger fish. As a result of his investment, he was having an outstanding year so far. He'd taken fifty ships to date, with eight hundred hostages, usually crewmen, and netted $20 million in ransoms paid. His spectacular successes included an oil tanker worth $90 million and two commercial tuna-fishing boats worth $20 million each. One of the boats was currently docked in the village of Eyl, where it was slowly sinking into the ocean as the result of a hole shot in the hull by one of his crew. He often warned them to shoot above the waterline so that the boat, once boarded, could be piloted back to shore for salvaging, but that particular ship had put up a fight, and the only way to take it was to disable it and kill everyone on board.

Now, however, several freighters had hired Darkview, an American security company, to protect their ships that used the Gulf of Aden trade route. In the last two months, Darkview personnel had managed to sink four of Mungabe's boats. In one incident the security company continued to chase his crew two hundred miles, not even stopping when they came within Somali territorial waters, as they were supposed to do. Darkview had captured the pirates and dragged them into Hargeisa to be tried. Mungabe had paid a princely sum to ensure their acquittal—it would not do to have any of his men sit in prison. Prison tested a man's loyalties, and Mungabe wanted no one to turn traitor on him. It was during the trial that he'd decided to launch his own offensive against the company that plagued him so.

"What type of ship do you want me to steal?" Mungabe said.

The waiter was back to take their order. Mungabe pointed to a fish dish, while the Vulture ordered in French. When the waiter left, the Vulture leaned in to him.

"A cruise ship. The finest in the world. It embarked on its virgin cruise from Dubai to Victoria in the Seychelles Islands a few days ago."

Mungabe settled back in his chair while he thought about what the Vulture had said. He didn't read papers, didn't care about world news, and had little interest in the politics of the West, but even he could see that taking the finest ship in the world would reflect well on him. Still, he frowned.

"The cruise lines don't come near Somali waters. Victoria is two thousand kilometers away. Too far. We've only taken ships at six hundred."

The Vulture raised an eyebrow. "Are you saying you can't do it?"

Mungabe felt a flash of anger. He could do anything. "I can, but for a very large price. What will you pay?"

The Vulture shook his head. "I pay nothing. You do this for the ship and its hostages; your usual take."

Mungabe laughed. This Vulture was joking. "I don't need a cruise ship. I need a fishing ship! They are at least useful after. What do you think my crews do when they are not pirating, huh? They fish. They use the hijacked commercial boats to do it. They do it for Somalia. Without my assistance Somalia's waters would be emptied by the rest of the world. They sneak into our territorial boundaries where the tuna lives, steal our fish by the tons, and leave nothing for us. We stop this plundering by the rich and give to the poor."

The Vulture smirked. "Spare me the Robin Hood story. You don't give anything to the poor. You keep it all for yourself."

Mungabe shook his head. "Still, I don't do this for the boat. You must pay."

The Vulture shifted. "I will pay you then, but in that case it is understood that I get both the ship and its cargo."

"Cargo? What cargo?"

The Vulture shrugged. "Pharmaceutical products. Not important for you, but I would like to have them."

The waiter returned with their meals. As he lowered the Vulture's in front of him, Mungabe thought he would retch. On the plate was a large lobster; its black legs, hard carapace, and beady eyes were revolting, as was the heavy, oily odor of the drawn butter that sat in a cup next to it. The sight and smell of it repelled Mungabe. Like most Somalis, he would never eat a lobster, which he considered the equivalent of a sea cockroach. It was a bottom feeder, eating the fecal remains of the rest of the ocean's creatures.

The Vulture sliced the beast in half with one deft cut from a long, wicked-looking knife. He twisted off a leg, put it to his lips, and sucked on it. He did all of this while gazing at Mungabe. Mungabe feared no man, but in that minute he wondered if he was dealing with a demon. He shook off the thought.

"I want two million dollars, *and,* as I told you last month, I want the American security company called Darkview put out of business. For that price I will hijack the ship. You get the carcass and cargo. I get any money on board and its passengers to ransom as I see fit."

"One million. No more. Plus, you pay all expenses."

"And Darkview?"

The Vulture waved a languid hand in the air. "It is already begun."

3

CAMERON SUMNER STOOD NEXT TO A LOUNGE CHAIR ON THE deck of the *Kaiser Franz* cruise liner and stared at the horizon, waiting. The chair was one in a long row of chairs, all occupied by passengers clad in swimsuits, baking in the sun. The woman to Sumner's right, noticing his preoccupation with the horizon, did her best to capture his attention.

"I see you watch the ocean every day after your workout. It's beautiful, isn't it?" the woman, an American, said. Sumner eyed her. She wore a string bikini on a figure with full hips, fake breasts, and striking, artfully streaked hair. Her lips were painted a bright coral, and her forehead didn't move when she spoke. Her husband, a good ol' boy from Texas who owned a string of car dealerships, spent his days in the ship's casino drinking gin and playing blackjack. His wife spent her days watching Sumner swim laps in the pool or run on the track. The woman's question marked the first time she'd worked up enough nerve to speak to him.

"It is beautiful," he said. He grabbed a towel and dried his dripping body, while the American woman looked at him with bright, avid eyes.

"So what brings you on a cruise ship alone?"

"I work for the company that owns the *Kaiser Franz*." Sumner kept his answers short to discourage more conversation.

"How *interesting*." The woman breathed the words.

Sumner did his best to contain his annoyance. His patience ran thin these days. He slipped on a pair of track pants, sank into a nearby lounge chair, and thought about Caldridge. He'd been having dreams of her, some so vivid that he thought he might be able to touch her, some so frightening that when he would reach her after a slow-motion chase, he would find himself to be too late and his anguish at her death would overwhelm him. He pulled up a mental picture of her: light brown hair a little past her shoulders, green eyes, a straight nose with no upturn, and a lithe, athletic runner's body. He sighed and kept his eyes on the water.

The ship's sundeck ran the width of the foredeck. In the center was the rectangular lap pool. Lounge chairs, each with a bright blue cushion, filled the rest of the available space. A small walkway ran along the railings. Sumner spent much of his time on the sundeck, because it allowed him to view both sides of the vessel.

The ship itself was smaller, more intimate, and much more luxurious than the larger cruise liners out of Miami. It boasted mahogany-paneled staterooms with flat-screen televisions, marble bathrooms, and thick Persian carpets. Each room had a private butler assigned to it. They'd embarked from Dubai, passed through the Arabian Sea, and were deep into the Indian Ocean on their way to the Seychelles Islands. It was ten in the morning. Only half the sundeck chairs were taken.

The woman shifted in her chair to lean toward him. Her blond, highlighted hair and overly manicured nails were the antithesis of what Sumner liked in a woman. He said nothing as he finished drying off. He grabbed a pair of Ray-Ban sunglasses and stretched out on the lounge chair, basking in the sun while he continued to keep watch.

"Are you working on this trip?" The woman interrupted his reverie. It was all Sumner could do not to sigh out loud.

"I'm headed to the Seychelles to check on our land-based operations."

"How *interesting*," the woman said again.

Sumner continued to scan the area, his eyes hidden behind his sunglasses. The ocean swelled in calm, regular waves. A waiter worked his way through the lounge chairs, handing out complimentary juices to the sunbathers. Another employee followed, offering a spritz of mineral water to cool them.

The German family walked along the deck rail toward Sumner. He felt a prickle of awareness shoot down his spine. Sumner worked for the Southern Hemisphere Drug Defense Agency and had been hired out to the *Kaiser Franz* in response to a vague piece of intelligence suggesting that trouble sailed with the ship. The trouble was thought to be drug-related, but nothing in the communiqué detailed the precise nature of the problem. An assignment off the coast of Africa carried the added benefit of getting Sumner as far away from the Southern Hemisphere as possible. His last assignment had disrupted a major drug cartel in Colombia, and his employers feared retaliation.

Sumner reviewed the ship's manifest and had settled on three potential groups of passengers as the ones he would watch: a Russian traveling with his mistress, a Frenchman traveling with two other businessmen, and this German family—two parents with their grown daughter. The father, a businessman in his late fifties, had the build of a steelworker. His large stomach hung over his expensive pants, throwing a shadow across his black loafers. His face bore the bright red hue of a man whose skin was unaccustomed to the outdoors. He held the *Frankfurter Allgemeine* newspaper in his hands and looked surly.

His wife, also somewhat north of fifty, was as thin as he was wide. Her blond hair—her natural color and none of it highlighted—ended at her ears in a blunt cut. Her blue eyes and cool, superior attitude telegraphed that she was from Hamburg, where blond hair and cool eyes abounded. Her manner telegraphed her dislike for her husband.

The daughter, a shy beauty with blond hair and a fresh, almost translucent complexion, was twenty-four. Six years younger than Sumner and light-years more innocent, she, too, would cast glances at him whenever their paths crossed, but she hadn't yet gotten up the courage to talk to him.

The father turned his head to gaze at the horizon. The woman next to Sumner was speaking again.

"Harry says we don't need to travel anywhere, that there's nothing to learn. But I think you should always see how the other half lives, don't you?"

Sumner refrained from commenting on the fact that she was unlikely to see "the other half" while sailing on the sea in a yacht with massive suites and private butlers, but he assumed the woman meant well. Before Sumner could respond, Harry himself walked up to his wife.

"Whatcha doin', sweetheart?" He boomed the question at his wife, towering over her in her lounge chair. He thrust his hand out at Sumner.

"Harry Block. Pleased to meet you."

"Cameron Sumner."

Sumner rose to shake Block's hand. Based on his own six-foot-two-inch height and weight of 175, Sumner estimated that Block stood a full two inches taller and weighed an easy 300 pounds. He was built like a linebacker, with a doughy face, hair just starting to gray at the temples, and shrewd eyes, despite his easygoing exterior. Sumner watched Block size him up.

"No need to stand. Didn't mean to bother you." Block shook Sumner's hand in a vise grip.

Sumner squeezed back. Block's wife sat up.

"This is Harry, my husband, and I'm Cindy. Harry, hon, he works for *Kaiser Franz*."

"You a cabin boy?" Block hollered at Sumner.

"Harry!" Cindy hit Block on the arm.

"What's wrong with that? It's honest enough work, ain't it?" Block turned innocent eyes on Sumner. Sumner hid his amusement.

"I'm not a cabin boy, no," he said.

The German family was upon them, walking along the rail. Sumner felt the father's presence at his right, then behind him. He heard the wife speak to the daughter in German. Since Sumner spoke fluent German, eavesdropping came easy.

"Americans are so loud," she said. Sumner kept his eyes on Block while he strained to hear the German girl's response.

"But friendly, I think, Mother." She spoke in low tones.

Don't be fooled by Harry, Sumner thought.

The father stepped past him. Out of the corner of his eye, Sumner could see that he continued to stare at the ocean. Sumner redirected his attention to Block, who was speaking.

"What's the point of all this 'cultural differences' mumbo jumbo? Folks from Africa to Mexico count their money the same as us, is what I say. So what do you do for *Kaiser Franz*?"

Sumner glanced back at the water. He saw the dot speeding toward them. He felt a surge of adrenaline that made his scalp tighten and his fingertips tingle.

He slipped a black T-shirt over his head. The dot grew larger every second. Soon it was joined by another. Sumner heard the distant roar of the cigarette boats' engines. The craft hurtled toward them at an impressive speed.

"Block, get Cindy and the others off the deck. Tell the waiters to move everyone below."

Block looked shocked. "What?"

"Mr. Block, do it. Now."

"Well, I never been ordered around like that," Block said.

Sumner didn't stay to see if Block obeyed. He sprinted across the deck to the stairs that led to the bridge, clambered up them, and burst onto the small walkway that surrounded it just as Captain Joshua Wainwright stepped out.

"Pirates," he said.

Sumner nodded. "Coming fast. Use the LRAD."

Wainwright, a competent, friendly man in his early forties, snapped an order to his second-in-command. They pointed a large gun in the direction of the cigarette boats, now well within a mile of them.

"Hit it," Wainwright said.

The Long Range Acoustic Device released a beam of high-pitched sound at the boats. Over 150 decibels of concentrated noise blasted through the air, like a sonic boom. Sumner winced as the sound assaulted his eardrums. He saw the driver of the lead cigarette boat clap a hand over one ear.

They continued to hurtle toward the *Kaiser Franz*.

"Again," Wainwright said. He watched the cigarette boats through binoculars.

The LRAD blared again. When the sound faded, Sumner could hear the tourists screaming on the deck. Still the cigarette boats kept coming. Sumner grabbed a second set of binoculars. The pirates looked like Somalis, dark-skinned and thin. They stared at the cruise ship with undisguised greed in their eyes. He watched one of them hoist a large gun to his shoulder.

"They've got RPGs," he said.

"What the hell is that?" Harry Block's loud voice echoed on the bridge.

"Sir, you don't belong here. Please get belowdecks." Wainwright waved at an underling, who stepped up next to Block.

Block shook off the crew member's grip on his arm like a horse shaking off a fly. "I said, what the hell are RPGs?"

Sumner lowered the binoculars to glance at Block. "Rocket-propelled grenades."

"Holy shit," Block said.

EMMA SAT UP. A HEAVY CLOUD OF ASH HUNG IN THE AIR, BLOT-
ting out the sun. She flinched as people hurtled past her going in
every direction, some coming so close that she put her arms up to
protect herself. Sirens howled far in the distance. Downed runners
lay all around her. Three behind her were moving, though they remained on the ground. Several others staggered to their feet. One
man drew a deep breath, inhaled the lingering ash, and began a violent coughing fit.

She took stock. Her back from neck to tailbone ached where she'd
landed in the dirt, her arms, previously wet from sweating, were
caked in dust that clung to the moisture, and an eighteen-inch scrape
of road rash covered her right leg and throbbed. She glanced at her
feet and was surprised to see only filthy socks. At mile thirty her feet
had ballooned in response to both the extreme heat and the long,
pounding distance, and she'd retied her running shoes loosely in order to accommodate the swelling. At mile thirty-three, even the loose
shoestrings had hurt, and she'd opened the laces as far as she could
without losing the shoes entirely.

She sat in the dirt on the side of the path, twenty feet from the
asphalt. The blackened hull of the vehicle smoldered while a small
group of onlookers huddled fifty feet away, watching.

Emma felt her skin begin to crawl. Whatever medication the man
had pumped into her was taking effect. She took a quick glance at
the trail. The competitors flowed off the road and onto the shoulder

to avoid getting anywhere near the burning car, then reentered and continued forward, using their feet to put distance between them and the site of the carnage. More than twelve thousand runners attempted the Comrades each year, a grueling eighty-nine-kilometer race between Durban and Pietermaritzburg. One had to qualify for the Comrades. Many competitors had successfully completed races like Hawaii's Ironman and so were made of tough stuff. It was a "gun to gun" race, meaning that the competitors were required to complete the distance within eleven hours or be disqualified. When the clock struck twelve, the race was over. The bulk of the competitors passed the finish line between hours ten and eleven. Emma's qualifying time put her in one of the fastest groups, a good thing in this instance, because the ten/eleven athletes hadn't yet come this far. The bomb could have hit many more.

Now these experienced ultra runners took one look at the gaping crater twenty feet from the course and broke into a sprint, running away as fast as their trained legs could take them. There was no stopping the herd without creating an even more dangerous situation, and the few handlers that worked the course at this mile marker didn't even try. They watched helplessly as the athletes stampeded past them.

Emma's heart began to gallop, and a strange euphoria overwhelmed her. Jumbled thoughts ping-ponged through her head, ranging from crazy paranoia to calm scientific logic. Her mind screamed, Go, go! Run away! Then, Oh, God, what the hell did he inject into you? and next, Get to your hotel room and close the door—they're coming! Somewhere in it all was another thought, born from her chemist's experience, that calmly informed her, If it's a chemical weapon, there's nothing the hospital can do for you now. What sent her fear spiking was the sound of a helicopter, coming closer. Her mind flashed onto a scene from her ordeal in Colombia just a few months before. Panic gripped her.

Before she knew what she was about, she stood up and looked for her shoes.

She squinted in the sun, putting her hand to her eyes to stop the glare. The smell of burning rubber filled the air, and bits of ash blew in circular eddies, brushing across the dry, packed earth. She skirted the burning vehicle and spotted her shoes fifteen feet behind her on the side of the course. She sat down to put them on, but before she did, she took a look at her feet. They were far less enlarged. In fact, they were back to their normal, pre-race size. The effect was almost like a cartoon, where a balloon deflates with comic speed. This, the panic, and the otherworldly high told her that the medication was making a circuit through her body. She put the shoes back on with shaking hands, retied them tighter than before, reentered the path at the location where she'd been ejected, and started once again to run.

Her feet felt feather light, her heart continued to pound, but her breathing settled into a rhythm that she usually achieved at the start of a race, not at the finish. Her legs flew with renewed energy fed by a jagged anxiety. Emergency vehicles coming from the opposite direction screamed past her, not using the road where the racers were but driving in the dirt culvert on the side, kicking up clouds of dust as they did. She swept past runner after runner, catapulting herself down the path. Her head ached with the precursor of a headache, but the pain was nothing compared to the exhilaration she felt since being stuck with the pen. She moved faster and faster, reaching per-mile speeds that were a personal best for her this late in the game, yet still she felt no real strain from the blistering pace.

She blew past the other competitors, all of whom were showing the extreme fatigue that was common in the last few miles of an ultra and for some was magnified by the pace they drove themselves to maintain since coming upon the burning vehicle. Some stopped to throw up on the shoulder of the road as their stomachs rejected the combination of runner's gel and liquids that constituted the whole of their sustenance, while others subsided to a dejected walk, their bodies curving from the waist up like a question mark, the result of their muscles' weakening strength. Some fell on the side of the path and lay there, taking shallow breaths. For them the race was over. This was what the Comrades could do to a runner.

Half an hour later, Emma still ran at breakneck speeds. Several police vans drove up next to the course, heading in the same direction as the runners. One pulled parallel to Emma, and she watched as a race official leaned out of the back window. He placed a bullhorn to his lips.

"Keep going straight! Do not deviate from the path for any reason. Avoid all cars parked on the roadside. Emergency personnel are assembled at the finish, and fire-department crews are checking every vehicle for suspicious cargo. Any runners who wish to stop should step to the side and wait. A rescue bus has been dispatched that can drive you to a safe location."

I'll be damned if I'll stop, Emma thought. Rather than calming her, the sight of the officials elicited a paranoiac's reaction. Emma wanted to get away from the truck. It took all her willpower to stay on the course and allow it to pace her. She kicked up her speed, running faster.

Two and a half hours later, she crossed the finish line. Her legs still felt powerful, but the paranoia had decreased to manageable levels. Along with the receding terror came the return of rational thinking. Now a secondary type of fear gripped her, because she realized that she should have left the course two hours earlier and headed straight to a hospital for testing. The risk she'd taken in waiting was astronomical. Even so, she realized that whatever had been pumped into her was clearly not designed to kill her immediately. In fact, she had never felt stronger at the end of an ultra than she did at that moment.

Ambulances lined the corral set up to cordon off the finishers from spectators. Runners milled around, some shaking, others crying, and the rest standing in numb silence. Media trucks, their roofs covered with satellite dishes and bristling with antennas, were parked in a crazy-quilt fashion on the outside of the gated area. The reporters leaned over the temporary fence, holding their microphones aloft as they attempted to interview the runners. Paramedics worked on several people who had collapsed, from either the heat or fear, or both.

The Comrades maintained a fully functional mobile ICU manned by doctors and nurses and prepared to assist any runners who fell into distress during the competition. A quick glance told Emma that she would not get anywhere near it in the time she needed to. At least fifty stretchers containing downed runners lay in a widening circle around it, while triage nurses worked through the injured.

Emma handed her timing chip to the attendant waiting to accept them, veered away from the ICU, and headed to the tent erected by Price Pharmaceuticals, a client of hers and the entity charged with post-race drug testing. She walked with a grim determination. She needed to know what had been pumped into her, and she needed to know it fast. Who better to check for a performance-enhancing drug or an illegal substance than the drug testers themselves?

A young woman guarded the door to the VIP area. Emma flashed the red wristband that showed she was a Price-sponsored athlete and stepped inside. Tables set up at the back held large water bottles, bowls of fruit, bagels, and a caterer's carafe of coffee and tea. Nurses staffed a makeshift lab in the right corner. One, named Karen Stringer, spotted Emma. She closed her eyes briefly, as if in relief, and hurried over. Karen and Emma knew each other from the work that Emma's company, Pure Chemistry, did for Price. When she reached Emma, Karen threw her arms around her.

"Thank God you're all right! We've been wrecks around here since hearing the news of the bombing." Karen pulled away to take a look at Emma. Before she could speak, Emma interrupted her.

"I know. I'm a mess. I was near the car when it exploded." Emma displayed the road rash on her leg. "Compliments of flying into the dirt. Can I get it cleaned and a bandage? And if I give you a urine sample, can you test it for any banned substances? I need a drug test right away."

Karen frowned at her. "Actually, you look better than anyone I've seen so far, even the winners. You're not limping? I swear you're the only one. We've had a wave of injuries, heat prostration, and dehydration. And why in the world do you need a drug test? We only test the medalists."

Emma took a deep breath. "The bomb blew me off the path. While I lay there, a man walked up to me and injected me with something."

Karen's face took on a horrified expression. "Injected you? That's awful! Forget the drug testing, you need to go to ICU or the hospital right now."

"No! That won't work. People are lined up ten deep in front of the ICU, and the local hospital will take hours, probably even days, to obtain lab results—and that's assuming they even have the necessary equipment." Emma waved a hand at the nurses' station. "You can test me right here, use Rapidtest."

Rapidtest was an investigational new test that Price was developing, able to provide preliminary results in thirty minutes. It was not approved by any racing body as yet, but Emma thought it would give her some quick answers. "Whatever additional testing I need, I can handle at the Price offices."

Karen looked dubious. "Rapidtest can only test you for performance-enhancing drugs, not for anything life-threatening. You should talk to the police right away."

Emma nodded. "I know that, but whatever it was, it doesn't *seem* life-threatening. It sent me flying down the path and gave me an extremely paranoid reaction, but that seems to be all. Even so, I could be wrong. You'll be able to narrow it down a bit. At least tell me what it isn't, if not exactly what it is. Please, test me *now*."

Karen stared at her a moment, then handed her a sterile collection cup. "I'll have to draw blood as well. It's going to take me some time, and you shouldn't hang around here waiting. When you're done, give this to me and go straight to the police. Write your name and cell number on the label. I'll call you with the results."

Emma provided Karen with a sample before heading to the opposite corner of the tent, where the Price athletes kept their gear. She pulled out her cell phone and powered it up. Dialed the number she was told she could dial anytime, day or night.

"This is Banner. Leave a message." The beep came after.

"Mr. Banner, it's Emma Caldridge. I'm sorry to have to call you so soon after Colombia, but I need your help. Something strange is happening here."

She left her cell number, then hung up. As she walked out of the tent toward the van that would take her back to the hotel, she felt her head pound. That pain had remained constant, but a new pain was growing. The pain of knowing that someone was after her.

5

EDWARD BANNER, PRESIDENT AND CEO OF DARKVIEW, SAT AT a desk and faced a raised dais behind which sat three United States senators and seven congressmen. Banner's attorney sat on his right, taking notes on a legal pad. Banner's phone lay on the desk in front of him, switched to "silent." He saw an "unknown" number appear on his telephone screen and noted the 786 area code. He let it go to voice mail.

"Mr. Banner, can you tell this committee why you chose, unilaterally, to disobey direct orders from your superiors at the Department of Defense and assist Mr. Cameron Sumner and Major Miguel Gonzalez in their ill-advised and destructive actions in Colombia?"

The question came from the esteemed Senator George Cooley, a self-proclaimed devout man who prided himself on his conservative views but who kept a wife in a clapboard house in the South and a mistress in a condominium in D.C. The senator was doing the bidding of an oil conglomerate and a major contributor to his campaign. He was searching for a scapegoat in what he called the "shameful Colombian incident" and had decided that Banner would fill the role.

Banner's part in the rescue of the Colombian hostages had earned him the highest praise from the media and was the subject of endless magazine and newspaper articles. His military background, coupled with his impeccable credentials and exceptional good looks, had made him a minor celebrity and the crush of scores of women. His refusal to capitalize on the media feeding frenzy by declining all requests for interviews, photo shoots, or speaking engagements only served to boost his enigmatic image. Dressed in a dark blue suit, a muted gray silk tie, a crisp white shirt with French cuffs, and discreet silver cuff links, he managed to appear imposing, down-to-earth, and competent all at the same time. In contrast, the senator, a tall man with a thin, pinched face and avaricious eyes, looked like a particularly mean ferret. He knew better than to allow the meetings to be televised.

Banner considered the senator a blowhard, but his righteous claims that he "owed it to the American people to get to the bottom of the incident in Colombia" posed a threat to Darkview, something Banner took quite seriously. Banner also respected the office the man held, even if he didn't like the man. Therefore he answered in as pleasant a voice as he could muster.

"At no time did I or Darkview ignore the orders of a superior. Darkview was charged with the task of rescuing the passengers of Flight 689. The mission was still authorized when I flew to Colombia. Mr. Sumner and Major Gonzalez were coming to the aid of one of the passengers on the downed airplane, a woman named Emma Caldridge."

Senator Blowhard waved an impatient hand in the air. "We all know who these men were claiming to save, but at what cost?"

Banner nodded. "Whatever cost is claimed, it was justified. The rescue mission ended up crippling one of the biggest drug cartels in the world. A feat that I would expect this committee to applaud rather than condemn."

Senator Blowhard leaned forward. "You and your cohorts managed to destroy the largest oil pipeline in South America in the process. This committee has been assigned the job of determining whether the rescue mission could have been undertaken without such an extreme act of destruction." Blowhard peered at a notepad in front of him. "Now we understand that Mr. Sumner never returned to the United States. Is that correct?"

Banner nodded. His attorney leaned in to him.

"Edward, the court reporter can't take down nods. You need to reply out loud."

Banner glanced at the female court reporter tapping on the keys of her device. He smiled at her in apology. She flushed red. He turned back to the senator.

"Mr. Sumner is a member of the Southern Hemisphere Drug Defense Agency. After the mission they deemed it too dangerous for him to return to his duties in Key West until they were sure that the cartel leaders were not seeking retaliation. Darkview agreed to hire him on an ad hoc basis and place him far away from his usual territory."

"Where is he?" Blowhard said. The committee members all looked up from their notes.

"He's on a sensitive mission at an offshore location."

"Which one of you blew up the pipeline?"

Banner's attorney leaned in to Banner's microphone. "Mr. Banner, if you know, you can answer. However, I don't want you to speculate."

Banner waved the attorney off. "I don't know the answer to that." Banner watched Blowhard shuffle some papers.

"You are aware that Ms. Caldridge appeared before this committee one month ago? That she was cooperative and forthcoming?"

Banner nodded again. "Ms. Caldridge is one of the bravest women I know."

"Then you are aware that she claims to be the one who caused the pipeline to explode? That if this committee finds any wrongdoing, she expects to bear the fault alone?"

"I have complete confidence in Ms. Caldridge. If she destroyed the pipeline, then she had a damned good reason to, and little other choice."

Blowhard looked irritated. "I have an affidavit here from Cameron Sumner. He also claims to have been solely responsible for the destruction of the pipeline. Now, I ask you, Mr. Banner, why is this man lying?"

Banner's attorney spoke up. "I object. It's a complete assumption that Mr. Sumner is lying."

Everyone ignored the attorney.

Banner shrugged. "Maybe he's not. Maybe they both did it."

Senator Blowhard snorted. "That's not what Ms. Caldridge said. Can you tell me why Mr. Sumner would lie to this committee under oath?"

Banner's attorney made a small, angry noise. "Don't answer that. It would be speculation on your part."

Banner shrugged. "To protect Ms. Caldridge from this committee's wrath?"

"Why would he do that?"

"Don't answer that," Banner's attorney said, a little louder.

Banner raised an eyebrow at the senator. "You've seen Ms. Caldridge."

The room exploded in laughter. Senator Blowhard looked annoyed as hell. Banner put up a hand for quiet.

"The last hours in Colombia were some of the most dangerous in my career. We were all under siege, dodging sniper fire from several directions and grenades from above. Any one of these things could have caused the pipeline to blow. It is conceivable that both believe themselves responsible for the explosion."

Senator Blowhard leaned forward. "Could *you* be responsible for blowing up the pipeline?"

Banner hesitated. Leaving Emma Caldridge and Cameron Sumner to shoulder the blame for the pipeline went against his personal code of ethics. If he could help them, he would. The room fell silent. Senator Blowhard got a triumphant look on his face, as if he believed he'd maneuvered Banner into a corner.

"You're under oath, Mr. Banner."

Banner nodded. Lying under oath went against his personal ethics as well, not to mention that it was illegal. He'd tell the truth and find some other way to help them.

"I'm aware of that, Senator. And no, I could not be responsible for blowing up the pipeline." The senator's triumphant look deflated in an instant.

"Why not?" he said.

"Because when I appeared on the scene, the pipeline was already blown."

Sporadic clapping echoed in the room. Senator Blowhard looked supremely annoyed. He made a note on his pad, then shook his pen up and down, the way people do when they've run out of ink. The pen splattered all over his paper. The senator wiped the ink off his fingers with a tissue before announcing that testimony for the day was concluded. Banner walked out of the meeting with the distinct impression that the testimony for the day might have been over but the trouble brewing for Darkview was just beginning.

6

EMMA WOKE IN HER HOTEL AT EIGHT O'CLOCK IN THE EVENING, disoriented. After a minute the horrible details came back to her. The bombing, the injection. She ran through her mind what the EpiPen could have contained: anthrax, ricin, botulinum toxin, HIV. All were deadly, none contagious. She sat up. Although the abrupt movement caused stars to dance in her eyes, she felt otherwise completely normal. Her stomach growled, but her head no longer pounded. The cell phone next to her bed rang, the persistent beeping getting louder the more she ignored it. She answered it to find Karen on the line.

"I finished your sample. We were unable to find anything untoward or illegal. You tested clean."

Emma hadn't expected a negative test. Whatever was pumped into her had increased her athletic ability tenfold. There was no way she could have run as fast as she did and still felt as good as she had without some sort of chemical boost.

"That's not possible. No trace of steroids? EPO for blood doping?"

"Nothing. If you had won this race, no one would know you'd been on medication. Just how much of a boost did this injection give you?"

"A huge one. I ran the last two hours faster than I've ever run. I reduced my split time by thirty minutes, and that's *after* mile thirty-five."

"And you have no other symptoms?" Karen asked.

"Only an extreme anxiety reaction bordering on paranoia."

"You were just blown off your feet in a blast. I would think it's natural to have some anxiety after that. In fact, you'd be crazy *not* to be anxious. Umm, Emma?" Karen sounded hesitant. "Could you have imagined the injection? I mean, you told me you were dazed for a few minutes after you landed."

Emma considered Karen's comment a moment.

"Unfortunately, I don't think I imagined him. And to be honest, if it weren't for the increased ability, I might entertain the idea. But the race splits speak volumes. There is no way I could decrease my time so dramatically so late in the game without the boost that injection gave me. Especially considering the condition I was in right before the blast. My feet were failing, my head was pounding from the heat, and I could feel dehydration setting in, but I was having a terrible time keeping down the gel. Whatever he pumped into me was a miracle drug. Maybe I'll run a few more extensive tests of my own. Can I have access to your temporary facilities here?"

"Of course, but first, did you go to the police?"

"Yes. I gave them a report. Do you have a key card for the lab?"

"You'll need to ask Mr. Stark for that. Do you have his number?"

Richard Stark was the CEO of Price. Emma not only had his phone number, but she was placing the finishing touches on a report that Pure Chemistry had prepared for him regarding a Price drug. The report contained devastating news, and she had hoped to delay speaking with him until after they were back in the States. As it was, she needed his facility, so she had to run the risk that he'd take the opportunity to ask about the findings. She hung up and called him. He listened in silence while she tried to make light of the reason for her need to use the temporary facility. She didn't want him to object and demand she go to a hospital, as Karen had.

"I used some new supplements and had an outstanding race. Too outstanding, actually." She told him that she'd given a urine sample that had tested negative.

"A negative sample? I wouldn't worry, then," he said.

"I just want to run down some ideas I have. Clarify a couple of things."

"Fine. I'm going there now before I take the corporate jet to Nairobi. Meet me in, say, an hour?"

Emma got up and packed to go. She needed to figure out what had been pumped into her, and soon. Once she did, she wasn't staying an extra minute in Pietermaritzburg if she could help it.

She shrugged into a pair of jeans, pulled on a T-shirt, and covered that with a lightweight linen blazer. She slipped on soft-soled black athletic shoes. She'd expected to stay in Africa just long enough to run the race. As a result she'd brought only the bare minimum in a small duffel.

She had a tiny makeup bag, a wallet that fit in the interior breast pocket of her blazer, as well as a thin metal case. The case contained a circle of lipstick, a square of eyeliner, a pot of transparent cheek color, and a small wand prefilled with mascara. The sleek case was designed by a high-end makeup brand, for sale to women who travel. Emma had formulated the colors inside it at Pure Chemistry. She placed a travel toothbrush and paste into an outside pocket of the duffel. She used the express checkout feature to pay her hotel bill and headed to the temporary labs.

The Price lab was located in a sleek building in downtown Pietermaritzburg. A doorman stood behind the reception desk. He nodded at her after she explained why she was there.

"Mr. Stark is waiting for you. Just take one of those elevators."

Stark was standing in the hallway when she stepped out of the car. He looked haggard, but Emma was aware of his reputation as a chronic workaholic, so his appearance didn't surprise her. His dark hair was wet, as if he'd just showered. Only thirty-five years old, he was tall, with brown eyes and clean-cut dark hair. Handsome in an East Coast, well-bred way, he owed his meteoric rise in the business world to his ability to focus on work to the exclusion of all else.

Married young and divorced three years later, Stark, Emma had heard, required only four hours of sleep a night, a trait that stood him in good stead as the head of one of the largest pharmaceutical companies in the world.

His dark chinos and blue button-down shirt with sleeves rolled to the elbows was one of the rare relaxed outfits she'd ever seen him wear. She was interested to note that the casual clothes became him. They took the edge off his usual aloof manner. He still wore his expensive Patek Philippe watch. If not for that, he could have been mistaken for a "regular" guy, not the multimillionaire CEO of a Fortune 500 company. His eyes settled on her, not with a smile, nor a frown, but with a reticent air. He held the door to the lab open.

"Ms. Caldridge, please, come in." He looked at his watch. "I should warn you that I need to leave for the airport in two hours." Stark turned right without hesitation. When he reached a door with the number 3 on it, he took out a key card that he placed on the magnetic reader. The door sprang open.

Stark flipped on the lights. The lamp reflected off the room's white walls, cabinets, and Formica countertops in a harsh glow, making Emma almost want to shield her eyes at first. The lab was large, but still a manageable size for one person to navigate, and laid out in a way that she thought was the most practical, with vials, pipettes, needles, and microscopes on long worktables within easy reach. Two Eppendorf microcentrifuges sat in the middle of each, along with test-tube holders. Emma headed to the nearest workstation, where labeled drawers itemized their contents. She removed surgical gloves, tubing, a needle with vials, alcohol swabs, and a Band-Aid and snapped on the gloves.

"What are you doing?" Stark asked.

"Drawing some blood."

"Whose?"

"Mine."

"Can you do that?"

"Yes. Unless you know how to do it?"

"No."

She handed him the tubing. "Wrap this around my arm, could you? I'll get the needle in, then you pull the plunger out. When the vial is full, you'll need to pop on another." She put three vials in a row.

Stark looked nervous. "Why are you drawing your own blood? The urine sample should have caught anything untoward."

Emma went for the truth. "I was injected with something. During the bombing."

Stark froze. Emma pulled open an alcohol swab to clean the inside of her elbow. When Stark still hadn't moved or said anything, she looked up. He was ashen. His face held a frightened look that was unlike any expression she'd ever seen on him.

"You look scared to death. What is it?" She was holding a needle in one gloved hand and a vial in the other. He reached out and gently took the needle from her. He placed it on the table.

"You didn't tell me someone had injected you. Tell me everything. Now."

Emma gave him a short version of the man with the pen.

"Could you have been dreaming it? You said you'd taken a pretty hard fall."

Emma was getting a little tired of people suggesting that she'd imagined the attacker.

"I still can't account for my results. My feet had been swollen; they shrank back down, practically in front of my eyes. I was at the last third of the race, but my endurance increased a hundredfold." Stark looked away. He appeared nervous—frightened, almost.

"Did you tell the authorities?"

Emma shook her head. "I told a police officer at the finish tent, but he was preoccupied with the bombing. He gave me an address and number to call in order to create a report. I did that, and I'll contact the race organizers to tell them what happened after I get these test results back. Maybe there's nothing there." And maybe it's a group targeting me from my last adventure, Emma thought. But there was no need to add that to the mix for Stark. That issue could be addressed best by Banner.

Stark nodded. "Sounds right. There's nothing that can be done immediately." He shifted on his feet. "Can you give me an idea of what's in your report on Cardovin? As I told you, I have some unexpected business in Nairobi, and I won't be able to attend the scheduled meeting." He grabbed a stool, rolled it close, and sat on it.

Emma tensed. She had known that this moment would come, but she wanted to avoid it a little longer, if possible. She hated to be the bearer of such bad news.

"It's in my report. You can read it when you finish in Nairobi."

"What are you going to say to us?" Stark's voice was flat and brooked no further delay.

Emma took a deep breath. No sense gilding the lily. Best be out with it fast and leave no room for doubt.

"Cardovin doesn't work."

Stark went still. All Emma could hear was the muffled sound of a car alarm, somewhere in the distance. She shot a glance at his face. He stared at her with a look that was a combination of anger and disbelief.

"What do you mean?" Stark's voice was soft but held an intensity she hadn't heard from him before.

"It doesn't work."

"At all?" He sounded shocked.

"At all," Emma said. She felt some pity for him. The results were devastating. They would annihilate Price's profits for a long time to come. The stool squeaked as Stark leaned toward her, his motion followed by a faint whiff of his cologne.

"Do you realize you're telling me that a drug sold all over the world, that cardiovascular doctors in every teaching hospital in seventeen different countries prescribe every day, that represents over four *billion* dollars in sales for Price, doesn't work?" Now he sounded incredulous.

"Yes."

Stark shook his head. "You must be wrong."

Emma bit back a retort. "I am not wrong. My methodology will stand up to any scrutiny your scientists at Price wish to subject it to. The drug doesn't work. Period."

"If what you say is true, how do you explain the conclusions reached by Price's own scientists? Results that won us FDA approval? Clinical trials showing that not only does the drug work, but it works extremely well?"

Emma sighed. "Actually, at first I deliberately avoided reading their studies before undertaking my own, so as not to be swayed by their approach. Remember, you hired Pure Chemistry to test this drug and urged us to start from scratch. That's exactly what we did."

Stark nodded. "Go on."

"After, I went back and looked at every test with a positive finding. None of them tested Cardovin on its own. All of them tested it in combination with other, well-proven cardiovascular drugs, which is why Cardovin is approved only as an adjunct to those drugs. When it was combined in this manner, the results *were* slightly higher, but not as high as the marketing materials for Cardovin would suggest."

"And yours?"

"My study showed that it worked no better than a placebo." She returned to preparing to draw blood. Stark grabbed her wrist to stop her.

"No better than a placebo! Are you serious? Just what am I supposed to tell the board of directors? The shareholders? Price is due to report last quarter's earnings in a few days, and to project future sales. You expect me to tell them that our number-one seller doesn't work? Wall Street will eat us alive." Stark's eyes were hard, furious.

Emma shook off his hand. "How you reveal these findings is up to you. My job was to analyze the drug. I did that. But, to be honest, I'm a little surprised by the depth of your reaction. You knew over two months ago that Cardovin had problems. I saw the memo from your head scientist telling you that he felt further action was required to analyze Cardovin's efficacy. Price hired Pure Chemistry right after, so I assumed you were acting on the memo."

Stark was up and pacing. "I was told that the drug had some questionable results, but not that it was a complete waste!" He stopped prowling the room and straightened. He pinned her with a stare. "I want a copy of that report e-mailed to me at your earliest convenience. Until that time I wish to remind you that Pure Chemistry is subject to a confidentiality agreement. You are not to release these findings to any scholarly journals, or to anyone else, without our express consent." He delivered the order in a precise, clipped manner. It was all Emma could do to respond to him in a normal tone of voice.

"I'm aware of my responsibilities—and yours. Price cannot continue to sell a drug that it knows is worth no more than a sugar pill. Once your scientists review my findings and agree with them, Price will have to stop selling the drug. It's that simple."

"Nothing is ever that simple." Stark strode to the lab door. "Inform the guard when you're done here. The door will lock behind you." He was gone in an instant.

Emma sighed. The day was getting worse by the moment. She returned to the task at hand. She'd worry about Stark later. Right now she was far more concerned about herself. Filling the vials was much more difficult now that she was alone. She watched as the red plasma rose in each one. She still felt normal, which was impossible if she'd been injected with a chemical weapon on the level of what she suspected. Each hour she didn't react was further evidence that whatever had been pumped into her wasn't going to cause immediate, catastrophic harm. So not a fast-acting chemical weapon—then what?

Several street drugs caused some of the same symptoms she was having, absent the extreme endurance boost, but something told her that the EpiPen contained nothing so ubiquitous. The injecting device itself showed a level of sophistication that wouldn't be found in conjunction with a street drug. In that case one could simply hit her with a needle and achieve the same result. She finished, tossed the sharp into a hazardous-waste container on the wall, and applied the Band-Aid to the injection site. She took the vials to another workstation to begin testing.

Anxiety usually entailed a level of stress, this much she knew. Stress released chemicals into one's bloodstream; hormones triggered cortisol, cortisol triggered epinephrine. Too much of any of this would overwhelm her system, but one's body also had a mechanism in place to moderate the reaction. Hers, though, was charging ahead full bore. It was as if her moderating switch had been deactivated. An adjunct Rapidtest existed that could reveal the levels of stress chemicals circulating in her veins. She prepared to check for catecholamines: dopamine, norepinephrine, and epinephrine. She finished the test, then waited.

Forty-five minutes later, she had her answer. She was awash in epinephrine and dopamine. Her levels were so high that she was surprised she wasn't banging her body against the walls to try to alleviate the effects. In fact, she couldn't believe that such levels could exist without causing major physiological harm. One's body wasn't geared to accept this saturation of fight-or-flight chemicals. Had she been any less fit, she probably would have had a heart attack.

She labeled the remaining vials and brought them to a nearby workstation. A piece of paper taped to the wall above the station listed the name of one of the Price scientists that she knew. She tore off a Post-it to write a note, then hesitated, not sure just what she wanted. She scribbled on the pad, asking the chemist to test for ricin, anthrax, HIV, and botulinum toxin. She also requested information on dopamine uptake and wrote Banner's number as a contact.

Emma left the lab, making sure the door locked behind her. When the elevator doors shushed open, darkness greeted her. The soft African night held the sound of township music playing far in the distance. There was a pull about Africa that one was unable to ignore. Something vibrant, elemental, and dangerous all at the same time. Emma paused. She wanted to stay, to dance to the native music, let the magic take her. A post-race celebration was scheduled at a local nightspot, but she wasn't sure it was the safest place to be that evening. She unlocked her rental car, tossed the duffel into the trunk, and started her drive to the airport.

7

SUMNER WATCHED THE PIRATES PREPARE TO FIRE.

"Hit them again," Wainwright said. The LRAD blared. The pirates were closer now, and its beam worked much better at close range. Sumner watched the pirate holding the grenade launcher lower it and shake his head, like a dog flapping its ears, attempting to ward off the unbearable noise. They'd bought themselves some time, but not much else. The emergency sirens blared throughout the ship. Sumner watched the passengers surging onto the decks.

Wainwright snorted in disgust. "I'd love to know which idiot pulled the fire alarm. Carter"—he waved at a nearby officer—"tell the security detail to get those people into the center of the ship. They're sitting ducks on the decks." Carter nodded and jogged off the bridge. Wainwright turned to the other crew members. "I want this ship moving as fast as it can go, and I want it now."

Wainwright's crew responded with a calm that Sumner found impressive. The ship, all twenty-eight thousand tons of it, would never outrun the cigarette boats, but the added speed would help make it difficult to board.

"Why don't you just blow the bastards out of the water?" Block's voice held a note of hysteria.

Sumner gritted his teeth. The last thing he needed was a three-hundred-pound beef head panicking. Wainwright seemed to have the same concern, because he cut Block off at the knees.

"Mr. Block, maritime law does not allow us to carry heavy weapons. I asked you to leave. Don't add to my troubles here by asking stupid questions." Wainwright turned to Sumner. "Mr. Sumner? Any ideas?"

"You're asking a cabin boy what to do? What the hell kind of captain are you?" Block's voice had risen an octave. His face was flushed with anger or fear—Sumner didn't know the man well enough to determine which—and he thrust it at Wainwright.

Sumner stepped between the two men and faced Wainwright. "I have a gun."

"Now you're talkin'," Block said.

Wainwright ignored him. "What kind of gun?"

Sumner hesitated. The gun was a sniper rifle and banned on board a cruise liner. Using it would be a last resort. Before he could respond, the ship's radio crackled.

"*Kaiser Franz*, this is the USS *Redoubtable*. We've received a distress signal. Please advise."

Wainwright grabbed the radio. "Captain Wainwright, *Kaiser Franz*. We're in a standoff attack. Two cigarette boats armed with RPGs are preparing to fire on the ship."

"We're on our way. Six hours."

"Hell, we'll be dead in six hours," Block said. "Let Sumner here shoot 'em!"

Sumner had his binoculars out. He watched the pirate put the RPG back on his shoulder. "They're getting ready to fire."

Wainwright turned to the crew member manning the LRAD. "Put it on the highest level. Hit them three times, four seconds apart." He handed Sumner some earplugs. "They're close enough now that this level will damage their eardrums. We're behind the beam, so it won't be as bad, but no sense taking a risk." Sumner shoved them into his ears.

"What about me?" Block sounded petulant.

"Use your hands," Wainwright said. Block covered his ears with his palms.

The LRAD blasted. The two pirates in the second boat grabbed at their ears, covering them, but the pirate in the first boat, the one holding the RPG, didn't flinch. He aimed and fired.

The grenade slammed into the side of the ship, high up, above the waterline. It shuddered with the impact. Sumner didn't stay to watch any more. He sprinted off the bridge, back down the stairs, and ran belowdecks.

He ran through the halls listening to the voice blaring over the intercom, instructing all passengers to head to the casino immediately. The voice repeated the information in calm, slow tones. The casino was located in the ship's center, hemmed in by hallways on either side. Like all casinos, it lacked windows, so the gamblers would not be distracted by the rising or falling of the sun.

Sumner fought his way past frightened passengers who streamed through the narrow corridors. He ran past closed stateroom doors but stopped at the entrance to the casino. The majority of the *Kaiser Franz*'s 350 passengers huddled in the interior space. They lay on the floor, arms over their heads. Cindy Block sat nearest the door. Through force of habit, Sumner looked for the German family. He found the girl under a roulette table, shivering in a fetal position next to her mother, who had her arms wrapped around her. The father was absent. Sumner scanned the room, looking for the Russian and his mistress. The Russian sat at the bar swallowing a shot; the mistress sat next to him, looking terrified.

He continued down the hall, opened his cabin door, and slipped inside. He pulled a case from the closet. Made of titanium, it looked like a rectangular violin case with a webbed carrying strap. Sumner threw the strap over his shoulder and plunged out the door, running.

A second explosion rocked the *Kaiser Franz*. Sumner careened into a wall as the vessel pitched. Screams of terror echoed from the casino. Sumner's heart pounded in his chest, and he ran faster, with renewed urgency. He retraced his steps, past the casino entrance, up the stairs, onto the deck, and up the ladder to the bridge. A second RPG flew at the ship. This one was aimed high, at the bridge. It overshot and kept flying out to sea.

Sumner crouched on the deck surrounding the bridge and lowered the titanium case before him. Block, Wainwright, and the crew were back in the bridge. They watched him through the windows. Sumner set the code on a small padlock before flipping open the case. A Dragunov rifle with a telescopic sight nestled in the box's protective lining. Sumner pulled it out, checked the chamber, and crab-walked to the deck's side. When he was within three feet of the railing, he dropped to his stomach and crawled the last few inches, dragging himself by the elbows. He settled into position. He peered through the scope, targeting the pirate manning the RPG, and reined in his anger.

The shot was a difficult one. The *Kaiser Franz* churned through the ocean, slicing the waves, rising and falling with each swell. Wainwright kept the boat at an angle to the waves so as not to have to fight them the whole way, which would only serve to slow the ship. In contrast, the cigarette boats slammed head-on into each swell. Their superior speed ensured that they would always keep up with the larger craft, but their heedless trajectory caused the boats to buck. The pirates bounced along with each crashing wave, and the man holding the grenade launcher was hard-pressed to keep it on target long enough to fire with any accuracy.

Sumner waited until the *Kaiser Franz* reached its lowest point, then began its roll up. He fired when the boat was halfway to its peak. A large hole bloomed on the shoulder of the man holding the rocket launcher. He went down. Sumner could hear Block hooting through the windows. At least he thought it was Block—he didn't bother to look up. The first cigarette boat veered off, racing away from the *Kaiser Franz*. The second also started to loop away. Sumner targeted the second boat's captain. Waited for the roll, squeezed the trigger. The man flew forward with the force of the bullet that entered his back, high, at the shoulder. Sumner watched the passenger scramble to take over steering the boat, and then he swung back to aim at the first boat, but it was out of range, retreating as fast as its engines would allow. He watched the boats until they were once again tiny dots in the distance.

Block jogged over. "Hot damn! You can sure as hell shoot, boy, and that's the truth. I'll bet that's the first time you shot a man, right?"

Sumner put the gun back in its titanium case. Closed it and twirled the combination lock. He straightened to look at Block.

"That's the first time I shot a man without killing him," he said.

Block's mouth fell open.

8

CAPTAIN WAINWRIGHT CLAPPED SUMNER ON THE SHOULDER. "Good job. How long do you think it will be before they come back?" Sumner watched Block blanch. The possibility that they'd come back must not have occurred to him. But Sumner had no doubt they'd return. The *Kaiser Franz* carried rich passengers and a casino filled with cash. They'd take the money, kidnap the passengers, and strip the boat for its parts.

"A little before dawn, I would think. And I have bad news. I saw radar equipment. Can you switch off yours and alter course? Take a less familiar route?"

Wainwright pondered the question for a moment. "I hate to turn off the beam. It will help the *Redoubtable* find us."

"And the pirates," Sumner said.

Wainwright nodded. "As for the route we take, I don't even know how long we can continue. Depends on how bad the damage is. I've got the engine crew checking into it now. If we're taking on water, we'll need to put into port as quickly as possible."

"Back to the Seychelles?" Sumner said.

Wainwright shook his head. "Last radar showed the pirates were massed between us and the islands."

"They're herding us."

Wainwright's expression was bleak. "They seem to be."

"In which direction?"

Wainwright grimaced. "Somalia."

"Somalia? I didn't pay thousands of dollars to go to Somalia." Block's voice was loud and scared. Sumner thought the man had a right to be frightened. Somalia was one of the most dangerous places on earth. Mogadishu's port bustled with commerce, most of it illegal. It was likely that the pirates originated from there. Sumner would have preferred Mombasa, Kenya, although that country was in the midst of its own problems.

Wainwright turned on Block. "Mr. Block, leave the deck. Now, please."

Block looked like he wanted to argue. Sumner frowned at the man. Block glanced at the titanium case still in Sumner's hand, closed his mouth, and left the deck.

Wainwright turned to his first officer. "Let me know if there are any injuries, and tell me the minute you get a report from the engine crew. Radio the *Redoubtable* and tell them we'll need an escort to the nearest port."

After the officer left, Wainwright sighed. "This cruise line serves a very wealthy, very pampered clientele. Any number of bad elements in Mogadishu will see them for what they are: easy prey and big money in ransoms. I'll do anything to avoid Mogadishu." A small radio attached to Wainwright's belt crackled, and a voice poured from it.

"Bad news, sir. The *Redoubtable* radioed back and said they can't escort us anywhere."

Wainwright depressed a button on the device and placed it to his lips. "Why not? Twenty minutes ago they said they were on the way."

"They're under fire from the insurgents. Four cigarette boats are bearing down on them, and two helicopters. I didn't know the insurgents even had helicopters. We've been advised to change course and hightail it out of the area as fast as possible."

"What's our situation?"

"The lower decks reported in. No injuries. Two staterooms sustained damage. Satellite's sporadic, radar's out, but I think both can be fixed. We're not taking on water, but oil pressure is dropping like a stone. We're trying to determine why. Unless we can plug the leak, we're going to be floating dead in twenty minutes."

"Let's get the generators ready to go."

"Already gave that order. I have two men suiting up. When we can safely stop, they're going to submerge to see if there is any damage below the waterline that could account for the oil-pressure problem."

"Tell me when it gets too dangerous to continue. When it is, we'll cut the engines."

"That would be now, sir."

Captain Wainwright sighed. "Fine, cut them." He turned to Sumner. "We're grenade fodder." He rubbed a hand across his face. "Come on into the control room. Let's assess our options there."

Sumner followed Wainwright into the control room, where Wainwright's first officer, a plump man named Nathan Janklow, turned to greet them.

"We only have so much fuel. We're going to burn it at a ridiculous rate if we continue at the speed we need to maintain distance from these guys. We're crazy to even consider Mogadishu. Frying pan to fire," Janklow said. He was only in his mid-thirties but had the dour personality of a much older man. At that moment, though, Sumner agreed with him. Putting in at Mogadishu was a decidedly risky move.

"What about Berbera?" Sumner said.

"Berbera? That's a Somali port, isn't it?" Wainwright said. Sumner moved to a large map on the wall and pointed to the northern part of Somalia.

"It's in the separatist republic of Somaliland. No one really uses it. Technically, the area is a part of Somalia, but it's been run by the same warlord for over seventeen years now. Somaliland wants nothing more than to break away from Somalia, and they like Americans. They might welcome a chance to play protector. Show the world how different they are."

Wainwright looked thoughtful. "It's going to take longer to get there."

"I've heard the port's a broken-down mess," Janklow said. "Dilapidated as hell."

"So's our ship, at the moment," Wainwright said.

"They don't get much foreign aid, so there's no money for the port, or for anything else. The United States backs the transitional federal government in Mogadishu. And that government considers Somaliland to be squatters. They refuse to recognize the area as its own country," Sumner said.

Wainwright gave a short laugh. "What government in Mogadishu? The city is a complete disaster, where anarchy reigns supreme. How the hell did we end up backing them and ignoring the peaceful regime located in the same region?"

Sumner shook his head. "I have no idea. But tensions between the separatists and the transitional government are at an all-time low. The transitional government is pushing the U.S. to denounce Somaliland. If we go there, this administration will be put in a difficult position."

"They'll have to be realistic. I can't risk putting over three hundred civilians in at Mogadishu. It's suicide," Wainwright said.

"You're both assuming we'll get there, but it's likely we'll be attacked again long before we reach Berbera." Janklow was once again ringing the negativity bell, and again Sumner had to agree with him.

"Short-term, we need to get security patrols going. How's the perimeter system?" Sumner knew that the boat had an electrified outer railing to deter boarding in just such a situation, and that it was a recent addition.

"Second grenade took it out. Doesn't work," Janklow said.

"Guns on board?" Sumner spoke to Wainwright.

"Two stun guns and a couple of flare guns. No pistols. Your rifle is the highest-caliber weapon we have."

"And it's illegal," Janklow said.

Sumner nodded. "The only one who's seen it is Block. I'll talk to him. Ask him not to broadcast it throughout the ship. We'll have to double the security patrol. We should have at least two—one on either side and at the front and back—and they should work in shifts."

Wainwright shook his head. "We don't have the manpower for that."

"We'll need to recruit from the passengers," Sumner said.

"I don't want to alarm the passengers any more than we have to."

"If they're smart, they'll feel safer to know that we're taking steps to increase security. How about I start with Block? He already knows that we think they'll be back, and he said he hunts. Means he must be able to shoot."

"I don't like that guy," Janklow said, "and he sure as hell panicked just now."

"He's as big as a house," Sumner said. "Someone like that gets frightened, he can do some damage. One of those whippet-thin Somalis climbs over the fence, he can just sit on the guy."

Wainwright gave a grim laugh. "Let's hope it doesn't come to that."

"I'll put this gun away and go get him. Maybe he has some insight into the other passengers. Help us pick the security team." Sumner grabbed his gun case and headed out.

The ship's narrow hallways were empty. The passengers, ordered to their staterooms, had beaten a hasty retreat there. In the casino a dozen die-hard players sat at the blackjack tables, including the Russian and his mistress. They gambled with a joyless determination that reminded Sumner of the stories of passengers left behind on the *Titanic*, playing while the ship sank. He shook off the ghoulish thought. This ship would not sink. Not if he could help it. He jogged to his stateroom and shoved the titanium case back into the closet.

He found Block at the casino bar, nursing a scotch. Cindy was nowhere in sight. Sumner couldn't help but feel thankful for that. He didn't know how she'd handle her husband being tapped for the security team. He slid onto a stool next to Block, who didn't turn his head but said, "You're coming to ask me to keep quiet about what I saw, aren't you?"

Sumner hid his surprise at Block's cynical question. Something told him to lay it out plain.

"Only about the rifle. The rest you can shout to the world. Preferably the military world. Maybe they'll send a destroyer to help us."

Block snorted. "They'd better do it fast. Those pirates are coming back."

The bartender stopped in front of Sumner. She was an attractive blonde, with green eyes, and even under the plain black-and-white uniform Sumner could see that she had a perfect figure.

She put a cocktail napkin on the bar in front of him and gave him a professional smile. "What can I get you?"

Sumner didn't want a drink, but he ordered one anyway. "Maker's Mark, neat."

The bartender set the drink on the table, and Block raised his in a toast. "To killing the bastards."

Sumner held his glass in the air. "To winning."

Block paused, the rim of his tumbler at his lips. He lowered it a fraction. "Ain't that the same thing?"

"Not if you're bleeding out while you kill the last one," Sumner said.

Block shook his head. "Jesus, Sumner, what the hell kinda comment is that? Aren't you a little young to be so jaded?"

Sumner took a swallow of his drink. The liquor scorched his throat. Even though he hadn't wanted it, the whiskey seemed like the perfect solution to his problems. He kept silent. He didn't care to go into his experience in Colombia. When Block saw that he wasn't going to respond, he changed subjects.

"What's the plan up there with the officers?"

"Round-the-clock security beefed up by enlisting willing passengers to take shifts. Your name came up, since you said you could shoot. You *can* shoot, can't you?"

"You ever met a Texan that couldn't shoot?"

Sumner shrugged. "I'm sure they exist."

"Well, I ain't one of them."

"So you'll take a shift?"

Block nodded. "But don't tell me we're headed to Mogadishu."

Sumner shook his head. "We're going to a small port in the northern part of Somalia run by separatist rebels."

"I don't fancy the sound of that. Do we like these guys?"

Sumner took another sip of the drink. It was even better on the second go-around. "If by 'we' you mean the United States government, the answer is complicated."

"Then why the hell are we going?"

"The people are honest. In Somaliland the moneylenders leave stacks of cash unattended while they pray in church, and when they return, it's still there." Sumner thought the citizens hesitated to steal not out of honesty but out of fear of the controlling warlord, but he wasn't about to express his opinion to Block.

Block snorted. "They don't sound honest—they sound damn stupid."

"They won't kill us."

Block clinked his glass against Sumner's. "Well, let's get there quick."

9

MUNGABE SAT ON THE DECK OF A CHINESE TANKER FLYING THE Liberian flag and watched his two advance boats roar toward him. He was not pleased to see them. They were to make an initial strike against the *Kaiser Franz* and, if all went as Mungabe thought it might, board her then. That they were returning so quickly boded ill. The small craft came alongside the mother ship, attached themselves to the side, and prepared to unload. Within a few minutes, Mungabe watched his crew pull two injured men over the railing. Anwar Talek, his right-hand man, instructed that they be taken below to be treated. He strode across the deck toward Mungabe with his usual arrogant swagger. Mungabe thought Talek would try a coup against him one day—his ambition was such—but that day was a long way off. Mungabe was only forty, still strong, and had many years' more experience. He would not relinquish power easily. Talek reached the place where Mungabe sat under a protective awning and delivered the bad news.

"The tourists have guns," he said.

Mungabe snorted. "Since when do tourists from Europe have guns?"

Talek spread his hands wide. "I cannot tell you. Perhaps the boat carries Americans? Americans sleep with their guns."

Mungabe shook his head. "The Vulture told me the passengers are wealthy Europeans. If I had known it was filled with Americans, I would have charged more." He took a sip of the thick, sweet Turkish tea that sat on a low table before him and contemplated this development. In truth, he was a bit shocked. No cruise liner routinely carried weapons. Especially not those so far from the danger zones. He thought it not likely a coincidence that this one did.

"The Vulture is keeping secrets from us. He must have known that this ship might be carrying weapons."

Talek squatted down next to him. "What is in the cargo hold that this man desires so much?" Talek said.

"Medications, that is all."

Talek frowned. "Why? Surely these medications are not worth so much?"

Mungabe pondered a moment. "Some drugs can cost one thousand American dollars per month to take."

Talek whistled. "That's a lot. But still. Why does he pay?"

Mungabe hadn't really thought about it. "Who knows? The Vulture is the head of a large corporation. Perhaps the owners of the boat angered him and now he craves retribution. All I know is that he has the power to destroy the security company that is causing us so many headaches. This is one ship I will be happy to take."

"I think we should grab the medication, too. If it is worth that much, then we can sell it just as easily as he can."

Mungabe drank his tea without comment. It was these types of statements that convinced him Talek had no honor. He thought nothing of betraying the European. Well, Mungabe wasn't too concerned about it either, but he tried to fulfill his contracts whenever possible. Talek had a point, though. What was in the medication that the Vulture wanted it so badly? Mungabe knew an arms dealer who was connected to all things European. He would know if there was anything in the wind about the Vulture and his so-called medication.

Mungabe shifted in his seat. The harsh sun beat on the blue sea so that he squinted with the reflection. A long stream of sweat ran down his face, followed by another, hastened by the hot tea he drank. The smells of cinnamon, cardamom, and the tangy snap of salt filled the air, scents that brought to mind relaxation. Mungabe, though, was anything but relaxed. He felt his blood beginning to heat.

"What do we do next? Our crews are out, aren't they?" Talek said.

Mungabe nodded. He'd sent the bulk of his fleet into the Gulf of Aden, where they were engaged in various activities. Three crews charged toward two freighters off the Somali coast near Eyl, while two others were attempting to board some Japanese fishing vessels located in the Somali economic zone. All the while they did this, they were dodging the various warships from the CTG 600, a coalition of countries that had agreed to assist with security along the Gulf of Aden trade route. Mungabe focused his efforts in the gulf because ships taken there were likely to reap the highest profits. He'd sent only a skeleton crew to the *Kaiser Franz*, since he considered it to be the easiest of all targets to capture.

Easy, but not simple. The cruise liner sat far from the trade route. None of the small skiffs used by the pirates could reach ships this far from the Somali coast, and so Mungabe had sailed the tanker out first. The massive barge towed behind it several small skiffs and held barrels of gasoline that they'd use to refill their tanks. This far away from the safety of Somalia, anything could happen. Although he'd kept the CTG busy responding to his other activities back at the trade route, if even one carrier came this far to engage them, neither Mungabe nor his crew could do much in defense. The average carrier held an array of sophisticated weapons and helicopters that Mungabe had yet to acquire. The tanker could not outpace a carrier, and the faster skiffs would run out of gas long before reaching land. They'd end up floating on the open sea until they died.

The cruise lines knew that the pirate skiffs were ill equipped for long journeys, and so they continued to sail to the Seychelles Islands along a route that kept them far from the coast and the Gulf of Aden trade channels. They docked at several different ports along the way, and because maritime law regarding armament varied country by country, the pleasure ships carried nonlethal weapons and fire hoses only. The fire hoses were the most effective in repelling boarders, but those manning them could not be everywhere at once. Mungabe's men knew to attack from all sides.

Mungabe thought that the cruise ship would use its various defense techniques, but, once on board, the pirates with their rifles would carry the day. He doubted that any cruise liner's captain would order civilian passengers to fight bare-handed against armed men. Surrendering was the only way to avoid bloodshed. Thirty armed pirates could easily hold three hundred people hostage.

"Perhaps the American security company that protects the freighters also guards the cruise liner," Talek said. Mungabe's anger rose at the mere thought. It was well past time for him to mount a concerted attack against Darkview. He consulted his watch.

"Get the satellite phone. I mean to ask the European how the plans are proceeding on his end." Mungabe looked at the sky. "It's getting late. We attack again in the dark. We'll see if those new night-vision goggles work. Just send two more boats. Get the ship to fire its weapons. I want to know what type of firepower they have and make them waste some more bullets."

"Should we board her?"

"If you can. But don't risk any men. Just keep them scared and put some more holes in the ship. Remember, though, we are not to sink it. We need the cargo intact. The European said he will not pay if we damage his precious medication. We will keep stinging them until the rest of the crews return. When they do, we'll collect everyone and launch a final run. Until then keep me informed."

Mungabe's second assistant handed him the satellite phone. "It's about our crew near the economic zones, the ones that were attacking the fishing trawlers. They've been taken captive."

"By Japanese fishermen?" Mungabe said.

The assistant shook his head. "They weren't all Japanese fishermen. When the advance crew got closer, they said it looked like there were mercenaries wandering among the crew. They opened fire and killed three in our advance line. The second boats pulled back."

Mungabe's legendary anger surged to the forefront. "Who did such a thing?"

The second assistant raised his eyebrows. "Who else? The American company. Darkview."

10

BANNER STALKED OUT OF THE CONGRESSIONAL MEETING AND marched down the halls to the exit. He stepped into the sunlight and inhaled fresh air for the first time in six hours. He turned right to the Metro, jogged down the stairs, and boarded a train to Arlington, Virginia, where Darkview kept its offices.

The building that housed Darkview had a curved design, with green-tinted windows and fully grown landscaping. Darkview occupied the second-story corner suites, which accounted for 30 percent of the building's available space. Banner hit the staircase door and jogged up one flight, emerging at the entrance to his offices. He flung open the frosted-glass doors. Cameras placed at advantageous angles in the ceiling monitored every visitor, so Banner was not surprised when his receptionist greeted him without looking up from her console.

"Hi, Mr. Banner."

Alicia Compton was twenty years old and working her way through community college. She was diligent and friendly, and she sported short neon-red hair, double earrings in both ears, and heavy goth eyeliner. Banner was doubtful about the two small tattoos inked on her upper shoulders. One said PAX and the other VIRTUS. While Banner applauded the sentiments, he wasn't a fan of tattoos on women. When he'd commented about them to his vice president, Carol Stromeyer, who was responsible for hiring the girl, Stromeyer had warned him to keep his mouth shut.

"It's not appropriate to comment on them. She's smart, industrious, and honest. Frankly, employees like her are hard to find. She could be covered with them and I'd still be thankful to have her."

"She's quite pretty. Why ink her body? Used to be only drunken sailors got tattoos."

"You sound like you're in your eighties, not your forties."

"It's the truth, though."

"*I'm* in my forties. What if I told you *I* had a tattoo somewhere?"

Banner had only grunted in reply. But later, alone, he'd spent quite a few nights wondering just where Stromeyer's tattoo would be, and the fact that she might have one wasn't off-putting at all.

Now he strode into her office to find her standing at her desk staring at a small machine placed there that blinked red in a silent, hysterical cadence. Her light brown hair streaked with blond flowed over her face, obscuring half of it. A crease lined her forehead as she frowned at the device. She put up a hand for silence. Banner waited while she scribbled a note on a pad. She held it up for him to read.

"Bug detector. Was blinking before, went crazy when you stepped in. Drop your cell and meet me in the courtyard."

Banner removed his cell phone, placing it gently on her desk.

The courtyard began at the base of a sweeping stairway. The May air was just cool enough to deter any outdoor activity. They were alone and could talk in peace. Banner watched as Stromeyer, in a wrap dress and heels, moved with her characteristic efficiency of motion. Like Banner, Stromeyer was former military. When he'd first met her, she was wearing a uniform, and she marched rather than walked wherever she went. Since she'd joined Darkview, her march had softened a bit, as if she had exhaled and relaxed. He'd worked with her for three years, and each year she seemed to grow deeper into the vice-president role. She was able to change direction in a heartbeat and with a flexibility demanded by corporate America but not often found in the armed services. Most of their contracts flowed from the Department of Defense, though, and during those meetings she maintained her military demeanor.

She turned to him. "So who do you think is tapping us?"

Banner smiled. "Hello, Banner, how was the congressional hearing? Did you bury Cooley? Or did he bury you?"

She laughed. "I don't have to ask. I watched it on closed-circuit television in between signing endless copies of our expense report in triplicate. You did great, although I got concerned when you kept talking over Ralston's objections. We pay him a lot of money to protect you. You should listen to him."

"If Ralston got his wish, I wouldn't have said a word. I thought it better to give Cooley a little bit rather than shut him down entirely. By the way, I received a call from Emma Caldridge. She's in trouble." Banner filled Stromeyer in on the call and the cryptic message.

"You think this has anything to do with our phones being tapped?"

"Maybe. Tell me what you know."

"Even after our bimonthly sweep—which turned up clean, incidentally—I kept hearing clicks on the phone. I thought the noises were suspicious. I bought that little device two days ago. It searches for physical bugs at the actual location, and it confirmed that our offices are tapped. Now I just need to find the transmitter. But the way it went crazy when you walked in told me that your cell phone must be carrying a physical bug. Has it been out of your control?"

Banner shook his head. "Not at all. When I got the thing, I made sure to disable the GPS as well. Who would use physical bugs anymore? You don't have to get near the actual phones, or even into our offices, to tap them."

"I agree, but the machine seems to think we've got a bug. And there's more." She handed him a letter. "Got it today. It's from the IRS. We're being audited."

Banner read the terse request for information. "This is Cooley's doing, you know that."

Stromeyer took back the paper. "There's no end to the harassment. It's entirely possible he's behind the tap as well." She looked glum. "Where's Caldridge now?"

"In South Africa, running the Comrades ultramarathon."

Stromeyer frowned. "Where the bomb went off? Maybe she's right to be worried."

The sound of a closing door echoed in the courtyard. They both looked up the staircase to the broad terrace. A man and a woman, presumably employees from one of the offices in the building, stepped out. Banner watched as both people put cigarettes to their lips, lit them with plastic lighters, and inhaled, their eyes closed in bliss.

"Addicts." Stromeyer's voice was filled with good humor.

"I used to be addicted," Banner said.

Stromeyer raised an eyebrow in surprise.

"Why the shocked look?"

"I just can't imagine you doing anything so . . ." She waved a hand in the air, as if searching for the word.

"Weak?"

She laughed. "Unhealthy. You're such a fitness freak."

"Thank you," Banner said.

She wagged a finger at him. "Rigid self-control is not always a good thing. Everyone needs a vice, no matter how minor."

Banner jerked his head toward the stairs, and they both started up. "I'll bear that in mind."

"Let's bring Caldridge in. I don't like what's happening here."

Banner held the door for Stromeyer. "What do you think is happening?"

"I think someone's after us all."

KARL TARRANT WALKED INTO A SMALL PATHWAY BETWEEN TWO
ramshackle houses close to Capitol Hill in Washington, D.C. It was
eleven o'clock at night, and the working crowd, what little existed
in this neighborhood, was long gone. The seasonal spring day had
faded into a crisp evening. Cars whizzed down the street, each one
hitting a metal square in the middle that covered a pothole. The repeated clanging sound frayed Tarrant's already jangled nerves. His
teeth chattered in response to a chill that was not from the night air
but from within. He hadn't had a hit in over thirty-six hours. His
hands shook and his head ached as he waited for the one thing that
would make all his pains go away.

The African in the overcoat strolled toward him as if he hadn't a
care in the world. Tarrant felt a mixture of relief and disgust. Relief
because his physical troubles were at an end, disgust because the man
had botched the job Tarrant had hired him to do. The man stopped
before him.

"Here." He handed Tarrant a bottle marked IBUPROFEN. The bottle actually contained black-market OxyContin.

Tarrant was outraged. "One bottle? That's it? What the hell am I
going to do with one bottle, eh? Won't last a week."

"Relax. I put ten more in a bag and left them in our usual spot. I just
figured you'd be hurting by now and thought I'd bring you some relief."

Tarrant snorted. He shook out two capsules and swallowed them.
They stuck a little on the way down, but he didn't care. He needed

them, not water. "Glad you're so thoughtful. I only wish you'd done what I asked you to do."

The African shrugged. "We got her with the pen, didn't we?"

"What about the bomb? Who the hell did that?"

The man grinned. "I set that up. A little one, really. Took out the area around the track. Was a well-controlled explosion. I am good." The man's white teeth glowed against his dark skin, and his eyes gleamed with the touch of madness that afflicted all true arsonists. Tarrant thought killing the guy wouldn't have been the worst thing that could happen, except for the fact that he'd have to find another dealer.

"I don't know how a simple stick could turn into such a disaster. We could have stuck her anywhere," he said.

"But now they think it's tied to the bombing. Worked out well, don't you think?"

A man emerged from the shadows thrown by the trees lining the sidewalk. Streetlight beams traversed his body at an angle from shoulder to ankle, illuminating the muted silk tie, soft blue shirt, and dark suit that looked custom. Tarrant noticed that the African quieted in respect as the man approached. The newcomer stopped just short of the pathway's entrance, his face shrouded in the shadow of an overhanging eave. Tarrant felt his stomach turn. He thought the nickname of Vulture fit the man's thin, hardened features. The Vulture paid handsomely, but Tarrant detested him. He was evil incarnate.

"It did work well. I have to compliment you." The European-accented voice held no trace of sarcasm. The African exhaled softly, as if he'd been holding his breath. The Vulture turned to Tarrant. "And we could *not* stick her anywhere. It had to be at the peak of the race in order to assess the chemical's effect on the human body during extreme exertion. A little human clinical trial minus the federal oversight. And what about the chemical *you* love so much? I trust you'll be feeling better soon?"

Tarrant nodded. His throat was dry.

The Vulture held up two thick white envelopes. "Here's another five thousand for each of you and detailed information on the next job. I need you to persuade a certain gentleman to halt his operations in the Red Sea. Or, more specifically, in the trade route through the Gulf of Aden." Tarrant took one of the envelopes and shoved it into his pocket without looking at it. The Vulture had never shorted him.

"Dead persuaded? Or just hammered-into-the-pavement persuaded?" Tarrant said.

The Vulture shrugged. "Beaten first. Homicides draw too much attention. Of course, if the beating doesn't work, you can escalate the force. I'm aware that you have a reputation for killing people by accident."

Tarrant snorted. "Once my temper gets away from me, I have a hard time pulling back."

"If you end up killing him, be certain that his vice president gets the message, too."

"Is it true that you want us to stick the runner again?" the African asked.

"I understand that she got up and finished the race."

The African nodded. "She ran away, fast. Real fast. Is that what she was supposed to do?"

"Yes. But we also expected much more erratic behavior as well. No one seems able to confirm that aspect. If she was behaving within the bounds of normal, then the dose may not be enough."

The African frowned. "I hit her hard. Gave her every last drop. I thought the drug works better on fit people. Enters their system faster. If that's true, she should have turned into a lunatic."

The Vulture shook his head. "She did not. Not at all. Dose her again." He looked at Tarrant.

"Whatever. We'll get it done," Tarrant said.

"Good. I'll be in touch." The Vulture sketched a wave with his hand, walked to the curb, and reached a hand into the air, as if he was hailing a cab. Tarrant was just about to inform him that there were no cabs willing to risk this particular neighborhood at that hour of the evening when a large black sedan pulled up and halted. The Vulture swung open the door and disappeared inside. The car drove off.

"That man is a psychopath in a suit," the African said. "I won't be crossing him."

The drug was in full flower now, giving Tarrant a feeling of bravado. "He's just a rich guy in good clothes who's afraid to do his own dirty work," he said.

The African scoffed. "I'd like to hear you tell him that to his face."

Tarrant shrugged. "He's gone now."

"But he'll be back. Let's just be sure we get this Gulf of Aden guy good. I don't want to fail the Vulture. He'd start his testing on me. I wouldn't make it a week."

"We'll get him, don't you worry." Tarrant grinned like a fool all the way back to his car.

SUMNER TOOK THE FIRST WATCH, TEAMED WITH JANKLOW. THEY
walked the deck, moving in opposite directions. Every twenty minutes or so, they'd pass each other. Sumner's watch showed three
o'clock in the morning. He met Janklow in the middle.

"You know, taking this shift means that we're most likely to see
some action, right?" Janklow said.

"If we don't fall asleep first," Sumner said. A thought occurred to
him. "If these guys come back and actually board us, what can they
get? Besides the hostages and the money in the casino, I mean."

Janklow leaned against the railing for a moment. He pulled out a
pack of cigarettes and offered it to Sumner.

"I don't smoke," Sumner said. He watched Janklow light up, take
a deep drag, and blow out the smoke before answering.

"We're carrying some cargo as well. It's unusual, we don't often do
it, but it's for a charity. Our hold contains vaccines and pharmaceutical products that we were to deliver to Mombasa when we docked
there."

"Is it worth anything?" Sumner said.

Janklow shook his head. "Invaluable to the kids who need it, but
not worth a thing to the pirates. The whole idea is a bit of a boondog-
gle anyway, because some African countries are highly suspicious of
vaccines to begin with. They think the medicine is really a way for
the U.S. to poison their children. Sometimes we deliver the products
and they end up rotting on the dock."

"So we won't be able to use the cargo as barter to get us out of the situation."

Janklow took another puff. "Not at all. Our best bet is the money in the casino. But I doubt they'll settle for it. They'll want to ransom the passengers as well. Last month the Danes paid over a million dollars for five of their own. That's big business for these guys."

Sumner thought about the four men in the cigarette boats. They had looked like Somali fishermen: skinny and underfed. He'd be amazed if they had fifty bucks between them.

"Who's getting the money? It sure as hell isn't those four losers in the boats."

"The warlords. They finance the boats, guns, you name it. The guys actually doing the attacking barely make a living wage."

"I wish I could speak to them. I could tell them that the U.S. won't pay. I know this from personal experience."

Janklow looked at Sumner with a measured gaze. "I heard that you were held hostage in Colombia. The U.S. didn't ransom you?"

Sumner watched the ocean for a moment before answering. "Not a penny. But I ended up costing the kidnappers a lot more than they cost the U.S."

Janklow looked intrigued. "If I may ask, how did you get out of there?"

Sumner thought about Emma Caldridge. He caught himself smiling, which was something he didn't do too much of, before and especially after Colombia. He hoisted the gun higher on his shoulder. "I was saved by a beautiful mad scientist."

Janklow grunted in surprise. "Can you bring her here? We could use her help."

Sumner shook his head. "I want her to stay as far away from here as possible."

Janklow finished his smoke, ground out the butt, and tossed it into a nearby cigarette bin. "I don't blame you for that."

Sumner started walking again.

Janklow moved out in the opposite direction. "See you on the next turn."

Halfway around the deck, Sumner bumped into Block. "Out for a stroll?"

"I wish," Block replied. "Wainwright wants me to take over for Janklow. Something's going on with the damage, and he's needed there." He turned and fell into step with Sumner. "Anything happen so far?"

"No, but this is the 'hot' shift. You know that, right?"

Block sighed. "I told you, I used to hunt. Lots of animals come out at night. Don't see how these are any different."

Sumner couldn't argue with that. They met up with Janklow at the midpoint. He eyed Block with a sour expression that was even worse than his usual one. Sumner watched him manage a cordial nod.

"Mr. Block, what brings you on deck this late?" Janklow asked.

"Wainwright needs you in Stateroom A to inspect the damage. He wants me to spell you." Block waved toward the pistol holstered at Janklow's waist. "That little gun all you got?"

Janklow sighed and pulled the gun, holster and all, off his waist. He handed it to Block. "This is it."

Block scrutinized the pistol. "What the hell is this?"

"A stun gun."

The gun was bright yellow and had a square muzzle instead of a round one. Slightly thicker than an actual pistol, it came with its own holster in fluorescent neon.

"Why the hell is it so bright? This thing glows. I might as well be carrying a sign that says 'I'm over here, shoot me.'" Block waved the holster around. The reflective material left streaks of green light as it moved through the dark.

"It's considered rescue equipment. All rescue equipment is designed so that it can be located in the dark."

"How does it work?" Block asked.

"It takes a few seconds to charge. You flick this on"—Janklow showed Block a switch—"and when it's ready, you aim and shoot."

"Do I need to touch the guy? 'Cause let me tell you right now, I don't want to get that close."

Janklow shook his head. "It has two darts that shoot out on fishing lines with a range of twenty-one feet."

Block smiled. "That'll do for distance."

"But there's a hitch with the fishing lines. They both have to hit the target to work. Guy manages to avoid one and you won't complete a circuit. Nothing will happen except you'll be standing there trying to reload while he's madder than he was before. The extra charges are attached to the holster's belt."

"Great." Block sounded disgusted. "Anything else I should know?"

"Certain materials will stop the electrical charge."

"Like what?"

"Like a wet suit," Sumner said.

Janklow hid a smile, while Block gave them both a long look.

"Sumner, give me your rifle," Block demanded.

Sumner shook his head. "The Dragunov stays with me."

Block pointed a finger at him. "Probably every one of those pirates will be wearing a wet suit as he climbs over the railing. You can't keep that state-of-the-art weapon while you give your passengers these pieces of crap."

Janklow knocked out another smoke. Before he lit it, he aimed it at Block. "Have you ever even shot a sniper rifle?"

Block looked outraged. "I can shoot anything you want to hand me, and that's a fact."

Janklow gave an incredulous laugh. "Texans. You guys are the biggest exaggerators in the world."

Sumner started pacing again. Behind him he heard Janklow instructing Block on his patrol duties. Sumner turned a corner, and the only sound was the swell of the waves on the side of the boat.

But in the distance came the roar of a cigarette boat's engine.

13

THE ASSISTANT TO THE UNDERSECRETARY FOR INTERNATIONAL
security policy and procedure called Banner at one o'clock in the
morning. Banner noted the caller ID before he snatched the phone
off his nightstand.

"Mr. Banner, we need you at Department of Defense headquarters
immediately. There's been a problem in—"

Banner interrupted her. "Don't say it. My phones are tapped."

The woman began coughing. While she did, Banner pulled an
image of her up from memory. She was a mousy woman, about
thirty years old. Nondescript brown hair, ill-fitting dark suits with
button-down shirts and flat shoes. She was new, one of the few who
had lasted longer than a quarter of a year, and for the life of him he
couldn't remember her name. She got hold of herself, and he heard
her take a deep breath.

"Who's tapping you?"

"Probably the FBI, but I can't be positive."

"Oh." The woman sounded relieved. "The FBI is on our side."

"You would think, but I'm not so sure. Best you wait to fill me in
until I get there."

"I'm using a secure phone and calling your secure line. A tap is
unlikely. Are you always this cautious?"

Banner was up and rummaging through his dresser drawers, using
his ear to hold the phone to his shoulder. "Yes. And really, aren't you
just a little bit impressed that I am?"

His joke was rewarded with a small laugh. "I guess I am. We'll see you soon, then. And could you bring Major Stromeyer?"

Banner glanced again at the clock. He hated to bother Stromeyer unless it was urgent. No need for both of their nights to be ruined.

"Is it necessary? I could handle the meeting and let her sleep a little longer."

The woman coughed again. Banner thought it was a nervous reaction. He rushed to reassure her.

"Is there a particular reason you want her there?" he asked.

"No, no, it's just . . ." The woman trailed off.

"Go on."

"It's just that Major Stromeyer is so good at requisitions."

Banner slid on a pair of pants and sat on the bed to put on his socks. "Major Stromeyer is *great* at requisitions," he said. "I've often thought that Major Stromeyer could requisition a trip to the moon and do it in a way so that no one in the government would complain."

The nervous assistant heaved a sigh. "I always get my paperwork wrong."

Banner felt sorry for the young woman. Especially since she probably wouldn't survive another month in the job.

"I'll bring Major Stromeyer." He rang off and called Stromeyer. When she answered in a voice filled with sleep, he almost regretted his promise. "Meeting at the DOD as soon as you can."

She gave a small groan. "Is my presence required?"

"The assistant asked for you specifically. I forget her name. The mousy one."

"Susan Plower."

By now Banner had his shoes on, and one sleeve of his shirt. He headed to the door with the rest of the shirt hanging off him. He snagged his car keys from a leather tray that sat on a credenza near the front door of his town house.

"She says she's bad at paperwork."

"She's terrible at paperwork. We'll finish the meeting, and she'll get it wrong, and then Darkview won't get paid for an additional six months while I straighten it all out. I'll see you in twenty-five minutes."

Banner walked into a DOD conference room populated with various personnel. They all looked relieved to see him, which should have made him feel good about himself but somehow only made him wary. Since Darkview specialized in missions to "hot" spots around the world, he wished someone would tell him which area had blown up. He didn't have long to wait. He watched Stromeyer enter the room and, directly behind her, the new undersecretary for international security policy and procedure, Jonathan Rickell.

Banner didn't know much about Rickell except that he'd been hired when the new administration took office and that he had a degree in international studies from the same Ivy League school the president had attended. About fifty years old, fit and balding, with shrewd eyes and a reputation for having an explosive temper, Rickell had been polite but distant the few times Banner had met him. Banner couldn't get a handle on him.

Rickell waved them all into their seats. The Plower woman sat at his right. She glanced at Stromeyer before giving Banner a look filled with gratitude.

Rickell cleared his throat. "We've learned that the situation in Somalia has taken a sudden turn for the worse."

Banner wanted to groan out loud. He hated Somalia. He currently had ten security contracts for shipping companies plying the Gulf of Aden trade route, but none for security within Somalia. It was one of the few places he tried to avoid sending Darkview personnel, despite the fact that Somali operations allowed for premium pricing based upon the extreme danger. There were two other companies in the contract security business that routinely handled matters there and made great profits doing so. Banner wondered why they weren't represented at this meeting.

"Banner, I understand that you've been hired to protect some of the ships using the trade route and may have an operative in the Indian Ocean as we speak."

Stromeyer gave a little jerk next to Banner, revealing her surprise. Banner held still, but he felt the dread rising in him. No one, not even Rickell, should have known that Sumner was in the Indian Ocean. Whoever was tapping them must have leaked the information.

"I'm surprised to hear you say that. Where did you hear this?" Banner responded.

Rickell shrugged and turned to Plower. "Who told us that?"

Plower's face took on a frantic look while she shuffled through a stack of papers in front of her. After an awkward silence, when it became clear to everyone in the room that she was unable to divine the answer from the documentation, Stromeyer reached across the table.

"Ms. Plower, why don't you hand me the forms and I'll look for the information while Secretary Rickell continues with the meeting." Plower gave Stromeyer a relieved nod and shoved the papers at her.

"Well? Do you have an operative there?" Rickell asked.

"I may." Banner wasn't prepared to tell Rickell everything until he knew what had occurred.

"You may? If you don't, I'll use Synocorp. Your company is far too controversial at the moment. Last thing I need is Cooley questioning my choices."

Banner kept his voice neutral. "Why don't you tell me what's happening, and I'll tell you if Darkview can help."

Rickell looked annoyed. "Here's what's happening: Three hours ago the USS *Redoubtable* answered a distress signal from a cruise ship headed to the Seychelles Islands. Seems they were under attack by pirates. While we are of course concerned about people on this ship, we are also deeply concerned about the international ramifications of intercepting the pirates without proper authority. As you know, the insurgents control most of Somalia as of last month, and they have instituted patrols along the edge of Somali territorial waters."

"Who owns the ship?" Banner asked.

"It's registered in Liberia, flies the Liberian flag, is operated by a German shipping conglomerate, and is owned by the Bermudan subsidiary of an American holding company. The passengers are tourists from ten different countries, including the U.S."

"So who's the lucky country that gets to intercept?"

Rickell shrugged. "None, or all of the above. The UN coalition forces have taken over patrolling the Gulf of Aden trade route, so the UN is first in line."

"What have they done?"

Ms. Plower spoke up. "They've sent a strongly worded letter demanding the pirates cease and desist."

"That'll work." Banner's voice was dry.

"CTG 600 is in the area but under attack by another pirate cell, so it will be at least eighteen hours before they can address the problem."

"Who insures the ship?" Stromeyer said.

"A Bermudan insurance company. They've indicated that they will pay a ransom immediately should the pirates successfully take the ship and passengers. They feel quite strongly that the pirates should not be provoked into escalating violence. Deaths would only result in lawsuits. But we need to mount some action, because we're concerned about the cargo they're carrying."

"I thought you said it was a cruise ship, not a cargo ship," Banner said.

"It's both at the moment. It's carrying both tourists and cargo."

Rickell hesitated. Banner could see that he was weighing how much to tell about the incident. Banner decided to nudge him along.

"So what's the cargo?"

Rickell sighed. "It's carrying pharmaceutical supplies and vaccines."

Stromeyer looked up from the paper in front of her. "Sounds harmless enough."

Rickell shook his head. "We just received an intelligence report claiming that hidden within the boxes marked 'vaccines' are two vials of ricin."

Banner watched Plower's mouth drop open.

"Is that a bomb?" she asked.

"It's poison derived from the beans of a castor plant. Introduce it into the food supply and thousands could die."

"And the boxes marked 'pharmaceuticals'?" Stromeyer's voice was shocked.

Rickell shifted in his seat. "We're told they contain something more dangerous than ricin, but we were not informed of the exact nature of what's inside. Seems no one, not even our source, is sure what's in there."

"Which company manufactured the vaccines?"

"Price Pharmaceuticals," Plower said.

"Can they get us any closer? Is it chemical, mineral, explosive?" Banner asked.

"We think chemical. After all, chemical weapons are the future—everybody knows this."

Banner was already planning the rescue. "You said the *Redoubtable* received the call. Can they intervene?"

Rickell shook his head. "They're under attack from a small group of militants. I say small, but they're well armed. The *Redoubtable* is holding its own, of course, but there's no time to fight this battle and then get to the cruise ship."

"Don't you have some military in Djibouti? Why not have a guy parachute onto the ship?" Banner said.

"Our Djibouti team is training the African Union forces. When training's done, it's our hope that they will secure Mogadishu for the transitional government there."

"How much of Mogadishu does the transitional government control? I thought it was quite small," Stromeyer said.

"Three blocks," Rickell replied. He sighed. "I know it sounds like an impossible task."

Stromeyer shook her head. "Three blocks is more than most have been able to accomplish. Somalia's government was too failed for even bin Laden to control. He left within a month. And that guy thinks living out of a cave is normal."

"Where's the cruise liner?" Banner said.

"Their radar is out. We're not able to pinpoint their current location, but we think they were driven into Somali waters one hour ago, so we can't fly into that area."

Stromeyer's head snapped up from the documentation in front of her. "Oh, yes, we can. We have a UN resolution that allows any rescue ship to continue pursuit into territorial waters. Somalia welcomed the help."

Banner kept quiet and let Stromeyer handle the conversation. His men on Gulf of Aden security details were ordered to apprehend any crews that attempted to take one of his clients' ships no matter where they were. They relied on the resolution when they chased pirates into the zone. Banner wasn't about to let the criminals off simply because they crossed some invisible line.

Plower spoke up. "That was last month. Now the insurgents control entire swaths of Somalia. They just sent us a demand that the resolution be suspended. They've informed us that any ships crossing into their territory will be considered to be trespassers and fired upon."

Banner snorted. "Tell them to go to hell. Make them back off long enough to get us to the cruise liner. If they knew what's on it . . ."

"Under no circumstances must anyone in Somalia know what's on that ship!" Rickell said. "If they did, it would be overrun with criminals all looking to get at the ricin. We must maintain complete silence on this and continue on as we would in any other similar situation. Follow usual channels."

"And if the pirates successfully take the ship hostage?"

"Then we must guard the secret even more closely."

Banner saw Rickell's point. There was a good chance that even if the pirates were successful, they might never give the vaccines a second look. Generally when attacking a ship, they took it to a nearby port, docked it, and offloaded the passengers. If the ship was still functioning, they used it until a ransom was paid. If not, they stripped it for parts and left it to rot. "What's the name of the ship?" Banner slid a notepad closer to take the information. He'd break radio silence and let Sumner know to keep as far away as possible.

"It's the *Kaiser Franz* out of Hamburg."

This time Stromeyer stayed absolutely still. It was Banner who jerked in surprise.

"GIVE ME ALL THE FACTS YOU HAVE," BANNER SAID TO RICKELL.

Rickell nodded at Plower. "Go ahead."

"About an hour ago, the pirates attempted a standoff attack on the *Kaiser Franz* with rocket-propelled grenades. They managed to hit the ship twice before they were repelled."

"Repelled? How?" Stromeyer had stopped messing with the paper in front of her and was writing notes on a nearby notepad.

"That's the funny part. The passengers heard sonic blasts coming from the upper decks. We assume that this was the sound of the Long Range Acoustic Device that's part of the *Kaiser Franz*'s security equipment. But another passenger called his father in England and claimed that he heard gunfire coming from the ship as well."

"Why is that strange?"

"Guns are illegal on a cruise ship. It is unlikely that the *Kaiser Franz* has any."

"Could the passenger have mistaken the sound of the LRAD for gunfire?" Banner said.

Plower shook her head. "I thought that, too, but after the explosions erupted, the passenger said that the pirates manning the ships sustained obvious bullet wounds. They turned away immediately."

Banner kept quiet. He had a sneaking suspicion who was responsible for the shots. It was all he could do not to glance at Stromeyer. She took a deep breath, but before she could speak, Plower continued.

"Apparently the passenger's father spent some time in the English

Royal Navy. He told the son that only a highly trained sniper could have delivered such accurate hits. I checked with our experts here, and they agree. We immediately pulled the manifest."

"May I see it?" Banner kept his voice mild.

Plower slid a piece of paper across to him. The manifest listed all the passengers in alphabetical order. Sumner wasn't on it. Banner moved the list over to Stromeyer, who scanned it as well. She said nothing as she handed it back to Plower.

"Does it matter, really? Whatever was done saved the passengers and crew."

Rickell waved a hand in the air. "It matters a lot to the insurgents. They're claiming that the boat is a decoy for the U.S."

"Decoy for what?" Banner said.

"They believe that the boat is actually dumping nuclear waste into the waters off Somalia."

Banner rubbed his forehead. "Oh, great."

"Relax, Banner, we're not dumping nuclear waste. Although some countries are, and that's another problem we'll have to address soon. Whatever is in that hold is far more dangerous than some nuclear waste. We need to save that ship, and soon."

"Any aircraft carriers in the area? You could arrange for air surveillance and security while the ship heads to port."

"Not going to happen. The insurgents guarding the economic zone would fire on them in a heartbeat. This administration will not have another *Black Hawk Down* disaster."

Stromeyer put up a hand. "Wait a minute. I know about the territorial limits, but what's the economic zone?"

Plower visibly brightened, and Rickell nodded for her to answer. "It's the zone that only the Somalis can fish. The waters off Somalia are filled with tuna, and the big companies were taking boatloads of it, leaving the Somali fishermen starving. To address this problem, most foreign ships are not allowed to fish within a two-hundred-mile nautical range off the coast."

"Well, we're not going to fish, we're saving people. Tell them to make an exception in this case." Banner couldn't keep the annoyance out of his voice.

Rickell nodded. "The transitional government granted the request but warned us that the insurgents currently control the area."

"How long will it take for the *Redoubtable* to get near?"

"Assuming the *Redoubtable* finishes up with its own security issues in the next sixty minutes—eight hours to three days."

"Three days. Why so long?" Stromeyer asked.

"They're far away. You have to understand, we're talking over a million square miles of ocean. They can't be everywhere. They focus their efforts on the most likely areas of piracy. And those areas have been the trade routes."

"So no real help there," Banner said.

Stromeyer started gathering her papers together. "To recap: We've got one stranded cruise ship with hundreds of civilians and one, maybe two chemical weapons either lost or sitting within the territorial zone of one of the most dangerous countries in the world, and the U.S. can't, or won't"—Stromeyer gave Rickell a pointed look—"enter the area to help them."

Rickell nodded. "Can't. And yes, that's it."

Stromeyer looked at Banner. He caught the look but was planning the steps he would take to board the ship and the price he would charge to do so. He finished up and laid the number on Rickell. Who exploded.

"That's highway robbery! Darkview has a contract with us. Standard rates in that contract should apply."

Banner shook his head. "This isn't standard. First, I need to find a ship that's located off one of the most dangerous coastlines of the world. Second, I need to secure the ship while fighting off attacking pirates. And third, I need to bring in a highly qualified individual to assess this chemical—whatever it is—and who will agree to infiltrate the ship at great risk to him- or herself."

Rickell snorted. "By the time the expert gets there, the vessel will already have been boarded and the people held hostage. What chemical specialist would be crazy enough to actually join those poor people?"

"Someone in the area with something at stake on the ship."

"Who would that be?"

"Emma Caldridge."

15

SUMNER WHISTLED. BLOCK WAS AT HIS SIDE FIVE MINUTES LATER.

"What is it?"

"Listen."

The cigarette boat engine roar grew louder.

"Here they come." Block unsnapped the Taser from its holster and removed the safety.

Sumner pulled a walkie-talkie off his belt. Depressed the button. "We have visitors. Coming from the port side. Douse the lights."

Twenty seconds later the entire ship went dark. Sumner heard the babble of voices in the distance. The passengers in the dining rooms were responding to the blackout.

From the right came the dancing beam of a small LED flashlight. As it drew closer, Sumner could just make out Janklow's form, followed by a member of the ship's crew.

Janklow walked up to Block and Sumner. "How far?" he whispered.

"Listen," Sumner said. But the sound of the engine was gone.

"I don't hear anything."

"Me neither, not anymore," Block said.

"Listen for the sound of oars."

"They'd still have to see us," Janklow said.

"They could have night-vision goggles."

Janklow moved closer to the railing and looked along the ship's side. "That's way too sophisticated equipment for these guys. They're Somali fishermen, for God's sake."

"They had RPGs, a cigarette boat worth over eighty thousand dollars, and at least one AK-47. Night-vision goggles would be the least expensive piece of hardware from that list," Sumner said. The roar of the cigarette engine began again. He estimated it was over a mile away.

"We'll find out soon enough." Block sounded grim.

Sumner knew that the ship stocked a couple of Tasers, but no other type of weapon save the flare guns. Everyone, including Sumner, was dressed in dark, plain clothes per Captain Wainwright's orders. Sumner recognized the crew member accompanying Janklow as a man all the crew members called Clutch. Sumner thought Clutch had a mean streak. He was a bouncer and sometime bodyguard who walked around in a state of repressed anger. Sumner didn't know his story, but it couldn't have been a happy one. Clutch had a flare gun attached to his belt.

Something about the engine noise bothered Sumner. It was too obvious. The pirates had to know that the entire crew of the *Kaiser Franz* would be prepared for their return. Over two hundred employees on a large cruise ship carrying at least three hundred passengers. How did four skinny men expect to prevail against them? Sumner shifted his thinking to address the problem from their perspective. Thought about what he'd do given the same odds.

"I hope you're ready to shoot, Sumner. Because your gun is the only one that's got the range to kill them before they reach us," Janklow said.

The cigarette boat fell silent again. Sumner set his jaw and strained to hear. He disliked the silence. The quiet stretched on for five, then ten minutes. Clutch sauntered over, wearing an attitude as if the situation caused him no concern whatsoever, which was idiotic, as his title was head of security.

"They figured out that they're crazy to take us on. We outnumber them by so much that they'd have to be insane to even attempt this. That's why they stopped." Clutch spoke softly, but even so his voice held a note of arrogance that Sumner found annoying.

"Maybe," Janklow said. "Sumner, what do you think?"

Sumner hated to rain on the 'we're superior to them' parade, but he didn't agree at all.

"I think they're going to stay a safe distance away and blast the hell out of the ship with their grenades. They'll kill two-thirds of us, then they'll radio back to a larger ship that's floating nearby, and that one will proceed to board us."

Sumner couldn't see anyone's face, but he could have sworn that the silence that met him held a thread of stunned disbelief.

Block's voice came out of the darkness. "He's all sweetness and light, ain't he?"

16

EMMA RETURNED HER CAR TO THE RENTAL OFFICE AT PIETER-maritzburg airport and hopped a shuttle to the terminal. Her phone started rattling. To her relief, the caller ID showed that it was Banner.

"Ms. Caldridge, Banner here. How can I help?"

Emma felt herself relax. At that moment this was one of the only men she trusted. He sounded tired, his voice scratchy.

"What time is it there? You sound exhausted," Emma said. She heard him sigh over the line.

"I got called out of bed for an emergency and just got back here. I've been sleeping since then."

Emma hated the word "emergency." Especially when Banner used it. Darkview's emergencies were always dangerous and volatile. She didn't bother asking him about it. Darkview handled classified matters on a regular basis. He'd never tell her about it unless it was absolutely necessary.

"I'm afraid I'm being targeted," she told him.

"In what way? I heard about the bomb at the marathon."

"It's that, but there's something else. I've been hit with some sort of medication." Emma described getting stabbed with the EpiPen at the bombing. "I tested my blood later. I was floating in dopamine and epinephrine, which you probably know as adrenaline."

"What are the effects of these chemicals?"

"They can trigger a fight-or-flight response, but at the levels I saw, any reaction is possible, even heart attack or death. In my case it increased my anxiety levels tremendously, and . . ." Emma trailed off.

"And?"

She took a deep breath. "And it made me want to run."

Banner was silent a moment. "I don't want to appear facetious, but you were competing in an ultra at the time. Most people would say that wanting to run is normal for you." His voice held a friendly, amused tone.

Emma smiled to herself. "I guess that's true, but trust me when I say that this was strange, not normal. And my endurance increased a hundredfold."

"I do trust you. You tell me: Are there any drugs out there that can trigger dopamine responses and increase one's endurance? The only thing I know about is from a layman's perspective, and that would be steroids."

Emma paused. "Steroids can enhance physical performance, but they take a long time to work. There are several drugs that affect dopamine. Dopamine agonists, used for people with Parkinson's, will sometimes trigger addictive behaviors, but even those drugs wouldn't flood one's system indiscriminately at the saturation point that I'm experiencing." The shuttle bus reached the terminal. Emma grabbed her duffel and stepped out, heading to the departure area. To her surprise, she saw Stark standing there. He held a BlackBerry in one hand while pulling a roller bag behind him. He glanced up and locked eyes with Emma. She nodded and started toward him, talking all the while.

"I wanted to tell you right away." She paused. Since her experience in Colombia, she'd not been in touch with either Banner or Cameron Sumner, the man who'd helped her through the mess. Now she wanted to contact Sumner, but only Banner knew where he'd been whisked off to after their arrival in the States. "Can you tell me anything about Sumner? I'd like to know that he's okay." There was a pause.

"He's in the Indian Ocean. On a cruise ship that was headed to the Seychelles. It got waylaid by pirates, and now he's somewhere off the coast of Somalia."

"Somalia!" Emma couldn't believe her ears. She stopped walking; all thoughts of Stark flew out of her head. "Oh, God, tell me he isn't a hostage again."

"No. But there is a situation that I wanted to speak with you about. The U.S. thinks the ship is carrying vaccines and pharmaceuticals that have been tainted with ricin and some other, unidentified chemical. They don't want to alert anyone to the importance of the cargo by mobilizing a large force to take the ship back. It's moved into Somali territorial waters, which creates a unique situation."

"So let me guess," she said. "They want Darkview to infiltrate the ship covertly."

She heard Banner blow out a breath. "Something like that."

"I'm going," Emma said. "You said the vials possibly contain ricin and some other substance. Who better than a chemist to figure this out?"

Banner sighed. "I agree with you, and your name came up, but I'm afraid Major Stromeyer does not. She is, in fact, in vehement disagreement with me. She said it would be taking unfair advantage of you in light of your recent traumatic experience. And that *is* a compelling point for your not going."

"Tell her not to worry. Do you have a contact for me? Where should I go? Mogadishu?"

"Absolutely not. Insurgents just closed the airport. They're using mortar shells to attack any plane that lands. Can you get yourself closer to Somalia?"

Emma glanced up to see Stark headed her way. He would be at her side in the next few seconds. She needed to end the call. Watching him, though, gave her an idea. "How about Nairobi?"

"That would be perfect, actually. Send me a text message when you land, but keep it brief. My cell phone is tapped, as are Darkview's phones. This line is secure for the moment, but I'll be changing phones on a regular basis. Dump yours after you're done. I'll have a contact meet you there to transport you to Berbera, a small port town at the tip of Somalia, where another contact will take over."

Stark was upon her.

"I'm off. I'll be in touch." Emma hung up just as Stark stopped in front of her.

"Hello, where are you going?" he said. His attitude was stiff, but he seemed less angry than the last time she'd seen him, which she took as a positive sign.

"Turns out I'm headed to Nairobi also." Emma waved her cell phone at him with a smile. "Just got my marching orders."

Stark raised an eyebrow. Emma thought he looked as suspicious as hell.

"Do you have a visa for Kenya?" he asked.

Emma paused. She didn't. "Can't I get one at the airport?"

Stark shook his head. "Maybe, maybe not." He looked at her for a moment, as if deciding something. He nodded then, seeming to have come to some internal decision. "You're welcome to fly on the Price jet."

"If it's no trouble."

"Of course not. I had some questions for you anyway. About your report."

Emma did her best not to grimace. The last thing she needed was an extended grilling about her report, but using the Price jet would save time, something that she assumed Cameron Sumner didn't have.

17

BANNER CALLED STROMEYER TO TELL HER THAT EMMA CALDRIDGE was on her way to Berbera, and then he braced himself. He expected a tongue-lashing. After the DOD meeting, they'd talked in her car. Stromeyer looked as angry as he'd ever seen her. She'd made no secret of the fact that she did not agree with his plan.

"You can't send that woman into such a situation. Not so soon after Colombia. You know she's suffering from post-traumatic stress and is in no position to take on yet another risky venture." Banner had agreed, but he saw no other way.

"She has the expertise we need to analyze the vials, and she has a huge stake in the outcome."

Stromeyer pointed a finger at him. "You're using what you imagine to be her feelings for Sumner against her. You have no idea how she feels about him, and if she does care for him enough to do this, then she's *really* the wrong person for the job. You know as well as I do that strong emotions often lead the person having them to make mistakes. People in love will try to save their loved one against all odds, and usually they die right along with them."

"I agree in principle with what you're saying, but not when we're talking about Caldridge. She won't let that happen. She's tough and resourceful—Colombia's proven that, and she's already on the run. She'd be better off staying the hell out of the States for a while. And you know that none of these attackers will follow her to Somalia. They'd be insane."

Stromeyer made a disgusted noise. "You're insane for sending her there. You can't seriously argue that she's safer in Somalia than here. Go home and get some rest. I can only imagine that sleep deprivation has scrambled your brains."

Now Banner listened to the phone ring and crossed his fingers that Stromeyer had altered her thinking on the subject. When Stromeyer picked up the phone, she dispensed with the usual hello and said, "Tell me you've seen the light now that you've rested."

So much for a change of heart. "Caldridge just called me. She's agreed to go help Sumner. I suggest we meet at Darkview to work out the rescue logistics. Want me to pick you up on the way?"

"Why the escort?"

"Caldridge said someone hit her with a strange medication after the bombing. I think there's safety in numbers."

"In that case, absolutely."

Half an hour later, Banner arrived on a motorcycle in front of Stromeyer's condominium building. He removed his helmet and looked around. She lived in the Georgetown area, a quiet, elegant neighborhood with tree-lined streets. Banner watched as several residents of the neighboring houses opened their doors to collect the morning paper. They were all women, and they all looked suspiciously alike. Each one glanced down the street, each one spotted him on his motorcycle, and each one frowned at him.

Stromeyer stepped out onto her porch. To Banner she looked different from the other women. More animated, less of a cookie cutout. She wore dark jeans and a short navy trench coat that she buttoned as she jogged down the steps. Her hair was loose. A triangular-shaped bag hung over her shoulder. Banner watched her take in the motorcycle.

"Planning on losing a tail?" she said.

"The women in your neighborhood all look alike. And every one of them frowned at me on this bike. Do I look disreputable?" He offered her a spare helmet.

She finished buttoning her trench, tied the belt, and did some magic with the bag's straps that turned it into a backpack. She swung a leg over the cycle.

"This area isn't known for its diversity, as you've noticed. A whole group of people here only ride in chauffeured limousines. Men on bikes are suspect."

Banner prepared to start the engine. "Lacking diversity is one thing, but imitating each other is something else entirely. Why do they all look alike?"

"Beltway hair. Affectionately called 'helmet hair.' Designed to make the women look conservative. I'm surprised you haven't noticed it before now."

Banner shrugged. "I haven't really focused on it before." The motorcycle roared to life. He merged onto the street and headed to Darkview's offices.

He picked up the tail ten minutes into the ride. So must have Stromeyer. She leaned in to him at a stoplight.

"Brown Crown Vic."

Banner just nodded. He accelerated through the next intersection, barely making a yellow light. The Crown Vic stayed with him by blowing the red light. He sped up, splitting lanes and zipping past a MINI Cooper. The Crown Vic got caught behind the Cooper and a Honda Civic in the left lane. Through his rearview mirror, he watched the car swerve back and forth in an attempt to pass. He took an abrupt right turn, accelerated through the first half of the street, then turned left onto another. He kept zigzagging, taking pains to keep within the speed limit. The last thing he needed was to be pulled over. At first he thought he'd lost the tail, but after a few minutes he saw it turn onto the street behind him. It was over a block away, but still in the game. Even more so after he hit a red light.

"Alicia has a motorcycle," Stromeyer said. "I'll call her."

The light turned, and Banner concentrated on driving. Behind him he heard Stromeyer telling Alicia to lock the office door and giving her their location. He pulled up to an empty parking space next to a coffee shop. Both he and Stromeyer stayed seated. The Crown Vic slowed as it passed them. The passenger, a man who appeared to be in his late thirties, with hard eyes and a menacing manner, glared at them through the glass. The car inched to the corner, crossed the street, then pulled to the right and parked.

Banner shifted a little to be able to see Stromeyer. "Did you get a look at the passenger? That was one rough character."

"Can you hit the street and turn right? I told Alicia to meet us near the White House."

"What's the plan?"

"Divide and conquer. You're going to park the cycle. Alicia is going to swing by and pick me up while you head off in another direction. We'll meet back at the office."

"What's the point? Surely they know where we work."

"Make them think we're off to meet someone. It'll give us a few minutes to speak freely at the office. Our latest sweep came up clean, but once they return and point a microphone at us, we're back on tape."

Banner fired up the cycle, swung into traffic, and blazed right at the corner. He shot down the street, keeping an eye on the rearview mirror. The Crown Vic cruised along with them, easily keeping pace. Banner swayed through the cars, each time getting farther and farther away. He reached the corner of their appointed meeting place and idled, waiting for Alicia. She appeared a few minutes later on a battered yellow Suzuki. She pulled up and flashed a smile.

"We get to lose a tail, huh? I love this! I feel like a spy. So much better than answering phones." Stromeyer crawled onto the back of the Suzuki. Banner glanced behind them. The Crown Vic turned a corner.

"Go," Banner said to Alicia.

"See ya, boss." Alicia revved the Suzuki out of the spot and back into traffic.

Banner sped off the other way. He was the lucky one that the

Crown Vic decided to follow. He swerved down streets and around corners. The sedan lost more and more ground. After twenty minutes he couldn't see it at all. He changed course and headed to his office.

He entered the office and walked straight to the conference room, where he watched Stromeyer pace back and forth. Alicia sat at the table's head, nervously eyeing first Stromeyer, then him. She mouthed, "She's mad," at Banner when Stromeyer wasn't looking. Banner sighed. This much he knew. The phone on the conference room's table rang twice before being abruptly cut off on the third ring.

"What did you do with the phones?" he asked.

"Forwarded them to your cell."

Banner grimaced. Sure enough, his pocket started vibrating. He ignored it while Stromeyer continued to pace.

"Aren't you going to answer it?" Alicia asked. "I try to never let them go to voice mail."

"It's tapped," he said.

Alicia's eyes grew large. "So cool. Can I text my boyfriend and tell him?"

"No!" Both Stromeyer and Banner spoke at once.

Alicia put up a hand. "I was just kidding. Jeez, you guys are on edge today."

"Being hit with an investigation, audited by the IRS, followed by two goons, and having one's phone tapped does that to a person," Stromeyer said. She stopped wearing a path in the carpet and pointed a finger at Banner.

"Okay, I'm over it. She's made her choice, and for better or worse she'll need backup."

The phone started ringing. Alicia reached over to answer.

"Leave it," Banner said. "This is more important." After two short rings, the phone went silent. Seconds later his pocket started vibrating again. He ignored it. Stromeyer raised an eyebrow but said nothing.

Alicia pursed her lips. "What if it's someone important? Like the president of the United States?"

Banner laughed. "The president would never call here. At best he'd have one of his assistants contact us."

Alicia put her hands on her hips. "Even so. I'm taking Marketing 101, and the professor said that a company should endeavor to always have a living person answer its phones during business hours. Not to sends the wrong message."

"Alicia." Stromeyer's voice held a note of warning.

Banner retrieved his phone and looked at the readout. "I'll pick up this one."

"Yes." Alicia pumped a fist, waved at him, and swung out the glass doors, headed to her console.

"Just filing, no phone calls!" Stromeyer called after her.

Banner made an irritated sound and punched the green button. "Banner," he barked into the phone.

"Is this the Mr. Banner who knows Emma Caldridge?" The female voice on the other end of the line was soft and spoke with a slight Asian accent.

"This is he."

"I work for Price Pharmaceuticals. Ms. Caldridge asked me to analyze some vials of blood and to give you the results. May I proceed?"

"Certainly," Banner said.

"The blood was negative for ricin, botulism, and anthrax. Also for HIV. As for her dopamine question, please tell her that people like her who engage in extreme sports will often exist in a state of continuously elevated dopamine levels."

Banner wasn't sure how to respond to this information. "Is that bad?"

The caller chuckled. "No. But it does reduce their sensitivity to certain stimuli. The body learns to accommodate the levels by forming a tolerance, much like that formed by individuals addicted to substances. For example, a Formula One race-car driver may feel intense excitement during his first race, when his body dumps dopamine into his system, but over time he will lose the jittery feeling and adjust to the new levels. Likewise Ms. Caldridge, as an extreme runner, has probably grown used to the excess chemicals created when she runs. She is undoubtedly capable of functioning normally under higher blood-saturation levels than less acclimated people."

"And what would happen to those less acclimated?"

"I'm sorry to say that these people would likely behave in a highly erratic and possibly dangerous fashion. Moreover, excessive amounts—say, in successive doses—could stress the heart to levels that can kill."

Banner thanked the woman and hung up, not quite sure what to do with the information just given to him.

"That call was for Caldridge," he said. He consulted his watch. "She should be landing in Nairobi soon. I told her to wait at the airport before heading to Berbera."

"Good idea. We have a contact there. Ahmed. Remember him? I'll let him know to look for her, and I'll send Roducci to meet her in Nairobi."

Giovanni Roducci was a disreputable Italian who ran around Europe pretending to be an entrepreneur distantly related to the Borgias. Roducci could produce fake documents, real weapons, and any number of vehicles on a moment's notice. He fawned over Stromeyer. Whenever she called, they engaged in a spirited negotiation that usually ended with Roducci pretending bankruptcy and Stromeyer claiming she was robbed. Banner steered clear of these conversations. Roducci wore him out with his breezy gamesmanship.

"Roducci can get her whatever she might need to analyze the vials. He's a notorious gossip, so I'll keep him out of it until I can determine what she may require." Stromeyer headed toward the glass doors, trench coat in her hand.

"Aren't you going to yell at me about sending her?"

Stromeyer turned back. She shook her head. "Seems to me like she took matters into her own hands. It's not what I would have done if I were her, but she's proven she can take care of herself."

"I doubt she has a Kenyan visa."

Stromeyer halted. She held the door while she stood halfway in, halfway out. Banner could almost see her mind whirring. Working out the details.

"That's not an insurmountable problem. I'll get it arranged."

Banner followed her out of the conference room, his thoughts on the task ahead. The idea that a chemical weapon could soon be in the hands of pirates disturbed him, as did the fact that he had no idea of its composition.

And that didn't even take into consideration the ricin.

STARK ESCORTED EMMA THROUGH THE AIRPORT.

"Come on. We won't need to go through security," he told her.

Emma followed him to a private exit. Stark pushed open a metal door that led directly onto the tarmac. Jets lined up on both sides of them, glowing under the sodium lights. He walked toward a large, sleek number parked fifty feet away and proceeded up the ladder to the main door. The inside of the aircraft was plush but surprisingly compact. Each leather seat was the size of a commercial plane's first-class seat, but there were only eight of them in two groups of four. Each grouping had a small coffee table in the center, and one had a tray with a laptop already up and running. Two men were in the cockpit, writing on clipboards. The first smiled when he saw Stark.

"We're all set. Flight should be a breeze. We'll be there in time for your meeting. Strap in. We'll leave in ten minutes."

Stark put his bags in an overhead compartment and shut it. He lowered himself into a nearby chair. Emma did the same. True to the pilot's word, they were in the air within ten minutes in a smooth takeoff.

Stark spent the first twenty minutes of the flight taking call after call on a hands-free unit. He talked to various Price executives, two organizers of the Comrades race, and to the main office in the States. He would hang up, and the phone would ring again immediately. After he was done with the calls, he turned to Emma.

"Let's talk about Cardovin."

Emma took a deep breath. She wouldn't feel guilty about her findings, no matter how devastating they were. "You had some questions?"

Stark grimaced. "I have so many I don't know where to start. You said Cardovin does nothing to clear one's blood of the plaque that can form on arteries, but are there any conditions the drug can treat?"

Emma thought for a moment. She could see where he was heading, but she wasn't sure she wanted to make any statements she couldn't support.

"Are you thinking of an off-label effect?"

Stark nodded. "An off-label use would save us. We could still sell it, we wouldn't need renewed FDA approval, and the drug would be beneficial to someone."

Emma ran the clinical test results through her head. She didn't see how any of them would support off-label use.

"I don't think so. Most off-label benefits are noted anecdotally by the physicians who prescribe the drug for its approved use. I'm not aware of any for Cardovin."

"But what if there were a disease that it could affect?"

To Emma it sounded as though Stark were grasping at straws. "Can I speak plainly?"

He shrugged. "You were exceedingly frank back there in the lab. Why change now?"

"Any off-label use you could find for Cardovin won't fill a four-billion-dollar hole in your sales."

Stark stared out the window, saying nothing for a while.

"Price can't afford to lose billions in sales," he said at last. "If the stock plummets, we'll have to contract to conserve cash. Thousands will lose their jobs. Not to mention the loss to the shareholders. Price may never recover from the blow. It's imperative that we find a use for Cardovin."

"Price is constantly in research and development for new drugs.

Don't you have some new products in the pipeline for approval that can pick up the slack?"

Stark sighed. "We do, actually, but they're still in the clinical-trial stage. It could be two, maybe three years before the FDA approves the next one. We'll need operating cash in the interim. Cash that Cardovin would provide."

Emma saw his point. While she felt sorry for the loss of jobs, she saw no way to salvage the drug. If it didn't work, it was unethical to pretend that it did. In fact, Emma wasn't entirely certain that the prior sale of the drug wasn't bordering on consumer fraud. Her results were in line with several other previous studies, yet Price's marketing arm churned out glowing statistics regarding Cardovin's efficacy. The marketing materials were careful to use terms like "in combination with other drugs" when discussing the results, but it still seemed to Emma like too much hype given the actual reports. She was glad she didn't have to decide how to withdraw the drug. Price's lawyers had that unenviable job. She stared out the window, feeling her eyelids becoming heavy. It had been a long, strange day. She stared into the darkness and struggled to stay awake. Stark reached out and pressed a button. The lights in the cabin dimmed.

"Tell me again why you're going to Nairobi?" His voice helped revive her. Emma hesitated. Stark caught her pause. "You don't have to tell me if you don't wish to."

"Just on a business matter."

"It's pretty sudden business."

"It's for a company called Darkview. They tend to have sudden business."

"Ah, so it's for Banner."

It was a statement. Emma was surprised he even knew the name.

"How do you know about him?"

"Wasn't he the guy that rescued the Colombian hostages? He's all over the news. Cooley's committee is trying to bury him for blowing up the pipeline."

"That's him," Emma said.

"You trust this man?"

"With my life."

"Is he the only man you'd trust with your life?"

"In addition to my father, there's one other. His name is Cameron Sumner."

"Where's he?"

"I have no idea."

Stark gave her a searching look. She returned to gazing out the window. The low cabin lights and the hum of the engines calmed her. She stared at a reflective white area on the airplane's wing. It reminded her of a song about the lines running along the freeway. She heard Stark shift in his seat.

"You seem worried about him."

Emma sighed. "I am, but that's not what I was thinking about."

"What *are* you thinking?" Stark's voice came out of the gloom.

Emma found the question surprising in its intimacy. At first she thought not to answer. But then decided she should. Something about being in the dark, heading toward a shared destination, made her feel less wary of him.

"I'm thinking about the words to that song. About the white lines on the freeway."

"Joni Mitchell."

"It is hers, isn't it?"

"Yes."

"What are *you* thinking?" Emma asked.

Stark was silent a beat. "I'm thinking that no one has ever said that they'd trust their life to me."

They subsided into silence. Emma looked away from Stark. She thought everyone needed to have one person believe in them, depend on them, and, if the chips were down, trust them implicitly. That Stark didn't have such a person in his life made him seem isolated despite his outward success.

"Has anyone entrusted his life to you?" Stark said.

Emma nodded in the darkness. "I'd like to think that Patrick, my late fiancé, would have. And Cameron Sumner did in Colombia."

"Late fiancé? Did he die?"

Emma felt her throat constrict, as it always seemed to when someone asked her about Patrick.

"Car accident. Over a year ago. He was hit by a drunken driver. I wasn't with him when he died, but if I had been, I would have done everything in my power to save him." She shook away the thought. Thinking too much of Patrick usually sent her down a road that she found too hard to step off.

"I'm sorry."

"Thank you."

"And Cameron Sumner, was he right?" Stark's voice pulled her out of her melancholy thoughts.

"Right? What do you mean?"

"To trust you with his life?"

Emma nodded. "I think so."

She saw Stark turn his head toward her. "Would you do it again?"

"You mean, would I save his life again?" she said.

"Yes."

"Absolutely."

"This is someone you love, then," Stark said.

Emma shook her head. "The man I love is dead."

He looked at her. "Maybe no one has ever entrusted their life to me, but thousands have entrusted their jobs, money, and health to me. I don't want to let them down. I'll do whatever it takes to keep Price afloat."

Emma said nothing. Personally, she didn't equate saving someone's job or money to saving that person's life, but Stark's loyalty to Price was admirable, if a little extreme. Emma doubted she'd ever fight so hard for a corporation, but to men like Stark perhaps the company was everything.

They landed in Nairobi on an approach and touchdown that were as smooth as anything Emma had ever experienced. After a few minutes, the pilot emerged, looking tired. Stark conversed with him while his copilot opened the door.

Emma stuck a hand out. "Thanks for the flight. My first on a private plane."

The copilot smiled. "Did you like it?"

She smiled back at him. "I loved it. The only way to fly."

The copilot looked pleased.

Stark didn't join in the conversation. He gazed out the jet's door with a preoccupied expression on his face. Emma turned to see what he was watching, and her heart dropped. Two stoic-looking men in uniform stared back at her, their expressions grim. A third man, not in uniform but in dark jeans, a black sweater, and dark gym shoes, also peered up at them. He had curly black hair that hit just below his collar, a ring in his left ear, and a BlackBerry phone in his hand. He flashed a huge smile at Emma.

"Signorina Caldridge? It is I. Giovanni Roducci. Here to meet you!" Roducci spoke English with an Italian-laced accent and held his hands out in an expansive gesture.

Stark moved up behind her. "The two in uniform are from immigration, but who's the gigolo?"

"He is Giovanni Roducci. Here to meet me," Emma said. She gave Stark a warning look. "Please try to be cordial."

"Why?"

"Something tells me I'm going to need his help."

"Okay. But a bit of advice: Don't trust *this* man with your life."

19

THE CIGARETTE BOAT REMAINED SILENT. SUMNER STRAINED TO see through the darkness. He would have killed for some night-vision goggles. As it was, he tried to empty his mind of any thoughts and focus on his sense of hearing. He directed his eyes toward where he'd last heard the engine and was rewarded by the metallic clang of steel hitting steel. Definitely not a sound heard in nature. He attempted to see movement in the dark, but there was none. He waited. In order to heft the gun, the pirates were going to have to reveal their position with more noise. When they did, he'd shoot in that direction. Block sidled up behind him.

"Any idea where they are?" Block whispered.

"Directly in front and a little to the left of me."

"Close enough to shoot?"

"Impossible to say. They could be out of range."

Clutch moved to Sumner's left. "How'd you get that gun on board? It's illegal." Clutch spoke in normal tones. Block shushed him.

"Keep your voice down." Block sounded irritated. "Why the hell do you care if it's illegal? That gun just might be the thing that keeps us alive."

"I care because I'm in charge of security. It's my neck if the authorities decide that I was negligent." Clutch's voice held a surly note.

Clutch *had been* lax. Sumner had simply carried the gun on board in its case affixed with a decal inscribed with the name of a famous fishing-rod manufacturer along with the words "fishing gear." Neither Clutch nor anyone else had bothered to inspect the luggage. In fact, Sumner was surprised at the lack of security on the ship. It was well stocked with life rafts, vests, flare guns, and the other accoutrements needed should the ship flounder and sink, but other than the LRAD it was completely unprepared for an attack of a hostile nature. Given the waters it cruised, Sumner found this lack of preparedness puzzling.

"So we broke one rule." Block's tone was dismissive.

"Not one rule—lots of rules. Running dark like this is also against the law." Now Clutch sounded belligerent. Sumner thought his concern for proper procedure was too little too late, and ridiculous under the circumstances. He could only assume that the man's ever-present anger made it impossible for him to cooperate with anyone.

"Me, I'd like to live, thank you very much. The rules be damned," Block said.

Sumner heard another unusual clatter somewhere out in the darkness. "Hear that?"

"I did," Block said.

"Forty-five degrees to the left."

A whooshing came from that angle. Like the fizzing of a bottle rocket spiraling up. Sumner traced its progress with his ears, not his eyes, although there was a small light trail created by the lit fuse. His heart picked up a faster rhythm.

"What the hell is that? A grenade?" Block's voice was strained.

"Too quiet," Sumner said. "And it sounds like it's moving upward, not toward us." He put his rifle to his shoulder and tensed, waiting for the explosion. The blast came with a beautiful fireworks display. White bits of light shot heavenward, then tumbled down in an umbrella shape, brightening the sky all around. In the resulting glow, Sumner made out the shape of the cigarette boat as well as those of its occupants. There were four. They were just gray silhouettes in the distance, perhaps too far to be hit. Sumner aimed and fired anyway.

The rifle shot cracked through the night. He heard a yell, and then the air filled with the roar of an engine. The walkie-talkie on Sumner's belt crackled.

"Heard that." It was Wainwright. "I've got enough power for half an hour. Use it now?"

"Go," Sumner said.

The ship shuddered with the vibration of the huge turbines coming to life. The electricity flickered back on, bathing the entire deck with light. Clutch cursed from his position to Sumner's left.

"We can't see them, but we might as well have targets on our chests," he said. Sumner felt completely exposed. He hunched lower behind the railing.

Block appeared at his right. "See anything?"

Sumner didn't bother to respond. Instead he aimed again at the pirates' last location. He concentrated on listening. They were moving closer. He targeted only blackness but fired anyway. He heard a yell, which gave him a great deal of satisfaction. He most likely hadn't hit anyone, but they knew he was there.

"You're keeping them on their toes," Block said.

The *Kaiser Franz* started to move. Below Sumner came the swish of rushing water as the boat cut through it.

"Cover your ears." Wainwright's voice came from the walkie-talkies and echoed on the deck. The LRAD blasted.

"He get them?" It was Clutch.

Sumner shook his head. "Have no idea. They've got to be moving. Probably zigzagging to avoid us. See anything?"

"Not a thing," Clutch said. "And it's worse with the deck lights on. They're killing my night vision." He pulled his transmitter off his belt. "Douse the lights!"

"We've got a spotlight," Wainwright said. "We'll use the LRAD on them as long as we can see them."

The cruise ship picked up speed. Now Sumner could hear the pirates as they opened the throttle on their boat. The spotlight danced around the water, searching. Sumner still couldn't see them, but he heard them just out of the searchlight's range. Whoever was manning the acoustic weapon had heard the pirate boat as well. It bellowed again at the exact moment the floodlight caught them. The decibels bounced off the pirate ship.

"That was good," Block said. His words were swallowed by the boom of a grenade being fired.

Sumner flung himself back against the wall, away from the railing. He threw down the rifle and curled into a ball, protecting his head with his arms and presenting his back to the ocean. The grenade shot over his head, high. He heard it hit something before it exploded. This hit was close. So close that Sumner felt the heat and the pulsing wave of air that came after. Bits of shrapnel peppered the water. Thank God they're such piss-poor shots, Sumner thought. Had they even a modicum of skill, the deck would have been blown to pieces.

"That one sheared off the satellite dish. There goes our contact to the outside world," said Wainwright's voice through Clutch's receiver.

Sumner was bathed in sweat. He wiped his hands on his pants before retrieving his gun, then returned to the railing. The deck lights blinked off, plunging them into darkness once again. Even the searchlight was gone.

This time Sumner's hearing was useless. The air around him was a cacophony of sound. The LRAD blasted, leaving a ringing in his ears and rendering him functionally deaf. The water pounded against the hull as they carved through it, and in the distance came the screams of the passengers somewhere deep inside the ship's bowels.

"Block, shoot a flare," he said.

Block was flattened against the deck wall behind him. He rolled up next to Sumner. "I don't have a flare gun. I've got a Taser. Clutch has the flare."

Sumner heard the pirates. Another grenade shot could be only seconds away.

"Clutch, shoot a flare, now." Sumner snapped out the order in the general direction of where he thought Clutch was. He could hear the cigarette boat revving, first far out, then maintaining the same volume, then becoming louder. In his mind's eye, Sumner pictured the vessel making an arc away before returning to home in on the ship. The deck stayed dark.

"Clutch, the flare, now!" Sumner shouted.

"Where the hell is he?" Block said.

Before Sumner could answer, a flare shot out into the darkness to Sumner's left. The flaming projectile rose into the sky. While it didn't throw a lot of illumination, it was enough to once again expose the pirates' position. He heard them give a yell. He lay on his stomach, aimed, and fired. The flare died out before he could determine if he'd hit. To his relief, he heard the pirate ship veer away.

"Bastards are moving back again," Block said. He turned toward the spot where the flare had fired. "Good shot, Clutch. I was just starting to wonder where you were. What the hell took you so long?"

Out of the darkness came a woman's voice. "I am sorry, sir. My English is not so good, and it took me a moment to find the flare gun."

Sumner and Block both turned to look. The lights on the deck sprang to life again, and there stood the German girl, holding a spent flare gun.

20

"I'M MARINA SCHULLMANN," THE GIRL SAID.

Block stood up and put out a hand. "I'm Harry. And this here's Sumner. What's your first name again?" Block asked him.

Sumner stood. "Sumner's fine. Not too many people use my first name." He held the rifle down and slightly behind him. Marina's white-blond hair, chopped to her chin, blew around in the breeze, flicking over her ice-blue eyes. She had a reserved, cool way about her, which he knew from watching her was alleviated somewhat when she smiled, but she wasn't smiling now.

She pointed at the gun hanging by Sumner's leg. "This is what caused them to leave?"

Block shot Sumner a cautious look.

Sumner nodded. "It is. But it's illegal on a cruise ship, so I would ask that you not broadcast that I have it."

Marina looked surprised. "I am happy you have it. Who is Clutch?"

"The head of security. He had the flare gun. Did you see him over there?"

Marina shook her head. "I found the flare gun on the deck floor. No one was near me."

Sumner made a mental note to throw Clutch against a wall and explain the rules of engagement to him. The first being this: Never run and leave your comrades to go it alone during a firefight.

"How long before they return?" Marina said, getting right to the point.

Sumner was about to tell her that it could be anywhere from a few hours to a matter of minutes when Block broke in.

"They turned tail and ran. We may never see them again."

Sumner frowned. He wouldn't have lied to the girl. She struck him as no fool. He watched her take in the information and shake her head.

"That is not true, Herr Block."

Block shifted. "Now, don't you worry, miss. Sumner and me here got the situation as far under control as it can be, considering the circumstances. You should go back to your cabin and lock the door."

Marina raised an eyebrow. "I think the situation was better controlled when I shot the flare gun."

Sumner suppressed a smile.

"And we thank you," Block said, clearing his throat. But you still should go back to your room. Didn't I see you with your parents?"

A cloud passed over her face. "My mother is frightened for me, that's true. But I wanted to know what was happening. The ship's captain is not informing us. He only says that he has sent a distress signal and an American aircraft carrier in the region is coming to our aid. But this I don't believe."

Block gave Sumner a worried look.

"Why not?" Sumner said.

"The Frenchmen in cabin 216 said that Americans will not come to the aid in Somali waters."

"Did they say anything else?"

"Not to me. They moved away. Besides, it's rude to listen to another's conversation, is it not?" Marina gave Sumner a reproachful look.

Just what we need, he thought, a woman with a proper upbringing.

"And," she continued, "I do not speak French."

"That's a shame," Block said.

Marina looked a little annoyed. "Do you, Herr Block?"

Block grinned. "Hell no. I speak Texan."

Block's comment seemed to mollify Marina. She gave him a small smile.

"Is this your first cruise to the Seychelles?" Sumner's question sounded mundane, given the situation.

Block snorted. "Guys, I'd love everyone to get to know each other better, but those pirates are gonna come back. Don't you think we should be preparing for that?"

Sumner wanted to tell Block that he was preparing for it, but he couldn't. Instead he raised his eyebrows at Marina to encourage her to answer.

"No. My father made this cruise six months ago. He liked it so much that he suggested to my mother that we go with him this time."

Did he, now? Sumner thought.

"What does your father do?" Out of the corner of his eye, Sumner saw Block begin to protest the continued conversation. Sumner gave a sharp nod of the head to indicate that he remain quiet. Block must have understood, because he didn't comment.

"He sells armored cars."

Sumner thought Block would fall over with surprise.

"What kind of armored cars?" Block said.

"Kind?" Marina looked confused.

"What brand? Fords? Chevys? BMWs?"

Marina shrugged. "All kinds. They bring the car to our shop, and we take it apart and armor it."

Sumner wondered what the odds were of an armored-car salesman taking this particular cruise to the Seychelles.

"I'd love to talk to him about how he does it," Block said. "Bet I could sell a ton of armored cars to the guys in Mexico. That country is in the middle of a drug war."

Sumner appreciated that Block wanted to learn about the marketing opportunities for armored cars, but he thought the more interesting question was why an armored-car salesman was taking the same cruise twice only six months apart.

"Do you know the Frenchmen's business?" Sumner asked Marina.

She shrugged. "No. But there is a Russian with his girlfriend. He sells drugs throughout the Eastern Bloc countries."

"Legal drugs?" Sumner said.

Marina smiled. "Yes. A heart medication."

STARK AND EMMA STARED AT RODUCCI AND THE KENYAN IMMI-
gration authorities. Stark frowned.

"I can't afford to have Price involved in any scandal. If you get detained at customs, I'd appreciate your keeping us out of it."

"Of course," Emma said.

Stark moved next to her to stand in the open doorway. "I'm staying here for the moment. My meeting isn't for another two hours, and I'm going to use the plane as my office. Something tells me that you and those officials are going to be having an extended conversation. I'll just watch the proceedings from up here. Do you mind?" He appeared to be enjoying the moment.

"Not at all." Emma did her best to sound unconcerned. She stepped out of the plane into the damp, cool air and moved down the stairs with what she hoped was a pleasant expression on her face. When she reached the bottom, Roducci held out a hand.

"So nice to meet you!" He pumped her hand with a heartiness that Emma found disconcerting. "Major Stromeyer of Darkview Enterprises asked me to meet you upon your landing and to give you your traveling papers." He kept her palm in his grip and held her gaze a beat while he let the information sink in. He released her and produced an envelope from his back pants pocket with a flourish. "Here they are."

Emma said nothing as she opened the flap to pull out the papers.

"The letter is from the American embassy located here in Nairobi.

It confers temporary diplomatic status on you, as well as the immunity from prosecution that comes from that status."

The papers were written in the form of a letter rogatory and suggested that Emma be allowed entrance to the country. It explained that she would be stopping only briefly in Nairobi on her way to Dubai. A Post-it note on the paper said that she was to meet her next contact near the Price private jet in one hour and warned Emma not to call until she received a second, cleared line from the contact. Emma peeled off the Post-it and placed it in her pocket.

The second paper looked exactly the same, except it was translated into a foreign language. Emma flicked a glance at the two immigration officers. The one closest to her held out a hand. She offered him her passport and the letter rogatory. He said nothing as he read them.

"Allow me to explain," Roducci said. "Normally you would require a visa. This is no real problem, a mere fifty dollars in the terminal and even less for a transit visa to another location. However, Major Stromeyer indicated that she did not wish for you to be registered in such a fashion. The officers have informed me that you must stay here, in the airport, for the time needed to obtain another flight to Somalia, which they understand is your final destination. You are not allowed to leave the airport." Roducci looked at Stark, who still stood in the open doorway at the top of the jet's stairs. "I am required to ask if the Price company intends to ensure that Ms. Caldridge does not venture outside of the terminal for any reason."

Stark shook his head. "The Price company will ensure no such thing."

Roducci looked taken aback. "You won't?"

"I won't." Stark nodded to the immigration authorities. "If you will excuse me, I need to make some calls before I disembark." He disappeared back into the airplane.

One of the officers raised an eyebrow and made a "huh" sound as he watched Stark leave. Roducci looked flabbergasted. He moved the

Kenyans away from Emma and engaged in a spirited discussion with them. After a moment they nodded their agreement to something, Emma didn't know what, and headed for the terminal entrance. Roducci waited until they were out of earshot before filling her in.

"I have offered to ensure your compliance." Roducci looked less than pleased at the turn of events. "But I need your agreement that you will stay in the terminal. Normally I would assume such compliance in the face of a direct demand from the immigration authorities, but Major Stromeyer indicated to me that you are a woman with her own ideas about things."

Emma wasn't about to promise Roducci anything until she met with her contact and learned the next step. She smiled a reassuring smile. "I promise to inform you if my plans change."

Roducci looked stern. "I don't have the power to help you if you break the law. My relationship with African police is one of mutual distrust. So far they have not attempted to incarcerate me, but the threat is always in the air."

"I understand. And I hope that nothing untoward happens," Emma said. She wondered at Roducci's business but decided that the subject was best left alone. "Is there a first-class fliers' lounge? I'd love a shower."

Roducci looked hesitant. "Yes, but it will cost you twenty dollars, and shortly thereafter you will enter hell. Best to save your money. Perhaps you may gain access to the one maintained by the international airlines." He walked along with her to the terminal. "The man in the dark slacks. Is he always so disagreeable?"

Emma saw no reason to lie. "Yes."

Roducci gave an expressive shrug. "Life is far too brief to be so upset."

They made it to a lounge maintained by a consortium of international airlines, paid a fee, and entered. The room was a narrow rectangle. Ancient armchairs upholstered in an orange industrial fabric, tattered and stained, lined one wall, and laptop power stations lined another. After the plush accommodations on Stark's private jet, the spartan room felt depressing.

Travelers occupied most of the chairs and all of the power stations. Some read, while the vast majority talked on their cell phones. A group of Arabs sat in a far corner, the men wearing business suits, the women head scarves and black, cloak-type dresses. To Emma's right, a long counter held a Coca-Cola fountain and an industrial coffee-maker. Plastic-wrapped sandwiches sat on a battered tray. At the far end of the coffee counter was a hallway that led to the washrooms.

"I'm going there." Emma pointed to the sign.

"I will await you here. I understand that your second contact is due to meet you in the next hour." Roducci snatched a newspaper from a nearby rack and settled into a free chair.

The bathrooms matched the outer area, in both age and cleanliness. Fluorescent lights cast a bluish gray glow onto the tiled walls. The far end contained three shower stalls. Yellowed vinyl curtains hung from a horizontal metal pole spanning each entrance. Emma moved one aside. White ceramic tile with gray specks and grout colored black with mold encased the interior. With a sigh, she headed to a sink. She dropped her duffel on the floor beneath it. The soap dispenser of the first was empty. She pushed the second, also empty, as was the third. At the third she depressed the handles of the cold and hot water faucets. A weak stream of tepid water poured out. It stopped after twenty seconds. She washed up as well as she could, repeatedly hitting the handles while splashing water on her face and cleaning her hands.

When she stepped into the main room, Roducci was gone. She headed to the counter, grabbed a shrink-wrapped muffin and a carton of yogurt. A display held individual servings of cereal. She chose a box of granola, ripped the top off the carton of yogurt, and poured the granola into it, then wolfed down the mix. When she was done, she took another quick look around for Roducci. She had twenty minutes before the second contact was to meet her at the rendezvous, so waiting for him to reappear was out of the question. She'd have just enough time to hustle back to the landing field.

On the tarmac once more, she received another bad turn of luck. The Price jet was gone. She walked a little farther out to check the names on the long row of private planes currently resting in Nairobi. None matched the Price jet's configuration. At the tenth jet, she reached the very end of the airport. A chain-link fence rimmed the runway. Beyond that was a frontage road. Cars whizzed by. She stood for a moment, perplexed, when she felt a touch on her arm. A man in a bright yellow reflective vest frowned back at her. He waved toward the aluminum door.

"I was just looking for my jet," Emma said. The man asked her something. She didn't know what he was saying, but she took a stab in the dark. "It's the Price Pharmaceuticals jet."

He walked her to a small booth situated next to the aluminum door. A stool, a counter, a telephone, and a clipboard filled the tiny area, barely leaving enough room for the man once he stepped inside. His foot kicked a wastebasket on the floor. He muttered and shoved it up against the wall with the toe of his boot. He consulted the clipboard before picking it up and showing it to her. At the top was the name, registration number, and time of embarkation for the Price jet.

"It wasn't supposed to fly anywhere. This was its destination," Emma said. The man shrugged, either not understanding her or not caring.

The aluminum door behind her slammed. She jerked around to see Roducci. He, too, glanced around as if searching for the jet.

"No Price jet and no contact. I've been stood up," Emma said.

Roducci's eyebrows hit his hairline. "The contact did not appear and the disagreeable man left? I don't believe it!"

Emma didn't either. She looked at her watch. "Let's give it some time." She moved to lean against the terminal building to wait.

Thirty minutes later she decided that the contact wasn't going to show. Roducci sat on the ground next to her, his head against the wall. She tapped him on the shoulder.

"Do you have a secure contact number for Major Stromeyer?"

Roducci shook his head. "She calls me on mine. She purchases prepaid phones for temporary use and gives me the latest number. Currently I can only contact her through the Darkview offices' line." He frowned. "Not a good idea, as it will immediately reveal our location to anyone listening."

So calling Stromeyer was out. "Any idea who the contact may be?"

Roducci shrugged. "There are four Darkview personnel in Nairobi. Perhaps five. I know two."

"Can you call them?"

"Of course." Roducci dialed his phone and waited. Hung up. Dialed again and waited. Hung up. "No answer at either."

Emma looked at the jets all around her. "I'm standing in an airport. Seems to me I should be able to get my own flight to Hargeisa, or at least closer to it, don't you think?" she said.

Roducci's eyes lit up. "I have just the thing. A good friend of mine is a member of a fine, upstanding family. They have their own jet that is parked here. I will contact them to determine what it will cost for you to charter it." Roducci whipped out his BlackBerry and began thumbing it furiously.

Emma started back to the terminal.

"Where are you going?" Roducci jogged next to her as he held the phone to his ear.

"To check the monitors. There may be a commercial jet leaving soon."

"Please, please, not necessary, not to mention not likely. Who goes to Hargeisa anyway? Just let me discuss this with my friend. I urge you to settle down. All will be well." He followed her into the terminal, chattering into his phone in a language Emma didn't understand. She headed to a customer-service desk manned by two agents. Above the desk hung several screens that contained scrolling flight information. She stood in front of the monitors, watching the green letters advance across the display. Roducci continued with an animated conversation. He lowered the phone.

"My friend says that you can use the jet. He can have a pilot here within the hour."

Emma kept her eyes on the schedules. The flights to Mumbai were scrolling by. "How much?"

Roducci held another conference. He lowered the phone. "Two hundred thousand dollars. American."

Emma gave him an incredulous look. "Are you joking?"

Roducci seemed offended. "It is a two-hour flight from Nairobi, and the cost of fuel is astronomical at the moment. The fee is for a round-trip, because once you are delivered there, the plane must be flown back here, and that is assuming you don't get shot down on approach. The insurgents are firing upon aircraft."

Emma raised her eyebrows at him. "What a lovely thought," she said. "But that's in Mogadishu, not Hargeisa."

Roducci gave a dismissive wave. "Nonetheless, we are discussing Somalia, so anything is possible. My friend would like to receive his jet back in one piece. And by the way, the jet you are paying for is the top of the line. A Gulfstream of the latest model. My friend assures me that it has all the comforts of home. He bought it from a very extravagant Russian billionaire who is now dead."

The screen completed its circuit. There were no flights to any destination in Somalia.

"Tell him thank you very much, but the cost is too high."

"Major Stromeyer will perhaps assist you in paying for part or perhaps all of it."

"I doubt that."

"I can arrange it very quickly. I am able to procure whatever you desire. I have a corresponding agent in Africa who is quite good at this."

Emma had no doubt that Roducci could arrange anything in any part of the world, but now she was much more concerned about his prices. "Who would pay for the procurement?"

"Why, the American government, of course. Major Stromeyer sees to it that my invoices are paid. She is not as generous as some contractors who hire me, but she is fair."

"I would have to run any charges past her and Mr. Banner first."

Roducci grimaced. "Mr. Banner and I do not always see with the same eye. I prefer to negotiate with Major Stromeyer." A smile creased his face. "She is a beautiful woman, is she not?"

"Major Stromeyer is very nice. As is Mr. Banner, once you get to know him. I'm sorry you don't always see eye to eye."

Roducci shrugged again. "It's no problem as long as Major Stromeyer is there."

Emma stepped up to one of the women behind the customer-service desk. "I need a flight to Hargeisa."

The woman shook her head. "All flights from Nairobi have been suspended. Ethiopian Airlines maintains flights, but you will need to connect in Addis Ababa." She tapped on her keyboard. "A flight there leaves in two days. You'll have a twelve-hour layover, and you will arrive in Hargeisa late that evening."

"Is there no other way? It's very important that I get there."

The woman paused. "The United Nations relief organizations fly their personnel into Hargeisa. Go back to the main ticketing counter in Terminal One and look for this sign." She wrote on a small note-pad, tore the sheet off, and handed it to Emma. It bore the letters UNHAS.

"What does it stand for?" Emma said.

"United Nations Humanitarian Air Services."

Emma headed to the main terminal, Roducci hot on her heels.

"I don't think the UN air services will allow you to fly. You should take my friend's aircraft."

"Too expensive," Emma said.

Roducci nodded. "I see your point. Exactly." He began another conversation with his friend on the phone.

Emma found the UNHAS sign prominently displayed on a counter next to a long line of passengers waiting for ticketing on a commercial jet. The UNHAS agent had no takers. He looked European, with short-cut hair and wearing a dark polo shirt. He watched Emma walk toward him and flicked a look at Roducci, who was still chattering on his cell phone. The man glanced back at Emma, a question in his eyes and a smile on his face. She responded with her own smile.

"I need to get to Hargeisa, and I understand that UNHAS flies that route. Is there a way I can pay for a seat?"

The man nodded. "Are you a journalist?"

"Unfortunately not."

The man shook his head. "I'm sorry. We're only allowed to fly UN personnel and journalists with proper press identification and advance clearance."

Emma hesitated. "If I can arrange for the identification, would I be able to go?"

"If so, then yes."

She pulled Roducci aside. "Can you get me some forged press identification?"

Roducci snapped his fingers. "Like that."

Emma stepped back up to the agent. "How much?"

"Today Hargeisa costs twenty-six hundred dollars round-trip, but the price can fluctuate as the situation there changes. Check-in is tomorrow, five-thirty A.M. I warn you, the flight is a bit rough. We fly small planes with no catering service and no toilets. It's five hours, with a touchdown in Jowhar." Emma calculated the time. Even with the overnight stay, she would cut twenty-four hours off the commercial flight to Ethiopia.

"Do I bring you the ID and clearances?"

The man shook his head again. "That needs to go through the main office, and it will take fourteen days for a security check."

Roducci snorted. "Fourteen days is far too long. And twenty-six hundred dollars for no beverages, no toilets, and in a small plane? That's banditry!" He turned to Emma. "My friend believes he can arrange to have someone rent the plane for its flight back here. He will accept fifty thousand dollars for your leg of the journey. Really, Ms. Caldridge, this is a very good deal for a private flight *with* all the comforts of a private jet. I believe you should accept this offer."

The UNHAS agent looked taken aback. "Somalia is an extremely dangerous place. The insurgents target any planes that fly there. There's no guarantee that a private jet won't be shot down. Even our jets are fired upon despite their UN affiliation. Your only other option is to take a khat flight out of Wilson Airport."

Emma perked up. "Khat flight?" She was familiar with khat, a twiggy plant popular throughout Africa. When chewed, it provided feelings of euphoria and led to long periods of chattiness interrupted by bouts of stupor.

"We don't recommend the flights, but they make the trip daily and the insurgents don't interfere. Khat is very important to them." The agent's voice was dry.

Emma turned to Roducci. "Can you take me to Wilson Airport?"

Roducci sighed and clicked off his phone. "So much for promises to stay inside the terminal. Should the immigration authorities stop us, I will charge Major Stromeyer for the inconvenience." He waved her out of the terminal and cut across several lanes of traffic to a nearby parking lot. Once there he marched to a hulking black Mercedes sedan with tinted windows and a satellite radio antenna. He reached around her to open the passenger side. As the door swung open, Emma noticed that the panel was thicker than most.

"Armored?" she said.

Roducci nodded. "I work in many dangerous areas of the world. Nairobi is not nearly the worst by far. However, even I have not been to Somalia in three years. Whatever business takes you there, I would suggest you reconsider." He closed the door with a heavy thud, jogged around, and slid into the driver's seat. As he snapped the seat belt, he cast a glance at her.

"I'm going," Emma said.

"Yes, I can see that you are determined." He sighed and started the car.

Half an hour later, Emma stood next to Roducci and stared at an ancient Fokker airplane being loaded with burlap sacks.

"That tall man in shirtsleeves is the pilot," Roducci said.

The pilot, a deeply tanned, rugged-looking white man with brown hair in a ponytail that brushed his collarbones, oversaw the loading. He wore faded navy blue chinos, combat boots that might have been black but were covered in dust, and a sand-colored short-sleeved shirt with the tails out. He appeared to have skipped his morning shave. Emma guessed he was nearing forty. He nodded at Roducci and made a comment to one of the workers before walking over to greet them. He walked with a smooth, loose-limbed gait that telegraphed confidence. Emma adjusted his age downward five years based on his stride alone.

"Roducci. What brings you here?" The man spoke English with a slight South African accent.

Roducci shook his hand. "May I introduce Ms. Emma Caldridge? Ms. Caldridge, this is Wilson Vanderlock. He owns that rusting plane you see being loaded."

Vanderlock ignored Roducci's insult to his aircraft and gave Emma a considering look and then a slight smile. "What can I do for you?"

"I'd like to hitch a ride to Hargeisa."

"Are you an aid worker?"

"She's working for Edward Banner," Roducci said. For some reason Emma was glad when she saw surprise enter Vanderlock's brown eyes. Something about his manner made her think he had a conventional view of women, and her working for Banner conflicted with that view.

"Banner's creating a stir in Hargeisa. His company arrested some pirates and dragged them there to be tried."

"Why would that cause a stir? Aren't the authorities happy to see a pirate captured?" Emma said.

Vanderlock shook his head. "Half the authorities in the Puntland region have a hand in piracy. Darkview is seen as a danger to the trade. I'm not sure I want to be associated with Banner or his company."

Roducci stepped forward. "Since when are you against Banner?"

"I'm against trouble, and that's what Banner has right now," Vanderlock said. He cocked his head to one side as he gazed at Emma. "Where's your entourage? Banner's people rarely travel without one. Not if they want to live."

She didn't like the sound of that. She ignored the fear trying to make its way through her system. Since Colombia she'd become an expert at ignoring the fear. She extended her hands, palms out. "It's just me. If it makes you feel any better, Banner has no idea that I'm here, talking to you."

Vanderlock raised an eyebrow. "Then why are you?"

"Because I need to get to Berbera. Fast. And the flights through Addis Ababa will take time, which is something in short supply for me."

"What's causing the rush?" A look of keen interest entered Vanderlock's eyes.

"Private business" was all Emma said.

He nodded, accepting the fact that she wouldn't tell him. "Better I don't know, actually. I'll take you. It will cost you a thousand dollars American."

Roducci made a surprised noise. "Out of the question! I know for a fact that your usual rate is one hundred dollars."

Vanderlock shook his head. "She's not usual. If anyone gets wind of her connection to Darkview, I'm going to be in hot water."

"She just told you no one knows, except us three. And discretion is my business, so I will never speak of it," Roducci said.

Emma wanted to strangle Roducci. Even if Vanderlock's price was inflated, it was hundreds of times less than that of the private jet he'd just tried to foist on her. She interrupted the men.

"I'll pay you five hundred," she told Vanderlock. Roducci took a breath to say something, but she cut him off. "You tried to bamboozle a Russian's jet on me for fifty grand when you knew not only that khat flights were cheap but even a pilot who flies the route?"

Roducci gave one of his expressive shrugs. "A lovely woman such as yourself should travel in style."

Vanderlock laughed. "You tried to unload Sergei's jet on her, didn't you?"

Roducci's look went sour. "I simply tried to keep her safe." He jerked his chin at the Fokker. "You've kept that thing flying with duct tape and rubber bands."

"It hasn't let me down yet." Vanderlock turned to Emma. "Seven-fifty and it's a deal. But know that I won't be able to fly you back here. Kenya doesn't care who I fly out of the country, but I'm no longer allowed to fly anyone in."

Roducci snorted. "That's never stopped you before."

"Well, it will in her case." He looked at Emma. "You'll have to return through normal channels."

"And Somalia? Do they care who arrives?"

"Not on the route we're taking. And keep your association with Darkview quiet."

She nodded. "Can you take me to Berbera?"

"Sorry, but no. After Hargeisa I return here. The khat is driven to Berbera. You might be able to ride with it all the way, but I wouldn't count on it."

"You go straight to Hargeisa?" Roducci sounded surprised.

"First to K50, then Hargeisa," Vanderlock said. Roducci gave a small groan.

Emma didn't like the sound of that. "Where's K50?"

"Mogadishu." Roducci supplied the information, a grim sound in his voice. "It's an alternate runway just outside of the capital. The main airport is too dangerous to use."

Tension curled through her. The immense danger of what she was trying to do hit her.

Roducci touched her arm. "You should wait to fly to Hargeisa directly. Surely whatever Banner needs you to accomplish can wait for a safer flight."

Vanderlock took a pack of cigarettes from his breast pocket. He put one to his lips and held the box out to her. She waved it away without a word. She needed to think. Vanderlock returned the pack to his pocket, extracted a blue plastic lighter, lit the cigarette, inhaled, and watched her. She noted that he neither confirmed Roducci's opinion that she should wait nor disputed it.

"Mr. Vanderlock—"

"Call me Lock. Everyone else does."

"How long will you stay on the ground in Mogadishu before taking off for Hargeisa?"

Vanderlock blew out a stream of smoke. "Thirty minutes. Just long enough to offload the first half of the shipment." He took another drag off the cigarette.

Thirty minutes could be a lifetime in Mogadishu, but Emma thought the UN agent might have it right. She doubted that the insurgents would mess with them when they still had half a planeload of khat to deliver. She offered a hand to Roducci.

"Thank you for your help." She transferred her travel toothbrush from the side of her duffel to the pocket of her jacket and handed her bag to him. "Do you mind throwing this away? It's just going to weigh me down."

Roducci looked at her and frowned. After a short pause, he took her hand between both of his.

"I see that you have made up your mind. Lock will keep you as safe as is possible, given the area to which you travel, but should you need anything, please call me." He produced a business card. "My number. Contact me anytime, day or night. I will see to whatever you may need." Emma took the card. It didn't contain a name, just a series of different phone numbers and two e-mail addresses.

"No name?" Emma said.

Roducci smiled. "Just numbers. But they all work. And when they don't, they will direct you to another. Do not worry. My business depends on people who need items quicker than can be found through the usual channels. My customers know how responsive I am. And they also know that I can get them anything. But my specialty is arms."

22

"I NEED TO SPEAK TO YOUR FATHER," SUMNER SAID. "CAN YOU take me to him?"

"Of course," Marina said. "But why?"

"I have some questions." Sumner handed Block the Dragunov.

"Oh, yeah, now, this is what I need!" Block's eyes lit up. "Those pirates come back and they're history." Block was like a child with a new toy. He pretended to sight something in the distance. Sumner reached out and gently pulled the scope away from Block's eye. He bent the gun on its side and flipped a small switch near the trigger.

"What did you do?" Block said.

"Switched it from automatic to semiautomatic. I don't have a lot of ammunition. You have to make every shot count."

"I just switch it back if I need automatic?"

"Don't."

"But if I need it? The switch will set it back?"

Sumner had a terrifying vision of Block spraying the water with ammunition, all of it falling far short of its mark.

"No. The switch sets it back to auto or semiauto depending on how you depress the trigger. One pull will give you one shot. Hold it down and the gun will continue to fire until you release it."

"Hell, put that back. Saves me a step. I promise to use it semi until I need it auto."

Sumner shook his head. "Under stress you are far more likely to hold the trigger down out of sheer panic. Kind of like the way a new driver hammers the gas pedal instead of the brake when an accident looms."

"I'm no new driver."

Sumner reached out to take the gun.

Block danced backward, out of his reach. "Okay, okay. You win. I'll leave it on semi for now. Don't worry."

Sumner had a lot of concerns, but he kept them to himself. He turned to Marina. "After you." They headed to the lower decks. Marina took a hallway that wound toward the casino.

"He's gambling right now," she said.

"So he's not worried about the pirates?"

Marina seemed to consider the question a moment before responding. "He likely is anxious about them, but he greatly enjoys gambling, so that's where we will find him."

Sumner thought it best not to comment on Herr Schullmann's habits. In fact, when they reached the casino entrance, it became clear that many of the ship's passengers were escaping reality by losing their money. The casino hummed with activity. Bells dinged from the slot machines, dice landed on green felt with muffled thuds, and the dealers murmured in low tones as they ran the games. The area was surprisingly full, mostly with men. Sumner didn't see one woman gambling. Even the bartender who'd poured him a whiskey hours ago was gone. One lone female croupier dealt a hand of blackjack to the French businessmen. Sumner spied the Russian at a roulette wheel, sans mistress, and Herr Schullmann leaned against a craps table watching the thrower fling the dice. Marina made her way through the stations. She slid up against the rail next to her father. Sumner remained a step behind her. Herr Schullmann flicked a glance at his daughter, then returned his gaze to the game.

"What do you want?" Herr Schullmann spoke in German. His voice held a gravelly tone, like that of a smoker who'd destroyed his vocal cords. He was in the same dark slacks from earlier, but he'd changed into a polo shirt that did little for his paunch. Sumner pegged him as a machine-tool operator made good. He had little doubt that if he were to meet Herr Schullmann at his factory, he'd find him with his sleeves rolled up and dirt under his fingernails. Sumner was raised in Minnesota by a professor father who, despite his advanced degrees, spent a great deal of time hunting, fishing, and skinning animals with his brothers. The rest of the family remained steadfastly blue-collar. They were pipefitters, plumbers, and electricians. Sumner spent entire summers camping with his uncles. He knew how best to deal with men like Schullmann. The trick was never to underestimate them. What they lacked in finesse, they made up for in ferocity.

"I'd like you to meet Mr. Sumner," Marina told her father. "He works for the *Kaiser Franz*. He wishes to ask you some questions." Schullmann turned his head to look at Sumner. His eyes held a wary look.

"What kind of questions?" He continued to look at Sumner but spoke in German and addressed his daughter.

"Questions about how to armor something to withstand a rocket-propelled grenade," Sumner answered in German.

Schullmann raised his eyebrows. He waved at the croupier to cash him out. Then he gathered his chips, dropped them into a pants pocket, and headed toward the bar without another word. Marina followed him, her face set. Sumner wasn't surprised at all. His take on the entire family was that the parents disliked each other, and this meant that the daughter would be stuck in the middle. Probably had been her whole life.

Schullmann heaved himself onto a barstool and ordered a beer. He gave Sumner a curt nod that Sumner interpreted to be a request for him to order.

"Seltzer water, lime," he said to the bartender, now a young man with red hair and a towel thrown over his left shoulder.

"You don't drink?" Schullmann said.

Sumner offered a barstool to Marina. She took one two seats away from her father, leaving Sumner the one in between. He pulled the chair out a bit and slid onto it.

"Not when I'm on duty," Sumner answered.

"They come back?" Schullmann asked the question in a desultory manner, then swallowed a mouthful of beer. To Sumner it looked as though Schullmann wasn't concerned about the pirates at all. Which was strange. The man had his entire family at risk, yet he sat in the casino playing craps and drinking. Sumner quelled his distaste. He wasn't privy to the family dynamics and didn't care to be. All he needed was this man's knowledge about armor plating. He took a sip of the soda, enjoying the cool liquid. It wasn't until that moment that he realized how thirsty he was. He downed some more of it before responding.

"That noise—you must have heard it—was a grenade blast. They missed. We were implementing our own countermeasures, but it was difficult to be accurate given the darkness. Your daughter's assistance was invaluable. She shot a flare gun at the precise moment that we needed it. Without the flare's illumination, they might have been successful in their latest attempt to board."

Marina colored a bit at Sumner's praise. Schullmann acted as though he hadn't heard it.

"What do you want to armor?" he asked.

"The door to the bridge and a small section of the upper deck. Is it possible?"

"What did you say you are armoring against?"

"Rocket-propelled grenades." Sumner used the English term before switching back to German. "I don't know the German word for them, nor do I know the model."

Schullmann nodded. "Most likely an RPG-7. They're the most common launchers used worldwide. I am quite familiar with this weapon, as I have had many discussions about arming a car to withstand them."

"Can it be done?"

"On a car? With an additional nine-hundred-plus kilos of steel, an undercarriage that resists fire, run-flat tires, and a good driver trained to move that vehicle out of the hot zone during an attack—maybe, but not likely. The design of those explosives was based upon the Deutsche Panzerfaust antitank weapon. This is a powerful device. One hit is often enough. Two in the same general location will end the struggle. Arming the sides of the ship against a direct hit? You would need steel. Lots of it. And a way to cut it to fit the dimensions you require. At my factory we have large robotic arms that do this for us. The weight alone makes it difficult to do without mechanical assistance."

Sumner shook his head. "Not the sides of the ship, a small portion on top of the deck. Almost like a duck blind for hunting. Just something to hide behind when the grenades start flying. And I need it to be movable."

Schullmann grunted. "That is crazy."

"Surely you can improvise something? Anything is better than nothing."

Schullmann considered this. He drank his beer. "Plating is heavy. It has to be in order to work. Even a small amount to protect the bridge door would weigh many kilos. When it's put on a car, the auto becomes far less mobile. In this case one would have to move the shield manually."

"Could we put it on a dolly? Move it around that way?"

"One of those red dollies with rubber wheels that you see delivery-men use? Probably not. Best would be a flat dolly with iron wheels. Do you have one of those?"

"I would think so. If only to transport the luggage and other items that provision the ship. I'll ask the captain."

Schullmann ran a hand along his chin. Sumner waited, allowing him time to think. The German swallowed some more beer before speaking again.

"You could try cage armor."

"What's that?"

"Strips of steel spaced at intervals. Almost like a birdcage. It's ideal for grenades, because it deflects them before they reach the target. There is a problem, though."

Sumner thought he already knew what the "problem" was. "As they are deflected, they explode. So whoever is within range of the explosion will die."

Schullmann nodded. "It's a flaw. The cage system is used to wrap around an already heavily armored tank. It stops the grenade from piercing the armor, but it's the armor on the tank that protects the inhabitants inside from the explosion. Just using the cage without another wall of steel is not a guarantee of safety."

"But the cage is lighter and easier to make than armor plating."

Schullmann nodded.

Sumner stood. "Let's make it. I'll look for a dolly and some metal rails or steel rods that we can use to build a cage. I'll get the ship's mechanic to assist you."

"What about the design flaw?" Marina had been so quiet that Sumner had forgotten she was there.

"I'm not going to have anyone inside the cage. I'm going to use it for another purpose entirely."

VANDERLOCK WAVED EMMA TOWARD THE AIRPLANE. THE WORK-
ers were loading the last sack into the cargo hold. One had already
jumped into his pickup and prepared to leave. She heard his car radio
switch on with the motor. Township music filled the air. She paused
to listen to the sound of pulsing beats and women's voices.

"What is it?" Vanderlock said.

"Township music. It's the second time I've heard it. I love it."

"I grew up with township music. I hate it," Vanderlock said. He
grabbed her elbow to help her into the jet. The workers had wheeled
a small set of rolling metal stairs to the entrance. Emma stepped up
and into the body, with Vanderlock right behind her.

The jet's interior had been gutted. Only the first row of seats remained, the rest ripped out to allow maximum cargo space. Wet burlap sacks filled every available inch. Twigs, leaves, and bits of dirt
from previous flights covered whatever floor space remained visible.
The entire plane smelled of damp leaves, earth, moss, and a hint of
mold. Skeletal metal rails, and nothing else, separated the cockpit
from the rest of the plane. Emma peered at the controls.

"Can you fly?" Vanderlock said.

Emma shook her head. "Not at all."

He lowered his frame into the pilot's seat. "Join me." He indicated
the copilot's chair.

"You don't have a copilot?"

Vanderlock busied himself with the dashboard. "I often do, but he's away for a couple of weeks. If I flew with passengers, I'd be grounded, but with khat? No one cares. The shipments must go on." He snapped a headset onto his ears, checked that the workers had closed the doors, and flipped some switches. The props began to circulate. Vanderlock handed her a second headset over his shoulder, all the while making adjustments and checking the dash.

Emma held the headset and hesitated.

Vanderlock looked up at her. "Are you afraid of flying?"

If you only knew, Emma thought. "I'm afraid of crashing. Flying is okay." Despite the danger, uncertainty, and her exhaustion, Emma felt almost giddy with excitement. She'd never flown in the cockpit of an airplane that size, never thought she'd ever do so. The idea of experiencing flight from the nose of the aircraft rather than the bowels of the plane seemed safer somehow—the way riding in the front seat of a car was more pleasurable than in the back. She scrambled into the seat, snapped her seat belt, and placed the headset over her ears. Vanderlock turned and taxied for a minute to an empty runway. When they reached the beginning, he throttled the aircraft forward.

The ground passed under their wheels faster and faster as the plane chewed up the runway. The liftoff felt magical when viewed from the copilot's seat. One minute they bumped along, grounded, and the next they angled into the air, floating. Emma laughed out loud with the feeling of the jet pulsing upward and the view of only the vast sky in front of her. Vanderlock seemed to enjoy her excitement, because he smiled. He kept his eyes on the controls as he maneuvered the aircraft higher. When they reached cruising altitude, the plane leveled off. After thirty minutes he pressed some more buttons and visibly relaxed. He glanced at her, shaking his head.

"You're the first person I've known who has laughed while flying to Somalia," he said.

Emma refused to let her fear of what lay ahead eclipse the moment. "I love this," she said.

Vanderlock held her gaze. She couldn't read his thoughts.

"What do you do for Banner?"

"Ah. I can't say."

"Are you a mercenary?"

"I can't say."

"Are you his girlfriend?"

Emma snorted. "If I were, do you think he'd be sending me to Somalia?"

Vanderlock shrugged. "Word is he hires ex-military women. Wouldn't be unusual for those types to take dangerous missions."

"Tell me about the khat."

"Changing the subject?"

"Yep," Emma said.

Vanderlock settled deeper into the seat. "The khat is picked in Kenya, driven to Nairobi, flown out of Wilson Airport to Mogadishu, and from there distributed throughout Somalia. Speed is important, because khat stays fresh for only forty-eight hours. After that it's useless."

"How much is in here?"

"Five tons. And I'm not the only flight today."

"How did you get into the business of flying it?"

Vanderlock checked his dash before answering. "I always wanted to be a pilot, but opportunities were slim in South Africa where I grew up. I flew charter safari tours for a while, but dealing with rich tourists out of New York got old. Too much hand-holding for my taste. When a friend offered me the khat route, I jumped at it."

The whole explanation sounded a bit too pat for Emma. Give up a good job for making drug flights to the most dangerous place on the planet? Not likely, but she decided not to pursue it. Whatever secrets Vanderlock wanted to keep, they were no business of hers.

"Have you ever been fired on?"

He reached behind him to open a Styrofoam cooler shoved between a green duffel bag and the airplane wall. He pulled out a bottle of water and handed it to her, then opened another and took a huge gulp. He had stopped smiling.

"I had a close call just last week. Surface-to-air missile came within fifty meters. I banked pretty hard and circled to take a look. Nothing else happened, so I landed anyway. Shocked the hell out of me. I've been flying the same route for two years now without incident. The insurgents know me and this plane. I'm still not sure if it was a mistake, some kid playing with a new toy, or deliberate, but it's not a good sign."

Emma swallowed. Her throat had gone dry. "Any idea what might be happening?"

"Things are deteriorating. The pirate activity is handled by the warlords. They're cashing in to the tune of millions, but the rest of the maritime world is starting to push back. Banner's stunt sent a message that the warlords couldn't ignore. They're responding by ramping up their attacks on anything that moves."

Emma felt a flare of anger. "Why do you call it a stunt?"

Vanderlock raised an eyebrow. "Because he knew that the government in Hargeisa had no jurisdiction over those pirates. Hargeisa's in a section of Somalia called Somaliland. It's relatively peaceful by Somali standards, but it's not separate from Somalia and its government isn't recognized by the West. It's just an area some warlord decided to take over. In fact, there's no government in Somalia at all, so when the navy catches the pirates, they often just let them go again. Banner knew this but dragged them in anyhow."

Emma swallowed some water. "Sounds like he was making a point."

"That point being?"

" 'Don't mess with me. I won't let you go.' "

"He's making that point against some very sick characters. They're going to attack Banner and his people with all they've got. And that means you."

The fear grew. She tamped it back down. "I'll take my chances."

She sounded tougher than she felt. She only hoped that she was convincing.

"You sure are taking a chance." Vanderlock tossed the empty water bottle into a small garbage bag that hung from the wall on a bungee cord. "Listen, it may be none of my business, but something doesn't feel right here. When Banner moves personnel, he arms them to the teeth and they travel in groups for safety. His stealth guys operate alone, but they're armed as well. And you? You show up with Roducci, one of the biggest arms traders in the world, but you have no weapons, no luggage, and no escort."

Emma in no way wanted to have this conversation. It would only serve to scare the hell out of her. She'd get to the second contact and take things from there. If Vanderlock was correct, she'd be in "relatively peaceful" Hargeisa in three hours.

"*You're* not armed that I can see," she countered.

Vanderlock pointed to a long metal toolbox strapped flush against the wall on Emma's side of the plane. "Open it," he said.

Emma reached to the box, flipped open the metal clasp, and lifted the lid. An AK-47 rested on top of another, tubular-type device.

"What's the tube?"

"RPG-7. Shoots rocket-propelled grenades."

Emma closed the box.

"And then there's this." Vanderlock leaned forward in his seat, raised the tail of his shirt, and twisted away from her. A pistol nestled in a holster at the small of his back. "And this." He put his left foot on the plane's side, pulled back his pant leg, and slid a slender knife out of his boot. He held the weapon up for Emma to see before returning it to its place. "I showed you mine, now you show me yours." Vanderlock's eyes held a challenge. Emma chose to ignore the double entendre.

"Please concentrate on flying this plane. You're making me nervous," she said.

He resettled into the flight seat. "You don't have a weapon, do you?"

She felt her face flush. Truth was, she couldn't shoot with any accuracy. If she held an automatic weapon and fired hundreds of bullets per minute, she *might* succeed in hitting a target, but success was not assured by any means.

"No," she admitted. "I'm not a great shot."

Vanderlock shook his head in disgust. "Roducci has a trunk full of guns in that Mercedes of his. Least he could have done is given you one. Can you fight?"

Emma was confused. "What do you mean?"

"Karate? Tae kwon do? Anything?"

Now Emma was getting angry. She didn't need his derision just then. She pointed at his metal box.

"Judging from that little collection you just showed me, fighting will get me nowhere once the bullets start flying. Listen, I'm a scientist and I just need to get to Hargeisa. I'm counting on you to fly me there. After that I'll go my own way."

Vanderlock put a hand up as if to ward her off. "Fine. I'll get you there."

They lapsed into silence. Emma gazed out the window. The fear had won. It overshadowed her joy at flying. She wrestled it back to manageable levels. She took several long, slow breaths to calm herself while she stared at the ground below them. She remembered a bit of advice a soldier had once given her: When in the field, sleep when you can. The sun on the windshield bathed her face, and the plane's vibration soothed her. After a few minutes, her eyes grew heavy and she fell asleep.

She awoke with a start. Vanderlock had a hand on her arm and was shaking her. "First you laugh, then you sleep. You're a cool one."

Emma straightened up. She had no memory of falling asleep, and for a moment she was disoriented.

"We're landing." He pointed to a spot far in front of the plane's nose. "Over there is the city proper. Used to be a beautiful place back in the eighties. It's a little bit of hell now. But we're not going there."

Below them, battered buildings came into view amid the scrub and dust. Gaping holes and missing roofs revealed the extent of the destruction wrought by mortar shells. The entire landscape looked bleak, hot, and forbidding.

Vanderlock focused his attention on the panel before him. Landing the plane appeared to be taking all his concentration. Emma stayed silent, letting him work. They dropped lower and lower. A single runway cut into the sand came into view. Vanderlock aimed for it.

They bumped once before the plane settled into a fast taxi. Vanderlock lowered the flaps. The resulting drag pushed Emma against her seat belt. Near the end of the track sat several pickup trucks with men gathered around. Sunlight glinted off the guns slung over their shoulders. Their images flashed by as the plane shot past. When it seemed as if they would fall right off the runway, they stopped. Vanderlock worked some switches, and the propellers slowed. He turned to her.

"Welcome to Mogadishu. Also known as 'Baghdad by the Sea.'"

VANDERLOCK THREW OPEN THE DOOR AND SPUN BACKWARD.
Men swarmed at the entrance, each one yelling at the other and jostling for position. They hoisted themselves into the plane, competing to be the first inside. They clawed at the sacks, hauling them onto their shoulders. A Toyota pickup pulled parallel to the opening, and the men flung the khat into the truck's bed. When the flatbed was full, the truck tore off, its spinning wheels flinging bits of dirt and stones into the air. Another vehicle pulled into place, and the men kept the sacks somersaulting out. The plane shook with the frenetic activity. Sunlight filled the aircraft's interior, and along with it came a wave of heat. Emma stood but remained pressed against the back of the copilot's seat to stay clear of the frenzied men.

A skinny Somali fought his way into the cabin. He wore a T-shirt and dirty green cargo pants, and he carried an open clamshell mobile phone in one hand. A necklace with a carved antelope head swung on a rawhide string tied around his neck. Emma stared at it, trying to recall where she'd seen it before. The memory danced around in her head, but she was unable to pin it down. The man's face twisted in anger as he shoved at the workers. He shrieked, "Shit, shit, shit!" interspersed with words in a language that Emma assumed was Somali. Behind him came a young soldier whom Emma guessed to be no more than nineteen, perhaps twenty. He wore jeans and black Nike basketball shoes. An ammunition belt encircled his waist, and two more crisscrossed his chest, covering the logo on his T-shirt. Emma noted that out of all the men, he was the only one in jeans. An AK-47 hung from a strap on his shoulder. Skinny Man stepped up to Vanderlock.

"Shit—" he said, and followed up with some more words in Somali.

Vanderlock shrugged and replied in the same language.

Skinny Man turned his eyes to her, not with interest but with menace. Emma pressed back against the seat. Her foot hit the locker holding the guns. She pulled up a mental picture of them nestled in the case and wished she were holding one now.

Vanderlock began speaking again in Somali, but the young soldier interrupted him.

"You should speak in English. It is the only language you know well enough to be understood." The young soldier spoke in American English with no accent. Emma gawked at him. He caught her surprise and sneered at her.

"Yes, lady, I'm American. Like you?"

Vanderlock snapped out a sentence in Somali. The young man gave him a disgruntled look but subsided a bit.

Skinny Man jerked his head at Emma and turned back to the door. A worker carrying a large sack of khat blocked the exit. Rather than let the worker toss his burden and move out of the way, Skinny Man shoved him right between the shoulder blades. The worker yelped and fell out the door, landing face-first on the truck bed, the khat sack still on his back. The others continued heaving the sacks despite the fact that their colleague lay in the line of fire. Emma heard him grunt as two fell on him. He extricated himself and leaped out of the truck. He threw a look of pure hate at Skinny Man as he loped back to the plane's door.

Vanderlock moved next to Emma and bent to whisper in her ear. "Abdul wants us to step outside."

"Who is he?"

"That skinny one. He's a paid lackey for a warlord named Mungabe."

Emma heard Abdul scream, "Shit!" and didn't understand anything else that came after.

"How many times is he going to say 'shit'?" Emma asked.

"It's the only English word he knows. The khat is late this morning. These guys are a little strung out."

"Why does he want us outside?"

Vanderlock shook his head. "I don't know, but it can't be good. Normally I don't leave the plane. I let them unload, and then I fly away as fast as possible, because every minute wasted degrades the khat."

Emma flipped open the toolbox and hauled out the AK-47. "This thing loaded?"

Vanderlock looked alarmed. "Don't wave that around. These guys carry an entire arsenal with them. One aggressive move and they'll blow us apart. That's a last resort."

"They're not going to see it," she said.

"Shit! Shit!" Abdul was shrieking again, though at whom Emma couldn't tell.

She looked closer at the weapon, unfolded the butt, and flipped the firing switch to automatic.

Vanderlock raised an eyebrow. "I thought you couldn't shoot."

"I can't. I know how to use the firing switch and depress the trigger. But in semi I can't hit a target to save my life." Emma pointed the gun downward and slid it behind their bodies, propping it up against the backrest of the copilot's seat.

"At least if anything happens, one of us can reach it," she said. The young soldier came back into Emma's line of sight through the door. He stood on the far side of the truck.

"Abdul says get out here. Now."

The last vehicle peeled off from the plane, and the workers jumped after it, one by one, until only Emma and Vanderlock remained inside. Emma cut a quick glance at the remaining sacks. She estimated that 50 percent of the shipment was gone. The men had unloaded two and a half tons of khat in fifteen minutes.

"Are we going outside?" Emma spoke in a low tone.

"No way. Abdul can come to me. I'm not leaving my plane." Vanderlock settled next to her, leaving his left arm flush with hers. Emma felt sweat beginning to form wherever their skin touched. The physical contact with him was somewhat reassuring. That and the knowledge that he was armed and she was within reaching distance of the AK-47. Abdul marched up to stand next to the young soldier. He yelled again.

Emma felt Vanderlock's body go rigid. He reached under his shirt and pulled out his gun in a leisurely motion. He held it in front of him, nose down, for a second, chambered a bullet, and then lowered it to his side. All his actions were in slow motion and performed while he kept his eyes on Abdul. Abdul snapped the cell phone closed in a dramatic gesture. Emma heard the metallic click as he did it.

Vanderlock put out his hand and said one word. After a short pause, Abdul reached into his pocket and removed a small cylindrical object. He tossed it through the open door. It landed on the floor and rolled toward Vanderlock, stopping against the side of his boot. It was American money, rolled and secured with a rubber band. Vanderlock reached down, grabbed the money, and shoved the bills into his pocket.

Abdul barked out another order and jerked his chin at her.

Vanderlock shook his head and spoke in Somali. When he was finished, he removed the pack of cigarettes from his pocket and used his lips to pull out a smoke. He managed the maneuver one-handed, because his other hand still held the gun. A look of pure fury washed across Abdul's face.

"Shit—" He spit out a sentence. Bits of foam collected at one corner of his mouth flew in all directions as he spoke.

"What did he say?" Emma said.

"He wants you to go with him. He heard a rumor that you work for Banner. He intends to drag you before Mungabe for questioning."

Emma's heart began to race. "What did *you* say?"

"I told him you were my latest girlfriend. We met in Dubai on vacation, and you wanted to fly with me."

"Does he believe that?"

"He's not sure what to believe. My reputation is to change women fairly often, but that's not what's holding him back."

A bead of sweat ran along Emma's spine, stopping at her waistband. She kept her eyes on Abdul and her voice low. "What is, then?"

"Banner's reputation. He knows that Banner wouldn't let an operative travel alone, with me, and apparently unarmed. It's making him hesitate. That and the fact that you're a woman."

Abdul yelled a phrase. Within seconds the workers surrounded the open door. Two aimed at them from the ground, while three others hoisted themselves back into the jet. One shoved a gun tip into Emma's ear. The metal felt hot rather than cold, as if it had just been fired. A muscular man, his head wrapped in a white turban and his beard dyed bright orange, stepped next to Vanderlock. He shoved a rifle up under Vanderlock's jaw. Vanderlock kept his own pistol lowered at his side.

Emma pressed against the copilot's seat, but there was nowhere to go. She felt a portion of the metallic outline of the AK-47 against the back of her right thigh. Between the worker jamming the rifle into her ear canal on her left and Vanderlock flush against her on the right, she doubted she could maneuver it into firing position in the time she would need. She froze, waiting. She could smell the worker's sweat coupled with the odor of cigarette smoke that clung to his clothes. The warm, fetid air inside the plane blanketed her, and rivulets of her own sweat poured down her face. The only sound in the cabin was the tapping noise made by a large fly that bounced against a side window, trying to get out.

No one in the jet spoke.

Abdul talked into his cell phone while keeping his eyes on them both. His gaze flicked to Emma. He lowered the phone and spoke to the soldier in rapid-fire sentences. The young man nodded and gave Emma a contemptuous look.

"What's your name?" he demanded.

"Emma Caldridge." She was proud to hear that her voice sounded normal, almost calm. "Where did you live in America?" She was equally proud to hear that her voice did not shake during the longer sentence.

The young man preened. "Minnesota. My parents fled Somalia and ended up there. I've returned to work among my people to drive the Ethiopians out and restore Somalia to its prior glory." His eyes held the fire of a convert.

"You said you were American. Are you naturalized?" Emma wanted to keep the soldier talking about himself and keep the subject off her.

It didn't work. Abdul barked out a sentence before the young man could respond. "He wants to know if you work for Banner and his company, Darkview," the soldier said. Emma tried to shake her head but succeeded only in driving the rifle tip farther into her ear.

"I do not," she said. The soldier translated for Abdul, who conveyed the answer to whoever was on his phone. Abdul listened to his caller for a moment and snapped out another sentence to the soldier.

"Why did you come here?" the soldier asked.

"She came to be with me." Vanderlock spoke before Emma could.

"Why did you bring her?"

"Why do you think I brought her?"

The soldier made a disgusted sound. "You should keep your mind on business."

"Man does not live on business alone. Unlike everyone here, I don't chew the khat, so I can still get it up."

The young soldier straightened. "The khat makes you strong!"

"The khat makes you impotent," Vanderlock said. He switched to Somali. The men holding the rifles began protesting, appearing to argue with him. Emma admired his quick thinking. The topic reinforced the idea that she was there as a girlfriend and not as an operative but did it in a way that was far more effective than his bald assertion earlier.

Abdul yelled one word, and they all subsided. He pointed to a pickup truck parked behind him and started walking away while still talking on the phone, as if the matter were closed. The man holding the gun to Emma's ear pushed her forward.

"You're coming with us," the soldier said.

Emma's mouth went dry. She slid her right hand behind her and wrapped her fingers around the stock of the AK-47. She'd raise it once she was clear of Vanderlock's body. Vanderlock yelled in Somali to Abdul, who halted and turned around. The man pushing Emma ceased his shoving. Emma waited, her fingertips still on the gun stock behind her.

"Let me repeat that in English so everyone here understands," Vanderlock said. He gave the soldier his own contemptuous look. "You take her and I won't fly. The khat will be late. Mungabe can explain to Jamar why detaining one unarmed woman was worth spoiling a three-ton shipment."

Abdul sent Vanderlock a considering look. He spoke into his cell phone, lowered it, and pointed at Vanderlock while rattling off a sentence.

"Kill her and I still won't fly the plane," Vanderlock responded in English.

The young soldier snorted. "Then we'll kill you."

To Emma's profound surprise, Vanderlock laughed. "No you won't, smart-ass. I fly twenty-five tons of khat a week. You kill me and the three warlords that depend on me will hunt you, Abdul here, and even Mungabe down and throw all your corpses into the ocean to be eaten by the bottom feeders."

Abdul snapped an order to the young Somali. He kept his eyes on Vanderlock while the young man translated. Abdul gave Vanderlock a furious look before consulting with whoever was on the other end of his cell phone. After a moment he clicked it closed. He spit out a response to Vanderlock and waved at the guards, who released their hold on Emma. They moved to the entrance and jumped down. Emma slid her entire hand over the AK-47's stock but held it next to her leg.

The workers reached up and slammed the door closed. Vanderlock bolted it into place and turned to her.

"Let's get the hell out of here," he said.

VANDERLOCK REMAINED SILENT THE ENTIRE TIME THE PLANE climbed. Emma sat in the copilot's seat, the AK-47 still in her hand. She stared out the window, thinking about what had transpired and wondering who had leaked her identity. She would have bet that it wasn't Roducci. Perhaps a worker at the Nairobi airstrip with connections to Somalia? But they had spoken in English, and Emma didn't think any of the cargo crew could. Vanderlock sighed as they reached cruising altitude. He reached into the green duffel and pulled out a silver flask that was dented on one side.

"Open it, will you? I need a drink. And you can put away the gun. Nothing they can shoot will hit us up here."

Emma closed the folding butt and returned the weapon to the toolbox. She unscrewed the flask's cap and handed it back. He took a huge swallow and offered the flask to her.

"What is it?" she asked.

"Whiskey."

She took a drink. Her throat protested, she coughed once, and her eyes watered. She shivered as the liquid followed a path to her stomach.

"Not a whiskey drinker?" Vanderlock said.

"That would be correct." Emma gave the flask back to him. Within seconds she felt the alcohol's warming effect. "Actually, that's nice."

Vanderlock gave a soft chuckle. Then he sobered and shook his head. "I should have asked for two grand." He took another swallow and drew a deep breath. "You okay? That was close."

Emma nodded. "I'm more worried about your reputation."

Vanderlock shot her a surprised look. "I do well, but you're top of the line, so I'm pretty sure it's still intact."

She rolled her eyes. "Not that reputation. I'm concerned that they'll be suspicious of you from now on."

A pensive look passed over Vanderlock's face. It was clear he understood the risk.

"Abdul's been there one year. The last guy Mungabe used got blown up making an IED. He'd been in the position all of six months. If I keep my head down, there's a very good chance that Abdul will get himself killed and the whole situation will be forgotten."

"What about Mungabe? I assume he was on the phone?"

"Mungabe's nuts. Certifiable. But he's almost forty. Guess what the average life span is for a man in Somalia."

"Well, in the States I would say late seventies. In Somalia . . . maybe sixty?"

"Forty-six. So Mungabe doesn't have much longer to go either."

Emma shook her head. "How do you live like this?"

Vanderlock swallowed some more whiskey and gave her an incredulous look. "How do *I* live like this? Lady, you just flew into the most dangerous city in the world, unarmed, in a plane loaded with drugs." He pointed the top of the flask at her. "People who live in glass houses." He took another swallow and handed her the container.

"Oh, what the hell," she said. She drank some more.

"You act like it's a bad thing to drink whiskey."

Emma wiped her mouth with the back of her hand. The second shot succeeded in getting quite a good buzz going. She felt all her muscles relax and her jaw unclench.

"Whiskey *is* bad. I'm an ultra runner. Alcohol puts you off your game."

Vanderlock thought about that for a moment. "You ever run the Comrades?"

Emma sighed. "Just a day"—or was it hours?—"ago."

"Greatest footrace in the world. I used to watch it on television when I lived in South Africa." Vanderlock's voice was filled with pride. "I heard about the bomb. Whoever did that should be shot. Figures you'd be at that one."

"What do you mean by that?"

"You're trouble. Or trouble follows you. Either way. Take your pick."

"Maybe I run toward trouble."

Vanderlock nodded. "That'll work. But if you're going to keep it up, you'd better learn to shoot. You need someone to teach you."

Unbidden, an image of Cameron Sumner flashed in her mind, coupled with a feeling of longing. She tried to toss the feeling aside, but the whiskey's effect left her brain fogged and her discipline lacking. Instead of controlling her emotions, she felt like she wanted to cry. She shoved the flask back at Vanderlock.

"Take it, I'm done."

"It's just as well. Hargeisa's right ahead. Close it, can you?"

Emma capped the flask and tossed it into the open duffel.

"What the hell is that?" Vanderlock said.

Emma glanced out the windshield. In front of them, a huge column of black smoke billowed into the sky. At its base Emma could see flames. Whatever was burning, it was big.

"Is that Hargeisa?" Emma asked.

"That's not only Hargeisa, that's the airport." Vanderlock flicked a switch and started speaking into his headset. He finished and turned to her. "It's a private jet flying out of Nairobi. Blew up after landing. They want us to divert. I'm going to head to a small runway that I know of between here and Berbera."

"Blew up? That doesn't sound right. I thought you told me Hargeisa was peaceful," Emma said. As they drew closer, she could begin to make out a cluster of cars surrounding the conflagration.

"It is by Somali standards. This is unusual."

"Do they know whose jet it is?" Emma asked.

Vanderlock nodded. "It's owned by a company called Price Pharmaceuticals."

EMMA SAT IN STUNNED SILENCE WHILE VANDERLOCK MANEU-
vered the plane lower. They'd flown thirty minutes farther, and now
he aimed for yet another dirt runway in the middle of nowhere. They
landed with one bounce and rolled to a stop. Vanderlock stayed still.
Neither of them spoke. Outside the jet, clouds of dust kicked up by
the landing hung in the air, turning it an amber color. After another
moment he stood and stretched. Emma stayed put while she did her
best to gather her thoughts and push down the combination of sad-
ness underlain with fear.

Vanderlock gave her a searching look. "Did the bombed jet rattle
you?"

Emma dragged herself out of the chair. The simple movement
broke the fright that had kept her paralyzed for the last half hour. She
nodded.

"My lab did work for Price. I flew on that plane from South Africa
to Nairobi. I met the pilot and the copilot."

He gave a small whistle. "What made you bail from that plane to
mine?"

"I didn't know it was going to Hargeisa. The president of the company was flying with me, and he said Nairobi was his last stop."

"I guess he was right, in a sick sort of way. Again, it's none of my
business, but if I were you, I'd get on the next flight home. Whatever
Banner has you involved in, it sounds as though it's escalating out of
control."

For the first time, Emma wavered. Vanderlock's face was set, and she knew he was right. But if things were escalating on land, she could only imagine what was happening at sea. She shook herself out of her stupor. She hadn't come this far just to quit.

"I need to keep moving," she said.

Vanderlock put a hand on her arm. His palm felt warm. "Where are you going?"

Emma rubbed her forehead, where a headache was forming. She no longer felt buzzed, just depressed and tired. "I should get back to the Hargeisa airport."

"That's thirty miles away."

She thought a minute. "What about the khat? Weren't you supposed to deliver it to Hargeisa? How will you get it there now?"

"I called the missiles and rerouted them here. I expect to see them in half an hour or so."

"The missiles?"

Vanderlock nodded. "It's what we call the khat trucks, because they travel so fast."

"Will they take me with them to Hargeisa?"

He kept his hand on her arm and cocked his head to one side. "Not giving up?"

"Not giving up," she said.

He made a sound of pure frustration. "I'm afraid I'm talking to a dead woman. Somalia has a way of devouring whatever falls in its path. Listen, I'll even fly you back with me to Kenya. I'll talk them into letting you into the country. If you'd like, I'll take you to Dubai. We'll have fun, I promise you." He gave her a smile that left no question as to the nature of the fun they'd have.

Emma believed that his concern was real, but mixed with it was a hint of swagger, as though he were confident that he could sway her with his charm. For a brief moment, she considered what it would be like with him. His freewheeling attitude was different from the straightforward friendliness that had been Patrick's approach to life, and as opposite from Sumner's brooding intensity as she could imagine. She didn't doubt that she'd enjoy being with him, but she wouldn't abandon Sumner to whatever fate he was facing in order to fly to Dubai with a man she'd just met. The decision was no contest.

"I'm not doing this lightly, I promise you. I need to go. But I thank you for the offer," Emma said.

Vanderlock sighed. "They'll take you to Hargeisa if I ask them to."

She smiled at him. "Thank you."

He snorted. "Don't thank me. To ride in a missile is to flirt with death at one hundred miles per hour." He gave the slightest shake of his head and moved around her. He bent down and opened the toolbox.

"Come on. I'll give you a shooting lesson while we wait. I'm not sending you out there without one."

Vanderlock put aside the AK-47 and reached in to get the rocket launcher.

"Are we going to shoot that?" Emma said.

He nodded. "It's the weapon of choice in Somalia. You'd better know how to use it."

They stepped into heat ten times worse than anything she'd experienced in Nairobi. She pulled an elastic band out of her pocket and tied her hair in a ponytail. It did little to make her feel cooler, but at least it stopped pieces of her hair from sticking to her face. The airstrip was nothing more than a dirt path carved into the road. Vanderlock waved her over to the far side of it. He dumped a dark green canvas bag onto the ground.

"This"—he showed her the tube—"is your basic rocket-propelled-grenade launcher." The launcher consisted of a two-foot metal tube attached to a long wooden stock that ended in what looked like a steel funnel attached to the bottom and facing backward. "Muzzle, stock"—he patted the wooden section—"and breech"—he pointed to the funnel. "You put the stock on your shoulder, hold the handle here, and pull the trigger. The rocket shoots out the front. Try it." He handed it to her.

She balanced it on her shoulder. A basic iron sight stuck out from the top. The wooden stock was worn smooth from age and use. Emma noted the wear and tried not to think about the destruction the weapon had wrought over the years. She lifted it up to test the weight. It wasn't heavy, but it was awkward. She wrapped her hand around the grip near the trigger.

"There's only one thing you need to know when firing. A stream of smoke and fire will shoot out of the back. That's called 'back blast.' You always need to check behind you before you shoot, because you don't want to hit a friendly with your back blast."

Emma sighted a tree in the distance. "What's my range?"

"Nine hundred feet, tops. Think less until you get proficient. And never, ever stand still after shooting. The back blast will reveal your position both in the day and at night. You shoot and run like hell for cover, because the other guy's going to target your blast to kill you."

Emma frowned. "So I only get one shot and then have to run? Not very efficient."

Vanderlock shook his head. "Not true. One shot is all you need, as long as it's a good one. These things took down the Black Hawks during the firefight in Mogadishu back in the nineties. The grenade is powerful." He reached into the canvas bag and pulled out a pointed metallic warhead and a pipe that looked like a toilet-paper tube, only thinner. "This is the grenade." He showed her the warhead. "You screw the booster on the back"—he attached the pipe—"and load it on the muzzle. Follow the guides."

Emma lowered the launcher to give him better access to the front. He put the warhead in place. When he was done, he shook out a cigarette, lit it with the stick lighter, took a drag, and scanned the area around them. He pointed into the distance while facing away from the airplane. "Aim toward that gnarled tree over there."

Emma adjusted her angle. "What if there's someone out there?"

"Highly unlikely. This area is remote, and even if it wasn't, we're in Somalia at one in the afternoon. The only people fool enough to be out in the noonday sun are us."

"What about the missiles? What if I hit them?"

He waved the hand holding the cigarette. "That would be bad, but they're coming from behind us, so I wouldn't worry. Also, I used a type of warhead that will explode after a set amount of time without impact. If you aim above the treetops, it'll explode up there."

"Good thinking," Emma said.

Vanderlock inhaled, blew out the smoke, and gave her a little bow. "Well, thank you. High praise coming from a scientist."

Emma smiled back before getting down to business. "Should I be prepared for a lot of recoil?"

"It's not bad at all, because the explosive pressure discharges out the breech."

She peered down the metal sight at a location twenty feet above the treetops, took a deep breath, and pulled the trigger. The warhead exploded out of the launcher with a blast that assailed her ears and a recoil that made her body jerk. She stumbled back a step, feeling the plume of heated air and fire run through the stock and exit the breech. Seconds later the warhead detonated, raining bits of shrapnel down on the trees.

"Wow," Emma said. Her ears rang. "That's an amazing amount of force."

Vanderlock watched her reaction with a sideways look and a slight smile as he pulled on the cigarette. "Yes it is," he said.

She heard the sound of an engine coming straight at them from the direction she had just anointed with her RPG. An ancient, dusty army-green jeep with no top appeared out of the trees. The driver aimed the vehicle toward them, pulling within ten feet before swinging it around and stopping.

The man killed the engine, hoisted himself out of the driver's seat, and jumped over the door. He was tall and slender, with beautiful dark skin and eyes, hair cropped close to his head. He wore khaki pants and a crisp white short-sleeved shirt and seemed unaffected by the heat. No sweat marred his forehead, and the shirt appeared fresh. In contrast, Emma already felt like a limp rag. Her damp shirt clung to her and a fine layer of dust covered her shoulder where the RPG still rested. The man stopped in front of her.

"Ms. Emma Caldridge?"

She nodded, too surprised to speak.

"I am Hassim. Major Stromeyer asked me to escort you to Berbera. I'm very surprised to see you here." He spoke in the singsong cadence of Africa, and his word choice seemed formal, as if English were not his native language.

Hassim put a hand out to Vanderlock. "Lock, how are you?"

Vanderlock put his cigarette between his lips and reached out to greet Hassim. "I'm good. Just giving Emma a shooting lesson."

"And me a heart attack," Hassim said.

Vanderlock grinned. "Sorry. Didn't think anyone would be out this time of day."

"You two know each other," Emma said.

Hassim nodded. "For five years now."

"Were you the one who was supposed to meet me in Nairobi?" Emma asked.

"That was Ahmed."

"What happened to him?"

Hassim's expression hardened. "He's dead. I found him lying in his kitchen."

Emma took a deep, shaky breath.

"I can't believe Ahmed would let anyone get that close," Vanderlock said.

"Whoever killed him was a professional. It would take nothing less to overcome Ahmed."

Emma lowered the RPG, which now felt heavy and hot and reeked of evil. Vanderlock took it from her. As he did, his eyes met hers.

He wore a grim expression. Emma didn't have to guess what he was thinking. He wanted her to abort the mission and go back with him. She thought he was struggling to keep from speaking his thoughts. He put the RPG on the ground next to the canvas bag. She looked back at Hassim.

"How was he killed?" Emma asked.

"No one knows yet. There were no signs of a struggle, no visible wounds, and no poison in the food in his pantry. The authorities think it was an aneurysm."

"Well, that's wrong. Ahmed was as strong as an ox," Vanderlock said.

"I agree. They're doing an autopsy, so we'll know more in a few days. Ms. Caldridge, are you ready? I'm to drive you to Berbera." He turned and walked back to the jeep.

Vanderlock stepped up next to her. "You'll be careful?"

Emma did her best to smile through the strain. "Now that I know how to shoot, I'll be safe."

He moved closer, his chest nearly touching hers. She looked up at him, read the speculation in his eyes, and waited. As she thought he might, he bent his head and kissed her. His lips were smooth and soft, and he slanted his head to deepen the kiss, slipping his tongue inside her mouth. When he was done, Emma was convinced that they would have had an excellent time in Dubai. She moved back a bit.

"If you find yourself in a tough spot, get a message to me through Roducci. He knows how to find me." He followed her to the jeep, where Hassim was sitting in the driver's seat, watching them with a serious expression.

"The doors are welded shut," Hassim said. Emma went around, stepped on the wheel well, and swung her leg onto the passenger side. She grabbed the edge of the windshield to lower herself into the seat. Hassim put on aviator sunglasses with a silver rim and handed Emma an identical pair. She checked out the maker's name stamped on the frame.

"Ray-Bans in Somalia?"

"Counterfeit," Hassim said. "There are two hats in the backpack. Can you give me the black one?" Emma fished out two bush hats. One black and one tan. She handed Hassim the black one and wore the tan.

"Later, Hassim." Vanderlock tapped the side of the jeep.

Hassim nodded, threw the jeep into first, and drove down the runway. When Emma looked behind them, she saw Vanderlock's back as he climbed into the Fokker.

They drove for about fifteen minutes, bouncing on a rutted single-lane road, before Hassim spoke.

"How long have you known Lock?"

"About seven hours," Emma said.

She couldn't see Hassim's eyes through his sunglasses, but she thought his lips twitched in amusement. He said nothing, keeping his focus on the road.

FORTY-FIVE MINUTES INTO THE RIDE, THEY CAME UPON A PICKUP truck parked on the shoulder. The cabin doors hung open on either side, and two men lounged on the bench seat, facing out with their feet on the running boards. One had an AK-47 slung over his shoulder, the other a rifle in his lap. They kept their bodies at right angles to the dash and watched the road. Hassim pulled into the shade of a nearby tree and waved them forward.

"Is this trouble?" Emma asked.

"No, they're with us. The government in Hargeisa requires that visitors wishing to take the Hargeisa-Berbera road hire SPUs, or special protection units, to accompany them. I picked these guys because they can speak rudimentary English."

"The road is dangerous, then?" Emma said.

"It can be, but it's the only road between the two cities, so we are required to use it. We'll spend the night in Berbera. They'll guard you while you sleep."

Hassim pointed at the dilapidated truck. "It can make it?" he asked.

The men nodded.

"Then let's go."

Two hot and dry hours later, they pulled into Berbera. Dust covered Emma from the neck down to her waist and encrusted her lips and face below the glasses. Berbera itself seemed devoid of people. Cinder-block buildings lined empty roads. Skinny mongrel dogs slunk into whatever shade was available. From somewhere in the

distance came the howl of an animal, along with the tinny sound
of Indian music. They drove along the outskirts of town to a rotting dock where the rusted hull of a speedboat without an engine
bobbed in the waves. A floating houseboat was tied to the far end
of the pier. Its flat, wide bottom made it look like a barge with three
masts, spaced evenly apart. The back was open to the air but covered
by a canvas roof that connected to the cabin area. Paper lanterns in
bright colors hung from the roof supports in a line. Hassim jerked
his head at it.

"It's a *dahabeeyah*. Egyptian, really. The lights are plugged into the
dock's power supply. They're off now but will turn on with a timer.
The windows are mesh, so you should get some relief from the mos-
quitoes." He pointed to a small wooden structure twenty feet off the
dock. "There's the outhouse, and you'll find paper in the boat. Sorry,
no running water to speak of, but there is an outdoor showerhead on
the side that is fed from an overhead tub, a rain barrel for washing up,
and a jug of drinking water."

Emma nodded. The *dahabeeyah* charmed her, with its paper lanterns. She remained silent, though.

Hassim peered at her. "You are quiet. I hope you're not upset. Unfortunately, there is no hotel. I promise you, this is somewhat better
than sleeping outdoors. We won't leave until dawn, so it was important I find you a safe place. It's clean, and the SPUs will watch you
through the night."

Emma shook her head. "I'm not upset. I'm pleasantly surprised.
It's perfect."

Hassim looked relieved at that. He reached behind her and into
the black bag in the back of the jeep. He pulled out a teardrop-shaped
backpack and a parcel wrapped in brown paper and tied with string.

"I'll show you the inside," he said.

True to his word, the boat was clean. A hanging curtain separated
the outdoor section from the cabin. To the right of the entrance,
against the far deck railing, sat the rain barrel. Its top was open to the

sky but covered with a wide mesh screen to keep out larger animals. Next to it was a tin tub, presumably for washing. Above the rain barrel rested another collection keg on a small platform bolted high up near the boat's roof. A rusted showerhead jutted out from the bucket's side, and a string hung down.

Hassim waved at the bucket. "It's a crude shower, but it works. Pull the string to release the water. Use it sparingly, though. The barrel empties fast and is filled only when it rains. We're entering the dry season, so what you use will not be replaced soon. Whatever's left is likely to be lost in evaporation."

The interior room consisted of one long rectangle, about ten feet by fifteen feet. It held no furniture, but colorful woven mats covered the floor. At the far end, a propane hot plate, an ancient coffee percolator—the type placed directly on heat—two dented pots, and two steel bowls containing silverware sat on a wooden crate. On the other side of the crate was a cooler.

Hassim walked to the center of the room and sat cross-legged on a rug. He placed the backpack and the parcel in front of him.

"This is for you. From Major Stromeyer."

Emma moved to sit opposite him. He handed her an American passport. She opened it to find a fairly recent picture of herself next to a false name and passport number.

"You don't want me to use my own?"

Hassim shook his head. "Not any longer. This one is issued not by the State Department but in Nairobi by a vendor near the Kibera slum. Nevertheless, it will get you past immigration in most countries of the world, with the possible exceptions of Switzerland and Israel."

He handed her the brown package. "Another gift from Major Stromeyer," he said.

Emma untied the string and unwrapped the paper. The parcel contained sleek black pants in a parachute-type material with ingenious pockets hidden in the legs, two gray T-shirts made by a running company in a technical fabric designed to wick away perspiration, as well as running socks and underwear. Emma checked the sizes. They were correct.

"Thank God for this," she said. Her relief was heartfelt. The clothes she wore were stained, filthy, sweat-soaked, and hot.

Hassim opened the teardrop backpack and withdrew an aluminum water bottle that he offered to her.

"What's in it?" Emma lifted the bottle.

"Water mixed with Red Bull."

"Not vodka?"

Hassim almost smiled.

It seemed to Emma that Hassim was too serious for his age, which she estimated to be about thirty, give or take a few years. She assumed he was a mercenary, like many connected with Darkview. Perhaps being a soldier for hire made one serious before one's time.

"The pack and what's in it are also for you."

The pack slung across Emma's shoulders diagonally. The strap contained a zip pocket suitable for a cell phone. She unzipped it and found just that. The credit-card-thin receiver had a minimum of bells and whistles. She held it up to Hassim.

"Will it get a signal?"

He shrugged. "It should. Cell phones are common. They keep the khat trade moving. I added a SIM card purchased from a nearby warlord's village, but I would be careful when using it. The phone contains a GPS signal tracker that I was unable to deactivate."

"Why don't they grow their own khat instead of hiring guys like Lock to fly it in?"

"The insurgents burned the fields during the civil war. Replanting would require cooperation between the various warlords, which is not likely to occur."

"Are you Somali?"

Hassim shook his head. "I'm from Kenya."

Emma zipped the phone back into the strap. A quick review of the rest of the backpack yielded a flat bubble pack of pills labeled "electrolytes," six packets of GU running gel, four PowerBars, three thousand dollars American in a thin bank envelope, and a compass. Emma smiled at the last item. After Colombia she had sworn that she would never be without a compass. She still wore the GPS wristwatch given to her by Banner when he'd appeared in Colombia, but the traditional magnetic type was sure to work under any conditions.

"And this is from me," Hassim said. He handed her a small bluesteel gun with an ankle holster. "I assumed you knew how to handle weapons and so was surprised when Lock said he was giving you a lesson. Would you like me to show you?"

Emma nodded. Hassim ran her through the loading, firing, and safety features of the gun. When he was done, he handed her a box of bullets.

"Extras," he said. She tossed them into the pack along with the gun.

Hassim stood and stretched. "We leave before dawn. The SPUs will return at dusk. There is food in the cooler for you. Please stay on the boat, and inside as much as possible. If you wish to shower, perhaps do so once the night has fallen. Although this area is usually deserted, it is best to remain anonymous." He parted the hanging curtain. Emma listened to his steps as he walked across the dock and then heard the jeep's engine and the crunch of the tires as he drove away.

Pillows lined the walls in the far corner, and a thick foam pad acted as a bed. Emma inspected all of it, taking care to shake out the pillows and look under the bed for scorpions. Seeing none, she removed her shoes, grabbed a pillow, covered herself with a small throw that was folded at the foot of the mat, and lay down. She spent the last three hours of daylight falling into and out of fitful naps brought on by the combination of heat and exhaustion.

At dusk the paper lanterns clicked on, sending small bits of colored light onto the boat's deck. A bare bulb in a protective cage threw a yellow glow in a desultory circle on the dock's weather-beaten boards. Moths and other insects fluttered in the beam. Emma made her way to the crate and found a kerosene lamp and matches. She lit the wick and adjusted the flame higher. Shadows flickered in the room.

When it was full dark, she roused herself again to rummage for food. She opened the cooler and found three apples, two oranges, a plastic bag with a type of round flatbread that looked like tortillas only spongier, a jug of drinking water, one can of salmon and one of tuna, and a small bag of coffee, all nestled in ice. She ate the bread, then pulled the ring tab on the tuna can and devoured the contents. She finished her dinner with a chaser of the remaining lukewarm Red Bull mixture.

On top of the crate was a threadbare bath towel. She stripped off her clothes, wrapped it around her, grabbed the lantern, and pushed aside the fabric door to the outside deck. The shower and rain barrel were on the side deck facing the water. A small sliver of soap on a rope and a bar rag hung from some nails pounded into the wall next to the shower. She pulled on the shower string to wet her body. The stream of water was weak, but so warm as to be almost hot. She lathered the soap everywhere, including her hair, and pulled again to rinse. She wrapped the towel around her once again.

Emma paused to gaze into the night. A slice of moon sent a stream of light across the undulating waves. The only sounds were the lapping of the ocean as it moved against the dock and the rhythmic creaking of some loose boards. Insects hummed somewhere on shore, and she heard the occasional splash of a fish in the water. She felt alone but not lonely. She looked at the stars and wondered if Patrick's spirit floated among them, watching her. She returned her attention to the water, and she prayed that the ocean was not preparing to swallow some more inconsequential humans who attempted to sail its waves.

THE LIGHTS OUTSIDE TURNED OFF. She moved back into the cabin, put on the clean clothes, and removed the gun, placing it next to her. Then she turned down the kerosene lamp and fell asleep on her first sigh.

MUNGABE LISTENED TO THE VULTURE GIVE AN EXCUSE ABOUT why Darkview still existed. He paced the length of the trawler in the early-morning hours, holding the phone to his ear and doing his best to keep his temper in check.

"We have a congressional committee pressuring Darkview to give answers on a job they completed four months ago, the American tax authorities are auditing its income, and a new offensive is on the way. Things are moving along nicely," the Vulture said.

Mungabe couldn't believe his ears. "That is nothing! Hire a man and shoot the head of the company dead. Why do you waste your time?"

The Vulture made a disgusted sound. "The man works contracts for the Department of Defense. Killing him will alert the authorities with their endless questions. I won't kill him until it's required. You should trust my judgment."

Mungabe wanted to laugh. Men like them didn't use the word "trust." "As soon as you can, kill him."

"Killing him won't stop the company. He has a vice president who will simply continue to operate it."

"Then kill him, too," Mungabe said.

"Her. It's a woman, and I will kill her once I have completed testing and have the information I need. But killing her still may not end the corporation. The only way to be sure that the company no longer functions is to remove its supply of funds. Without money every business starves. This company is no different. I am taking the necessary steps to stem its flow of defense contracts, squeeze off its private clients, and cost it time and effort in battling the tax authorities. Soon it will have to close its doors, only because it cannot fight on all fronts. Just stick to attacking the ship. I'll handle the rest."

If Mungabe could have killed the man right through the phone, he would have at that moment, for no other reason than the patronizing sound in the man's voice.

"I will have the ship by tomorrow. But I don't give it to you until Darkview is dead, do you understand?" The man on the other end of the line was silent so long that Mungabe thought he'd hung up.

"No one dictates to me," he said at last.

Mungabe could not believe his ears. Was the European threatening him? If he was, Mungabe would be sure that the man would not survive the week. "Is that a threat?" he said.

"Merely a fact. I suggest that we both work on our respective duties and talk again after you have taken the ship."

"And after you have destroyed Darkview."

"Yes," the Vulture said.

Mungabe hung up and immediately dialed Roducci. He would get to the bottom of the cargo question. When the man answered the phone, Mungabe dispensed with hellos and got right to the point.

"It's Mungabe. I'll pay you four thousand dollars to tell me what news you have heard about the cargo on a cruise ship in this area and an additional six on the delivery of three new RPG-7s."

Roducci hesitated. Mungabe could hear him breathing over the phone.

Eventually he said, "I'll give you information. You know I cannot sell you guns. Somalia is on a restricted list. No weapons."

Mungabe wanted to spit at the man. He sold his guns all over the world, but not to Somalia? He was a hypocrite.

"I've lost five RPGs in as many hours. I need some more weapons."

"Then call the Russian. He has no morals. He would sell fire to the devil."

"He cannot be found. His partners think he is dead."

"Ah, see what happens to those who mess with the restricted list?"

"Then transfer them to the Sudan. I'll—"

"Also on the list."

"Not all of it. But if you are so worried about bureaucratic lists instead of making money, send them to Kenya. The Russian used to deliver his to Mombasa port. I pick them up there."

Roducci sighed. "Mungabe, I am truly sorry not to be able to do business with you in arms, but the situation in your area is troublesome. You are stinging the shippers, the Western media is watching, and the companies that insure the ships are screaming for blood. They've had to pay out too much as a result of your activities."

Mungabe chuckled despite himself. He loved the idea that his work was being recognized the world over. He basked in the praise for a moment. Then Talek stepped up to him, listening to Mungabe's side of the conversation.

"Fine. I'll locate my arms elsewhere. For now I will wire you the money for information. What is the agent's name, and where can I find him? When you call me back, I want to hear all about the Western companies shrieking for blood. Send me the latest paper by e-mail."

"Read *Al Jazeera*. They report from their side of the conflict."

Mungabe snorted. "Arab trash."

"The *New York Times*, then."

Mungabe was getting angry. They were communicating in English, that was true, but only because it was the language of war the world over. The man knew he couldn't read that well, and especially not English. Roducci must be messing with him. "No English."

Roducci made an annoyed sound. "Stick to reading the Koran. I will tell you the news when your wire transfer clears. I'll call you back."

"Tell me now. You know I pay my debts."

Roducci chuckled. "You are a good client, that's true, but I wait for the transfer nonetheless."

Mungabe hung up. He waved Talek over. "Send Roducci four thousand dollars."

Talek brightened. "We're getting some more guns? Roducci sells the best. How did you convince him?"

Mungabe felt a flash of irritation. "He's not selling us arms. We're buying information. If there is anything special about the cruise ship's cargo, Roducci will have heard about it. In fact, he may even have sold it."

Talek nodded. "That's right. Roducci knows everything."

Mungabe returned to staring out at the ocean. He was no further in his quest to destroy Darkview. He looked at Talek. "How well can you read?"

Talek shook his head. "Not at all. When Barre went down, the schools were closed. I was sent home."

"You can read the Koran, can't you?"

Talek shook his head again. "A little. My grandfather read to me, but he died shortly after the schools' closing. My father can read, but he never taught me."

Mungabe wasn't surprised. When the Ethiopians took down the Siad Barre government in '91, most of Somalia fell into anarchy. The latest generation was barely surviving. There was no time for education. He didn't read to his children either. Actually, when he thought about it, he wasn't sure if any of his children were able to read. He made a mental note to ask his women.

"Why do you ask me this?" Talek sounded suspicious. "Reading is of no use." He sounded dismissive, but Mungabe saw the comment for what it was, a way for Talek to cover for his lack of education.

"I want to know what the media are reporting about our conquests here."

"They are singing our praises."

Mungabe snorted. "Perhaps not praises exactly." He thought a minute. "But when we take the cruise ship, they will speak about us with respect. That much I promise you."

The phone rang. Mungabe checked the display. It was Abdul.

"Hassim Reboude just drove into Berbera with the woman that Vanderlock claimed was his girlfriend."

Mungabe stopped pacing. "Are you sure it's the same woman?"

"A white Western woman with brown hair and light eyes. Who else would it be? I knew he was lying. She's the Darkview agent we've heard about."

"Or an aid worker," Mungabe said.

"So? We take her first and ask questions after."

"Did Vanderlock continue with the shipment?"

"Yes. He's probably in Nairobi by now. And there's more. The bombed jet at Hargeisa airport? It was owned by a pharmaceutical company."

Mungabe resumed his pacing, his mind whirring. "Who carried it out?"

"The insurgents. I don't know the whole of it, but the rumor is that a European paid them to do it."

The Vulture, Mungabe thought. The ship's cargo was the real prize, not the worthless cruise liner. Mungabe would take it all. "Where is the woman?"

"On the old trading boat near the fishing dock. There are two guards as well."

"And Hassim? Is he there?"

"Yes. He's arranged to take Ali's skiff."

"Stop him. And when you do, kill them both." Mungabe switched off the phone and smiled.

SUMNER FOUND CAPTAIN WAINWRIGHT ONCE AGAIN ON THE bridge. The ship continued to move, something Sumner considered to be a good sign. Wainwright waved him over to the ship's console.

"We got the radar up long enough to see them moving away. It went down again right after, but they were here." Wainwright pointed to a green blip that stayed frozen on the radar screen. "Do you think they're done?" he asked.

"Not at all. I think they're just heading back to get more grenades, crew members, or both. How long to Berbera?"

"Two days at least. More if the engines give out, which is a strong possibility. My real goal is not Berbera, but to go farther out from Somali territorial waters. The distance will give us a little more safety from the pirates and will allow foreign ships to come to our aid."

"How long does it usually take for aid to reach a boat under these circumstances?"

"Eight hours is average."

Sumner grimaced. "That's a long time."

"That's an assumption. I have no way of guaranteeing even that. And none of it's going to happen if we don't get out of territorial waters. Tell me about the sentry duty."

Sumner recapped the recent skirmish, leaving out Clutch's craven retreat but giving Marina her due as the one to fire the deciding shot. He also told him about Schullmann's cage idea.

"We've got a bunch of aluminum rods in one of the electrical rooms and steel supports for them. They're railing replacements. Feel free to use them. Steel sheets will be harder to come by. I don't know that we have any. Ask the mechanic if there's anything he can cannibalize for the metal."

"I also think we should arm the passengers," Sumner said.

"With what? We don't have arms for the crew, much less the passengers."

"The crew should be given knives from the kitchen. The passengers—screwdrivers, ice picks, anything they can use to fight as the pirates board."

Wainwright's face hardened. "Absolutely not. These guys carry AK-47s, and they won't hesitate to use them if they meet with resistance. Anyone fighting will be mowed down. I'd rather have the passengers taken hostage than risk a bloodbath."

Sumner rubbed a tired hand over his face. "Listen, I was taken hostage once, and it's not a situation I would wish on my worst enemy. These guys will drag the hostages to a deserted area and leave them in a pit. They'll barely feed them. The ones who don't die from the exertion and stress might die from starvation. It's my advice that the passengers be allowed to fight back."

"I appreciate your view on the subject, but I can't allow the situation to escalate. The moment those pirates climb over the railing is the moment we surrender."

Sumner could see that the subject was closed. "I understand. Then we'll just have to do our best to ensure that they don't board. How long can we continue?"

"Twenty minutes."

Sumner headed down to the mechanical room. Schullmann stood next to an engineer and directed him in broken English. The engineer responded in broken German. They appeared to be progressing despite the language barrier. Schullmann's sleeves were rolled to the elbows. He looked interested, less bored than he had in the casino.

Sumner took this as a good sign. He went to the man's side and told him about the railings.

"Is this steel the same as that which forms the ship's railings?" Schullmann asked.

"It is."

"The steel is soft, so I would not depend on it."

"I understand. All I really need is to deflect the grenade."

"It will do that, but not much more."

Another mechanic stepped up carrying a blowtorch and wearing protective goggles.

"I'll leave you to it," Sumner said.

He headed to the deck to check on Block, whom he found looking morose.

"What's the matter?" Sumner asked.

"I hate that they're out there. I thought about what you said. They're coming back, that's for damn sure. And even if they kill two-thirds of us, they'll still make a ton of money."

"Don't think about it. Never worry about something that hasn't happened yet."

Block gave Sumner a speculative look. "Tell me why you're really on this ship. You ain't no cruise-line employee, that's for sure. And you're a damn sight more competent than that loser head of security, Clutch."

Sumner sat down next to Block and rested his back on the far wall. He gazed into the darkness. "I'm a security agent and work for the government. I'm supposed to be far from the site of my last location, in order to stop any retaliation."

Block laughed a hearty laugh. His obvious pleasure at the irony of the situation made Sumner smile.

Block wiped his eyes and pointed a finger at Sumner. "You gotta be kidding me, right? What are you, some kinda shroud? You bring only bad luck."

Sumner couldn't help but agree with him. "It does appear that way, doesn't it? I'm a member of the Southern Hemisphere Drug Defense Agency. We generally focus on Latin America, but I'll go to whatever hot spot needs me. It's my job to be in the front lines. I don't relish the danger, but I do like the feeling that I'm doing something good for the world."

"No wife? No kids?"

"No."

Block looked relieved. "That's good. Once you've got a family, you no longer feel so free with your life. Kids anchor you in more ways than one."

Janklow's voice pierced the darkness. "Sumner, come with me. We've got a problem."

"I'll be back." Sumner placed a hand on Block's shoulder.

They moved through the ship. The halls remained empty. It was two o'clock in the morning, and Sumner hoped that most passengers were able to sleep, although he doubted it. Janklow took him to a door marked PRIVATE. He punched a number into a keypad, and the door clicked open. They entered a large cargo bay. Rows and rows of pallets lined the walls. Most were filled with boxes shrink-wrapped in plastic. Words like "tissue" and "detergent" were marked in black stencil. Janklow ignored these pallets and headed to the rear of the long, rectangular room. At the far end was a large wooden box stamped with the manufacturer's blue logo and covered in bold red with the words PERISHABLE, MEDICAL PRODUCTS. Janklow stopped in front of it.

"These were supposed to be vaccines and some sort of heart medication," he said.

"Supposed?" Sumner said.

"We've gotten word that buried somewhere in this box are two vials of ricin."

Sumner felt his mouth drop open. He prided himself on being the type of man who was rarely surprised, but now he was, and deeply so. He felt completely inadequate to address such an issue. The box in front of him was four feet high and wide. It could contain hundreds or even thousands of vials. From what he understood, ricin looked like any other clear liquid in any other vial. He wouldn't be able to analyze any one to determine its contents.

"Who told you this?"

"A man named Banner. He said you should know right away."

"We have a spare dish?"

"No. He sent an encrypted message on the computer right before they sheared off the satellite. He said to tell you that he's sending a chemist to analyze the vials, but that under no circumstances must you reveal the ricin to anyone else. Only Wainwright and myself know about what's in there."

"Of course not. But how does he intend to get his chemist on board? We're in the middle of a crisis and no one is coming to our aid, but a chemist will make it here? Doesn't that sound a little strange to you?"

Janklow heaved a sigh. "Who knows if they'll be successful? The chemist is coming with some operatives undercover in a small boat. They're going to try to slip through the net without the pirates or anyone in Somalia being the wiser."

"How will they find us? Wainwright switched off the tracking beam, and the radar's gone."

"Like I said, we had the radar up and running for a short while, and I sent out our coordinates then. We've continued to drift, but if they come soon, they may be able to locate us."

"Who's the chemist?" Sumner asked.

Janklow shook his head. "Someone from Darkview. They didn't say."

"Darkview employs security personnel, not chemists."

"Guess this is a chemist Darkview knows."

Sumner felt a feeling of inevitability wash over him. He shook it off and headed back to the deck to patrol. He'd learned long ago not to worry about things he could not change.

EMMA WOKE TO FIND HASSIM LEANING OVER HER.

"You're a quiet one, aren't you?" she said. If Hassim had been the type to smile, she thought he would have then. Instead he gave a shrug, just a tiny movement of his shoulders.

"Stealth is important in the bush. I am quite good at it."

Emma sat up. The wrap fell off her, bunching at her lap, allowing the cooler air to play around her shoulders. Even that fleeting perception wouldn't last for long. She felt the heat lingering just outside her presence, like a dog waiting patiently to get in the door. It promised to be a scorcher. Today Hassim was in dark-colored camouflage pants and lace-up combat boots. A dark gray T-shirt, not tucked in, completed the army look. He handed her a camping flashlight.

"Take this. It has an ultraviolet light."

Emma flicked on the flash. The bulb glowed blue. "Why ultraviolet?"

"To illuminate the scorpions."

She paused and looked at Hassim, but he was busying himself at the hot plate, his eyes on the task before him.

Emma got up, grabbed the roll of paper near the curtain's base, and slipped outside. It was still dark, but there was a sense that the sun was there, just under the horizon. She thought it might be four o'clock in the morning. The outhouse consisted of several haphazardly nailed boards twelve inches wide by eight feet high, creating a structure with a vaguely rectangular shape. Like a coffin sitting on its end. There was no roof, just two more thin boards to act as supports, but the door was hinged and had a rope handle. She swung it open and used the flashlight to check it out.

Inside, two thick, sawed-off boards rimmed the edge of a large hole, acting as a platform for one's feet. The entire setup was more like a Turkish toilet with walls rather than an outhouse. It smelled musty, but not like a sewer. It must have gone unused for some time. Five scorpions glowed in a dark corner, their bodies flush against the walls. Emma knocked on the wooden door, and they scuttled out through a hole in the boards.

Upon leaving the outhouse, she spotted another scorpion moving across the beaten earth path. It disappeared under some dried leaves. She made her way back to the rain barrel and peered through the mesh. Dead insects and a small drowned gecko floated in the water. The mesh wrapped over a couple of nails pounded into the rim of the barrel. She removed it and used it to scoop out the corpses, then replaced the screen and shoved the tin tub under the spigot that stuck out from the bottom. She used the soap on a rope to wash her hands but didn't bother to dry them. The water started evaporating in the heat almost immediately.

When she stepped back into the cabin, she saw that Hassim had lit the hot plate. He filled the percolator with water from the jug, dumped some coffee into the basket without measuring it, and placed the pot on the hot plate. He picked up an orange, holding it in the air with a questioning look. Emma nodded. He tossed it to her. She caught it, settling back down among the pillows to peel it. At the first break of the skin, the tangy, sweet smell of citrus floated up to her, and her mouth watered. She broke apart the sections and ate them, enjoying the sharp, clean taste.

"The flashlight worked. Lots of scorpions in the outhouse," Emma said. She ate another orange wedge.

"I hate scorpions." Hassim's voice was filled with loathing.

The percolator heated surprisingly fast. Within minutes dark liquid perked into the small glass top, sending a rich smell of strong coffee into the air. Hassim poured two mugs, handed one to her. Emma took a sip. It was exquisite. Better than that made from any electric pot, and even better than her press at home. She closed her eyes in bliss. When she opened them, Hassim was watching her over the rim of his mug with a look of amusement in his dark eyes.

"It's the best I've ever tasted," she said.

"The beans are African. Percolating them allows the flavor to become strong. Much better than the method of pouring water through a filter used by most modern coffeepots."

"A coffee connoisseur," Emma said.

"It is my favorite drink." Hassim finished his and poured some more. He topped off the mug Emma held out to him.

"When do we leave?" she asked.

Hassim glanced at a large diving watch attached to his wrist. "I stopped by to ensure that you were awake. I have one more matter to complete and will return in half an hour, at which time we will leave."

"It will be daylight soon. Is that a problem? I expected to leave in the evening, when we can use the darkness to our advantage."

Hassim shook his head. "Darkness is only of minimal assistance, because the warlords patrol at night. Plus, the pirates have night-vision goggles and radar. The best time is at eleven o'clock, maybe noon, when the khat arrives. Nothing gets done after it's consumed. Unfortunately, we cannot waste valuable hours waiting for that moment."

"I know all about khat," she said.

Hassim reached into the cooler and pulled out the bread. He split one before adding slabs of salmon to each half. He handed one to Emma.

"Not too many Westerners are familiar with khat. Did Lock tell you about it?"

Emma bit into the bread. Salmon was not her favorite, but she wasn't sure when she'd get her next meal, so she was determined to eat it all.

"Lock told me how it's transported, but I already knew about its effects. I'm a chemist. Among other things, my laboratory makes cosmetics for high-end companies throughout the world. I search for plants that may have an antiaging benefit. I looked into khat as a possible ingredient in skin-tightening lotions. To be used as a stimulant. Some clients were adding caffeine to their lotions to achieve the same effect, and since khat has a slight amphetamine action, I wondered if it could be useful."

"And was it?" Hassim said.

"It didn't do anything beneficial that we could determine, and adding it to a product would have triggered a need for FDA approval, which is way too expensive and time-consuming." She stood up to stretch. "What direction are we taking?"

"We're leaving from the beach. The first part of our journey is the most dangerous. We enter pirate-infested water. I was able to procure a boat, but nothing of the quality most pirates have access to, and I doubt that it would be able to outrun an attack. Piracy is big business here. Some say the only business."

"What do they normally look for in a target?"

"Generally freighters and fishing trawlers. Many countries fish illegally. They take in tons of tuna. When the pirates catch them fishing within the economic zone, the companies pay ransom very quickly and quietly in order not to be caught." Hassim finished his coffee. "Of course, they learned that the companies pay equally quickly for the lives of their crew members, and they are now hunting the boats outside the economic zone."

Hassim stepped past Emma holding the percolator's basket. Through the side window, she watched him stroll down the dock. He tossed the grounds onto the dirt. When he returned, Emma asked him the question that had been on her mind for the past hours.

"Any more news on the Price matter?" She tensed, waiting for his answer.

Hassim turned to look at her. "The jet was gutted. It will take a while to determine if anyone died in there. My understanding is that even a human body would have been incinerated, so they will need to sift through the ash to make the analysis."

"Anyone take responsibility for it?"

Hassim shook his head. "Not yet, but most think the insurgency is involved. The reasons are murky."

She stared out a slit in the curtained doorway and thought about Stark. She'd heard he had a preteen daughter from his first marriage. She wondered how that daughter was feeling. How hard it must be for a twelve-year-old to learn that her father was dead.

"You look very sad. Is it about the bombed airplane?" Hassim asked.

Emma felt her throat thicken. She swallowed before answering. "Just thinking about the pain for the families left behind."

"Why did you agree to this mission?"

Good question, Emma thought. Why *had* she? Because of Sumner, of course, but there seemed more. Hassim remained silent while he waited for her answer.

"I want to help a friend. His name is Cameron Sumner, and he's on that ship. . . ." Emma's voice tapered off. There was more to the answer, but she couldn't articulate what.

"Were you together?"

Emma didn't really know how to interpret "together." She decided Hassim meant dating.

"No, our relationship is not like that," she said.

"It's quite a risk to take for a mere friend."

Emma tried to explain. "He saved my life under very dangerous circumstances. I would return the favor." Even as she said the words, they rang false. She thought about the moment of longing on the airplane but once again veered away from analyzing it.

"And you found that you like the excitement." Hassim's comment was a statement, not a question. As Emma thought about it, though, she decided that he was onto something.

"Why do you say that?"

"The mercenary business attracts a certain type of person. Usually a wanderer, risk taker, and adrenaline junkie. Most of us have a huge thirst for the excitement that accompanies danger."

Emma thought about Hassim's insight. During her last ordeal, she'd wanted nothing more than for it to be over. But this one was different. This time she'd chosen the danger, it hadn't chosen her—at least not completely. She didn't want to think about the bombing and the man with the EpiPen. Those problems would be addressed when she got back, after she knew that Sumner was safe.

"How will we find the *Kaiser Franz*?" she asked.

If Hassim was surprised at her sudden change of topic, he didn't show it.

"Radar. We have last-known coordinates. We'll head there, then use radar to sweep the area." He put the coffee cup down on the cooler. "I should go. Please be prepared to leave soon."

Emma followed Hassim off the boat. The battered green jeep sat under the shade of a nearby tree. Two large black nylon carry bags filled the small trailer in the back. Next to them was an aluminum tool kit.

"The kit is for your use. It contains some of the equipment you will need to analyze the vials on the cruise ship."

Emma flipped it open. Most of the equipment looked used but still in good shape. A pair of heavy lead-lined gloves lay on top of the various aluminum bottles, along with three kits labeled HAZARDOUS MATERIALS DETECTION and INVESTIGATIONAL ONLY, NOT FOR SALE.

"Should I check this out? Is there any possibility of getting something different if I should need it?"

"Definitely not in Berbera. Probably not in Hargeisa, and Moga-dishu is off-limits completely."

Emma closed the toolbox with a clang and locked the latch.

"Then it will have to do. Let's go," she said.

They climbed into the jeep. The SPUs waved good-bye and headed to the town to hitch a ride on one of the converted land cruisers that regularly drove the Hargeisa-Berbera road.

The sun started its rise, and the darkness took on a slightly gray tone. Emma estimated that it was already eighty-five degrees, and she fully expected it to reach ninety-five before the day ended. She felt like she was in an oven.

"Is it always this hot?" she asked Hassim.

He nodded. "It will be worse soon, during dry season. Right now, the rains keep it wet, humid, hot, flooded, and cholera runs rampant."

Emma shook her head. "Sounds like hell on earth."

"That's a good description of Somalia."

They drove through Berbera. Only a few people were out. Most strolled listlessly in the shimmering heat, their dark bodies creating moving shadows in the early dawn.

"Not a lot of people."

Hassim dodged a mongrel dog that jogged in a crooked pattern across the street, its back legs bent in a curve away from its front legs.

"Many have already fled inland, away from the heat."

They drove down a pockmarked road, bouncing in holes and spewing rocks and gravel behind them. They turned a corner, and Emma gasped. Suddenly she was looking at one of the most beautiful beaches she had ever seen. White sand stretched in a graceful sweep for more than a mile. Blue waves tipped with cream washed over them, before retreating back. The sun rose, staining the sky overhead with pink. No garbage, people, or other signs of civilization marred it.

"It's gorgeous," Emma said. "I was wrong about Somalia being hell on earth. This is heaven."

Hassim navigated the jeep a little farther onto the sand.

"Some of the best diving in the world is here. The UN workers used to come here to snorkel and fish. There are other beautiful areas of Somalia that could be developed if the country could only shake its perpetual violence."

He switched off the engine, and they sat in silence. The only sound was the pounding of the surf and the occasional cry of a seabird. Emma stared at the ocean, mesmerized by the endless blue, and a thought came to her. Somewhere, out there, Sumner was on a death ship.

31

BANNER'S PHONE BEEPED ON HIS DESK, INDICATING THAT AN IN-ternal call from Alicia was coming through. He hit the speaker button.

"What's up?" he said.

"Two men here to see you." Alicia's voice sounded strained.

Banner picked up the phone. "Are you on speaker?"

"No, I understand that the defense secretary is more important. I'll let them know you will only be a few minutes."

They must have been standing directly in front of her, forcing her to talk in riddles. She was giving him a chance to leave through the back door in his office that fed directly into the stairwell. Banner appreciated her quick thinking, but he wouldn't even consider leaving.

"Do they look strange?" he asked.

"Yes. But that computer hasn't been quite right in a long time." Her cryptic words, coupled with the strain in her voice, told Banner that something bothered her about the visitors.

"Got it. Send them in. Just give me a chance to activate the camera." Banner reached under his desk and hit a small button on the console's interior portion. A short click confirmed that the camera hidden in a vase on the credenza behind him was on and recording. The feed went straight to Alicia's and Stromeyer's desktop computers, with an additional stop at another location where it was downloaded and stored.

The door swung open, and Alicia walked in trailing two men be-hind her. One was dressed in a trench coat, the front unbuttoned. The second was the rough-looking passenger in the Crown Vic that had tailed him from Stromeyer's house. Banner felt his fingertips tin-gle with a little fizz of adrenaline-generated electricity. He stood but made no move to shake their hands.

"Gentlemen, how can I help you?"

The rough-looking character smirked. The other man stepped aside for him. So Rough-Looking was the leader, Banner thought.

"We're here to talk about your security operations."

Banner waved them to the chairs positioned opposite his desk. "Please sit down."

The leader shook his head. "This isn't a social call. We're going to give you the facts of life. First"—the man held up his index fin-ger—"we know you're running an operation in the Gulf of Aden. An illegal operation. You're arming your security guys in violation of international law. Second"—another finger went up—"you're putting hundreds of lives at risk by placing that guy on a civilian cruise ship."

Banner raised an eyebrow. He'd bet the rough-looking character wouldn't know international law if it came up and bit him on the ass. "What's your name?"

"Agents Tarrant and Church."

Banner raised an eyebrow. "Agents? Of what?"

"None of your business."

The other guy snickered.

Banner had had enough. "Listen, *Agent* Tarrant. I have a lot on my plate today, and a visit by two men making vague threats is not on my to-do list. Tell whoever sent you that I'm operating within in-ternational law, I'm not impressed with either of you, and get the hell out of here." Banner moved toward his office door. Church stepped into his path. Banner stood his ground, which resulted in his getting a potent whiff of stale cigarettes and bad patchouli cologne that wafted off the second loser.

"We know you're doing your vice president. I'd hate to see her get hurt." Tarrant gave Banner a sardonic grin.

Banner rarely lost his temper—a source of pride, because he thought losing one's temper was the mark of an amateur. He looked at the sniggering Tarrant and wondered just who was behind the intimidation, because it was clear neither Tarrant nor Church was the brains of any operation. He wondered if they had any idea how difficult it would be to take out Stromeyer. In a straight fight, he'd bet on her every time. Before he could say a word, the office door opened and Stromeyer strode in holding a cup of coffee and a gun.

"Edward, would you like some coffee?" she asked.

Banner raised an eyebrow but remained quiet. Stromeyer never called him by his first name—no one did. It was their personal code that meant *be prepared*. She was going to either shoot the gun or throw the hot coffee—or both. He tensed. He watched her turn toward Tarrant, who took a look at the gun and shoved his own hand into his jacket.

She threw the coffee. It flew at Tarrant in a perfect arc, her body flying with it. He dodged to the side, whether in an attempt to avoid the coffee, Stromeyer, or both, Banner couldn't tell. Stromeyer stumbled two steps forward before catching herself. She still held the gun, but now she stood over Tarrant, who had fallen onto the floor. Two more drops of coffee fell on his sleeve from the cup.

"Don't move, Mr. Tarrant. If it's a gun you're reaching for, it had better be licensed, because you're on *Candid Camera*." Her voice was calm, collected. Behind her, Church took a step closer.

"I wouldn't if I were you, Mr. Church. The camera feeds directly to a security station that will notify the D.C. police," Banner said.

Church stepped back.

"I don't know what you think you're doing, aiming a gun at a federal officer." Tarrant's voice was harsh, but he'd pulled his hand out of his coat and stayed put.

Stromeyer looked at the gun in her hand, and an expression of surprise came over her face. "Oh, I *am* sorry. I forgot I was even holding it. It's been misfiring, and I was going to have it checked out after I delivered the coffee to Banner. But of course then I slipped." She bestowed a solicitous smile on Tarrant. "It didn't burn you, did it? And what agency did you say you work for?" Tarrant remained quiet. He got up, brushing coffee off the sleeve of his trench coat, only managing to smear it instead.

Banner walked to the door and held it open.

"This meeting is over. It's been informative. Next time you two *agents* decide to come here spouting threats, you'd better have a warrant."

Tarrant laughed an ugly laugh. "I don't need a warrant to beat your ass."

Banner pointed at the door. "Get out."

Tarrant walked over to Banner. When he came even, he leaned in close. "Shut your operation in the Gulf. It's illegal, and after the Colombian matter no one's gonna believe you when you say it ain't. Darkview's finished. Better find yourself a new job quick." He sauntered out the door. Church followed, his face suffused with red from suppressed anger. He managed to bump Banner's shoulder as he passed. Banner wanted to brush himself off to rid himself of any part of the man's touch. Instead he stood still and watched them both leave.

32

BANNER'S PHONE RANG THE MINUTE THEY WERE GONE. STRO-
meyer had followed the men out, probably to ensure that they vacated
the premises. He punched the speaker button on the base. Might as
well use the feature, he thought, since the whole world was listening
to his conversations anyway.

"Mr. Banner, Senator Cooley calling, please hold while I connect
you?" Cooley's secretary sounded impersonal, professional, but Banner was still irritated. As far as he was concerned, Cooley should
place his own calls, like the rest of the business world. He made a
mental note to have Alicia place the next call to Cooley.

Cooley's supercilious voice came over the line. "Mr. Banner, I'd
like to meet with you at my offices. New information concerning the
pipeline has come to light. Oh, and I've signed a subpoena in which
we demand that you provide the committee with every piece of paper
related to Darkview's contract in the Colombian matter."

For a brief moment, Banner considered demanding that Cooley
tell him about the pipeline over the phone, but the tap held him back.
Depending upon what the information was, he might want to hear it
directly from Cooley in a safe environment.

"When?" Banner said.

"Thirty minutes from now."

"I'll be there." Banner clicked off the speaker. He grabbed his motorcycle helmet on the way out.

He drove into the underground parking lot attached to Cooley's

office building. The minute he left the sunlight, cool, damp, grease-
filled air hit his face. Fluorescent lights cast a harsh glow over the gray
concrete. Banner had felt his anger growing ever since he'd hung up
the phone. Cooley was gunning for Darkview and showed no signs of
letting up. The subpoena sounded like yet another attempt to dig up
dirt that Banner knew didn't exist. He wasn't concerned about what
the subpoena would find—he knew that Stromeyer would never have
a paper out of place—but he *was* concerned about the impact such
a move would have on the company's reputation. Cooley knew that
clients of security companies like Darkview relied on discretion and
wouldn't like to do business with a company that government inves-
tigators were targeting. Likewise, the Department of Defense would
eventually steer clear of a contractor that brought with it even a whiff
of impropriety. Cooley had been unable to bring Darkview down in
a legitimate fashion, and now it appeared he was going to try a smear
campaign. Banner parked the cycle, removed his helmet, and headed
for the elevators, brooding. At that moment he could have happily
smashed something. He heard a noise from a corner of the lot but
ignored it while he continued to fume.

Twenty seconds later three men appeared from behind a stone support. All three focused on Banner. Two were black guys, over six feet
but slender. The third was white, about five-eight, with a basketball
for a stomach and arms like a stevedore's. He carried a heavy Maglite
flashlight. They were an incongruous bunch. Like a motley group
of thugs brought together only by their love of destruction. Banner
slowed to a stop. It was apparent they were focused on him. He began
to make the calculations he'd been making his whole life when con-
fronted with impending violence.

Banner stood six feet, weighed 170, and had the advantage of experience. As former Special Forces, he knew how to fight. Over the
years he'd learned a little about many martial arts, cherry-picking the
moves he liked and adding them to his repertoire. Still, three against
one constituted formidable odds. He sized up the men and did some

quick reckoning. The tall ones looked like a couple of inner-city gangbangers accustomed to fighting dirty. Banner thought he caught the glint of some brass knuckles in the hand of one. The little guy was the oldest and meanest of the three, and once he got his hands on Banner, his strength would come into play, but his girth was going to slow him down. The short one must have known this—hence the Maglite. Despite the weapon, as long as no one pulled a gun, Banner thought he had a decent chance to survive. In fact, he thought they intended for him to survive. If killing him was on their agenda, they wouldn't have shown themselves so early but would instead have jumped him from behind. They were there to deliver a message and then beat the hell out of him to drive the point home. Banner waited for one of them to speak. He focused on the short guy—who, sure enough, started talking.

"You're getting to be a pain in the ass," the short one said. "Our shipping friends tell us that you've got guys running around the Indian Ocean firing on their fishing boats. They don't like it." He slapped the Maglite on his palm.

Banner shrugged. "I'm sorry to hear that. Tell your friends to stop firing on legitimate trading vessels and we can all go back to living peacefully."

"Tell your guys to fly home. They don't belong there."

"No," Banner said.

"You've got thirty-six hours. We're here to show you what happens when people don't do what we want. We're gonna give you a little preview."

Banner stared down at him. "Listen, jerk. I don't have anything you might need except maybe the instructions for a really good diet." The gangbanger on the right laughed.

The short one's face flushed red. "You won't be so cocky when you end up in the emergency room."

Banner shook his head again. "I'm not the one going to the emergency room. I'm only asking once for you three to move on. If not,

I'm going to have to hurt you, and I'd hate to do that." Banner freed up his hands by dropping his helmet on the ground.

The skinny one on the left came at him so fast that Banner was impressed. He had his hand cocked back, ready to deliver a blow. There was steel on his knuckles, and he covered the ground between them in a couple of seconds, but the move was a straightforward attack, which made it easy to avoid.

Banner dodged the punch on the inside. He opened his hand wide and used the space between his thumb and index finger. He hammered this spot into the man's Adam's apple, keeping his arm slightly bent to absorb the blow but moving forward into the attacker. As he did, he closed the rest of his fingers around the guy's neck and squeezed.

The skinny one made a strange gargling noise from his windpipe. He arched backward, as if he were doing the limbo, while Banner followed him down, trying his best to crush the man's throat. The other two came at him at the same time. The short one grabbed Banner around the waist, trapping his left arm to his body and holding him in place while the second one aimed a fist at his temple. Banner avoided the main force of the punch, but the hit still whipped his head to the side, making him see stars. Pain radiated through the bones of his face along with the scrape of a dull point ripping his skin open. The temple shot forced him sideways. He dragged the short one with him, like a load of ballast. Banner felt his own blood pouring down his cheek. He lost his grip on the first guy's neck, but he was down anyway, rolling around on the cement, holding his throat and making wheezing noises.

Banner stumbled over the first one's body while he wrestled to free himself from the short one's grasp. The man was like a pit bull with its jaws clamped down. He held on to Banner so tightly that Banner was finding it hard to breathe. Number Two had a grip on the sleeve of Banner's leather jacket and was using him like a speed bag, raining a series of short punches on him. The jacket softened the blows, but each one created a burst of pain. He quit with the rapid hits and aimed a jab straight for Banner's face, looking to drive Banner's nose into his forehead. This time Banner saw the brass knuckles with spikes on top as they came at him. He managed to twist his upper body to the side, getting his face out of range. Instead he felt the fist with its metal-tipped payload piston into his rotator cuff. The same rotator cuff that had taken shrapnel fifteen years before and still ached at the slightest change in the weather. Even with the leather as protection, Banner knew that the blow might take him down. The gangbanger had found his Achilles' heel.

White-hot pain reverberated through his arm and into his chest. It felt like someone had driven a two-foot blade directly into half his body. Mixed with the pain came a surging volcano of anger. He turned toward the gangbanger in a blinding rage, yanking his left arm out of the short one's grip. Now he had a better range of motion, despite lugging the short one around like an anchor. He drove his right fist into the guy's solar plexus with such force that odds were he wouldn't survive. As he folded forward, Banner raised his knee into his face. Number Two dropped like a stone.

The short one still had a vise grip on Banner's midsection. Banner catapulted himself backward, onto him. They fell together. Banner heard a loud crack as the man's head hit the pavement. His arms finally loosened. Banner wrenched himself out of the other man's grasp, rolled himself sideways, and rose up to his knees. The short one was already on all fours. His hands scrabbled around on the floor. Banner watched his fingers close over the Maglite. He jerked, as if attempting to stand.

Banner's left arm was useless, his temple wound dripped blood onto the concrete, and he had no weapon. All he had left were his feet. He staggered to his cycle. He heard the last guy behind him but forced himself to keep his eyes on the ignition. Even raising his left arm enough to hold the handlebar sent waves of pain through it. He jammed the key into the ignition. The cycle started on a roar. Banner drove it off its kickstand and raised his boots into position while he skidded around a turn.

Twenty minutes later he pulled into his garage. His face still bled, and his left arm shook with pain. He watched the electric garage door close while he sat on the cycle, unable to move. He pulled his cell phone out of his pocket to call Stromeyer and tried to raise it to his ear, but the upward motion, even from his uninjured shoulder, sent a twinge of pain across his chest. He ended up holding the device at waist level while he sent a text requesting that she meet him at his house.

He dragged himself into the kitchen, headed toward the ibuprofen that he kept in a cabinet above the sink. But when he contemplated the pain level that reaching up for it would create, he decided against the maneuver. Instead he opened a nearby drawer, fished out a long wooden spoon, and knocked the bottle off the high shelf into the sink. He swore under his breath at the childproof cap. The pain wasn't letting up, the blood from the cut on his face was congealing, and he felt a swelling beginning at his shoulder. He would need to ice it quickly, or the rest of the week was going to be all about agony.

The doorbell rang. Banner took it as a good sign that whoever wanted to see him had the decency to actually ring the bell. The three in the garage would simply have smashed in a window. He walked to the door, still clutching the recalcitrant ibuprofen bottle. He checked out the newcomer through the peephole. It was Stromeyer. He opened the door.

Her eyes widened at the sight of him.

He thrust the bottle at her. "Can you open this?"

She nodded and stepped inside. He closed the door, throwing the dead bolts before waving her into the kitchen. Stromeyer had the bottle open by the time they got there. She didn't say a word, and he was too busy clenching his teeth against the pain to engage in any conversation. She shook out two pills, took another look at him, and shook out two more. She filled a glass with water and handed it all to him. He downed them in one gulp and put the glass in the sink before extracting a Ziploc bag from a nearby drawer. He filled it with ice, wrapped it in a thin dishcloth, and placed it on the counter. Now came the hard part.

"Can you help me take off the jacket? I got hit in the shoulder."

She sucked in her breath. "The bad one?"

"Yes."

Stromeyer took off her own coat, threw it over the back of a nearby chair, and stepped toward him. She peeled the leather back from his chest in a careful motion. At the left shoulder, she took care to raise the fabric enough that she could hold it open while he eased his arm out. Every move, no matter how subtle, sent fresh waves of pain through him.

"The shirt, too," he said.

She unbuttoned his shirt and repeated the careful motion. They both gasped at what was revealed. The spiked brass knuckles had left deep indentations on the tip of his shoulder. Several purple swellings were set in a precise row where the spikes had punctured the flesh. The whole mess was a mottled red heading to black. He went over to the counter to retrieve the ice.

"You'd better wait to put that on until after you're lying flat." Stromeyer sounded matter-of-fact, but when he looked at her, he could see strain around her eyes.

"Afraid I'll faint?" Banner said.

"Yes."

He nodded. "You may be right." He turned to go.

"Let me wipe the blood off your face first," she said.

"I'll lie down. You can do it then."

He made it to the bedroom and sat on the bed. He stared at his booted feet. He didn't think he had the energy to remove them. Stromeyer appeared and knelt before him. She eased off his boots, and he swung his legs onto the bed. Once he was flat, he put the ice on his naked shoulder. Just the weight of the bag made him want to shriek in pain, but he knew that if he could stick it out, the ice would work wonders.

"Your jeans are covered in blood. Let me get them off," Stromeyer said.

Banner said nothing. She eased them down. Normally he would have been embarrassed to have her perform the chore for him, but he found that he didn't really care just then. She unfolded the blanket from the foot of his bed and covered him with it.

"I'll keep watch and call the police. You have a gun?"

Banner went to reach for it but decided against moving. "Under the pillow."

Stromeyer slid her hand beneath his head.

"Other pillow."

She leaned over him to reach under the second pillow. He smelled her perfume, a happy citrus scent that seemed incongruous given the circumstances. She removed his nine-millimeter. He watched her check it.

"I'll hold on to this. Try to sleep."

Banner fell into unconsciousness. He never heard her leave.

EMMA WATCHED AS A BLACK FOUR-WHEEL-DRIVE VEHICLE OF AN indeterminate make drove out of the shrubbery lining the beach. It came toward them, its wheels churning through the sand. It pulled within five feet of the jeep and stopped. A white man swung out of it wearing khaki-colored cargo pants, a Guns N' Roses T-shirt, and a pistol in a holder attached to his waistband.

"What's up, Nick?" Hassim sounded concerned.

Nick glanced at Emma and back at Hassim without replying. He had shaggy black hair that was hacked off at his collar in a choppy fashion, as if someone had taken a knife to it rather than scissors. His skin was tanned a honey color.

Hassim grabbed the top of the windshield, hauled himself upright, and jumped over the door. "She's okay. She works for Banner."

Nick looked visibly relieved. He gave Emma a curt nod before directing his attention back to Hassim. "We've got a problem. Our contact, the one who promised us the boat, wants another two days. He claims he's got something he needs to do."

Hassim snorted. "You know what that means. He's got a couple of hostages that he wants to transport first."

"Yeah, but who? They haven't taken a ship that I'm aware of."

Hassim looked thoughtful. "Last kidnapping I heard about was a Turkish freighter."

"That crew's long gone. Their company paid up a month ago."

"Where's he now? Or, more important, where's the boat?"

Nick waved back toward the beach behind him. "Anchored two miles down. I just saw it as I drove in."

"Anyone on it?" Hassim reached into a small area directly behind the seats. Emma watched him as he fished around under a green tarp. He withdrew an assault rifle.

"Not that I saw."

Hassim checked his weapon. "Then let's go. I've already paid that guy. If I let him get away with taking the money and not delivering the boat, I'll never be dealt with straight again." He turned to Emma. "Do you want to come?"

She was up and over her door in a flash. "I don't want to be left here, if that's what you mean. Do you have a gun for me?"

Hassim stopped in midstride. "Didn't I just give you one?"

"I mean a semiautomatic."

Nick looked amused.

Hassim stood still. Then he shrugged in apparent resignation and headed back to the jeep. He extracted another AK-47 out from under the tarp and handed it across to Emma, over the jeep's seats. She hefted it, feeling its weight. It appeared in fine working condition. Oiled, with a carrying strap that was relatively clean, it was set to automatic. Emma switched it to semiautomatic.

"Sure you want to do that?" Hassim asked.

You have no idea how sure, Emma thought. "I don't want to auto-fire indiscriminately. I'm a terrible shot and likely to kill one or both of you in a bout of friendly fire. I've had a sum total of three lessons on how to use a gun."

Hassim's eyebrows hit his hairline. "In that case by all means."

Nick laughed. "Glad that's settled. Climb into the car. I'll take you to the boat."

They piled the rest of the duffels and chemistry equipment into the Land Rover. When they were finished, Nick hit the gas. The car dug in even further as a result of the added weight. Emma watched sprays of sand fly out from under the wheels, but the four-wheel drive managed to propel the vehicle forward. They drove for ten minutes before coming to a dirt road cut between the palms. It led away from the beach. Nick turned onto it. Here they moved quicker, although potholes filled the road. Emma held on to a handle above the door as they bounced along. The path turned to parallel the beach. After a few minutes, it became gravel, then curved back in the direction of the ocean. When it appeared as though they'd drive straight onto the sand again, Nick took a sharp left and killed the engine.

"The boat sits in a small cove up ahead. I think we should finish the trip on foot. We'll need to move as quietly as possible." Nick whispered the instructions before he carefully opened the driver's door. Emma eased out of the car as well. She shut the door not by swinging it closed but by placing it against the side of the car and pressing it.

Nick went first, Hassim followed, and Emma brought up the rear. Her heart took on a crazy rhythm, and beads of sweat popped out on her forehead. She did all she could to walk softly. The only sounds she heard were the crashing of the waves on shore and the cry of seagulls, but these were so loud that she was concerned they'd miss the telltale step of a prowler behind them.

After five minutes of skulking through the trees, Emma could see the prow of a boat bobbing up and down. It was anchored ten feet from the sand's edge. Nick waved them into cover. Hassim moved behind a tree. Emma followed his lead. Now she had a view of the entire vessel, and she was underwhelmed. It was a small cabin cruiser. So small, in fact, that she wouldn't have been confident taking it out on a local lake, much less the ocean. From what she could see, there was a little cabin up front, and enough seating on each side of the open back to seat six, three on each side.

"*That's* the boat we're taking on the ocean?" Emma said.

Hassim turned his dark eyes on her. "It's seaworthy. The *Kaiser Franz* was only about seventy-five miles out at its last known location, so we don't have far to go." He looked at Nick. "So we know the boat's here. Where's the owner?"

At that moment two men came out of the trees, assault rifles slung over their backs. They scanned the area before waving behind them. Three Somali women emerged. All three balanced large bundles on their heads. After them came two more men with guns. They carried a large crate. Once their feet hit the sand, they staggered with its weight. The entire entourage headed to the boat.

"They're provisioning," Nick said, "but I don't see any hostages."

Hassim shrugged. "Maybe they're carrying arms to the mother ship. That box looks heavy enough. Whatever they're doing, they're not taking my boat. Let's make a circle around and check out the road they used. I'll bet Ali's there."

Nick gave Hassim an incredulous look. "You're using Ali?"

Hassim nodded. "Why does that surprise you?"

"Ali *always* delivers. He's the most reliable thief in Puntland. He'd never leave you high and dry if he could help it. Whatever's up, he must really need that boat."

Emma didn't like the sound of that. The change of plans could very easily be born of desperation or coercion. Hassim, though, seemed unimpressed.

"*I* really need that boat. And this is the first time I've ever used Ali. Somalia isn't my usual stomping ground. Perhaps this guy thinks he can mess with me."

Nick shook his head back and forth. "No way. Ali may not know you personally, but everyone knows that you work for Banner and that Banner doesn't allow anyone to mess with his people. If they did, there would be a small army of former Special Forces guys crawling up their ass within days."

Hassim looked doubtful. "Banner doesn't work this area much at all. Ali may not know his reputation."

Nick snorted. "Ali knows, believe me."

Hassim hitched his gun higher on his shoulder. "Whatever's going on here is not my concern. I have a time-sensitive situation that requires my intervention. I need the boat, I paid for the boat, and I'm going to take the boat."

Nick put up his palms in surrender. "Hey, I'm with you. Let's go get the boat."

Hassim moved out from behind the tree. Emma followed, and Nick brought up the rear. They jogged through the trees, following a jagged path from trunk to trunk. After a couple of minutes, they emerged at the beginning of the road. From the looks of it, Emma guessed that it was the road the Somalis had just used to deliver their provisions. Hassim hesitated behind another tree.

"They most likely have a Land Rover around here somewhere. It's doubtful they carried that crate the entire way on foot. Let's go down, farther away from the shore, and impound their car. If they want it back, they'd better bargain."

Fifty feet along, they came upon a Range Rover parked dead center in the road. Emma was surprised to see that it was the latest model. Behind it sat an old white panel van. They watched both vehicles for a few minutes. Nothing happened.

Nick shifted. "No one's here. How about I canvass the road on the back end, leading to the village?"

"I'll head farther down the ocean side," Hassim said. "When you're done, come join me." He turned to Emma. "You stay with the cars. It's the safest place under the circumstances. They're not likely to get past either Nick or me."

Emma shouldered her gun. "I'll check both vehicles. If there are any weapons on board, I'll drag them here." She watched both men head to their various destinations. Silence settled over the clearing. After a minute she slipped out from behind the tree and walked to the Range Rover. The door opened with a smooth swing. A gust of superheated air washed over her. The inside of the SUV was like an oven. Despite the temperature it still contained a new-car smell. The incongruity of such a beautiful vehicle in Somalia struck Emma as evil. Nothing good had bought this car. She scanned the backseat first, looking for evidence of weapons, peering into the cargo area. Sand was scattered on the carpeting, but on the whole the interior was clean. She lowered herself onto the front seat. The leather was so hot that she felt the warmth seep through her clothes. By now she was sweating freely. Rivulets of perspiration streamed down her sides.

She fished around the glove compartment, the ashtray, and the console. A canteen sat in the passenger's foot well. Next to that was what appeared to be an aluminum water bottle. The driver must have tried to stash them out of the sunlight. A small burlap bag tied at the top with string sat on the console between the front seats. Emma opened it to find twiggy khat leaves, still fresh. They hadn't started chewing yet, which was unfortunate, because they wouldn't be impaired when they came upon Hassim and Nick. She gave another cursory look around and backed out of the Rover.

The sun struck her, though it was a bit cooler when compared to the SUV's interior. She headed to the van, ignoring the front area and moving straight to the rear doors. If any weapons existed, they'd be there.

She reached for the handle and yanked her hand off it. The metal scorched her palm. She wrapped her fingers in the edge of her T-shirt and used it as a protective layer. She grasped the handle again and swung the door wide. Another blast of hot air hit her. She peered into the cargo area and gasped.

There, staring back at her, was Richard Stark.

SUMNER STOOD ON THE PORT DECK NEXT TO THE SWIMMING pool and gazed at the cage armor. It sat in a circle of light cast by the overhead lamps. Herr Schullmann supervised a mechanic wielding a torch. Red and yellow flames sparked as he welded one piece to another. It was a grid of metal rods erected on a movable dolly. The bars ran horizontally, spaced six inches apart and held together by vertical support beams. The entire grid measured four feet high by five feet across. It was mounted at the end of the rectangular flatbed, which allowed a man enough space to crouch behind it on the platform. Schullmann moved to stand shoulder to shoulder with Sumner while he watched the mechanic work.

"It is almost finished. What do you think?"

Sumner walked around the dolly. The beams did not appear to be bolted to it. He looked underneath. Schullmann had welded several beams at a ninety-degree angle to the upright supports. These were six inches apart. They managed to slide over and under the dolly's platform, stabilizing the entire grid without the need to nail it down. But what caught Sumner's attention was the piece of steel attached to the back of the grid. It looked like a door, complete with a glass porthole. He walked over and tapped on it.

"Where did you get the steel plating?"

Herr Schullmann jerked his head at the mechanic. "It's the metal door to one of the engine rooms. We took it off its hinges."

"So maybe it will protect against a blast after all. I'm impressed. This is excellent, Herr Schullmann," Sumner said.

Schullmann shrugged without smiling, but Sumner thought the man was pleased with the praise.

"It is movable as well as removable. If it needs repair, we can simply slide it off."

Sumner nodded. "I noticed the way you attached it. Almost like a paper-clip bottom, with supports on each side of the flatbed."

"But you know, even with the solid door, it will not necessarily protect the person hiding behind it, right?"

"I know."

Block walked up to them. He eyed the armor. "Helluva contraption you got there." He moved around it, checking it out from all angles. He reached over to pull on the bars. The system didn't shake. "Solid. You sure do know your armor, don't you?" Block extended a hand to Schullmann. "I'm Harry Block. I sell cars in Houston. You must be Marina's father."

Marina, who was standing next to Sumner, translated for her father.

Schullmann brightened. "What example of cars do you sell?" His English was passable, Sumner decided.

"You name it, we sell it."

"SUVs?"

"Hell, yeah."

Sumner could see a long conversation ensuing, and he had no time to spare for it.

"Any action out there?" he said.

Block broke off his patter with Schullmann. "No. But Clutch is back. He's drunk. I wanted to punch the guy, but he's so damn impaired, wouldn't be sporting."

Sumner was finding Clutch's behavior to be more and more strange. He made a mental note to ask Wainwright how the man managed to become chief of security. He checked his watch.

"It's late. You want to be spelled?"

Block nodded. "Cindy came by about an hour ago. I promised her to get some sleep."

"Give Janklow your weapon. I've got to get some sleep myself."

"I thought you went to do that already."

"Didn't work out."

"So go. But this time, sleep, will ya?"

"First we've got to set up the armor." He turned to the mechanic. "Can you get it to the first deck level? The area nearest the ladder."

Block snorted. "You think these guys will be able to board?"

"I don't *think* they'll board, I *know* they'll board. The only question is from which side?"

The entire group fell silent. Sumner glanced at Marina. Her face had lost all its color. He wished he could assure her that she was safe, but he couldn't. Odds were they were soon to be attacked. The only questions were who would live, who would die, and who would be kidnapped.

He put an arm around Marina. "Why don't you get some sleep? You may need it later."

She shook her head. "I won't be able to. I'm too afraid someone will climb in the porthole."

"Come with me."

Sumner took her by the hand. He nodded at Block and Schullmann before walking her to the decks. Block pursed his lips but refrained from commenting. Schullmann hardly noticed that his daughter was leaving.

Sumner escorted Marina to the kitchens behind the main restaurant. It was deserted. Pots hung from hooks overlooking a long steel prep table. The walls on each side were lined with sinks, counters, and bins labeled as containing food, spices, and various utensils. Sumner walked over to a wooden block with black knife handles sticking out of various slots. He pulled one out. The steel made a sleek slipping sound as he removed it. He handed it to Marina.

"Take this and keep it with you. They won't need it tonight. You can return it in the morning."

Marina gazed at the knife with a disappointed air.

"What's the matter?"

She shrugged. "I would prefer it if you stayed with me." She gave him a direct look that left no doubt as to what she was saying.

Sumner was surprised at the offer. He couldn't remember the last time such a thing had happened to him, and for sure he couldn't recall saying no. He could only hope circumstances would turn around soon and he could say yes. With Marina he was sorely tempted. He'd come to like her in the short time he'd known her. He admired the way she kept her dignity around her difficult father, and how she'd fired the flare gun. If he weren't so sure the pirates would return soon, he would have liked nothing better than to keep her company. But the pirates' inevitable attack occupied his mind and dominated his thoughts. He needed to focus on survival, and sleep was essential to his ability to function. Once he was horizontal, it was imperative that he rest. He paused a moment while he tried to marshal his tired thoughts. He wanted to explain why he wouldn't stay in a way that spared her feelings.

"I can't stay with you tonight; I'm needed on the deck. But don't think for a minute that I don't wish I could."

She smiled. "I understand." She showed him the knife. "I will take this. Thank you."

"Let me escort you to your cabin."

They left the darkened kitchen, moving down the dimly lit hallways.

"Why are the halls so dark?" Marina asked.

"They're trying to conserve energy. The ship is on generator power only."

They turned a corner. Marina's mother stood in front of her door, a frightened look on her face.

"You are safe! I was worried about you." The woman eyed Sumner. Marina introduced them, speaking in German. Frau Schull-mann's eyebrows rose.

"Herr Sumner, you speak German?" she said.

"I do." Sumner kept his voice neutral. Marina's mother was wound tight. Her lips were pinched together, creating hollows under her cheekbones. She clutched at Marina's arm, and her eyes widened as she took in the wicked butcher knife. Sumner sought to put the woman at ease. "It's from the kitchen. I suggested Marina sleep with it nearby. Just in case."

Frau Schullmann visibly relaxed. "It's good. Marina, would you like me to stay with you as well?"

"That's not necessary. You're just next door."

"I'll wish you both good night, then," Sumner said.

He headed to his own stateroom and threw the metal bar that locked the door. He set his watch alarm to wake him in thirty minutes, hit the lights, and crawled into the bed fully clothed.

WHEN BANNER WOKE, IT WAS FULL DARK. THE HOUSE HELD A quiet, restful feeling. His shoulder, however, was less than restful. In fact, it was throbbing in a persistent rhythm. The ice pack remained full of not-yet-melted ice. Stromeyer must have replaced it recently, but for the life of him Banner couldn't recall her doing so. He heaved himself to a sitting position, catching the ice bag as it dropped off his shoulder. He headed straight to the shower, studiously avoiding looking in the mirror. While the hot water was not the greatest for his swollen shoulder, it did wonders for his mood. He dressed and strolled to his living room, where a light glowed through the open door.

He found Stromeyer there, sitting in his favorite reading chair, next to his favorite reading lamp, her feet on his favorite ottoman. She had a stack of paper next to her, along with a glass of red wine, a plate of cheese, and a highlighter pen. Banner's gas fireplace threw flickering color around the Oriental carpet on the floor, and in the background his integrated music system played soft jazz.

"How do you like the chair?" he said.

Stromeyer looked up at him, and a smile lit her face. "How do you feel?"

He wanted to shrug, but the movement would cause unnecessary pain, so he settled for rocking his left hand back and forth. "Okay. Shoulder is bad, but not as bad as it could have been."

She rose. "Do you want to sit?"

He waved her back down. "You stay there. I'll use the other one." Banner sank into a matching chair opposite Stromeyer. She went to a minibar set in a corner of the living room, poured him a shot of his preferred cognac, and walked across the room to hand it to him. He noticed she was barefoot. Her toes were painted a nude color.

"How long have I been sleeping?"

Stromeyer settled back into her prior position, folding her legs underneath her. "Eight hours. The police were here. At first they insisted that I wake you up. I refused, and I opened the door to the bedroom so they could see you. One look at your face and they agreed that the interview could wait until after you woke." She picked up a business card off the cocktail table in front of her. "Here's the detective's number. He said just call the interview in. He'll take it from there."

"How bad do I look?" Banner was so busy focusing on his shoulder pain that he'd forgotten about the temple shot. He reached up to touch it gingerly. There was a swelling that felt like a small egg, but it didn't throb nearly as much as the rest of him.

Stromeyer cocked her head to one side as she assessed him. "Like you've been in a car accident. The side of your face is a lovely black with red around the edges. Not to worry, though—I don't think you'll have any lasting marks. Your good looks remain."

Banner snorted. "Who cares about my looks as long as everything continues to function?"

Stromeyer took a sip of her wine. From her expression it appeared as though she wanted to reply, but she refrained. She held the cheese plate out to him. "Hungry?"

Banner leaned forward to pluck some cheese from the platter. "Starving. Want to go to dinner? There's a great trattoria around the corner. Run by an entire Italian family. It's not fancy, but the food is outstanding."

Stromeyer nodded. "Sure. But before we go, I have some bad news and some much worse news."

Banner didn't like the sound of that. He grimaced and took a swallow of his cognac. "Okay, go ahead."

"Ahmed never made contact with Caldridge. He was found dead in his apartment."

"Who found him?"

"The neighbors called the authorities after they smelled a stench. No signs of a struggle. The authorities are conducting an autopsy."

"And Caldridge? Is she still in Nairobi, then?"

Stromeyer shook her head. "Roducci said she insisted on flying a khat flight into Somalia. Vanderlock flew her."

Banner leaned back in the chair. "That's a lucky break. Vanderlock's fairly reliable."

"The Price Pharmaceuticals jet went up in flames after landing at the Hargeisa airport."

Banner stilled. "What in the world was a Price corporate jet doing in Hargeisa?"

"No one seems to know."

Banner took another sip of his cognac while he digested this information. "A bomb blows up at an ultra where Price is a sponsor and Caldridge a Price-sponsored athlete. During the race someone targets Caldridge and injects her with a performance-enhancing drug. And now the Price jet blows up in Somalia. Quite a set of coincidences."

Stromeyer nodded. "Too many coincidences for my taste, but I can't figure out if all of this is somehow tied into your getting beaten up."

Banner pointed his shot glass at her. "I beg to differ. I wasn't beaten up, I was the one doing the beating."

Stromeyer raised an eyebrow. "Perhaps you should go look in the mirror."

Banner always took pains to avoid looking in the mirror after any pummeling. In his experience the aftereffects of a beating were always worse than the actual injuries. It was better not to dwell on them. Otherwise he might think he was more broken than he really was.

"I have a hunch the whole thing is tied to Price somehow. The mousy assistant—"

"Susan Plower."

"—said that Price manufactured the vaccines. Maybe whoever's at the bottom of this got wind of Darkview's mission to secure the ship and they're covering all bases. One of those bases includes threatening me."

Stromeyer looked pained. "That's a bad thing on so many levels, I don't know where to start. If you're correct, then they must already know what the ship is carrying. And if *that's* true, then all this secrecy is wasted effort. We might as well send in seven different aircraft carriers to surround the ship and escort it to port. You think they tapped our phones and that's how they heard we were hired?"

Banner considered her suggestion. "Doubtful. The DOD call came through on this home line. We've never detected a tap here." He stood up. "Let's go to dinner. Maybe it will all become clearer on a full stomach."

The night air was fresh, with more than a hint of summer. Banner enjoyed this time of the year, and he found himself relishing the walk through his neighborhood. The only dark spot on the evening was right before they left, when Stromeyer had insisted he carry concealed. He had a license to do so but rarely did. He'd spent so many years carrying guns that he was loath to do it on civilian territory. Besides, he figured Stromeyer had one on her person somewhere. He thought his weapon was overkill. Also, Banner preferred a shoulder holster, but his injury didn't make that feasible. Currently the gun was located at the small of his back in a holster that wrapped around his waist. He wore a casual blazer to hide the bulge of the gun.

They made it to the restaurant, ordered dinner, and, as if by mutual consent, changed the topic to current events. It was only when the espresso order came that the subject veered back to their immediate circumstances.

"Are you going to sleep at the town house?" Stromeyer asked.

Banner sighed. "No. I'd be an easy target. I thought I'd pack a bag and head to the airport hotel."

"And from there?"

"Dubai."

Stromeyer didn't seem surprised at all. "You're due to speak at the local Rotary Club."

Banner groaned. He'd forgotten all about it. "Can you cover for me? Tell them I've been in some sort of accident? God knows it wouldn't be far from the truth."

"Of course I can cover for you. I expect to see Cooley there."

"Cooley! Why?"

"He's a member. Didn't you know?"

Banner put his espresso cup down a little harder than he intended. The noise of it hitting the saucer clanged through the room. He really disliked Cooley.

"All the more reason for me not to go. You do the speech. If Cooley's there, pull him off to the side and tell him just what happened to me in the basement of his office. Let me know if you think he was involved in some way."

Stromeyer shook her head. "I'd be shocked if he was. He's a jerk, I'll admit that, but he doesn't seem to be the type to beat up rivals." She caught the waiter's eye and made a writing motion. He appeared at their table with the check.

Banner took it, extracted his business credit card, and slapped it down on the vinyl wallet that held the bill. Ten minutes later they were back outside and working their way toward the town house. Banner's arm throbbed, his face hurt, and his torso felt as if someone had used it for a punching bag—which, when he thought about it, was exactly what had happened. What he wanted more than anything was to sleep in his own bed that night. He turned the corner to his house, and three of his best men were lounging on the front steps. They all stood up to greet him and Stromeyer.

"Hey, Banner," Gage Johnson said. Gage worked most of England and Ireland for Darkview. He was a trained knife fighter, and so he thrived in settings where guns were not the norm. He was in D.C. for only a few days on a brief layover from Los Angeles before heading back to England. Standing next to him were Steven Cardill and Tyler Walter. Both worked Northern Europe.

"To what do I owe the honor of your visit?" Banner asked.

"We heard about your close encounter with several of D.C.'s finest criminal elements. We figured you might need some security. Are you up for a poker game? Should keep us occupied most of the night."

Banner stepped into the pool of light thrown by the outdoor lamp, and he watched the men grimace.

"That's bad," Tyler said.

"Don't tell me. I haven't looked yet. But I'd like to sleep in my own bed. If you guys stand guard, I'll be more than grateful. But I'll pass on the poker game. It's all I can do to stay on my feet."

"Major Stromeyer, you could be the fourth."

Stromeyer shook her head. "I'm out, sorry. I've got to prepare a speech for tomorrow. My car is parked just down the street."

"I'll walk you," Gage said. Stromeyer waved at them all before leaving.

Half an hour later, Banner dozed off to the murmur of conversation and the thud of thrown poker chips emanating from his kitchen. Once again he was thankful for sleep.

36

"THANK GOD, YOU'RE ALIVE," EMMA SAID. THE GAG IN STARK'S mouth made it impossible for him to respond. The van's interior was stripped to the metal sides. Stark sat with his back against the wall separating the cabin from the cargo area. His tied hands rested in his lap. His face was bright red, alarmingly so. He looked about to pass out from the heat. Emma jumped into the vehicle and went straight to remove the gag. Stark bent his head forward to give her easier access to the knot.

When the fabric fell away, Stark said, "Water." His voice was hoarse, almost a croak.

"There's some in the car parked ahead of this one. Let me help you out of this furnace, and I'll go get it." Emma turned to the cloth strips binding his wrists and ankles together. After a minute they, too, unwound. She scooted backward with Stark following. He staggered onto the ground.

"Let's get the water and go back to hide in the trees."

Stark said nothing while Emma retrieved the canteen. She gave it to him and watched while he took huge gulps.

"Better?" she asked.

"You have no idea." He took a deep breath.

"Let's get out of the open. Last thing we need is for the crowd that brought you here to come back."

Stark followed her to her hiding place. Emma crouched down

behind a tree. When Stark joined her, she asked him the question that couldn't wait any longer.

"Who suggested that you hire me to review Cardovin?"

Stark rubbed a hand over his eyes, whether in irritation or resignation, Emma couldn't tell.

"Do we have to have this conversation now?"

She nodded. "Absolutely. Bumping into me in the airport wasn't just a coincidence, was it? You're in this up to your eyeballs, Mr. Stark. I just can't figure out how I play into the situation. And think before you answer, because if you lie, or try to hedge, I'll leave you here to deal with whatever comes."

For a minute he said nothing. Then he nodded, almost to himself. "We were pressured by a lobbyist claiming to have ties to both the FDA and the members of Congress who were threatening to conduct an investigation into various drug products."

"Members of Congress? Not Cooley."

Stark grimaced. "The lobbyist said that Cooley would be one of the senators assigned to review certain products. We were told that if we hired you, it might go easier on us."

"Easier? How?"

Stark shrugged. "The lobbyist seemed to think that Cooley would see any opinion written by you or your company to be unbiased."

"What a crock. Cooley is gunning for me, not listening to me."

"At the time we hired you, we weren't aware of that. The investigation into the pipeline bombing wasn't yet in full swing. The press was still fawning over Banner, his company, and you," Stark said.

Emma thought about Stark's comment. It was true that in the early days of her return to the States, both she and Banner were media darlings. Banner dodged the limelight every chance he could, and since he was a security-firm contractor doing business with the Department of Defense, the press was unable to hound him too aggressively. When they did pepper him for answers, Banner simply parroted "state secrets" and they'd back off. Emma, on the other hand, had no such convenient excuse to avoid scrutiny. She simply kept repeating the tired line that she was shocked from her ordeal and did not wish to discuss it. As a result the press hovered nearby almost continuously, waiting for a chance to report her story. During that time both she and Banner were hailed as heroes who'd helped save airline passengers. It wasn't until after the full extent of the pipeline damage became apparent that the oil companies started calling for blood. Cooley led the charge.

"I got injected after the bombing. Do you know with what?"

"That had nothing to do with Price," Stark said.

"I don't believe you," Emma said.

"I'm telling the truth." He took another swallow of water.

"Did you know Cardovin had problems?"

"I told you. We knew that some test results showed an inconsistent effect, but on the whole we thought the product had enough efficacy to merit its marketing. We, or at least I, had no idea it would prove to be worthless. To be frank, I'm still not sure whether to believe that."

"What happened in Hargeisa? Are the pilots alive?"

Before Stark could respond, the sound of gunshots cracked through the quiet. A group of birds flew upward from the trees about a hundred yards away. Answering shots followed. Emma pulled the pistol out of the holster attached to her ankle. She handed it to Stark.

"Can you shoot?" She kept her voice soft and low.

"I've been skeet shooting since I was a kid."

"Ever shot a pistol?"

"I'll figure it out." He held the gun in his right hand and stared down the path, as if the discussion were over. Emma reached out, wrapped her palm around his wrist, and pulled his arm sideways, toward her. While she did this, he kept the gun's muzzle pointed in the general direction of the shots. At least he knew enough to aim the gun away, she thought.

"Watch," she whispered. She flicked the safety off, then pushed his hand back so that the gun was once again aligned with the path. Stark colored a little but said nothing.

They waited.

The three Somali women who had carried the provisions burst out of the trees, with terrified looks on their faces and running for all they were worth. Their head scarves flowed out behind them. After, with their backs to the path, came two of the four men. They held their assault weapons at the ready. Stark raised his pistol. Emma stilled his arm. He cast her a quick look; she shook her head no, and he subsided.

The men ran to the Range Rover, flinging open the door. Within seconds Emma heard the engine turn over and then roar as the driver punched the gas pedal but must have failed to release the clutch. The motor whined while the car stayed in place.

The final two men, the ones who had carried the crate, came next. One turned around and released a volley of shots. The rifle visibly rattled in his hands. Bits of bark from nearby trees burst into the air. When the shooter was finished, he jogged into the Rover.

The last man headed for the back of the van. He yanked the rear doors open. Emma would have given anything to see his reaction once he realized that Stark was gone, but the panels blocked her view.

Seconds later the man came around. He had a grim look on his face. He ran to the Rover and leaped into the backseat. The driver finally released the clutch, and the car shot forward, careened sideways as it circled left, and sped down the path, away from the ocean. In less than a minute, Hassim and Nick came into view.

Emma stepped out from the path. "They're gone."

"For now," Hassim said.

"I think I found our hostage." She waved Stark forward. Both Hassim and Nick stared at him.

"Who are you?" Nick said.

"Richard Stark, CEO of Price Pharmaceuticals."

Hassim got a knowing look on his face. "You didn't die in the fire, then."

"Thankfully, no," Stark said.

Hassim looked wary at this latest piece of information, and Emma didn't blame him. Stark's miraculous escape seemed too good to be true.

"I want to hear what happened, but not now. We only have a few minutes. That crowd will run to the village to collect assistance. We need to get on the boat and out of here immediately."

Hassim turned and started a slow jog toward the ocean. Emma, Nick, and Stark fell in behind him. When they reached the area where their own vehicle was hidden, they grabbed the chemistry duffel. The waves crashed on the beach. Along with them came the bodies of jellyfish. Over fifty spread out on the sand—large ones with pink umbrella forms, smaller blue ones in a crescent shape. They lay on the beach, baking in the sun.

"Watch out for the jellyfish," Hassim said.

"Why are there so many?" Emma asked.

Hassim took the duffel from her and handed it to Nick. "The corporate trawlers are overfishing, removing tons of sea life and upsetting the balance. The jellyfish bloom when their natural predators are reduced or gone. When they migrate in masses like this, they can be extremely dangerous. The ones on the beach are a small fraction of the schools that we will find in the water."

Stark stopped when he saw the small craft bobbing in the water. "What are you doing?"

Hassim indicated to Nick that he should keep moving. Nick continued forward, picking his way around the beached jellyfish. He began wading into the water. Emma paused to listen to Hassim and Stark.

"We need to get Ms. Caldridge to a cruise ship that requires her assistance. We'll use this boat to get there," Hassim said.

"Are we all going?" Stark sounded suspicious.

Hassim shook his head. "Not Nick. He'll drive the car back to Berbera."

"I'll go with him," Stark said.

Hassim shook his head again. "No you won't. Everyone in Berbera knows Nick. His presence there will go unnoticed. But that will not be the case if he appears with a Westerner. I won't put him at risk."

Stark stopped cold. Emma could tell he was going to dig in his heels.

"I'll take the risk. Nick can drive me to Hargeisa."

"The Hargeisa-Berbera road is monitored by the pirates. Even with SPUs I can't guarantee that you won't be subjected to a revenge attack."

"SPU?" Stark said.

"Special protection units," Emma said. "They're security guards who ensure your protection along the road. But I think you should listen to Hassim. He knows what he's talking about."

Stark looked aggravated. "Are you sure about that?"

"He works for Banner."

"Ah, the vaunted Banner. Then get *him* on the phone. Perhaps he knows what we should do."

Hassim made a disgusted noise. "You deal with him," he said to Emma.

He turned and headed out to the cabin cruiser. Emma gave it one last shot.

"Listen, I know you don't want to get any deeper into this, but you're not safe here, and we have to go. Either you come with us or Nick and Hassim will leave you to fend for yourself."

Stark gave her a long, pointed look. "Don't you understand? I've just had the most harrowing twenty-four hours of my life. All I want to do is get to civilization and go home. You're off on some wild-goose chase for this Banner guy. What makes you think I want to go along?"

The discussion was cut short by Hassim yelling from the boat. "Leave him! We go!"

Emma sighed. "You're right, I'm heading into a mess, but staying here is a mistake, too. It's yours to make, though, so I'll leave you to it."

She started wading toward the boat. Nick was on the way back toward shore. He high-fived her as he passed.

"Luck to you," he said.

Emma reached the ladder and pulled herself up. She heard a splashing behind her. She looked back to see Stark heading toward them.

"What did you say?" Hassim said.

She shrugged. "I left the decision to him. I think he realizes that he's in an untenable situation. The problem is, I can't tell if he's the source of our troubles or another innocent victim." They watched Stark come nearer. He climbed onto the deck.

"I really think I'm going to regret this," Stark said.

"Ashes fly back into the face of the one who throws them," Hassim replied.

"What does that mean?" Stark said.

"It means don't press your luck," Emma said.

SUMNER WOKE WHEN THE SUN WAS PEEKING THROUGH THE STATE-
room windows. His alarm remained silent, which puzzled him. He
turned to look at the glowing numbers, only to realize that he'd slept
right through it. He sat up in a flash. He'd slept far longer than he'd
intended. He splashed some cold water on his face and headed to the
upper deck, where he found Clutch sitting on the port side, cradling
a stun gun in his lap while he drank from a steaming mug of coffee.
The ship seemed becalmed.

"What's going on?" Sumner said.

Clutch gave a desultory shrug. "Not much. Turbines are off. Wainwright's hoping to keep some juice in case the pirates come back. But,
like *I* said, they're gone. They must know by now that we can't be
taken. This whole sitting-watch thing is a joke."

It was all Sumner could do to continue conversing with the guy.
Instead of responding, he turned to look out to sea. It was full day,
and the heat was rising right along with the sun. Here and there, crew
members went about their usual duties, which added to the surreal
nature of the tableau. It was as if nothing untoward were happening,
or had happened.

"And Block?" Sumner said.

"Went to sleep five, maybe six hours ago. Janklow and Wainwright, too. Soon as they come back I'm letting one of them sit watch.
This is stupid."

"Who has the sniper rifle?"

"It should be obvious that I don't."

Sumner reined in his anger. "I was asking you if you knew who did."

"Probably Block. He was treating the thing like it was his baby. Didn't allow anyone else to use it, which was stupid, because we might have needed it these past hours while he slept."

Sumner noted that this was the first intelligent thing Clutch had said so far, though he couldn't help being pleased that Block didn't just give the gun to Clutch. Sumner didn't think the man had the temperament required to handle the weapon.

"I'll go find it," Sumner said.

Clutch shrugged. "Whatever."

Sumner took another deep breath. The man sounded like a disaffected teenager. Sumner revised that thought almost immediately. A teenager would have realized the danger they were in and would have had the quick reflexes and inclination to be of some help. Clutch had neither.

Sumner headed to the hallway between decks. Before he could make it there, he heard the roar of a cigarette boat's engine. He spun around to see Clutch lurch upward. The coffee in his cup sloshed all over the deck. He gave Sumner a frantic look.

"Go get that gun!" he shrieked.

Sumner fled back down the stairs, taking two at a time. A loud alarm erupted, and on the PA system he heard Janklow's voice over the blaring noise saying, "We are under attack. Please clear all decks and return to your staterooms immediately. Repeat—" The burst of a rocket-propelled grenade drowned out the rest of the warning.

Few people were in the halls. One woman sobbed as she ran. A couple worked their way past him. The man had his arm around his wife, who looked so pale that Sumner thought she might faint. For the first time since the ordeal began, the casino appeared to be empty. He caught a glimpse of a lone bartender restocking glasses. The man shoved the dishwasher crates to the side. Seconds later Sumner heard a noise behind him. He took a quick glance to see the bartender hot on his heels.

Sumner took a right turn into the hallway that held Block's stateroom, just as Block stepped out of the door. He held the Dragunov in his right hand and looked ready to kill. A relieved expression passed over his face when he saw Sumner.

"Here's your gun," Block said. He lobbed the weapon at Sumner. "Go get those bastards. I'll be right behind you."

Sumner caught the rifle and spun back to retrace his steps. He heard the blare of the LRAD. He didn't think the weapon would work this time. The pirates now knew it existed and would have taken measures to protect their eardrums.

Soon he was back up on the swimming-pool deck right below the bridge landing. Once there, he shielded his eyes from the sun to take stock of the attackers. Four boats streamed toward them. Two were high-powered speedboats, the other two were a more basic design. The first three stayed abreast of each other, separated by about forty meters. The fourth and final boat brought up the rear. It was at least half a mile away from the first three, but moving straight toward them.

Sumner halted, took aim, and fired at the closest ship in the formation. They were out of range, but he was counting on their hearing the report and responding. They must have, because the two end boats in the formation split off in different directions, while the lead boat visibly slowed.

He clambered up to the bridge deck.

Janklow was watching the pirates through a set of binoculars.

"They're splitting up to take us from all sides," Sumner said. "What's the ETA for some assistance?"

"Not happening," Janklow replied. "Three other ships were captured in the last twelve hours. Seems these guys are busy. The CTG 600 is still trying to contain the damage, because one of them is transporting nuclear waste. We're on our own. But take a look at that last boat, the one bringing up the rear, and tell me if you see what I think I see." He unwound the glasses from around his neck and tossed them to Sumner.

Sumner put the binoculars to his eyes. His heart sank at the sight.

Janklow moved up until he stood shoulder to shoulder with Sumner. "Either that's a Western woman holding an assault rifle or I'm going crazy."

"You're not crazy," Sumner said.

"Then *she* is," Janklow replied.

EMMA STARED AT THE *KAISER FRANZ* AS IT PLOWED THROUGH THE water. It seemed like a large, slow elephant compared to the quick rabbits that chased it. They'd been following the pirates for two hours on radar, trying to keep their distance in order to be able to surprise them when the time came. During that interval Emma watched the tiny green dots converge on a larger dot that represented the *Kaiser Franz.*

Hassim had laid out the plan as they did. "We'll stay behind until it becomes necessary to reveal ourselves."

Stark, however, was not playing ball. "Do you mean to say that we're deliberately following them?"

Hassim turned his dark eyes on Stark. "They intend to hijack the cruise ship that Ms. Caldridge needs to board. We will attack them as they do so."

Stark sat down abruptly. He turned to Emma. "Did you know that this would happen?"

She nodded. "I did."

He looked incredulous. "You mean to tell me that you *intend* to insert yourself into this situation?"

Emma nodded again.

"My God, you're as crazy as the rest of them."

It was Hassim who cut short Stark's complaints. "I'm sorry to inform you, but most of the world exists in a realm of constant life-or-death struggle. You Americans enjoy a relatively peaceful existence, compared."

Stark put up a hand. "An existence that I'm more than willing to go back to, thank you very much."

Hassim snorted. "Then you should have thought twice before you flew your private jet into Africa to sell your products."

Stark looked pissed. "What are you saying? That because Price sells vaccines, heart medications, and HIV drugs in the Third World we deserve to be caught up in the maelstrom? Those medications save thousands of lives. I shouldn't have mine taken because I provide them."

But Hassim would not back down. "I'm saying that if you want the benefits of selling the drugs here, then you must accept the risks." He turned the boat toward the pirates. "They're close now. Let's reveal ourselves." He opened the throttle, and the small craft moved forward even faster. "There's a rocket launcher in the under-seat storage. Pull it out."

Emma lifted the seat cushion. There, nestled in the cabinet, was an RPG. She maneuvered it out of the space, lowered the seat, and placed it on the cushions. She pulled out the grenades and started to assemble one.

"Could you please show Mr. Stark how to shoot it in case we need to switch weapons?"

Emma checked out Stark's response. While it was clear that he was dumbfounded by the circumstances in which he found himself, he visibly gathered himself up and nodded to her. She wanted to sigh in relief at that. She needed him present and willing to assist if they were going to survive this thing. She showed him the launcher. As she talked him through the operation, Hassim added some additional instruction.

"Be sure to watch your back blast, both of you. I did not have the time to weld a cover on it."

"Back blast?" Stark said.

Emma showed him the rear of the tube. "The exhaust shoots out of the back with a powerful force. It can fry anyone too close to it.

You need to look behind you to ensure it's clear before firing. Also, it leaves a visible vapor trail, which has the unfortunate consequence of revealing one's position in the dark."

"Have you fired one of these?" Stark said.

"Yes."

Stark stilled, watching her. Just as she began to feel uncomfortable, he turned his attention back to the rocket.

Emma heard an alarm in the distance. A barely audible voice chanted a warning. The next warning, though, came through loud and clear. A recorded voice spoke in English and echoed over the water. "Warning! Do not approach. Leave the area immediately."

Stark turned to Hassim. "Do these guys understand English?"

Hassim pursed his lips. "Probably not. But they should be bright enough to figure out that the cruise liner does not wish to be boarded."

Out of nowhere came the blast of the most excruciating noise Emma had ever heard in her life. Stark yelled in response, holding his ears and lowering his head. There was another, cracking sound, and the pirates began to split up.

"They're going to attack from all sides," Stark said.

Hassim grimaced. "We're moving as fast as this engine will allow. Get ready, we'll be in firing range soon."

Emma held on to a side rail, her assault weapon at the ready, as she watched the *Kaiser Franz* loom larger. She could see movement on the upper outside decks. One man in a white uniform stood on the highest level. He appeared to be staring at them with binoculars. Another man, slender and dressed in jeans and a T-shirt, stood with him. A frisson of recognition ran down her spine as she gazed at the second man. Despite the fact that she was too far away to make out any features, she knew, without a doubt, that it was Sumner.

STROMEYER TOOK A CIRCUITOUS PATH TO THE ROTARY MEETING.
While anyone could have seen from the organization's Web page that
Banner was scheduled to speak that day, the most dangerous time for
her would be en route. Once there she'd be surrounded by the other
attendees, a much less desirable target. Getting there, though, was
going to be time-consuming. She started from her house, leaving
out the back door and jumping the neighbor's fence. The neighbor's
name was Stan, and he took his morning coffee in a sunroom facing the yard. Stromeyer often jumped his gate when working on a
particularly sensitive matter, or when she wished to avoid the press.
Stan was a sixty-year-old former analyst at a right-wing think tank.
Stromeyer considered herself a centrist, leaning toward liberal. Their
divergent political views didn't hinder the relationship in the least.
Each of them had worked long enough in Washington to realize that
most issues in the world were neither a simple black nor white but a
complex shade of gray. They both lamented the violence that pockmarked the globe.

Stan was in his solarium when Stromeyer swung her leg onto his
side of the fence and placed her toes on the overturned wheelbarrow
placed there. He cranked open a casement window.

"I hope this doesn't mean that the witch-hunt is getting you down,"
he said through the screen.

Stromeyer smiled at him. "Just being cautious. If you see any
shady characters floating around, you'll be sure to call me?"

"I'll shoot them first, then call you. How's that?"

"Works for me," Stromeyer said.

She waved good-bye before running past his garage to the alley behind, where Alicia was waiting for her. They rode Alicia's cycle to the nearest Metro stop. From there Stromeyer took the train to a location three miles from the Rotary club, doubling back in a cab to the front door of the imposing redbrick building. The cab turned in to the circular drive and stopped.

She was thirty minutes early. The lobby was empty, with the exception of one lone man behind a reception desk. Stromeyer stepped up to him.

"I'm the speaker. I know I'm a little early. Is there somewhere I can get something to drink before we begin? Perhaps some lemonade?"

The man pointed to the lounge entrance on the far left side of the lobby. "Over there is the lounge. The bartender isn't on duty yet, but you can get a water bottle from a refrigerator behind the bar. Senator Cooley's there, pouring himself a stiff one."

Stromeyer doubted that. Cooley was a notorious teetotaler. When campaigning in the South, he would put on cornpone airs and call alcohol "the devil's brew." Stromeyer thought it was an act, but no one had ever seen Cooley take a drink, so perhaps she was wrong. She strode over to the doors that separated the lounge area from the lobby. They were heavy leather-covered panels with studs outlining the perimeter. She hauled them open and stepped inside.

The doors closed behind her with a swishing sound. It was dark in the lounge, which was paneled in gleaming mahogany. A thick carpet covered the floor, and leather club chairs were scattered in small seating configurations. On the far wall was an elaborate carved-wood bar. The bottles of liquor gleamed in the faint light. Cooley stood at the cushioned edge, his back to Stromeyer. He didn't turn when she walked across to him, leading her to believe that he didn't hear her.

"Go away. Can't a man even have a drink in peace?" Cooley slurred his words. When Stromeyer came abreast of him, she was aghast at what she saw. Cooley stood belly to the bar, with an entire bottle of Jack Daniel's in his hand. It was already half empty. Stromeyer looked for a glass but couldn't find one anywhere on the gleaming wood top. The lack of drinkware didn't seem to faze Cooley, who took a huge swallow of the amber liquid straight from the bottle. He lowered the container a fraction while he raised an eyebrow at her. "You look like you've seen a ghost."

Stromeyer gathered her thoughts. Something was very wrong here.

"Senator, I'm surprised to see you drinking, especially this early in the day. I understood you to be a teetotaler."

Cooley put the bottle down with a thud, resting it on the bar but never taking his hand off it. He looked about to weep.

"I am. Been sober twenty-five years." He gazed at the bottle in his hand. "But guess that's all over now. Gotta start from square one." He took another huge gulp. "Right after I finish this bottle." He took another swig. He was drinking so fast that Stromeyer was becoming frightened. It was as if the man were possessed.

"Maybe you should hand me the bottle. You've had a lot in a very short time. It can't be good for you."

He shook his head. "Never *was* good for me. Practically ruined my life, way back then. But I can't give you the bottle. What you don't know, but I do, is that once I start, I don't stop." He shook the bottle at the shelves lining the back of the bar. "I'll drink everything on those shelves without stopping." He took another swallow, and this time when he lowered the bottle, Stromeyer could see tears forming in the corners of his eyes. He wiped them away with the back of his free hand. "'Course, in those days I was what my first wife called a mean drunk. Now it looks like I'm a sloppy drunk." He made a sound that was halfway between a sob and a gulp. "But I gotta finish off this whiskey and get the next. So go away and leave me to it."

Stromeyer reached out. She wrapped her palm around the neck of the bottle above where his fingers grasped it. A fine line of blood ran down his hand.

"Senator, you're bleeding." Stromeyer pointed at a small puncture wound.

He nodded. "It's nothing. Man bumped into me in the lobby and hit me with his pen."

"What type of pen?" Stromeyer couldn't keep the sharp sound out of her voice. The revelation that he'd been stuck with a pen rattled her. Just like Caldridge, she thought. But Cooley was six thousand miles away, so the odds of the two things' being connected seemed remote.

He shrugged. "White one. Dug into me. Doesn't matter." He didn't release the bottle.

"Let go. I'll take it. Something's not right about this."

For the first time, he seemed to really look at her. Focus on her. "You're Darkview's vice president."

She nodded.

He snorted. "You must be loving this. The great man falls. Bet you always thought I was a liar."

He was so close to the truth that Stromeyer could feel her face coloring a little. She shook off the embarrassment.

"If you've been sober for twenty-five years, what possessed you to drink now?"

Cooley shook his head in what looked like true bewilderment. "I can't tell you. I was only in the building a few minutes, and then I had the most overwhelming craving for a drink. I was here and with Jack in a heartbeat."

Stromeyer tried to imagine a substance that would force a man to drink, but nothing came to mind. Cooley unwrapped her fingers from the top of his hand, breaking her train of thought.

Once again he was focused on her.

"You look scary smart just now. I can almost see the gears turning in your head."

"I'm thinking you were poisoned," Stromeyer said.

He had the bottle halfway to his lips, then stopped. "Poisoned?"

Stromeyer nodded. "Fast-acting. Somehow triggered a drinking binge."

He stayed frozen, holding the liquor in the air. "Drugged in order to drink?" He burst out laughing. "Now, that's a good one!" He brought the bottle closer to his mouth.

"Stop it!" Stromeyer snapped out the order. She used the tone she'd utilized for years in the military, when some grunt was insistent on doing some foolish thing that was going to get him killed, demoted, or both. Like the men before him, Cooley stopped. The whiskey stayed in midair.

"Put that alcohol down! Quit acting like your actions are out of your control. A man who's been able to avoid drink for twenty-five years certainly has the wherewithal to avoid succumbing to a poison, for God's sake. If you were drugged, then as soon as it fades, you'll be back to where you were. Nothing lost, nothing gained. Status quo. Now, do it."

Cooley put the bottle down with a clink. He shoved it at her. "Here."

Stromeyer took hold of it. A garbage can lined with plastic sat in the corner of the bar. She tossed the Jack Daniel's at it. It flew in and crashed to the bottom.

"You'd better get out of here. There's an entrance to the kitchen in that corner." Stromeyer pointed to a set of swinging doors. "Leave that way. Hit the Metro and go home."

He straightened. "Yes, sir!" He snapped out a salute. The action made him stagger sideways, ruining the effect. He waved her aside. "Out of my way."

"I'm not in your way."

"Oh." He paused. "I meant that metaphorically, of course."

Stromeyer rolled her eyes.

He peered at her. "Do you scare Banner as much as you're scaring me?"

"Nothing scares Banner."

Cooley looked as though that answer made sense to him. "I'm learning that." He staggered to the kitchen door and was gone.

Two hours later Stromeyer stood in Darkview's reception area watching men in jackets labeled FBI carry out box after box of Darkview's files, two of their computers, and even their telephone console. Alicia sat on the long couch in the waiting area and watched the procession with wide eyes.

Stromeyer's cell phone rang. She flipped it open. "Stromeyer, that you?" It was Ralston, the attorney.

"They're almost done here."

"Get yourself to a safe location where you won't be overheard."

Stromeyer went through the swinging door down the hall to the very end. She stood opposite the back stairwell door that was Banner's favorite way to leave the premises on the sly.

"I'm alone," she said.

"Their subpoena is good. It was issued by Cooley's committee as a part of their investigation into the pipeline bombing. Apparently Cooley signed it two days ago. Right now no one is able to find him. Seems he dropped out of sight."

"Will it help if we find him?"

"Conceivably. He could halt the seizure. Or, if he's feeling particularly benevolent, he could return the boxes altogether."

Stromeyer watched as a group of agents headed toward her. All wore the same black pants and black windbreakers. She stepped aside while they swarmed past her down the stairs. Several jostled her.

"Last time I saw him, he wasn't himself," Stromeyer said.

"Maybe that's good. Because in his usual mode he seems to be bent on destroying Darkview."

Stromeyer hung up the phone, her stomach churning with worry.

EMMA HANDED THE ASSAULT RIFLE TO STARK. HE TOOK IT FROM her without comment.

"It's on semi. I can't shoot, and neither can you—"

Stark looked about to protest. Emma put up a hand to silence him.

"—*despite* your years of skeet shooting. I'd recommend that you keep it on semi most of the time. Its recoil is hard to control when it's on autofire." She grabbed the RPG and lifted the cushioned seat on the boat's side. She attached a rocket to the weapon's muzzle before turning to Hassim.

"Get us as close to the lead craft as you can. They'll try to take out the captain and anyone piloting the boat first. When the *Kaiser Franz* slows, the others will begin bombarding it."

Stark gave Emma an impressed look. "Where'd you learn that?"

"It's only logical. If you want to stop a car, you can either kill the driver or disable the car. Or both. Even with RPGs they may not be able to disable a vessel that large, so going for the bridge makes the most sense. Plus, without a captain the crew and passengers will be less likely to put up a fight."

Hassim turned the boat to follow the lead pirates. "You should work for Banner. You're a natural," he said.

Emma wasn't sure if Hassim meant it as a compliment or not, so she remained quiet.

"Our real problem," Hassim continued, "is getting them to regroup.

We need all three on one side so we can drive around the other side and have you climb up the back."

They surged toward the *Kaiser Franz*. By now the Somalis were within firing range of the ship. Emma, Hassim, and Stark, though, were not. Emma watched with a helpless feeling as the lead attacker fired his own rocket launcher. Flames shot out of the back as the missile climbed toward the cruise liner.

"They're too far!" Hassim yelled over the sound of their own boat's engines. "That was a waste of a grenade." Sure enough, Emma was pleased to see the grenade self-destruct a full twenty feet in front of the ship.

The popping sound of gunfire was followed by a yell. She watched a pirate in the lead boat fly back. He landed on the boat's floor, out of her range of vision.

"That was a nice shot," Hassim said.

Emma looked at the men on the topmost deck. Sumner was no longer standing but was a dark mass on the edge, by the guardrail. He was on his stomach aiming a gun.

"I know that man. He's an expert marksman," Emma said.

Hassim looked thoughtful. "Is he the one that you're coming here to help?"

She nodded.

Hassim pointed his chin at the messenger bag at her feet. "Take the bag with you. There are some grenades in there you can light and throw if you need to. Roducci sent them. He insisted you have them."

Emma aimed the RPG without comment. "Tell me when we're within range," she said. She didn't want to make the same mistake the pirates had and fire too soon.

Hassim eyed the screen before him. "I'll tell you in detail. Stark?" Hassim didn't turn his head.

Stark stepped up.

"Your weapon has a firing range of a hundred fifty to two hundred fifty meters. The RPG can get about three hundred. More, in the hands of an expert. Let Caldridge shoot first, then cover her by targeting anyone who looks like he's even thinking of retaliating."

Stark moved up behind Emma.

"Don't stand there," she said.

He started. "Oh, right. Back blast. Don't fire that thing without warning me," he said.

They came within four hundred feet of the lead pirates. By now Emma could make out the people on the *Kaiser Franz*, as well as a large gash on the vessel's side. The ship was huge compared to the tiny boats surrounding it. It churned through the water but seemed unable to maintain a steady pace. At one moment it appeared to surge forward before slowing and then surging again. It was like a barely functioning car lurching in its last throes.

The pirates shot another grenade. This one aimed true, headed right to the deck where Sumner waited. Emma held her breath. A cracking sound echoed in the air. The pirate holding the RPG went down. A second gunshot was followed by the grenade exploding in midair.

"Get ready to fire," Hassim said.

Emma aimed at the lead pirates.

"Now," Hassim said.

She fired. The rocket catapulted out of the tube just as the boat hit a wave. She stumbled backward. She kept going in that direction to allow Stark to step forward. He aimed, held the position for a second, then fired. Emma saw the gun buck on recoil.

Her grenade exploded five feet from the back of the pirate boat. Shrapnel rained down on the inhabitants. They were close enough now that she could hear their yells as the bits of exploded ordnance pelted them. She couldn't tell if Stark's shot was wide or not, but he followed it up with another that did hit its mark. A pirate at the boat's rear dropped like a stone. She saw a muzzle flash from Sumner's gun as he fired another shot and the pilot fell, hitting the side of the small craft and tumbling overboard. There were three men left in the boat. The two other pirate ships appeared from behind the cruise liner and roared toward the front.

"Here come the troops. Excellent. When they bunch up together, we'll veer off to the back," Hassim said.

The attackers formed into a roughly triangular pattern, joining the lead ship in firing at the *Kaiser Franz*'s bridge. Several flashes of muzzle fire from Sumner told Emma that he had turned his attention to the new attackers. One pirate in the second boat raised a rifle in their direction.

"Time to go," Hassim said. "Hold on."

He put the craft in a tight right-hand turn. Emma stumbled to the side with the curve.

"Good hits, both of you," Hassim said. "Stark, take the RPG." He looked at Emma. "You should get ready to board." She reloaded the RPG and handed it to Stark.

"Watch my back blast," he said. She scrambled to the other side. Stark aimed and fired. Flames leaped out the back of the tube an impressive distance of at least ten feet. Emma grabbed the messenger bag, slung it over her left shoulder, put her teardrop backpack on the other shoulder, and hauled the large duffel to the boat's edge.

"I'm ready," she said.

The *Kaiser Franz* loomed closer. They were in its shadow, skirting the ship's side, heading to the rear of the enormous vessel. As they did, Emma looked up at the portholes for the lower-level staterooms. One framed the anxious face of a man. He caught Emma's eye, and his widened as they looked at each other. They kept moving, and the man disappeared from view.

"Let me get off another shot before you turn behind," Stark said. Hassim nodded and manipulated the throttle, powering down the boat. Stark aimed the AK-47 off the back. He fired off ten shots in quick succession. A cry went up.

"Got one at least." Stark's voice held a grim note of satisfaction.

"They're not following us right now. The guy with the gun on the cruise ship is keeping them busy."

"I'm cutting around the back," Hassim said. He made another hard right, curving behind the liner and angling across its wake. They bounced into the air with the force of the waves.

Emma stared at the wake in dismay. Black oil poured from a hole in the ship's hull. It flowed out behind in a long stream. She didn't know where it originated from, but it didn't bode well.

Stark tapped her on the shoulder. "Are you sure you want to do this? That ship is going to stall soon. When it does, those pirates will be crawling all over it."

Emma *wasn't* sure. Now that she was there, she understood the extreme danger in which Sumner had once again found himself. The pirates alone were trouble enough, but once they got hold of the ricin, they would be armed far above the crude explosives that they currently carried. Whatever happened, they could not be allowed to obtain it.

"I'm going," she said.

Stark ran an angry hand through his hair. Before he could say anything, Hassim spoke up.

"I'll get as close to that aft ladder as I can, but it's still going to require that you leap. I suggest you leave the duffel for last. Once you're on the ladder, I can try to hand it to you."

"If we miss?"

"We can't. It will drop like a stone. The mission will be over. Finished."

"So not an option," Emma said.

"No."

"How about I lose these two other bags and just jump with the duffel?" Emma said.

"The duffel's too heavy. It will hinder you. If it does, then *you* will drop like a stone. I'd rather you get on the ladder. If we can't get the duffel to you this time, we'll swing around and give it another try."

"Well, at least let me take the ricin testing kits." Emma zipped open the duffel and grabbed three of the boxes labeled BIOHAZARD DETECTION KIT. She shoved them into the messenger bag.

They moved closer to the ship. The sounds of exploding grenades intermingled with the whooshing of the waves that buffeted the little boat. Hassim slid the craft up to the ladder hanging off the *Kaiser Franz*'s side. He yanked the steering wheel to the left when a wave threatened to slam them against the larger vessel. The spray from the wake blew in the air, misting Emma. She grasped the handrail and prepared to move over the edge. The rail was cold and slick with a combination of water and oil. She scissored one leg, then the other over it and hung from the side, facing forward, her feet on the very edge of the deck where it met the hull. The weight of the two packs seemed to steady her, but the boat was slippery underfoot, and she couldn't imagine what would happen once the ungainly duffel was added. It was sure to unbalance her.

"Next try!" Hassim yelled to her. He stayed parallel for a moment before angling closer.

Emma kept her concentration on the approaching ladder. She bounced with every wave that hit them. At four feet away, when the ladder was opposite her, she leaped.

Her oil-slicked hands slipped on the rails. She managed to grab one with her right hand but missed with her left. Pain shot through the fingers of her right hand. The knuckles felt as if they were being pulled apart from the weight of her body as she hung there. Her grip was loosening with each swell of the wave. She swung back and forth, trying to grab anything to lessen the pain in her fingers. She managed to get a grip on the ladder's side rail. Once she did, it was easier to maneuver her feet onto the rungs. She turned to Hassim, who stayed with her but once again parallel and at a safe distance.

"Throw me the pack!" she said. Hassim looked at her, the ladder, then lifted the pack. Before he could throw it, Stark put a hand on his shoulder. Emma watched him lean closer to Hassim while the two men talked. They reached some agreement.

"Get ready. I'm coming with the pack," Stark said.

Emma was speechless. That he would go from calling her crazy for boarding the vessel to joining her in the madness was remarkable. Before she could respond, the Somalis came around the back of the cruise ship, hurtling straight for them.

"Go!" Stark yelled.

Emma needed no further encouragement. She started up the ladder as fast as she could. Behind her she heard Hassim's engine noise increase as he opened the throttle. The boat shot away, leaving her alone to scale the side. She looked up. The climb seemed to last forever. She moved as efficiently as she could, given the motion of the boat, the slipperiness of the ladder, and the weight on her back. Out of the corner of her eye, she could see the pirates approaching.

When she was ten feet from the top, she heard the cracking sound of gunfire from above. The pirates behind her yelled. She was three feet from her goal now, and moving with a speed that would have impressed her had she the time to admire it. She was at the top when she heard the sound of an RPG being fired.

A hand reached over the side, grabbed a fistful of her shirt in the back, along with the strap of one of the packs, and she felt herself being physically hauled over the metal railing. She gave whoever was pulling her onto the deck some help by pushing off her toes, vaulting over the side in a heap of limbs, still flying forward, unable to stop her trajectory. She catapulted headlong into the man's body, the weight of hers throwing him backward onto the deck. She landed on top of him. He grunted in her ear as the fall took the breath out of him. He grabbed her around her torso, rolled her, reversing their positions, until her back was on the hard wooden planks and he was on top of her with his head against her cheek. She looked up and saw a strange steel wall looming over them, with a porthole in it. She stared at it, fascinated, wanting to close her eyes to avoid seeing the grenade strike them but finding it impossible not to watch.

The grenade hit the wall from behind and angled from right to left. It exploded on impact. Emma felt her eardrums shiver with the sound, popping as if she were on a plane at thirty thousand feet. With the cacophony came a blast of heat and wind. The wall twisted with the force of the warhead. It curved to the side and bent in half. The entire contraption flipped into the air, and Emma caught a glance of flying shrapnel as the wall cartwheeled to their right. Bits of metal flew in every direction. She closed her eyes when it rained on them, before opening them again. The object hammered back onto the deck and rolled in a crazy, lopsided fashion, flinging off parts as it did. It came to rest twenty feet away and stopped. One thin bar swung from a metallic thread that kept it attached to the debris.

The man on top of Emma raised his head, and she got her first full look at him. Sumner loomed over her, his face a mixture of anger and disbelief.

SUMNER ROLLED OFF HER AND CRAB-WALKED ACROSS THE DECK to the far wall, where a rifle lay. He returned to the railing, staying low. The cruise ship kept surging in fitful starts and stops, making it hard for Emma to stay put. Sumner, too, seemed to be having trouble. She watched him brace his shoulder against the railing and his foot on the deck. He wore black gym shoes with rubber soles that squeaked on the polished planks. A large man stepped out of a nearby door. Emma recognized him as the person who had stared at her while she was trying to board.

"Block, get down," Sumner said. The man hunkered down before crawling to Emma.

"Can you shoot?" she asked.

Block raised an eyebrow. "Yes."

She lifted her pant leg at the ankle and pulled out the gun. It seemed as if she was forever giving her gun to someone else to shoot. She handed it to Block.

He smiled. "Finally I get a real gun. Sumner's been hogging the rifle. What are you going to use?"

She reached into the messenger bag and removed two grenades. "Do you have any matches?"

Block handed her a small book of matches embossed with the words *KAISER FRANZ*.

"I'll light these and throw them if I need to."

Block looked intrigued. "How about I give *you* the gun and *I* throw the grenades? I might be able to throw farther than you."

"Good idea," Emma said.

"Block, do you have a radio?" Sumner asked.

"I do," Block said.

"I don't hear anything. Call Janklow and ask him what's happening on their end."

Block pulled a walkie-talkie off his belt and depressed the button. "Janklow, they gone?"

Emma moved up next to Sumner with the matches still in her hand.

"You should get inside. I don't want you to die from a grenade," he told her.

"I'm staying."

Sumner didn't say anything. He turned back to stare out to sea.

"Janklow says they're gone. Took off all at once. Like they got an order to retreat or something," Block said.

Sumner visibly relaxed. Emma felt a breath rush from her body, as if she'd been holding it for a very long time. She heard Block's walkie-talkie rattle again. A man's voice flowed out of it.

"The crazy Western woman, is she on board?"

Emma snorted. "Is he talking about me?"

Sumner nodded. "You think he's wrong?"

"About what, that I'm crazy?"

"Yes."

"As crazy as you are," she said.

Block laughed behind her. "Yeah, Janklow, she's here and giving Sumner what for."

The walkie-talkie emitted another squawk. Emma heard the man's voice again. "Ask Sumner if she's the beautiful mad scientist."

Sumner allowed a trace of a smile to cross his face but said nothing.

Block depressed the button. "She's beautiful, and she's nuts to join us, so I guess the answer is yes."

Sumner grabbed a rung of the railing and pulled himself up to standing. "This is Emma Caldridge. Caldridge, Harry Block."

"Pleased to meet you, Ms. Caldridge," Block said.

Sumner handed Block the rifle. "Can you take a watch? Ms. Caldridge and I have a lot to talk about."

Emma watched Block heft the gun with obvious pleasure. "I sure will." He handed Emma her pistol. "Don't hurt him. He's the most depressing guy I've ever met, but I'm getting used to having him around."

She was surprised. "Depressing? Not at all."

Block grunted. "Just ask him what our chances of surviving are and then tell me if you don't think he's depressing."

"Our chances of surviving just got a whole lot better," Sumner said.

Block looked happier. "Let's hope you're right."

Sumner waved Emma to a nearby door.

The minute they passed through it, she turned to him. "I'm glad you're alive. I was afraid I'd be too late."

The hallway was dark. All the lights were off. The ship continued to move in fits and starts, but it was slowing. The surges were not as violent, the slowing less pronounced. Emma leaned on the wall to brace herself against the movement. Sumner supported himself by placing a palm on the same wall, next to her head. Emma thought he looked exhausted. His dark hair hung in clumps, and deep circles rimmed his eyes. He rubbed his face against the arm that held him steady. When he was done, he gave her one of his intense looks, but it was tinged with another emotion Emma couldn't identify.

"Did Banner send you?"

"He wanted to, but Stromeyer was against it. I sent myself."

Sumner took a deep breath. He shook his head. "You shouldn't have come."

"I had to."

"Colombia not enough excitement for you? You needed more?"

"I couldn't live with myself if you died and I hadn't tried to help. And besides, what about you? Are you a danger junkie or something?"

He put his head down and looked at the floor for a moment before looking back into her eyes.

"I'm furious that you took the risk, but at the same time very, very glad to see you."

His voice sounded like gravel rolled over, as if he hadn't slept, but there was no mistaking the emotion behind the words. Something small in her uncurled, as if the constant hold she kept on her emotions were relaxing for a moment. Instead of the usual rush of despair and grief that followed whenever she released her vigilance, she felt calm. Perhaps for the first time in days. Sumner leaned toward her, lowering his head to hers.

From down the hall came the sound of several people approaching. Emma watched Sumner fold back into himself, almost as if he were physically pulling himself together. He stepped away from her, breaking the connection that had passed between them.

"Heading to hot spots is my job," he said.

Emma sighed. "And chemistry is mine."

He grew serious. "There's ricin on board."

She nodded. "I know. I was supposed to have a kit to identify it. But Banner's contact was unable to throw it to me on the ladder. I only hope he and Stark got away."

Sumner straightened. "Who's Stark?"

"Richard Stark. The CEO of Price Pharmaceuticals."

Sumner got a strange look on his face.

"What? What's wrong?" Emma said.

He grabbed her by the hand. "Come with me."

Sumner steered her into the bowels of the ship. When he came to a door with a keypad, he tapped in a code. The door swung open. He led her to a large crate with the word PRICE stamped all over it.

"What's this?"

He took a deep breath. "This is where the ricin is."

Emma felt her heart plunge.

"Could he be involved?" Sumner said.

She thought about Stark. Ran the events of the past days over in her mind. "Oh, yeah, he could definitely be involved." Still, she didn't want to believe it.

Sumner seemed to catch her reluctance. "What's he like?"

Emma thought about Stark. "Driven. Smart. Tough."

"Ruthless?"

She nodded. "In business? He has that reputation. He told me he'd do anything to ensure that Price stayed viable."

"And personally? Ruthless there as well?"

Emma wasn't sure. "He lives to work. Nothing else seems to matter, but he does have a daughter."

"What do you think of him?"

The question was a good one. She had no real answer for it.

"I don't trust him, but I can't tell you why. He's never done anything to hurt me that I know of."

A plump man with a dour face, wearing a white uniform, stepped into the cargo area. He ran his eyes over Emma.

"This the chemist?" he said.

"Nathan Janklow, meet Emma Caldridge."

Janklow shook her hand. "What do you think of our little problem?"

"The ricin?"

"The pirates. Without them we'd quietly sail into some port and have the experts remove the ricin just as quietly."

Emma turned her attention back to the crate. "Do we know who claimed that ricin is in there?"

"Banner informed us," Sumner said.

That solved that. Emma wasn't about to question anything Banner said. Ricin protocol required a whole host of cautious steps and protective equipment that was currently back on the little speedboat floating somewhere on the ocean. Emma could only hope that Hassim and Stark were alive and still able to drive the boat.

"Normally I'd follow hazmat procedures, but in this case I think we just cover up as much as possible and get to it. We don't have a lot of time."

"What are normal procedures? Space suits?" Janklow said.

"Protective clothing, of course. But ricin isn't readily absorbed into the skin, so we can proceed with something less and still survive the encounter. It's inhalation that I'm worried about. I don't suppose that you have anything like respirator masks?"

Janklow thought a minute. "We have temporary fire masks. I say 'temporary' because they consist of a simple plastic hood that goes over one's head and contains a respirator filled with enough air for forty-five minutes. They're not meant to be a full-fledged mask but instead are designed to buy a person time to get out of a smoky area."

Emma gazed at the crate. It was wooden, with an outer layer of plastic shrink wrap. There was a risk just opening it, but the danger rose exponentially with each layer they unpeeled.

"Any protective clothing?" she asked.

"Will work coveralls do? We have some in the mechanical room."

"Gloves?"

"Rubber or cloth? I might also be able to dig up some surgical gloves in the infirmary."

"Surgical with a heavy workman's glove over it would be great. We'll use the combination during the crate's initial breakdown, and I'll strip mine off to the surgical layer during the testing phase, when I'll need some dexterity. I suggest we save the masks for after we get through the first layers. Maybe a simple face mask from the infirmary will help."

"Can the ricin particles infiltrate a standard face mask?" Sumner asked.

Emma wasn't sure, but she thought it could. "Probably, but it doesn't hurt to wear them anyhow."

"Let's get to it," Janklow said.

Forty-five minutes later, Emma, Sumner, Janklow, and a man named Clutch were dressed in heavy mechanics' jumpsuits and work gloves. Emma had rolled her suit at the sleeves and the pant legs to allow her to use her hands and to walk unhindered. She watched while Janklow and Clutch used crowbars to pry off the crate's vertical slats. Once those were removed, the only thing standing between Emma and the vaccine vials was another layer of shrink wrap and the individual cardboard boxes that housed the vaccines. The second layer of plastic was off in no time. They were down to the boxes.

Emma couldn't see inside them, but if the vaccines were packaged like other vials she'd seen, each large box would contain four smaller ones that in turn would contain twelve vials. There were thirty-six large boxes, which meant they had 1,728 vials to analyze. Something told Emma that they'd never get through them all before the pirates regrouped. She needed a strategy to both physically arrange the vials and check each as rapidly as was feasible.

"Lay them out on the floor. Don't put the mask on until the last possible minute. Only wear it while you look through each small container."

Sumner grabbed a large box and lowered it to the floor. He used a razor knife to slice open the top, then removed each smaller carton and began lining them up. Janklow joined him. They worked with a quiet efficiency. Emma helped, all the while trying to dredge up facts about ricin from her memory.

"You said it doesn't easily penetrate the skin. Does that mean that if it gets under our gloves or clothing, we won't die?" Janklow asked the question while moving boxes back and forth.

"Washing with soap and water will work." Emma was sure of that.

Two women stepped into the room. The first was young, about

Emma's age, with white-blond hair and a pretty, open face. Her eyes flicked around before locking on Sumner. She smiled when she saw him, a shy smile. It was clear she was attracted to him, and Emma felt a small twinge of something. She tamped it down, in order to stay focused. Sumner nodded at the women, but he looked back at the boxes, and it was clear his mind was on the problem before him.

The second woman was a bit older, perhaps nearing forty-five, dressed in jeans and a white sleeveless top that hugged the curves of an impressive chest. She had long caramel-colored hair streaked with blond. Her eyes locked on Sumner as well, but she had a determined air about her. Emma thought she was there to deliver an ultimatum. After a minute, when Sumner finally looked up from his work, the second woman spoke.

"Harry's on the deck holding your gun and telling me to stay in my room, but I want no truck with that. I want to help." She indicated the woman next to her. "And Marina does, too."

Marina nodded. "I can't stand the waiting."

To Emma they seemed an unlikely pair. The first woman had a German accent, while the second had a southern drawl. One looked as pure as the driven snow, the other like a steel magnolia. The second one appeared the type of woman who wasn't about to let anyone or anything get in her way. Emma watched the proceedings while continuing to unload the boxes.

The southerner walked up to her. "I'm Cindy, Harry's wife."

"Emma Caldridge. You shouldn't be in here." Emma kept her voice mild, but what she wanted to do was throw up her arms and warn them away.

Janklow stepped in. "Ma'am, you're not allowed to be here without protective clothing."

Cindy's eyes narrowed. "Why?"

Clutch stopped working. "Because it's a cargo hold. The door to it is marked 'Private,' did you see that?" His voice held a harsh

note. Emma didn't like Clutch. His every word since meeting her—
and the words were few—had been either an order or a challenge.

"The door was open. What's in the cargo?"

"Ma'am, please leave. You can't be here, and that's it," Janklow
said.

"A chemical weapon," Sumner said.

Cindy's mouth dropped open. Marina's eyes widened. They both
froze.

"At least we think that's what it is," Sumner continued. "We're not
telling the rest of the passengers for obvious reasons. But once we
open these cartons, you could be at great risk, so unless you're serious about helping, you both need to get as far away as possible."

Clutch made an angry noise. "What the hell are you telling them
for? I thought this was supposed to be a secret!"

Sumner returned to removing the boxes. "They're not going to be
on the deck shooting, but we are. We die in the next few hours, someone should know what's in here."

Emma was starting to see why Block thought Sumner was depressing. His clear-eyed view on things was a bit disconcerting.

He jerked his chin at the two women. "You want to help, there are
two more jumpsuits in the mechanical room. Left out the exit and
third or fourth door down."

Cindy and Marina stood still. Emma kept unloading, but she
couldn't help feeling a little sorry for the two women. They had
more problems than they'd realized. To their credit, though, neither
seemed like the type to fall into hysterics.

Cindy turned to Emma. "Harry said you're a scientist. Give me
the lowdown."

Clutch made a noise and started toward Cindy. Janklow stepped
in front of him. Once Clutch subsided, Janklow moved closer to the
women.

"No lowdowns until you are both properly dressed. I'm not kidding."

The women looked at each other. Cindy took a large breath. "I'm not staying." She pointed at Clutch. "*Not* because I'm afraid. Just because I agree with Sumner that if y'all die once you open the boxes, then someone should be alive to tell the tale." Touché, Emma thought. She was starting to really like Cindy.

"Possibly ricin, maybe mustard gas, or maybe a new weapon not on our radar screens yet," Emma said.

"What about anthrax?" Marina said.

"Or anthrax," Emma agreed.

"What does ricin look like, and how does it kill?" Cindy asked.

Janklow made an impatient noise.

Emma waved him off. "Two-second explanation. Then they'll go."

Cindy nodded her agreement.

"It's odorless and colorless, although in liquid form it may appear a bit cloudy, depending on how carefully it's prepared. It kills by inhalation, ingestion, or injection. The three *I*'s. Regarding odds of death, worst is injection, obviously, because it's shot into your system at maximum toxicity. If it's camouflaged as a vaccine, I'm thinking that injection is the intended delivery method. But while injection is bad for the guy who gets hit, it's good for us, because injection is not a feasible method for mass destruction. It's impossible to inject hundreds of people at once, and even if you could, ricin is not communicable, so there's no compounding effect. Plus, if injection is the plan, then the ricin will be inside a sealed container, in a liquid form, awaiting use. It'll be easy to dispose of, and we'll live."

"Assuming the pirates don't kill us," Janklow said. Emma didn't respond to his comment.

"If not by injection, what about inhalation?" Cindy asked.

"Inhalation is bad. Especially aerosolized fine particles that can infiltrate deep into your lungs. Ingestion is also bad. This stuff gets sprinkled on your food, you're getting sick, no doubt about it."

"How do we know we've been infected?" Marina said.

"Flu-like symptoms. Destruction begins at the cellular level. There's multi-organ dysfunction, then death."

Marina paled. Emma couldn't blame her. It was a dreadful scenario.

Cindy stepped back. "We're going now. Ms. Caldridge, would you mind coming to talk to me after?"

"If I live after I open these cartons? Certainly."

Cindy nodded. She spun on her heel and left, Marina trailing in her wake.

Emma turned back to the job of lining up the vaccines. "Nice women," she said.

42

STROMEYER WOKE TO SUNLIGHT STREAMING THROUGH HER WIN-
dows, the singing of birds, and a pounding on her front door. She
threw on a robe, picked up the gun she kept on her nightstand, and
headed to the foyer. She put an eye to the peephole. Stan stood there.
The fish-eye's distortion turned his head into a balloon that sat on his
shoulders. She swung the door open.

"Ready for our weekly chat? I brought you the paper." Stan
boomed the words in a hearty voice that was nothing like his actual
tone. "Boy, I really enjoy these mornings."

Stromeyer had absolutely no idea what he was talking about, but
she stepped aside to let him in. When he was through the door, she
took a quick glance outside. She saw nothing questionable and so
closed it.

"What in the world is going on?" she said.

He held the paper up and let it unfold. SENATOR COOLEY FOUND
DEAD! screamed the large letters on the front page.

"Oh, no," Stromeyer said.

"It gets worse. The article implies that his investigation into the
Colombian pipeline bombing played a role in his death. It says the
FBI raided Darkview's offices yesterday looking for clues."

Stromeyer reached for the paper. "They were at our offices yesterday, but it wasn't a raid in response to his death; they were executing a
subpoena signed while he was alive. Dead men don't sign subpoenas."

"And you have stalkers. Two guys. One sitting in a car three spaces down the street and another in the alley. Mean-looking. You shouldn't leave the house alone. Maybe you call Banner? Ask him to escort you?"

Stromeyer waved Stan into the kitchen. "Banner's on a plane to Dubai via Frankfurt. Mean guy about thirty-five? Pockmarked face? Bad khaki trench coat?"

Stan nodded. "That's him."

"Alley or front? He claims to be some sort of agent."

"Alley," Stan said. "He doesn't look like an agent. He looks like a thug."

"He's got issues."

"Do these issues involve stepping over the line? Because if they do, I still have contacts in the White House. I can make some calls, get them to back off."

Stromeyer contemplated Stan's offer. It was tempting, but she hated to waste it on Tarrant and Church. She had bigger problems to address.

"Can you get our side of the story placed in the paper? Let people know that we're being targeted, too?"

"Targeted? How? And by whom?" Stromeyer told him about Banner's being attacked after his meeting with Cooley. She kept the incident with Cooley to herself.

"I'll talk to a few people. Get the ball rolling. Meantime let's go over the fence to my garage. You can hunker down in the car's front seat and they'll never know you've left."

Stromeyer held up the coffee carafe.

Stan extended his mug for a refill. "I'm actually finding this to be much more interesting than retirement."

She shelved the carafe and headed down the hall. "Anything for you, Stan," she called behind her.

Thirty minutes later Stan turned at the top of the street in front of Darkview's offices. News vans lined the road. Press crews hung out in front, drinking coffee from paper cups and looking bored.

"This is not good," Stromeyer said.

"To be expected, I guess. Want me to take you somewhere else?"

She sighed. "No. I'll get out here. I'll go in the back." She grabbed her tote. "Thanks, Stan. I owe you."

"Anytime. In fact, take this." He handed her a small remote on a key chain. "It's for my garage. Feel free to cut through on your way to the fence."

Alicia manned the reception desk, looking determined. She held an enormous white phone receiver with a coiled cord that Stromeyer had never seen before.

"I told you, Mr. Banner is out of the country." Alicia listened for a moment. "Mr. Banner is not running away from you. He's doing his job, which often takes him out of town. If you want to leave a message, I'll be happy to give it to him when he gets back." Alicia listened some more. "I can't tell you where he is." Stromeyer marched across to Alicia. She put her palm out for the phone. Alicia handed it to her. The caller was still talking, his voice flowing out of the receiver. "He wants an interview with Mr. Banner," Alicia said.

Stromeyer put the phone to her ear. "You can have an interview anytime you'd care to fly to Mogadishu." She hung up.

Alicia giggled. "Guess that ends that." A concerned look crossed her face. "Mogadishu? Is he going to be okay?"

Stromeyer patted her on the shoulder. "He's in Dubai." She pointed to the phone. "Where'd you get it?"

Alicia beamed. "My grandmother had a couple of spares. She said they were called Trimline phones, which is funny, because they're huge. I put one in your office. I figured we need something, since they took the console, and I didn't have time to buy one this morning. But a lot of calls are going to voice mail. It's driving me crazy. I need some real equipment if I'm going to do my job right."

"You're doing great. I'll retrieve the ones that you miss." Stromeyer's office phone was the same style as Alicia's, but Stromeyer's was a strange shade of avocado green.

Stromeyer leaned back in her chair, thinking about Cooley, the FBI subpoena, and her stalkers. The phone rang, pulling her out of her reverie.

"Major Stromeyer? It's Susan Plower. I need to talk to you."

"If what you're about to say is at all classified, you shouldn't say it over the phone."

"Are you still having problems with it being tapped?"

Stromeyer wanted to say it was more like problems with her ancient phone technology.

"Just being cautious." She gave the name of a coffee shop near Plower's office. They agreed to meet in fifteen minutes.

Stromeyer passed a harried Alicia on her way to the back stairs. She heard Alicia say, "Mr. Banner is in a highly volatile country doing his best to keep us all safe from terrorism. When he's done there, I'll be happy to give him any message you'd care to leave." Stromeyer found herself laughing down the hall. Alicia was a gem.

Susan Plower was frantic, however. She sat on a high barstool at a counter that ran along the coffee shop's storefront window and sipped a coffee while her eyes darted around the room. A look of abject relief came over her face when she spotted Stromeyer. She was wearing a shapeless suit with a jacket that was too boxy for her small frame and an A-line skirt with flat loafers. A huge briefcase overflowing with paper sat on the counter next to her coffee cup. Stromeyer ordered a large coffee and sat down next to Plower.

"What seems to be the problem?" she said.

Plower gave a hurried look around the room, then leaned in to Stromeyer. "Undersecretary Rickell has gone off the deep end." Plower whispered this information. Her voice was so low that Stromeyer was concerned she hadn't heard the woman correctly.

"Deep end?"

Plower nodded. "Can you ask Major Banner to go get him? Bring him home? We'll take it from there."

Stromeyer was getting more confused by the minute. There were any number of security personnel that Plower could have turned to if protecting Undersecretary Rickell was on the agenda that day. Stromeyer was positive that Plower knew this as well.

"Did you contact the FBI to find him?"

Plower shook her head. "No, never. He would hate it if they saw him in his current condition. He's a very proud man."

He's an asshole, Stromeyer thought. She tried again.

"Perhaps you can give me a clue as to his condition."

Plower leaned even closer. "He's somewhere in Germany, gambling. He's been there for two days. My sources tell me he hasn't slept, barely speaks, and refuses to leave the table even to eat. He drinks only the alcohol that the waitress brings."

Stromeyer felt the beginnings of fear start at the base of her spine. Rumors that Rickell had a problem with gambling had swirled around him for years. Despite this, his star kept rising. Those in the know claimed that Diplomatic Security agents had hauled him out of several tight spots before the secretary of defense issued an ultimatum: Either Rickell cease or he was fired. Rickell accepted an embassy post in a small country in Europe, where he'd entered a program for his addiction. Three years later he was appointed to his current position. During his tenure as undersecretary, Rickell had studiously avoided casinos or gambling in any form. Stromeyer heard that once he attended a charity ball where bingo was being played as a way to raise cash. Rickell had made an excuse and left before the games began.

"What would you like me to do?" Stromeyer said now.

"Could you send Mr. Banner to get him? I know that Darkview can keep a secret."

"Banner's headed to Dubai. He lands in Frankfurt first, but I'm not sure he'll be willing to divert to handle this. Time is of the essence, as you know."

Plower looked crestfallen. She placed a hand on Stromeyer's arm. "Could you go? It's not ideal; you're a woman and Undersecretary

Rickell is . . ." She appeared embarrassed to say anything further.

Stromeyer helped her out. "Undersecretary Rickell is a sexist jerk who doesn't give women enough credit and therefore won't take advice from one?"

Plower choked on her coffee. She pinned Stromeyer with a surprised look. "He's not *that* bad! I was going to say that he thinks of himself as a bit of a ladies' man, and I doubt he'd like it that a woman as pretty as you witnessed him in that condition."

Stromeyer was beginning to see why Plower had kept her job all these months. She seemed to base every decision on whether the course of action would serve Rickell's best interests. He was a jerk, but even he must have realized that not every assistant would do so much to protect the boss's back.

"I can't go. I'm needed here to run Darkview, but I promise to have Banner check it out before he continues to Dubai."

Plower's BlackBerry buzzed. She eyed the message, then paled.

"What?"

"He's gone. I asked the casino's manager to tell me if he left."

"Call him back. Find out what he knows," Stromeyer said. She watched while Plower hit the redial button.

"It's Susan Plower. Thanks for calling me. Do you know where he went?" She sat silent while the manager poured information into her ear. After a minute she thanked the man and hung up.

"Well?" Stromeyer said.

"He left several hours ago. He said he was headed to another game in what he called 'a famous area of Frankfurt.'" She gave Stromeyer another frightened look. "Do you know of any famous gambling areas in Frankfurt?"

Stromeyer pondered the question. "In fact, there are a couple of famous casinos nearby. One in Bad Homburg."

Plower sagged against the counter, like a balloon that had deflated. Stromeyer felt sorry for her.

"Don't look so glum. There's one bit of good news in this picture: I'll send Banner a text message right now asking him to wait there until he receives further instructions from me."

Plower nodded her head forcefully up and down. "Tell him to go right to this Bad Homburg casino."

Stromeyer was already tapping out the text. She put up a hand to Plower. "Hold up. We don't know if he's there. I hate to send Banner on a useless trip."

Plower hauled her overstuffed briefcase off the counter. "It's not a useless trip. Rickell must still be gambling. What other explanation could there be for him not checking in with me? He's due to speak in"—she consulted her watch—"eighteen hours, and he doesn't even have a copy of his itinerary." She thumped the briefcase with her hand. "It's in here, for God's sake. Oh, no, Major. He's gambling, you can bet on it."

"Once he's back to normal, I want you to ask him if at any time in the last three days he could have been poisoned."

Plower's head snapped up from her BlackBerry, where she'd been tapping her own text. "Poisoned?"

"Yes. Delivered in the form of a prick from an EpiPen. If so, then call me on my cell. I need to know as soon as possible. If Banner finds him, I'll have him interview Rickell. We need to determine if he indeed was the subject of a poison plot."

"And if he was?"

"Then he'd better be careful. I think Senator Cooley was poisoned, and now he's dead."

MUNGABE WATCHED HIS LATEST CREW COME LIMPING BACK TO the mother ship. Three men were dead, two injured, and none had ever reached the *Kaiser Franz*. Mungabe set his teeth together while Talek asked the questions.

"What happened? How is it three boats were unable to take the cruise liner? A bunch of weak tourists overcame you?" Talek screamed his derision at the crew. One of his lieutenants screamed back.

"We were hit from behind! A second craft hid in the shadows, waiting to attack. It launched grenades at us as we fought forward."

"Who was on this boat?" Mungabe asked. The crewman turned to him, fear in his dark eyes.

"An African. Maybe Kenyan, I don't know, and two Westerners. But, Mungabe, this is the thing—I could have sworn that the boat they used was Ali's."

Ali the thief held few loyalties, but generally he would not cross a warlord unless under great pressure. Whoever paid for the boat held enough power to frighten Ali or was many times smarter than him. Mungabe lowered himself to his deck chair to think. An assistant brought him a pot of hot tea, bowing as he backed away. Talek began his screaming once again, but Mungabe flitted a hand at him to silence him.

"You"—he pointed to the crewman—"go below and tend to your injured. Be prepared to tell me everything that occurred."

The man nodded and limped away, keeping his eyes averted from Talek's the entire time.

"Talek, get Roducci on the phone. He has not given me the information I need, and by now the wire transfer must have cleared."

Ten minutes later, Roducci's voice flowed out of the satellite receiver's speaker.

"There is rumor of a significant sale going down soon in your region."

"What arms are they selling?"

"Not arms, a weapon. Chemical. Some say it is a new poison."

Talek's eyes widened as he listened. "Where is it?"

"There are many different stories, some impossible to believe, and it is difficult to say which is true, but there is one that says the weapon is on a freighter somewhere in the Gulf of Aden trade route."

"Why do you say the stories may not be true? Tell me all the rumors."

Roducci sighed over the line. "One source told me that the weapon may actually be hidden on a cruise liner. There are some buyers on the ship, having a vacation while they wait to cut a deal."

Mungabe smiled to himself. So the Vulture's precious cargo was actually a weapon, not a medication. "What kind of weapon is it?"

"Chemical. But there's more. The rumor is that the buyers are other arms traders and are actually being set up. The seller has no intention of holding the auction. Rumor is that the seller lured them onto the ship but intends to either attack the ship or sink it. Either way he gets rid of the competition. You wouldn't happen to know anything about this, would you?"

Mungabe was impressed with the Vulture's duplicity. No wonder he let Mungabe take the proceeds from the ship and its hostages. He was using Mungabe to eliminate the competition.

"And who owns this ship?" Mungabe said.

"A German conglomerate. But I wouldn't attempt to take it, if the rumor is true."

Mungabe snorted. "Why not?"

"Because the word is that the ship is protected by a company that I know well."

Mungabe knew what Roducci would say next. He felt his face flaming at the thought. "And who would that be?"

"Darkview. An American—"

"Do not say that name to me! I have taken steps to destroy it. By now both it and its president must be dead."

Roducci scoffed. "Hardly. I know the president and the vice president, and they—and their company—are very much alive. In fact, I just handled a matter for them. I don't know who tells you Darkview is no more, but you should not listen to them. They lie."

"Who from Darkview is protecting the ship?"

"You want names?"

"For several thousand dollars, I deserve names," Mungabe said. He heard Roducci blow out a breath in aggravation.

"I've heard that two Darkview agents are there. A sniper and a chemist."

"And their names?"

"This I do not know."

Mungabe thought Roducci did know, but he didn't bother to press him.

"Chemists don't scare me. Tell me about the shooter."

"The gossips say that he can shoot the eyes out of an eagle at five hundred paces."

"He is the mercenary, and the chemist guards the drugs. These two men will not live to see tomorrow."

Roducci coughed for a minute before catching his breath. "The sea is vast. There are any number of trawlers you can harass. Perhaps you leave the cruise liner alone. Nothing good will come of attacking it."

Mungabe stood up to increase his presence, even though he knew Roducci could not see the gesture. "Do you question my ability? I will kill them all!"

Roducci sighed over the line. "Think, Mungabe. If Darkview agents are protecting the arms, then it is likely that the American military hired them. You are buying trouble. I doubt that the ship will be taken without a battle. You don't need the money. Why do you do this?"

Just like a Westerner, Mungabe thought. They had no understanding of the greater glory beyond this world. They only fought to live; they did not embrace death.

"I do this to ensure my place in the afterworld."

Roducci burst out laughing. "You do this to buy another Range Rover and some more khat. You also do this because you are in too deep with the Vulture."

Mungabe sucked in a breath. Roducci's information went farther than Mungabe liked.

"But you should know that even though the Vulture is losing against Darkview, he will not die, because he fails to do his own fighting. He hires people like you to do it for him, and after you die, he walks away, beating the dirt off his palms. So think carefully before you take on the sniper and the chemist."

"I should not have paid you. You disrespect me," Mungabe said.

"You paid for the truth, and that is what you got. My advice will keep you alive. Take it."

Mungabe punched off the speakerphone in response. He dialed the Vulture's number.

"What do you want?" The European didn't bother with a greeting.

"You haven't eliminated Darkview. You broke our agreement. Therefore I am no longer honoring it. I'm going to take the chemical weapon after I take the ship." Mungabe felt enormous satisfaction when he heard the Vulture's quick intake of breath over the phone line.

"You broke *your* end of the deal. You were to have taken the ship by now, but you haven't. You failed."

Mungabe's brief feeling of superiority disappeared. He wanted to reach through the phone to throttle the Vulture.

"There are Darkview agents on board. You didn't tell me this. Had you done so, I would have put all my men on the job. I thought I was dealing with a bunch of soft tourists. You lied to me."

"I didn't know Darkview agents were on board. This is the first I have learned of it. However, I have one of my men there. Tell me which ones are the agents and I'll arrange to kill them."

"Like you killed Darkview's president? He still lives."

"Tell me. My operative can use the weapon on them. They'll be dead in half an hour, and you can take the ship."

"I don't know who they are. I just know it's a sniper and a chemist. My contact refused to identify them."

The Vulture said nothing for a moment. "I'll have *my* contact hit the entire ship. This will disable it once and for all, and then your men will be able to walk on board. We'll put an end to this back-and-forth fighting."

"Oh, no you won't. Those hostages are mine to ransom. You will not kill them."

"Relax, Mungabe." Now the Vulture's voice took on a soothing tone. "The stick won't kill the passengers. The weapon will disorient them. Only the weak and old will die with the first dose. It kills all on a double dose. I will tell my operative to hit everyone once, then wait to see if the Darkview agents reveal themselves. When they do, only they will be hit a second time."

Mungabe liked the idea of weakening the enemy from the inside. "Do it."

44

EMMA FINISHED LINING UP THE SMALLER BOXES. SUMNER AND Janklow completed their allotments before standing back as well. Clutch had left twenty minutes earlier to get an update on the pirate situation from Wainwright.

"Remember," Emma said, "ricin is odorless and colorless. What we're looking for are any vials that appear to have been tampered with, or any vials containing liquid different from all the others, or crystals rather than liquid. If you find one, put it aside. I have only three testing kits, so we'll test just the suspicious boxes. Ready?" The men nodded. "Let's get to it."

Emma slid her temporary fire mask over her head, turned it on, and bent to open the cartons. She still wore gloves but had removed the heavy work coverings, leaving the surgical gloves in place. She opened the top to find twelve sealed vials. She carefully removed each one, turning it back and forth before replacing it in its own little section. The first box looked innocuous. Each vial was in place, each contained the same-looking fluid, and each had a sealed top that appeared to be intact. She headed to the next, performing the exact steps. As she did, she cast glances at Sumner and Janklow. They worked with an efficiency that matched Emma's, and in silence.

Forty-five minutes later, she straightened. She'd completed her allotment and found nothing. Each vial appeared to be factory-sealed, and each contained liquid that was similar in color and amount. Nothing appeared to be out of the ordinary. Sumner finished his vials and stepped back. Janklow was last. He, too, stepped back.

"Nothing tampered with on my end. Yours?" Emma said.

Sumner shook his head. "Same here. Janklow?"

"All looks in order to me." Janklow sounded relieved.

"Then let's pick three random boxes, and I'll test one vial from each."

Sumner picked three at random and handed them to her. She pulled out one vial from each, lined them up on the floor, and opened her kits. Each kit contained a test tube nestled in a small plastic stand. Emma placed the stand next to the vial it was to test.

She nodded at Sumner. "Can you open the first vial and pour it into the tube? Wait three minutes. If ricin is present, it will set off a chemical reaction."

"What type of reaction?" Sumner was already opening his vial.

"You'll see a luminescence. The liquid will literally begin to glow."

They dumped the vaccine vials into the test tubes and waited. At three minutes the tubes remained the same.

"The intelligence must have been wrong. False alarm." Janklow reached up to pull off his fire mask.

"Leave your mask on. We should have a few more minutes at least," Emma said. She gazed at the vials, trying to decide their next step. Just because the vials were intact and the three random controls were clear didn't mean that they were safe. Conceivably one could have added the ricin at the factory before the tamper seal was put in place.

"We need to destroy them all. It's the only way to be sure."

Sumner nodded. "I agree."

Janklow looked grim but nodded also. "What a shame. The children need these vaccines. How do we go about it? Do we even have the right equipment to do that?"

Emma shook her head. "Not really. We need to heat it to eighty degrees centigrade for an hour. Generally you'd incinerate them.

Water boils at one hundred, but I don't think we should just dump the ricin into boiling water, because the particles could escape into the air with the steam. We'd end up killing ourselves. We would need to trap the steam as well." She waved at the next large crate that also had the word PRICE stamped on it. "What's that supposed to contain?"

Janklow checked a clipboard that hung on a hook at the door. He flipped through the pages. "A heart medication."

"Do you know which one Price makes?" Sumner asked.

"Cardovin. Has to be," Emma said. "Let's open it. See if it's really Cardovin in there or if we find some more vials. Then we can decide how to proceed."

Sumner picked up the crowbar left by Clutch and applied it to the crate's slats. He ripped off two from the side before moving around to the back. He stopped cold.

"Caldridge, come look."

Emma stepped forward, Janklow next to her. Sumner pointed to the rear of the crate. It was clear someone had already ripped off the plywood slats. Two were missing from the center. The broken pieces sat on the floor. The remaining splintered slats formed a rough opening, like a window, allowing access to the boxes inside. Someone had slashed at the boxes with a cutter. Their cardboard sides were shredded. Pieces of paper and bits of plastic from the shrink wrap hung from the opening. The inside of the carton looked like it had been ransacked. Several round plastic containers marked CARDOVIN were strewn around. Some lay on their sides, others were upended on their caps, and one lay on the ground at Emma's feet. It was clear that the container had been full, but the box was less than one-third filled.

"Someone removed handfuls of these pill bottles," Emma said.

Sumner nodded. "Maybe the ricin was in here all the time."

"Didn't the intelligence report say that the ricin was in a vaccine vial?"

"Maybe it was wrong. Someone could have put ricin in a powder form in one of these and transported it with the heart medication.

Whoever it was, though, got to it before we did. Now we just have to figure out where it is on this ship."

"Has anyone disembarked since this whole pirate thing began?" Sumner spoke to Janklow, who shook his head.

"No. And only Ms. Caldridge arrived. Whoever did this is still on board."

Emma wanted to kick something. She was too late. The ricin could be anywhere. She plunged her hand into the opening and moved it around, sifting through the remaining pill bottles. Her hand closed on a long, thin object at the bottom of the container. She pulled it out and held it up for Sumner and Janklow to see. It was a white EpiPen.

"Gentlemen, here's your weapon."

Janklow looked confused. "An antiallergy pen?"

Emma's mask gave out. She pulled it off. Sumner and Janklow did the same. Suddenly she wasn't worried about ricin inhalation anymore. She was beginning to doubt that it had ever been there in the first place.

"This is some sort of dopamine and epinephrine accelerator."

"I know what dopamine is, but what's epinephrine?" Janklow said.

"You probably know it by its former name: adrenaline."

"What happens when these substances are accelerated?" Sumner asked.

"In my case, my reactions alternated between panic attacks, the urge to run away, and the need to drink."

Sumner frowned. He cleared his throat, looking concerned. "Caldridge, those are the classic symptoms of post-traumatic stress disorder."

Emma fixed him with a look. "Which I have, we know this. But my symptoms before getting stuck just entailed nightmares and headaches. Since I got stuck, these other problems have arisen."

"Do you know if anyone else is being attacked and having the same reactions?" Janklow said.

Emma didn't know, and there was currently no way to find out. She shook her head.

Janklow sighed. "The existence of the EpiPen doesn't rule out ricin. We still have to address what to do with these vials."

She turned her attention back to the task at hand. Janklow was right. The vials remained an issue. Sumner stood over them. He seemed to make a decision.

"I saw some empty aluminum barrels in the mechanical room. Let's put the vials back in the small boxes and put the boxes in the barrels. We'll seal them up, slap a skull and crossbones on them, and hide them someplace where they're unlikely to be found if the ship is boarded."

Emma felt Sumner's eyes on her.

"What are you thinking?"

"That this ties back to me. Stark told me that a lobbyist insisted that Price hire me to analyze Cardovin. That Cooley would go easier on them if I backed their results."

Sumner's eyebrows rose. "Since when does Cooley help any of us?"

Emma nodded. "I know. He's out to get us. Which leads me to believe that there's a player here behind the scenes who's manipulating this entire thing. It must all go back to the pipeline somehow."

Sumner waved Janklow to the door. "Let's get the barrels and pack the vials. We don't have much time. Those pirates aren't giving up."

BANNER STOOD IN THE AIRPORT IN FRANKFURT READING A TEXT message from Stromeyer describing Rickell's suspected condition and asking him to track the man down. He estimated that Rickell had a twelve-hour lead on him, easy. Banner headed to the rental car desk to get a vehicle. He would drive to Bad Homburg himself. No need for a driver to witness Rickell's condition. The fewer witnesses the better. Once in the car, he called Stromeyer.

"I have bad news," she said.

"Is it about Cooley? I already saw it on the Internet."

"That and Agents Tarrant and Church are tailing me. I would never have made it to work if it weren't for Stan." She described her escape route through Stan's garage. "I'm cutting through his property so often that pretty soon I'm going to have to pay the man for an easement."

Banner smiled a little at that as he drove the car. It had started to rain, and the windshield wipers slapped back and forth in a soothing rhythm.

"Tell me about Rickell. What's his favorite game?"

"According to Plower, he's an avid poker player."

"At least he's smart enough not to get caught playing publicly at a craps table. How do you think this poison works?"

"It seems to remove one's inhibitions and accelerate addictions."

Perhaps Rickell was thinking about gambling when they hit him and it triggered old behaviors. And Caldridge was in a dangerous spot. She probably already had running away on her mind when she was hit. Stromeyer's explanation made sense. Perhaps the drug identified emotions bubbling under the surface, acted on them, and brought them to the fore.

"If you get anything further, let me know. I'll check Bad Homburg and call you when I'm done."

Banner stayed in the right-hand lane, letting all faster traffic pass him while he brooded about the FBI, Darkview, and Cooley. The harassment was all tied to the pipeline, but he couldn't figure out how the pen poisonings connected to it. His phone rang. He shoved the earpiece into his ear before answering. A quick glance at the screen identified Stromeyer as the caller.

"New information just came in. He's been spotted at the Bahnhofsviertel."

"*That's* not good," Banner said.

"Why? Is it a casino?"

"It's a quarter located near the Frankfurt train station that has a lot of prostitutes."

Stromeyer didn't say anything for a moment. "Well, that's not *all* bad. I mean, prostitution is legal in Germany, isn't it?"

Banner swung the car into a side street and began a three-point turn in order to reverse direction and head back to Frankfurt. At this rate I'll be in this car all night, he thought.

"I hope this intelligence is reliable," he said to Stromeyer. "I don't want to spend my evening driving back and forth between Bad Homburg and Frankfurt. And yes, prostitution is legal here, but I imagine that the good folks in America will be less than enthused once they discover their undersecretary for international security policy and procedure is doing some field research by visiting hookers in foreign countries. Not to mention his wife. Is he married?"

"I haven't the faintest idea," Stromeyer said.

"Give me a name, a street, anything. Otherwise it's going to be a long night visiting brothels."

"That's all I've got. Guess you'll just have to bite the bullet. Who knows? Maybe some of the girls will be interesting."

Banner groaned. "Sure. They'll all be students working their way through medical school."

"From good families fallen on bad times," Stromeyer said.

"Well raised, with excellent manners."

"That, too." She was laughing now.

"I'll call you when I find him. In the meantime watch your back. Don't go home without an escort, and don't stay there without security."

"Want some good news?" Stromeyer said.

"Yes."

"Plower arranged for their office to pay last month's invoice in full."

"The one who's bad at paperwork? I'm surprised she even knew where to find the bill."

"I gave her a copy. Good luck locating her boss. If you save him, we just might get hired again. We need the work. Since the raid, the phones are ringing off the hook with reporters calling for a story, but not one new client. This keeps up for long, we're going under."

"I won't quit until I find him. But every minute he keeps me from Dubai is another minute that Sumner and Caldridge are placed at further risk. At some point we'll have to pull the plug here."

"I know. Good luck. Don't do anything I wouldn't do."

"I've yet to figure out what you will or won't do."

"Be safe out there, and when you come back, I'll run it down for you."

"Now, there's an incentive." Banner listened to Stromeyer's laugh before clicking off the phone.

46

TARRANT DRANK FROM A HUGE CUP OF COFFEE WHILE HE WATCHED Darkview's back door. A white EpiPen sat on the passenger seat. He'd decided it was time for the Stromeyer woman's hit. She was no longer any use to him, and he needed a way to get to Banner. Show the man that they meant business. The Vulture had approved killing her at last. Everyone knew that Banner depended on his vice president to keep the corporation humming. Without her he'd have a hell of a time surviving. She did all the intricate paperwork required to ensure that the defense contracts kept flowing.

Tarrant was going to enjoy watching her spin out of control. He would inject her, throw her in the panel van he currently sat in, drive her to a secluded area, watch her die, and bury her body. Let Banner wonder for the rest of his life what had happened to her. Served him right. He should have caved earlier. Dismantled Darkview and disappeared. Of course, Banner wasn't going to live much longer either, but still . . .

Tarrant opened the ibuprofen bottle and threw back a pill with a coffee chaser. His schedule was one pill every four hours. He'd started them after injuring his back in a car accident. The injury had healed, but the pills remained. The entire problem almost got out of his control after a bad incident when he was working a joint deal with a particular drug cartel. His job was to rough up one of the cartel's American-based contacts suspected of skimming off the top. Tarrant took him to a secluded area in handcuffs and beat him with a bicycle chain, all the while demanding to know where the money was. The contact never revealed the stash's location, and he died of his injuries. Tarrant regretted killing the man before he could get him to talk. The cartel leader listened to the story and seemed to accept that the money was gone, but from that moment forward, Tarrant felt a presence at his back, hovering, like an ominous black cloud. He knew that it was the dead man. He popped more pills to keep the cloud at bay. Soon after, small incidents arose where Tarrant suspected that the cartel leader thought he'd scammed the money for himself. He felt he was being watched. The cloud remained, and sometimes Tarrant thought he heard laughter from behind him. He upped his pill schedule.

Tarrant's phone rang just as the Stromeyer woman stepped out the back door. He was tempted to ignore it, but a quick glance told him that it was the Vulture. He shoved a hands-free wire into his ear and answered.

"She's just coming out. Can I call you back?"

"No." The voice on the other end of the line spoke with the authority of someone who expected to be obeyed. Indeed, few ever crossed him. Not if they valued their continued existence on this earth. Tarrant tamped down his irritation and did his best to keep a level voice.

"What, then?"

"Banner didn't get beat, he did the beating. That's the second thing you've botched. Tell me why I shouldn't kill you now."

Tarrant felt sweat pop up on his forehead. Matters didn't get better when he saw two men step next to Stromeyer. That they were bodyguards would not be immediately apparent to most, but Tarrant had dealt with enough trained fighters to tell that these two were not to be messed with. They were lean and tall, and both looked supple enough to move quickly in a fight.

"You didn't let me use my usual guys, remember? You insisted on freelance, and quality control suffered. Every time one of my operatives was charged to do the attacking, the job got done."

"Killing Cooley was an act of sublime stupidity. He was to be a test case, not a dead man. The police have an autopsy planned."

Tarrant felt his heart racing. Now he had two ghosts hovering at his back. "That was unfortunate. I didn't expect him to die."

"I told you, two sticks and they die."

"I know."

"You'd better hope the drug works the way we've been told. I don't need an autopsy confirming foul play."

Tarrant's stomach went sour.

"And Rickell's safely in Europe."

Tarrant wasn't going to take the fall for that. "We weren't able to get the guy alone after Church injected him. The loser gambled like some sort of robot. He sat at that table morning, noon, and night. Then he took off before we could grab him."

"The runner got away, Rickell got away, Banner got away, and now Banner's VP is marching around with two Darkview bodyguards."

Tarrant felt nausea rising. That the Vulture knew already about Stromeyer's security contingent meant he had another operative watching her. If he did, Tarrant would be rendered redundant. Once redundant, he'd be taken out. He scrambled to maintain his position.

"Listen. Cooley got hit, Rickell got hit, and Caldridge got hit. You wanted that to happen, it did."

"I want Banner hit before he gets to Rickell."

"Where are they?"

"Frankfurt."

"Germany? I don't have any guys in Germany."

"Your African friend does. Call him. I want this done."

"What about Cooley? I mean, do the police know anything?"

"You mean, do the police know you did it? No. I'm using my contacts to throw suspicion on Darkview. Everyone knows that Cooley was gunning for them. That means your guys need to get to Banner. Stick him, get some video dirt on him after he starts acting strangely, hit him a second time, then plant some evidence on him."

"And the VP?"

"Kill her."

Tarrant shut down his cell. The device danced in his shaking hand. He reached for the glove compartment, opened it, and pulled out a brown paper bag. He extracted a bottle of tranquilizers he used in those times when he found it impossible to sleep, pressed open the safety cap, and swallowed two. He threw the car into drive to tail the woman, his hands clutching the wheel.

BANNER PULLED THE CAR'S LEFT WHEELS ONTO THE SIDEWALK
as he parked in front of a dark wooden door. A neon sign hung over
it that said ARIES EROSCENTER. To the right was a framed poster with
a graphic of a man and a woman entwined in a sexual position. Both
were naked, with shadows artfully arranged to hide the woman from
view. The man's naked back was exposed. Under the picture, the lo-
gos of the biggest credit-card companies in the world were proudly
displayed. Banner folded in the car's sideview mirrors so as to avoid
getting them clipped in the narrow lane before stepping up to ring the
bell. He waited for a response, eyeing the LED light glowing from
a camera placed in a discreet location above his head. When a clicking sound indicated that the lock was sprung, he pushed through the
entrance.

It was a dramatic lobby. Black and white marble tiles set in a
geometric pattern adorned the floor, and a plush black velvet couch
hugged one wall, with two large red wing chairs facing it. A man
whom Banner guessed to be about fifty sat behind a paneled reception desk watching a computer monitor. He was bald, with a thick
neck and broad shoulders, but despite his large physique he seemed a
cut above the average bouncer. He wore a dark brown sweater with a
shirt underneath, and reading glasses hung from a chain around his
neck. He nodded at Banner.

"Welcome. Can I help you?" The man spoke in English.

"Is it so obvious that I'm American?" Banner said. He was seek-

ing to put the man at ease, to form some sort of connection before
plunging into the reason for his visit.

The man smiled. "Yes."

"Are you the owner?"

The man shook his head. "No. I'm the manager. Can I help you?"

"How much does it cost?"

The manager slid a rate card at him. "Ninety euros cover charge.
We give you a key for a locker, a robe, and slippers. You can shower,
then take one of our saunas. Upstairs we have a bar, a lounge, and a
wellness center, as well as a theater."

Banner glanced at the card. The man had given him one translated
in English. The fees listed were not exorbitant but rose according to
the time spent. One fee was for what was euphemistically called a
"sleepover." Banner thought it was an unfortunate choice of the English word. While it was a direct translation, he suspected that the
establishment probably didn't understand the childish connotation.
Or at least he hoped they didn't.

"I'm looking for a particular patron."

The man frowned. "We don't reveal our clients. They depend on
our discretion."

Banner pretended to sympathize. "I understand, but this particular
client is quite famous, and if he were to be found here, it would throw
both him and this establishment into an unfavorable light. I'm sure
your owner wouldn't care to have that happen."

The manager seemed to consider this. "You can pay the fee, and
then you are free to look around. If he's not busy in a room, you may
find him between sessions in one of the common areas."

The last thing Banner wanted to do was go padding around a
brothel in a robe and slippers. He was even less enthused about the
idea of watching a bunch of other men padding around in robes and
slippers. But by far the worst thing would be to find Rickell in a robe
and slippers. Unfortunately, it was possible that he'd end up doing
just that before the night was over. If he did, Banner didn't think he'd

be able to sit in a Department of Defense meeting with the man ever again.

He sighed. "I don't want to throw my weight around, but I am willing to arrange for the authorities to come here and run a search."

The manager waved a hand at the sofa. "Please sit. I'll get the owner for you."

Banner sat. Ten minutes later a tall, striking middle-aged woman with blond hair, a willowy body, and a regal air walked toward him. She wore impeccably fitting tailored pants with a white silk blouse and peered at him through expensive eyeglasses that lent her a serious, professorial air. Banner stood to greet her. If she was indicative of the quality of the women inside, he was already impressed. She held out a hand to him.

"I'm Isabelle Kartiner, the owner here. I understand that you wish to speak to me?"

"I do. I'm looking for a particular client who may be inside. If he is, I need to arrange to get him out without anyone noticing."

Ms. Kartiner gave Banner a sad smile. "I apologize, but we will be unable to help you. Our clients insist on maintaining their privacy. We wouldn't last a week if it were discovered that we were free with their information."

Banner tried another tack. "Then I won't ask you to find him, but perhaps I can ask you questions that may reveal whether it's worth my while to remain?"

She smiled. "I think it would be worth your while to remain in any event. Our girls are the best at what they do. I'm sure we could find one to suit you."

"Thank you, but I don't normally frequent places like this."

Ms. Kartiner gave him a shrewd look. "Generally I wouldn't believe that statement, as many of our newer patrons claim to be novices to the trade yet really indulge themselves frequently. However, it occurs to me that a man with your looks would have little need to come here for female companionship."

Banner smiled. She had delivered the compliment with an aplomb he admired.

"I imagine that the men who patronize your establishment don't come here because they are unable to obtain female companionship on the outside. I'll wager that they have other impulses that drive them to engage in such a transaction."

Ms. Kartiner looked amused. "That's true. And you? Do you have any impulses that you'd like to explore?"

Banner shook his head. "Just the impulse to locate my friend." He pointed to the entrance. "Do they all leave through this door?"

She smiled. "Yes. Do you wish to wait and see if he appears?"

"I do."

"Please, make yourself comfortable. This isn't our main sitting room—we have a bar and lounge area upstairs, but only paying guests are allowed to proceed to that level. Nevertheless, I'll have a drink brought to you. There is the magazine rack"—she pointed to a Lucite rack that held magazines behind transparent sleeves—"and newspapers in every language are on that wall"—she pointed to a wooden ladder that held folded newspapers. "What would you like to drink?"

"A double espresso would be greatly appreciated."

"Of course." She glided away, her heels making a clicking sound on the marble floor.

Banner watched her as she left. As professional as she was, it was clear to him that she wouldn't give him the information he needed. Despite what he'd told her, he didn't have the time to sit in the lobby waiting for the off chance that Rickell would emerge from the upstairs rooms. He was going to have to work on the manager some more.

Ten minutes later a stunning cocktail waitress appeared carrying a black tray. This one was young; Banner estimated that she was no more than twenty-five, with long, shiny brown hair and brown uptilted eyes set in an exotic face. She wore a short black dress that revealed miles of leg and high stiletto heels. She placed before him a narrow silver tray containing a black-and-white demitasse cup filled with thick, sweet-smelling coffee, a tiny silver spoon, and a glass of water. She bestowed a practiced, seductive smile on him.

"Can I get you anything else?" She also spoke in English, but with a slight Eastern European accent. Banner handed her a five-euro bill.

She refused the offer. "Frau Kartiner said that you were not to be charged."

Banner placed the money on the tray. "Tell her thank you."

"Shall I escort you inside? Frau Kartiner suggested that I ask you."

Banner was beginning to understand why Frau Kartiner was the owner of the establishment. She had excellent marketing skills.

"I'll just stay here, thank you," Banner said.

The young woman looked surprised. "You're not going in?"

Banner shook his head. "Not my habit."

A look of yearning came over the woman's face. All the practiced seduction was gone. "Then why are you here?"

"I'm looking for my friend. An American man about fifty years old."

The woman looked puzzled. "There aren't any Americans here right now. Only locals and a group of Asian men in town for a convention."

Banner frowned. "Are you sure?"

"Oh, yes. You see, it's early yet. While we have walk-ins, they don't typically occur until much later in the evening. The early hours are usually filled with the regulars and preregistered conventioneers."

Banner considered the girl worth her weight in gold, because he was now free to move on. He followed up his four euro bills with twenty more.

"Thanks for saving me a lot of time sitting here. Do you have any ideas where my friend might be? Are there any other establishments nearby?"

She seemed to consider his question. "Does he have a specific requirement? If he does, that would narrow down the choices." Banner knew nothing about Rickell's predilections, if he had any at all. If Rickell had been drugged, it meant his judgment was impaired. He could be acting in a manner foreign even to himself.

"None that I know of."

"Try the Speakeasy. Two streets down and left. It's not as nice as here, but the American GIs like it."

He could only hope that Rickell was not so impaired as to walk into a cathouse loaded with American army men. Banner would go there last.

"Anyplace else? He likes poker. Are there any places where he could play a game?"

The waitress turned toward the manager and fired off a long question in German.

The manager shook his head. He directed his attention to Banner. "None of the houses have girls and a casino together." He shrugged. "Doesn't mean that call girls don't work off the books in casinos, but that's the same everywhere."

Banner downed his espresso in one gulp. "How about an off-the-books game in a regulated house?"

The manager gave Banner a knowing look. "Try the VIP Lounge. It's a block north on the diagonal. There's no sign, just a small plaque that says 'Private Club.' They often get a game going there."

"Thanks." Banner stood. The whole time he'd been there, not one man had entered. "Is business always this slow?"

The manager smiled. "Not at all, but there's a championship soccer game on television tonight. Business is always slow when that happens."

Banner didn't bother to hide his surprise. "Soccer trumps women?"

The manager nodded. "In Germany soccer trumps everything."

to the bridge. She stripped off the mechanic's jumpsuit and shoved it into a drawer just as the electricity went off, plunging her into darkness. She fumbled along a wall to the exit.

The halls were slightly more lit than the cargo area. She made her way toward the bridge, running a hand along the wall to keep her bearings. She heard the fizz of electricity as it surged in fits and starts into the lightbulbs. The area in front of her flickered.

She turned a corner and stopped. People filled the small area, stretching in a long line thirty feet back from a door marked NURSE. Cindy and Marina were squeezing past the waiting patients. Cindy spotted Emma and gave her a nod.

"What's this line about?" Emma asked.

Cindy looked uncomfortable. "Come over here." She led Emma away from the entrance, stopping after they turned the corner. "That's the line of people asking for drugs."

"Drugs? What do you mean?"

"I mean drugs. Tranquilizers, sleeping pills, you name it. The nurse is pretty near the end of her rope."

"Can I talk to her? I just need to ask her a question. Of course I'm happy to help in any way I can, but I'm not licensed to dispense medications, so there's no way I can assist her with that line."

Cindy started back toward the office door. "Follow me."

They made it to the nurse's office door. The people in the front of the line frowned at their intrusion. One man said, "Get back in line. We were here first."

Cindy put her hands on her hips. "She's not here for medication, Captain Wainwright sent her. She needs to speak to Nurse Miller."

The man subsided a bit. "Are the pirates gone? What's the captain doing? We're going to die out here! I tell you, when I get back to Phoenix, I'm demanding a refund. This trip has been a disaster."

"I understand completely," Emma sympathized. "Captain Wainwright is keeping a close watch on the radar. He's an excellent captain." Emma kept her voice soothing. The man seemed a bit mollified by her manner.

"He's a good man, I know. I don't mean to imply that he's not, but I'm so anxiety-ridden over this situation that I can barely control myself. Why, just an hour ago I thought I would explode. I'm really here for my wife. She threatened to jump off the railing into the sea during the last attack." The man's eyes filled with tears. "She's never done anything close to that before. I calmed her down, but I can't watch her day and night. I came to see if the nurse can give her some anti-anxiety medication." The man sighed a jagged sigh and then patted Emma's arm. "You go ahead on in. I'm not usually like this, all teary-eyed and such." He rapped once on the closed door before opening it for her. "I'll wait till you're done."

Emma walked into a tiny waiting area with comfortable couches and a desk. Behind that was a hallway. A woman sat at the desk, writing on a small pad. She had chestnut hair that ended at a high widow's-peak forehead and was pulled back into a severe ponytail. Her skin was so pale that Emma could see the blue veins underneath. She wore a white coat and a name tag that read ANN MILLER. She finished writing, ripped off the paper, and handed it and a small pill bottle to the female passenger sitting in front of her.

"Take one every four hours on a full stomach." The woman, who looked to be about sixty, gripped the bottle so tightly that Emma could see the knuckles on her hands whiten. She opened the bottle, took out a pill, and swallowed it right there. The move screamed desperation, and it stunned Emma with its intensity.

"Don't you want some water?" Cindy sounded as shocked as Emma felt.

The woman colored. "No." She mumbled the word, her head down, before bolting out the door. Ms. Miller frowned as she watched the woman leave. Two large creases appeared on her forehead, as if the skin were papery thin.

"Are you the chemist who boarded the ship?" she asked Emma.

"Yes." Emma offered her hand to shake. "I'm Emma Caldridge. Is that line normal?"

Ms. Miller looked surprised. "Good heavens, no. These people are just begging for medications. They all want tranquilizers—I'm going to run out very soon—and most want sleeping pills as well."

"They're scared," Cindy said.

Ms. Miller frowned. "So am I, but I can't just dispense tranquilizers willy-nilly. I'm turning away anyone who has no history of needing them. But I must say, some of the reactions I'm getting are scaring me."

"Scaring you? Why?"

She swallowed. "They're insisting. Some are threatening violence if they don't get what they want. Their behavior is strange, to say the least."

Shouts of "Come on!" and "Where is she?" echoed from the hallway.

"They're getting restless," Cindy said.

"I'd better get back to work." A look of exhaustion spread across Ms. Miller's face.

Emma put a hand on the woman's arm. "Ask each of them if they recall being stuck with a pen or feeling a jab at any time prior to their symptoms. Ask them if they recall feeling a rush from inside."

Ms. Miller frowned. "You think they've been drugged?"

"I *know* they've been drugged. I would just like to know who's doing it. Ask them all who was near them at the time of the stick. I'll be on the bridge if you get any answers."

Emma continued wending her way to the bridge, with Cindy and Marina accompanying her. They made it to Deck Three without incident and were fifty feet from the stairs that rose to the exit to the pool deck when a group of people poured into the narrow space behind them. All three women turned to look. They were face-to-face with a crowd of men, all led by one with a beer bottle in his hand and anger in his eyes. His face was flushed and his color high. Emma watched him labor for breath. Behind him the others jostled one another to get a look at what blocked their passage. All the men had wild looks on their faces. Two had facial tics. Emma watched as the muscles under their skin twitched in a regular rhythm.

"Where the hell you going?" the man with the beer bottle said.

Emma aimed for a soothing tone. "We're just headed to the bridge."

The man's face flushed brighter. "Get out of our way. That's where we're going. We're going to handle this situation for the captain. We're done sitting here waiting for those pirates to come back and kill us. We're gonna act."

Emma hesitated. The last thing she needed was a confrontation. The lead man noted her pause.

"I said, get out of the way." He moved closer, and the entire group shuffled along with him.

"Emma, let's keep going up." Cindy was behind her, tapping her on the shoulder. Emma could hear the strain in the woman's voice. She didn't want to alarm Cindy, but she wasn't moving. This crowd was not going to the bridge—not past her, at least. She stood her ground as she spoke to the women behind her.

"Go tell Wainwright what's going on here."

The men moved closer.

Cindy's hand clutched Emma's shoulder. "Not without you."

"Yes, without me."

"Marina, go. I'm staying here."

The men moved closer. Emma could smell the beer from the bottle. The lead man's breathing hitched even more. She wished she could calculate how long it had been since he'd been stuck. If recent, he wasn't going to come to his senses anytime soon.

"Just shove her out of the way!" a man yelled from the back of the mob. He spoke with an English accent.

Before Emma could react, the lead man did just that. He put his hands on her shoulders—the one holding the bottle was fisted—and he pushed. Emma staggered backward. She grabbed at a railing set along the wall. If not for that, she would have fallen. She regained her balance and continued to face the men but took one step back. She needed to stay upright. If she went down, she was sure they'd trample right over her in their rush to the bridge. The lead man moved closer. This time he took a final swig off the beer bottle and then raised it high.

"I don't want to hurt you, lady, but you need to get the hell out of my way," he said.

Before Emma could respond, a whizzing sound came from the back of the crowd. A man yelped. She heard something hit the carpeted deck with a thud. The entire group turned around to look at the new disturbance. Emma took advantage of the moment to move up the stairs, backward, keeping her face to the crowd. Cindy stayed right behind her, moving in unison with her. From this position Emma had the added advantage of being above the men's heads and could see past them.

Sumner and Block stood at the far end of the hall. Emma made out the shape of a square device in Sumner's hand that looked like a gun with a boxy muzzle. His face held its usual determined look as he calmly went about reloading the weapon. Block looked far less calm. In fact, he looked furious. His color was as high as that of the men around him, but Emma thought it might be induced from pure rage rather than a drug.

"What the hell do you think you're doing, pushing a woman?" Block's voice pulsed with anger. Emma heard Cindy gasp. The men began to step toward him but stopped when Sumner held up the stun gun.

"Anyone comes closer and he gets to go lights-out courtesy of fifteen thousand volts."

The men stopped. Sumner flicked a questioning look at Emma. She nodded to let him know she was unhurt. A man from the center of the group yelled in a language that sounded like Russian.

"*Sprechen Sie Deutsch?*" Sumner said. The Russian shifted into German without missing a beat.

"*Ja, drecksack!* Get out of our way. We're going to the captain."

"You've all been drugged," Emma said.

The crowd fell silent and turned back to Emma.

"What do you mean, drugged?" The beer-bottle holder spit out the question.

"Just what I said. Someone on the ship is drugging the passengers. I want you all to think—did you feel any type of stick or sting followed by a surge that might have been a chemical entering your system?"

A man in the center of the crowd spoke up. "I did. A guy fell against me. I felt the sting and the rush right after. I didn't think anything of it."

"What did he look like?" Emma asked.

The man, a younger passenger with ginger-colored hair and a large-framed body, hesitated. "He was a ship employee. He wore a white uniform. But I don't know which one."

Emma wasn't surprised at this information. Only ship employees had access to the cargo bay where the vials were located.

But before she could respond, the ship's alarm went off.

49

BANNER STEPPED INTO THE VIP LOUNGE. THE VIBE HERE WAS completely different from the Eroscenter. This club evoked the feeling of men's social clubs in an era gone by. Heavy paneling covered the walls, dark velvet draperies lined each window, and leather chairs with matching ottomans faced a fireplace with an elaborately carved mantelpiece. The smell of old cigars and new cigarettes permeated the air. Three silver-haired men strolled past the reception desk, headed up a flight of carpeted stairs to the second level. As in the establishment before, the VIP receptionist was a somewhat beefy man. Banner stepped up to him to begin his rap.

"I'm—"

"Here to check out the poker game."

"The Eroscenter called you," Banner said.

The man nodded. "You'll need at least two thousand euros to join, but that will cover your initial chip allocation of five hundred, all your food and drinks, and one session with the girl of your choice after the game."

"Steep," Banner said.

The man shrugged. "It's a good game. You could win, and if you don't, at least you'll leave here fed and happy."

Banner chuckled. The man had a point. "Do you take credit cards?"

The man shook his head. "Not for this. The game's off the books. We need cash."

"I don't have it."

"There's an ATM down the street to the right."

"Don't they usually have five-hundred-euro limits?"

The man nodded. "Maybe you come back tomorrow. Least now you've seen the place."

"How about I give you five hundred cash? That will cover my chip allocation. I'll pay for food on the card, and I won't touch the women."

"You're gonna want to touch the women."

"I don't doubt that, but beggars can't be choosers."

The man considered the offer. "Okay. But you change your mind about the women, you're gonna have to leave the game and go to the main area of the club. They take credit cards."

"It's a deal."

The man pointed to the stairs. "Up there. Second door on your left. Give the guard the cash. Good luck."

Banner thought he'd need it. He headed up the stairwell. At the top was a long hall with several doors on either side. A young man reading a paper sat in a chair with its legs tilted and its back against the wall. He dropped the chair legs to the carpeting when he saw Banner and stood. Banner handed him five hundred euros. The young man opened the door.

"Play well," he said with a smile.

Banner stepped into a rectangular room. A circular table, positioned in the center, acted as a focal point. A stained-glass lamp hung over it, illuminating the green felt top. Five men sat with cards in their hands. Off to the right, three women, all dressed in thong bathing suits and high heels, hovered near a wet bar. They were model thin, on the verge of emaciation. Each one gave him an assessing look as he walked in, and each one smiled after the look.

Rickell was on the far side of the table. Deep circles rimmed his eyes, and his hair was plastered to his head as if by sweat. His skin was a pasty white, and his lips were cracked. He had a stack of chips in front of him, but something told Banner he wasn't winning. He didn't have the look of a winner. Banner stepped closer to the table, into the light. Two of the men glanced up from their hands with irritated expressions on their faces. He was interrupting a hand. Rickell never lifted his eyes from his cards. When the other men halted, Rickell looked up. His face took on a resigned expression.

"So they're searching for me," he said.

Banner nodded. "Time to go."

Rickell shook his head. "No."

Banner had expected this response. Rickell probably viewed himself as Banner's superior in many of the ways that counted. Without Rickell's signature, Darkview wouldn't land the lucrative DOD contracts that kept the company humming. Banner, however, viewed no man as his superior. Either they partnered with him in ventures where both gained something or they stayed away. Rickell's office had hired Banner to bring Rickell out, and that's what he'd do.

"We leave now. I haven't much time."

"No."

The men at the table waited, watching them both with interested eyes.

"I'll drag you out of here if I have to. I've been hired to get you, and, as you know, my company delivers. I can't afford to fail. Not given the current climate surrounding Darkview. Plus, I've got mouths to feed."

Rickell snorted. "You don't have any children."

Banner didn't bother to correct him. "I've got office and equipment costs, three hundred and twenty operatives worldwide, a vice president, and a secretary with an expensive tattoo habit who's putting herself through school."

The player to Rickell's right gave a soft laugh. He was one of the silver-haired men who had taken the stairs before Banner. His eyes sparkled with enjoyment. Banner was glad someone was having a good evening, because it certainly wasn't him. He took a step toward Rickell.

The men at the table shifted. The smiling man raised an eyebrow, lowered his cards to place them facedown on the felt, and spoke in German to the others. Their chairs scraped backward as the players stood. One of them indicated to the girls that they should leave.

"*Schnell,*" he said. Even Banner knew that meant "fast."

The girls moved with an alacrity that impressed Banner, given the shoes they wore.

Rickell rose, staring at him the whole time. He was two inches shorter than Banner's six feet, but fit. Banner thought he'd be easy to beat. Unless the poison gave him superhero powers, Banner didn't view him as any risk in a fight. None at all. His only problem was going to be subduing Rickell without doing any real harm to him. He would have to pull all his punches.

"I could beat you, you know," Rickell said.

The other players' heads swiveled to watch Banner's response.

Banner kept a level stare. "You've got a lot of skills, Mr. Rickell, but fighting isn't one of them. You benefit from living in a country where the rule of law prevails. I've spent most of my life infiltrating those where none exists. It's going to be no contest."

The smiling man gazed at Banner with a look of respect. No one spoke.

Rickell waved at his chips. A man emerged from a darkened corner at the back of the room. He placed a holder on the table, counted out Rickell's chips, and wrote a number down on a pad of paper. He slid the pad toward Rickell and handed him a pen. Rickell signed the receipt without really looking at it.

"You keep that under lock and key?"

The banker nodded.

"Let's go," Rickell said.

Banner stepped aside. "After you."

The other players seemed to sigh in unison. The smiling man caught Banner's eye and nodded once. Banner returned the gesture.

They made it down the stairs, out the door, and into the narrow lane before they were attacked.

The man came out of nowhere. He raced toward Rickell, his hand outstretched. Banner caught a glimpse of a white-handled weapon in the man's right hand. Rickell stumbled back as the man hauled off to stab him. Banner threw himself between Rickell and the attacker, knocking the man's arm out of the way. He swung his left fist into the man's temple. The attacker grunted, falling back, his arms flailing. Two more men came around the corner.

"Rickell, move!" Banner said. Rickell scrambled up. His expensive leather shoes slipped on the pavement, forcing him down again. Banner grabbed him by the arm, propelling him upward and dragging him down the street, in the direction of his car. He heard the men's feet pounding behind them. Banner let go of Rickell while he pulled the ignition key out of his pocket. He hit the button to open the doors. The taillights flashed in response.

"You see that?" Banner yelled to Rickell.

Rickell angled toward the vehicle.

Banner was a foot from the car when the men reached him. He swung around to face them. They were two swarthy-faced foreigners with undisguised hate in their dark eyes. One carried a knife. Banner tried to see if the other was armed, but the man's hand was covered in shadow. The knife wielder stepped forward, his hand flying out to stab. Banner stepped off the line of attack, grabbed the man's arm, holding it away from his body while he pulled back to punch the man with his right hand. The man tried to yank his arm out of Banner's grasp. Banner held it tightly while he pistoned his fist into the man's nose.

The sound of collapsing cartilage echoed through the narrow lane. The second man was on Banner, grabbing him around the neck, doing his best to haul Banner's face down toward the pavement. He plunged a needle into Banner's skin where the neck met the shoulder. Banner felt the surge of some unknown chemical enter his veins. His skin heated like it was on fire. It might have been adrenaline running in his system, but the force of it was unlike anything he'd felt before. He pulled out of the other man's grasp with an ease he shouldn't have possessed. The man had such a grip on Banner that the maneuver caused Banner's flesh to twist as he wrenched his throat free. He felt his skin abrade from the friction, creating a burn across the back of his neck.

The Eroscenter door flew open, and the manager catapulted out of it with a policeman's baton in his hand. He swung it in an arc, catching the first man across the arm that was still holding the knife. The attacker dropped the weapon with a cry of pain while blood poured out of his nose from Banner's punch. He was off, running back down the lane. The second man released Banner in an instant. He sprinted away, following the other guy. Banner stood still, his breath heaving. The passenger door on the car opened, and Rickell stepped out. He gazed at Banner but remained silent.

"Are you okay?" the manager said. "I saw you being attacked. The camera recorded it." He indicated the camera over the Eroscenter's door. Before Banner could answer, Frau Kartiner stepped out of the entrance, a worried look on her face. Behind her hovered the young cocktail waitress.

Banner took a deep, steadying breath. The strange fizz ran through his veins, and his skin crawled. He wanted to continue fighting. When he saw Frau Kartiner, his urge to fight turned into something different. The force of his desire made his body heat up and his mouth go dry. He stared at her, unable to take his eyes off her.

Frau Kartiner's eyebrows flew upward, and she took a step back. Color suffused her face. The cocktail waitress watched them both, but when she saw Frau Kartiner's face redden, she bestowed a fascinated look on her boss. The manager stared, too.

"Are you injured?" Frau Kartiner's voice was a whisper. Banner didn't trust himself to speak. What he needed was for her to move away.

"Thank you," Rickell said. The waitress and the manager turned to acknowledge him. Banner and Kartiner stayed frozen. "We'll be going now. Banner?" Rickell prodded Banner.

Banner swallowed a dry gulp. "I owe you all." He was surprised at how normal his voice sounded.

Frau Kartiner's face relaxed. She smiled a genuine smile. "You be careful. You are welcome. Anytime." She emphasized the "Anytime."

Banner slid into the driver's seat, put on his belt, and drove out of the narrow lane. After a minute of silence, while he negotiated his way through the busy area, Rickell shifted.

"Want to tell me what's going on?"

"We've been poisoned."

Rickell was silent so long that Banner thought he didn't hear him.

"What are the effects?" he said at last.

"I'm not sure. Some sort of heightened fight-or-flight response. Old behaviors renewed—it's why you gambled. Emma Caldridge, the chemist we're using for the cruise-line rescue, thought maybe it was an adrenaline by-product, or a dopamine enhancer, she wasn't sure."

"Was she poisoned, too?"

"Yes. As were Cooley, you, and now me. You have a jet at your disposal?"

"I fly commercial. Why?"

"I need to fly to Berbera, and I need the *Redoubtable* to pick me up."

"You found the cruise liner?"

"We did. It's under attack, but well outside the zone. We need to finish this thing."

Rickell hesitated.

"Don't give me any more international-law craziness. It's outside the zone. The insurgents can't reach it for the moment. Please arrange for the *Redoubtable* to send a helicopter to take me the rest of the way. It's about time we shut this whole pirate crew down."

"You had some intelligence about this ship before it sailed, didn't you?"

Banner nodded. "But it was incomplete. The German conglomerate that owned the ship thought maybe one of the crew was dealing drugs from various ports. We heard that a group of European arms traders were on the ship in preparation to attend an auction to buy some more product. I borrowed an agent from the Southern Hemisphere Drug Defense Agency to sail with the ship."

"Who?"

"Cameron Sumner."

"The Colombian disaster."

Banner sighed. "I wish everyone would stop saying that. The Colombian thing is over. We did nothing wrong."

Rickell nodded. "I know. I'll help wrap that up when I get back."

They drove for a while, Banner navigating the narrow streets to hit the main road to the airport. He heard Rickell chuckle.

"I was losing that game, but I was ahead overall. For the first time ever, I was ahead. If you hadn't stopped me, I would have put it all back on the table. But thanks to you I'm ahead. It's a good way to go out."

A half hour later, Banner pulled the car up to a spot on a road near the runway at the Frankfurt airport. He killed the engine and sat in the silence.

"I can't tell you how relieved I am to know that the gambling returned because of a poisoning," Rickell said. "Have you ever had an impulse that you couldn't control?"

Banner thought about the moment he'd wanted to continue fighting, and when he stared at Frau Kartiner. He'd controlled himself, but just barely.

"No, but I've been close," he said.

"Well, it's a frightening thing when your body craves what your mind rejects."

Banner didn't reply.

Rickell reached for the door. "Thank you for getting me."

"You're welcome."

"Don't die out there."

Rickell slammed the door and walked away.

50

BANNER'S PHONE RANG TEN MINUTES AFTER HE LANDED IN BER-
bera, Somalia. He glanced at the readout. The number listed was un-
familiar. He punched the green button.

"Banner here."

"It is Giovanni Roducci."

Banner snapped to attention. Roducci wouldn't call him if he'd had
an opportunity to speak to Stromeyer. Something was up. "Yes?"

"I have just learned that both you and Major Stromeyer may be
targeted for death."

Banner did his best not to let his mouth drop open. "Who's targeting us?"

"A man called the Vulture. He is a corporate raider from Europe.
Lots of money that he spreads around. No one really knows his true
identity, because he operates out of a tangled mass of offshore shell
corporations, but it is believed his influence reaches into the highest
levels of society. Unfortunately, he uses the influence to harm those
who get in his way."

"How have I gotten in his way?"

"You haven't. You got in the way of a Somali warlord. This warlord cut a deal that included wiping Darkview off the planet."

"What does the Vulture get in return for killing me?"

"He gets the warlord to capture a cruise ship that carries several
dealers waiting to bid for the formula for a new drug. Once the warlord captures the ship, he takes the dealers hostage and gives the

Vulture the cargo. The Vulture wipes out his competition in one clean sweep, and no one will suspect he's behind the attack. After all, pirate attacks have become quite common in the past few years, so it will be considered just another act of piracy."

"Is Major Stromeyer aware of this?"

"She is. I contacted her first, of course."

"Of course," Banner said. He was surprised Roducci even bothered to let him know. Sometimes he thought Roducci would like nothing better than to see Banner out of *his* way.

"What did Stromeyer say?"

"She told me that you had already placed bodyguards around her in response to some recent threats. Then she asked me to warn you. She would have done it herself, but she was concerned about a wiretap."

A man in military clothing stepped up to Banner. "Your helicopter to the *Redoubtable* is ready," he whispered at Banner. Banner acknowledged him with a nod.

"Thank you, Mr. Roducci."

"Anytime, Signor Banner."

TARRANT SAT OUTSIDE STROMEYER'S HOUSE. He'd had no opportunity to hit her with the pen all day. The two bodyguards never left her side. He checked his watch. He'd been sitting in the car for over three hours. He needed to do something soon. Take some action. He reached into the glove compartment, extracted two more pills, his last, and downed them with a whiskey chaser. His nerves were uncommonly jittery. A knock on the driver's-side window startled him. He saw only dark knuckles and antelope cuff links. It was the African. Tarrant lowered the window.

"I thought you would never get here. I'm out," Tarrant said.

"Yes, you are," the African said. He pointed a gun with a silencer at Tarrant's head and shot him. He walked calmly away, flipping open a phone as he did. "It's finished," he said.

"And the woman?"

"Alive."

"Good."

The African was confused. He thought the woman was supposed to be targeted for elimination.

"Why don't you want her dead?"

"She received a confidential communication from an arms trader, mentioning my involvement. She started digging, looking for my identity. She is quite adept at obtaining information. She notified the DOD that if she or Banner is injured or killed, they are to activate an investigation."

The African felt a stab of fear. "Does she know us?"

"Not yet, but it is best that we subside for some time."

"And Mungabe?"

"I'll deal with Mungabe."

The Vulture hung up.

EMMA WATCHED THE CROWD OF MEN STAMPEDE. THEY TURNED as a group toward Sumner and Block. The two men moved to the side to let the panicked passengers run past them in their rush to the casino. Emma sprinted to the bridge, Cindy close at her heels, and pounded on the door. The captain's second officer opened it. Emma, Cindy, Sumner, and Block pushed into the room, which was already filled with Wainwright, Janklow, Herr Schullmann, Marina, and several ship employees. They all stared at a radar screen set into the *Kaiser Franz*'s control panel.

"You fixed the radar," Sumner said.

"It's jerry-rigged from some old parts we found in storage," Janklow said. "Although right about now I wish we hadn't managed it."

The radar showed thirty green dots massed at a spot not far from the ship.

"What do you think?" Wainwright said to Janklow.

Janklow rubbed a tired hand over his face. "Maybe it's a meeting?"

Wainwright nodded. "I agree, but what are they meeting about?"

"New tactics being discussed? Sumner?"

"I think they're getting ready to do this thing right."

Block groaned.

Sumner ignored him while he pointed at the dot closest to shore. "That's the mother ship. They're going to make a concerted attack."

Emma was appalled. If the dots represented individual pirate boats, then they were soon to be overrun. Her head started pounding. She wasn't ready to be a hostage, and she wasn't ready to die. She looked at the men assembled around her. She was as helpless to stop this thing as they were.

The massed dots were moving toward them. Ahead of the entire group, and also moving toward them, was a lone dot. It was nearly upon them. She pointed to it. "Who is that?"

Wainwright handed her a set of binoculars. "Have a look." He pointed beyond the bridge's window to the sea. Emma couldn't make anything out. She put the binoculars to her eyes. A small boat sprang into view. While the driver's face was unrecognizable because he was behind a water-splattered windshield, the second man's face was not. It was Richard Stark.

"That's Hassim and Stark. The two men who helped me get here."

"Are they friend or foe?" Wainwright asked.

Good question, she thought. Hassim she could vouch for, at least. "The driver is an agent for the Darkview company. The passenger is the CEO of Price Pharmaceuticals."

Wainwright gave her an incredulous look. "Since when do CEOs of major Fortune 500 companies end up on the high seas being chased by Somali pirates?"

Emma had to agree. Stark was not to be trusted. "Since I don't know. Some very strange things have been occurring at Price, and he's in the thick of them."

"Do we let him board?" Janklow said.

Wainwright nodded. "I'm not leaving the Darkview operative to die out there. We'll haul them both on deck and sort it out later." He thought a moment. "Is everyone accounted for?"

Sumner spoke up. "Not Clutch. I haven't seen him in hours."

"Come to think of it, you're right," Janklow said. "When we're done here, I'll go look for him."

Hassim's boat made it to the side of the *Kaiser Franz*. Janklow and two crew members lowered a ladder. Hassim came up first, Stark second, carrying Emma's duffel.

"Hassim, what happened?"

"We never got far. They're everywhere."

Stark climbed over the railing. Emma couldn't read his face. He looked as tired as she felt.

"Why are you here?" she asked.

"To stop it."

"What are you stopping?"

Stark sighed. "Can we go belowdecks? Speak in private?"

Emma shook her head. "No. There's no time. In case you weren't aware, there are thirty boats coming this way. Besides, I'm not going anywhere with you in private. You tell me what you know now, in front of these witnesses. Which one of the vials has ricin in it?"

Janklow and the crew members stayed where they were, listening.

"None. There is no ricin. It was a hoax. It's the AX 2055."

Emma thought a moment. "That was an experimental drug Price was testing."

He nodded. "It's an investigational drug that had a small effect on those with neuromotor problems. It also increased one's endurance dramatically, by as much as eighty percent within a few minutes of injection, while acting on the dopamine receptors. Like many dopamine drugs, it had the side effect of increasing addictive behavior. But, unlike others, it worked too well. Rather than taking years for a person to develop that particular side effect, with this drug it happens quickly and with an aggression we've rarely seen. And it has a dark side."

"Other than the fact that it can ruin people's lives by driving them into destructive acts?"

Emma let her sarcasm show. She was so furious she was having a hard time even looking at him.

"Much worse. On the second application, it kills."

"How do *I* figure into all this? Why did you hire *me*?"

"I knew several months ago that Cardovin didn't work. With Cardovin dead in the water, we needed a cash infusion fast. I went to an investor known for his interest in undercapitalized companies. The investor offered to keep us afloat while we tested AX 2055 but insisted that your company be hired in the bargain. The investor was a major contributor to Cooley's campaign, and he claimed that Cooley wanted you hired to keep an eye on you. I didn't mind—your reputation was solid, and I'd get the money. The company would survive."

"Who would buy such a drug?"

Stark took a deep breath. "At first we thought of athletic teams, people weakened with immune disorders, Parkinson's, or any group that required an endurance or a dopamine boost. We ran mice tests and were preparing for approval to begin human clinical trials, but the mice died on the second stick and precluded that completely. Then it disappeared."

"Disappeared?"

Stark nodded. "The drug and its files were stolen from our lab. We reported the theft, and I considered that to be the end of it. Until you told me that you'd been stuck and what happened after. I knew it was our drug. Before it was stolen, we'd been preparing a trial using endurance athletes. We'd inject them after they'd exercised to exhaustion and see if the drug served to boost performance. Whoever stole it was running their own back-alley clinical testing."

Emma didn't believe his claims of complete innocence. "You mean to say that you knew I'd been hit with an illegal, untested substance that kills on the second ingestion, yet you neither warned me nor told anyone else of your suspicions?"

Stark got angry. "I wasn't sure! It was only after I was kidnapped in Nairobi that I realized the stolen product was out there, ready to be sold on the black market. They wanted to know where they could get the formula and some more product. They were going to hit world leaders. Get them to behave irrationally, then either blackmail them or stick them twice and kill them. I insisted that we didn't have any.

After it was stolen, we didn't make any more." The ship ground to a halt. "What's going on?"

"We're out of time," Sumner said. He looked at Stark. "You're going to the bridge deck." He turned to Block, who had walked up a few minutes earlier. "Take him with you. Keep him in your sight at all times." He pulled the duffel out of Stark's hands and gave it to Block, who opened it and looked inside.

Block's face lit up. "Now, ain't that a beautiful sight? It's an RPG."

"Have you ever shot one?" Janklow asked.

Block looked annoyed. "Why do you keep insisting that I don't know how to shoot?"

"I'll teach him," Hassim said.

Block nodded at him. "Thanks. Harry Block here. I'm from Texas."

Hassim almost smiled. "Hassim. I'm from Kenya."

"Now that the formalities are over, let's fire up these babies and blow the bastards away."

Hassim turned to Janklow and Sumner. "How many boats are coming?"

Sumner grimaced. "Between twenty and thirty."

If Hassim was frightened, he didn't show it. Neither did Sumner. Emma thought them both the most unflappable men she had ever met. She turned to look out to sea. The pirates, if they were out there, could not be seen by the naked eye just yet. Then she looked down at the water next to the boat and gasped. Hundreds of jellyfish floated next to them. Huge schools of the gelatinous creatures passed by, their pulsing bodies moving them through the water with their long tentacles flowing out behind.

Sumner came to the railing to stand next to her. "What are you looking at?" he said.

"Jellyfish. Masses of them."

Sumner gazed at the schools, saying nothing.

A thought occurred to Emma. She turned toward Hassim. "How will the pirates board us?"

"They use grappling hooks to attach themselves to the ship's side, usually near an existing ladder, but if one is not available, they will place their own after they're sure the skiff is attached."

"So we'll know where they'll be coming over if they do get that close."

Hassim nodded. "Affixing the grappling hooks, attaching a ladder, and climbing up all takes a little time, so yes, you can predict where they will appear."

"Can we collect these jellyfish without killing them? Use a net?"

Hassim strode over to the railing. "Those are box jellyfish. Terribly dangerous. Too many stings—"

"Too many stings and a human will go into a form of anaphylactic shock. It's perfect."

Hassim shook his head. "These fish will not help us. The pirates will board directly from the skiff. They won't go into the water first, so there is no chance that the jellyfish will sting them."

"That's not what I'm thinking. I'm thinking we collect a bunch of these, put them in shallow pans at the top of each stationary ladder. When the pirates swing a leg over to board, they step on the fish and get stung. I'm not suggesting we wait around for this to work, but it will be quick and easy to set up and we have very little to lose."

Hassim frowned in thought. Janklow moved to the railing to check out the jellyfish.

"Jellyfish won't always sting. There's a good chance the majority of them will be too shocked themselves to do any harm to anyone else," Janklow said.

"I would never underestimate the sting of a box jellyfish. People have been stung by fish that have been baking on the sand for hours," Hassim said.

"And if we pour fresh water on them, it may encourage them," Emma said. "Nematocysts fire from all sides if they're hit with water, even dead or dying ones."

Block marched to the ship's rail and looked over. "You sure about that?"

Emma shook her head. "Not entirely. But I'm fairly certain that the tentacle will react to the water with a sting of its own."

Cindy touched Emma's arm. "Let me work on this. I'll ask some crew members to help me net them. The kitchen should have bus pans we can use."

"And could you leave some bottles of water nearby?"

Wainwright emerged from the door that led to the bridge. He looked grim. "They're massing in formation just on the outer fringes of radar. It's as if they're preparing to mount an assault on an aircraft carrier, not on a cruise ship."

Sumner nodded. "I think we need to arm the passengers." Wainwright looked about to interrupt, and Sumner put up a hand. "We can tell them to fight only if threatened by an unarmed man. Warn them to surrender to anyone holding a gun."

Wainwright thought a moment. No one spoke. Stark stood off to the side. Emma noted that he looked as serious as the rest. Wainwright appeared to reach a decision.

"This doesn't feel like an ad hoc attack, it feels like a planned offensive. Let's get all the passengers back into the casino. I still won't arm the passengers, just the cruise-ship employees. I'll have them guard the casino entrance. The repair crew is working on the oil-pressure problem. With any luck we'll regain some mobility."

Emma stared out to sea. Nothing broke the endless blue water except the cresting white tips as the waves undulated. She turned back to analyze the deck, the stairs up to the bridge level, and the control room within. An idea came to her.

"Cindy!"

Cindy stopped and turned, half in, half out of the entrance to the stairs.

"Can you also get me some buckets, a jug of bleach, and a bottle of ammonia?"

Cindy looked perplexed. "Sure, but why?"

"We're going to make a chemical weapon."

Sumner gave Emma a considering look. "Mix them?"

Cindy started, her eyes wide. "You can't mix ammonia and bleach. My mother told me that when I was little. You mix them and you get—"

"Chlorine gas," Emma replied.

"—dead," Cindy said.

"You'll need an enclosed area." Sumner was looking upward, toward the bridge.

Emma pointed to the stairway. "When they board"—she shook her head—"*if* they board, we retreat up that way. They should follow us. We set the bucket at the top. Is there a second exit?"

Sumner nodded. "At the far end of the bridge room. It leads to the ship's interior stairwells."

"Last person in mixes the cleaners, retreats through the stairwell into the bridge, and slams the door behind himself. Or herself."

Sumner turned to Emma. "I'll fill everyone in here about the chlorine idea, but where's Clutch? Could you and Janklow go find him? Maybe do a quick sweep of his room. I'd feel a whole lot better if I knew where he was. I'll take Block, Hassim, and Stark to the bridge to watch for the pirates' approach."

Emma jogged next to Janklow, who moved through the halls with the alacrity of someone familiar with every nook and cranny. They reached Clutch's door five minutes later. Janklow banged on it, and they waited. They were met with silence. Janklow slid a master passkey into the electronic door lock and pushed the handle. The door swung open. They stepped inside.

Light streamed through a porthole, illuminating the small crew quarters, accompanied by the sickly sweet smell of decaying flesh. Clutch lay on the bed, one arm flung outward. His eyes were open, his face immobile in death. In his hand was a white EpiPen.

Janklow jerked backward. "Jesus!" he said.

Emma stepped closer. She peered at two puncture holes in Clutch's arm, right above the wrist. At his feet lay two more open boxes filled with EpiPens. They looked unused.

"He stuck himself, I think," Emma said. "He must have liked the initial dopamine surge and wanted to try it again." She went over to the porthole and closed the covering. The room descended into gloom.

Janklow shook his head. "This is creepy. Let's get out of here. I'll tell Wainwright."

Emma bent down to pick up one of the boxes. "We'll bring these with us. You never know when we may need them."

Janklow took the second. "I hope not. I don't want to get close enough to those guys to be able to use these."

They closed the door and left Clutch there. Emma hoped he was happier in the next life. She also hoped she wouldn't be joining him anytime soon.

MUNGABE SAT IN THE LEAD SKIFF ROARING TOWARD THE *KAISER Franz.* He wanted to show his crew that he was determined to take the ship. While the other attempts had proved futile, this one would succeed. Talek rode with him. He held an RPG that contained a loaded grenade and had a red scarf attached to the tube. He thought the scarf, given to him by a woman three years before, was good luck, and so he carried it everywhere. Abdul and the American Somali made up the rest of the boat.

The tiny craft bounced along the ocean in a constant banging rhythm. Mungabe jumped along with it, keeping his eyes forward. He determined not to show any weakness before his men. He hefted an AK-47 onto his right shoulder, his intention being to kill the sniper who was causing them trouble. Mungabe thought himself a very good shot. No Westerner would beat him. Not when he had a Kalashnikov in his hand.

As they neared the boat, he gazed at it with the pride of someone who already believed he owned it. It was magnificent. Small by oil-tanker standards, but still large enough to be imposing, sleek enough to be elegant. Mungabe could now understand why the Vulture wanted the vessel. But Mungabe had already decided to take it for himself. The Vulture hadn't fulfilled their deal, and so neither would Mungabe. This much he knew.

The ship floated in the ocean, still. Mungabe's men had managed to disable it. It was like the large bulls he had seen on his one visit to

India. They were considered sacred and so had lost any instinct to fight. No longer smart enough to move when something bigger, more ferocious was approaching them, and too stupid to care.

Mungabe gave an order to stop when his men came within four hundred meters of the boat. He wouldn't risk an RPG attack until everything was prepared. He leaned toward Talek.

"Tell the rest to surround it." He watched as his crews separated, forming a circle with the cruise liner in the middle as the target. The satellite phone rang. Mungabe waved an aggravated hand at the device. A crew member grabbed the receiver and handed it to him.

"It's me," the Vulture said. "Do you have control of the ship?"

"Have you destroyed Darkview?"

"Yes."

Mungabe felt his anger erupt. "You lie! I'm taking the ship, the passengers, *and* the poison. If you value your life, you won't come to this part of the world again."

Mungabe heard fast breathing over the line, as if the Vulture were running a race.

"You cross me and you won't live to see the next month," the Vulture warned.

Mungabe laughed. "Come and get me, Vulture. But don't wear those fancy suits when you do, because you had better be prepared to fight." He hung up the phone. He'd deal with the Vulture later.

He waited while his men gained their positions. The large craft hadn't moved.

"Hand me some binoculars," Mungabe said. A crew member dropped a set into his hand. Mungabe peered at the *Kaiser Franz*. There was no movement on any decks. The satellite dish and the spinning dish that operated the radar were gone. They were off the grid, then. He skimmed the glasses over the boat's windows, looking for passengers, crew, anyone. He saw nothing. Talek moved up next to him.

"Where's the crew?" Talek said.

"It's a trick. They're on that boat, you can be sure."

Talek lowered his own binoculars to look at Mungabe. "It's a foolish decision. Better to fight us off with grenades." Talek eyed the ship. "Perhaps they don't have any? It's against the law for such a ship to carry heavy arms."

Mungabe doubted that the ship had no weapons. Darkview fought without honor, ignoring the laws of its country in favor of winning. "Darkview ignores international law whenever they decide to. They have grenades, you can be sure."

"They have never shot them before."

Mungabe pondered that. It was true. In all the prior skirmishes, the cruise liner had yet to fire a grenade. Only the sniper had shot at them. Mungabe shook his head. No, that was wrong. Darkview had grenades. He wouldn't allow them to lure him in with such a trick.

"Are the men in place?"

Talek nodded.

"Then let's move. Tell them we fire the first grenades in unison. After that may the best boat win. The first crew over the side gets a bonus."

Talek grinned. He put his RPG on his shoulder, its red scarf hanging down his back. "That will be me. I could use a bonus."

Mungabe laughed. He picked up the walkie-talkie, depressed the button, and said, "Go!"

EMMA WATCHED THE PIRATES mass around them from her hidden position behind a deck door. There were almost thirty boats, each with a crew of four. She couldn't see the men's faces that clearly through the small crack she allowed herself to peer through, but she didn't have to. That they were vastly outnumbered was apparent. Emma's tiny gun, Sumner's Dragunov, Hassim's RPG and few grenades—these were not going to be enough to win this battle. Emma patted the leg pocket of her cargo pants. She held ten EpiPens. Stark had made it clear that although someone would die from two sticks, it would take too long for death to occur for the pens to be of any help. In fact, Stark thought that using the pens would work against them, due to their tendency to heighten the fight-or-flight response.

"We'll be adding to their rage, not diminishing it" was how Stark put it. Nevertheless, Emma had handed out all the pens from the boxes they found in Clutch's room, with instructions to stick the pirates twice if they could. Likewise, everyone was given a squeeze bottle of fresh water spiked with rubbing alcohol to shoot at the pans of jellyfish or into the eyes of the boarding pirates. Emma's sat on the floor at her feet. Sumner sidled up next to her.

"You okay?" he asked.

"Good as I'll ever be," she said. "I wish I had an RPG instead of a small gun and some pens."

"You think the pens will work?"

Emma nodded. "I do, despite what Stark said."

Sumner nodded. "I'm with you. It's all we've got going for us at the moment."

There was a roar as the assembled boats began their charge.

"Here they come," Sumner said.

53

EMMA WATCHED THE SKIFFS SHOOT TOWARD THEM. SUMNER held the Dragunov, and he stepped out onto the deck as they approached. He waited in the shadow of a small overhang along the wall for the moment that they were close enough to hit. The pirates began their own volleys at three hundred meters away. They fired in unison, launching grenades at the *Kaiser Franz*, aiming high. The luxury boat shook with the force that hammered into it. Explosions rocked the ship, blowing out windows, sending shards of glass catapulting twenty feet into the air, and raining bits of metal and splinters of wood everywhere. Two grenades shot past Emma's hiding place, too high to hit anything. She could smell the sulfuric chemical burning at the rockets' tails as they whizzed by.

Sumner stepped out of the shadow and returned fire. Emma watched the driver in the lead boat drop. From twenty feet to Emma's right came the burst of their own RPG being fired. Hassim held the weapon. Emma could see him standing at the very edge of the deck rail. His back blast nearly scorched a life ring hanging on the wall ten feet behind him. Hassim's grenade traveled straight toward his target like a heat-seeking missile. The first skiff's hull shattered at the prow, sending planks flying upward. The pirates screamed, jumping out of the craft into the water. Emma heard more shouts as the men landed in the jellyfish-infused ocean.

Sumner fired again, but it did little to slow the pirates' progress. They unleashed grenades at the ship in sporadic bursts, and as they neared, their aim sharpened. Most of the ordnance met its target. They were close now. Sumner picked off pirate after pirate, but the sheer number of them ensured that they would succeed in boarding the ship. Emma saw the flash of steel as the first grappling hooks flew over the railing thirty feet to the left of them.

The hooks cued Cindy and Marina, who emerged from their hiding places behind a door. They crouched over as they slid four flat dishpans across the deck. Marina shoved one under the first hook, which had been thrown next to a ladder built into the *Kaiser Franz*'s side. Cindy pushed hers beside it, in line with the first. Three more grappling hooks flew into the air, clattering onto the deck. Cindy yelped when one grazed her shoulder before it fell onto the planking. The metal prongs rattled as they were drawn back. Two fell harmlessly into the water when their hooks failed to grab on to anything. The third caught the base pole of the railing and stuck there. Cindy rammed another pan under the last. Both women scuttled back to the metal door.

The *Kaiser Franz* emitted a huge metallic sound, belched a cloud of oily smoke, and groaned to a start. They were moving. Emma heard muffled cheers from the passengers hiding in the lower decks. The ropes attached to the grappling hooks pulled tight while the boat hauled them along. Sumner moved closer to the railing, firing shot after shot into the attached skiffs. Emma sidled up next to him, removed the safety on her gun, and glanced over the side.

Four skiffs dragged in the cruise liner's wake, each one filled with Somalis. Two aimed assault rifles upward. One fired off a volley at Sumner and Emma. Sumner dove to the deck, but Emma was already as flat as she could get, so she concentrated her attention on the shooter. She responded with her own series of shots, catching the man in the shoulder and causing the others to dive for cover. Empty bullet casings ejected from the pistol's side, flying to the right and landing on the wooden planks with plinking sounds. She held the gun with two hands, as Hassim had taught her, but she still had a difficult time controlling the weapon's recoil.

Six more hooks flew over the railings at various points. Sumner crawled next to her, lay on his belly, and aimed at the men. He started picking them off as they grabbed on to the ladder to haul themselves upward. The vessel's movement served to slow the pirates' momentum, but even so they were climbing fast. The ones using makeshift ladders fell off them when they hitched sideways from the combination of ocean waves and moving target. Emma reloaded with the last of her ammunition. Each shot was going to have to count.

The first group was at the top of the railing, and four swung a leg over to board. Their weapons were slung across their backs, and a quick glance at the first two showed that they wore heavy work boots with thick steel-reinforced soles and long pants. Emma wanted to groan. Although they stepped directly into the dishpans, they didn't react. Even if the tentacles had fired, the men weren't feeling the sting. The first on board managed to stumble over the lip of the pan. He catapulted forward, arms flailing. Emma darted toward him, a pen in her hand. She plunged it into the back of his arm as he fell to the deck.

Emma swung back to watch the other two. One crumpled to the planks from a shot fired by Sumner, while the fourth wasn't quite over the railing. He wore sandals and slammed one foot into a pan. He didn't react but seemed intent on swinging his second leg across the railing. Marina darted from behind a lifeboat. She skidded to a stop four feet from the man, pointed a squeeze bottle at him, and emptied the water into the pan. The man howled, stumbling over the pan's lip and dropping to his knees. Marina spun back to run for cover. There was the sound of a crack, and her body flew forward with the force of the bullet entering it. She slammed face-first onto the deck, and a blooming red stain formed on her shoulder. She lay flat, unmoving.

Emma felt an arm wrap around her throat from behind. The man she'd hit with the pen was choking her. She fought for air as he tightened his sinewy arm on her neck. She could smell his sweat and feel his bicep bulge with his effort. She still held the spent pen in her hand.

She dropped it and scrabbled in her pants pocket to grab another. Her fingers closed on the slim plastic piece and she pulled it out, held it low, and plunged it backward, into the man's thigh, which was the only part of his body she could reach. Seconds later she felt him begin to jerk in a spasm. He kept his arm locked around her throat as his body twitched.

Sumner was up and running toward her, his weapon held in both hands. He swung the butt of the gun high, above Emma's head, aiming for her attacker. She felt a puff of air as the steel whiffed past her hair. The gun hit the pirate with a thudding sound. He collapsed, taking Emma down with him. She untangled herself from his arm and rolled to the edge of the railing to get away.

Her heart plunged as she looked downward. The pirates were swarming over the side of the boat, slamming makeshift ladders against the side to crawl up. One man, still inside a skiff, yelled orders, his face contorted with rage. He held an assault weapon at the ready while his eyes raked the ship—looking for what, Emma didn't know. Sumner moved to stand above her, a foot on either side of her body. He continued to fire at the pirates, but it was only going to be a matter of minutes before they were overwhelmed. The raging man's eyes locked on Sumner. He raised his gun to shoot.

From that moment forward, Emma felt her world switch into slow motion. She hauled the arm that held the pistol out from next to her body, preparing to shoot the raging man. Sumner, too, shouldered his weapon to aim, and the pirates continued to crawl upward. The raging man, Emma, and Sumner fired at the same moment. The raging man went down, a bullet in his heart, and Sumner dropped, landing on Emma.

The weight of his landing on her squeezed all the air out of her lungs. She felt the warm flow of blood ooze onto her cheek. Sumner groaned and stayed still, his body heavy on hers. Emma wanted to scream, but her shock at seeing his blood seemed to freeze her lungs. She twisted to slither out from under him. He moaned again, twitched, and slid off her. She watched him reach for the Dragunov with his left hand. Blood poured from his right arm. A pirate loomed over them both, holding his gun like a baseball bat. Emma rolled onto her back, aimed her revolver, and pulled the trigger.

The gun gave a hollow click, barely audible. Nothing happened. The pirate's eyes, which had widened at the sight of her pistol, narrowed. He flipped his own rifle back into firing position. Emma pulled a pen from her pocket and jammed it into the pirate's foot at the arch. She left it hanging there, grabbed another, and jabbed him again. When she glanced up, she saw that the man was shaking, trembling, his mouth jerking. He still held the gun, but it hung down at his side while his muscles spasmed. His finger was curled over the trigger, and the gun erupted. Bullets hammered into the deck in a crazy pattern all around her. She found her voice and started yelling, pushing herself backward, bumping into Sumner, who still lay behind her, while she used her feet to scuttle across the planks.

Several more pirates appeared at the railing, grasping the horizontal slats and climbing hand over hand.

"Sumner, can you shoot?" Emma threw the question behind her. She felt him move in response.

At that moment Block burst out of a nearby door. He stopped, then aimed and shot a stun gun. Emma watched darts attached to trailing wires zip out of the front and connect with a pirate's chest and shoulder. He yelled and dropped to the deck, writhing. Behind Block came Herr Schullmann and Stark, who wielded a long steel pipe. He stepped up to the men at the railing, pulled back the pipe, and slammed it into the nearest pirate's skull. The man let go, falling backward into the sea. Block fired again, hitting a second pirate who had succeeded in getting one foot over the railing. His eyes rolled up in his head when the electricity entered his body.

Schullmann gazed down the deck, and Emma heard him give an anguished cry when he saw Marina lying on the boards. He ran toward her, ignoring the chaos all around him. A pirate aimed at her from the railing, preparing to shoot her again. Schullmann threw himself toward her as the man fired, and his body jerked when the bullet entered his chest. Block was reloading when more pirates reached the railing. Emma stood up and turned to help Sumner rise. His right arm was slick with blood.

"Go to the bridge deck!" Stark yelled. He kept swinging the pipe, slamming it onto the hands of the pirates as they grabbed at the slats to climb upward. A grenade, fired by Hassim, flew past the railing and exploded when it hit a skiff floating below them. Emma figured he had one warhead left. Hassim disappeared around a corner, heading to the other side of the ship. She could only pray that he didn't meet a new pirate force on that side.

Sumner was up, but he seemed to sway on his feet. Block reached out to grab his elbow and steady him.

"We've got to retreat up the stairs. Emma, you out?" Sumner's voice was strained with pain.

Emma nodded. "Only the pens."

"Then go!"

Sumner placed the Dragunov strap over his head and jogged to Herr Schullmann and Marina. He checked for Schullmann's pulse, then shook his head at Block. Together the men lifted Marina, Block carrying her body while Sumner held her legs. She hung from their grasp, her hair flowing downward.

Emma reached the stairwell door at the same time as Block. Stark was next. She stepped back to allow Sumner and Block to maneuver Marina's body through the doorway. The young woman's face was parchment white and immobile.

Cindy darted in next. "Here." She shoved some pens into Emma's hands.

Emma stepped in the stairway last, swinging the door shut as she did. A pirate's fingers wrapped around the edge. She grabbed the interior handle with both hands, and the two of them engaged in a tug of war, with Emma trying to keep the panel shut and the pirate at-

tempting to yank it open. She let one hand go long enough to slam a
pen into his index finger so deep that she felt it rattle against bone. He
let go. She closed the door.

The stairwell felt cool and dark after the heat from the decks, and
the sounds were muted. She scurried to the top of the stairs, where
their first two buckets sat on the landing. She took a deep breath and
held it as she dumped the first bucket's contents into the second. The
door opened, and sunlight flooded into the stairwell. The Somalis
flowed into the narrow passageway. Emma hurled the empty pail at
the men charging up the stairs. She didn't stay to watch but ducked
through the door leading to the bridge, closing and locking it behind her.

Every window in the bridge was shattered, but only two had actual
holes in them. The remaining sections were cracked in a crazy splintered pattern, like the windshield of a car. The panels with the holes
were opposite each other, as if a grenade had passed straight through.
Block and the others were already across the room and out the other
side. A long smear of blood left a trail on the floor. Emma wondered
if Sumner had taken a bullet in a major vessel and was bleeding out.

She jogged across to the second set of buckets. At five feet away,
a wave of toxic air washed over her. The others must have already
mixed the gas. The door behind her burst open, and several men
staggered into the room, bringing with them a second wave of nox-
ious fumes. One dropped to his knees and started vomiting. His gun
skittered across the floor toward Emma. The others gasped in huge
gulps.

Emma reached for the door, but before she got there, the fumes
overwhelmed her. Her eyes burned, and each time she inhaled, it felt
as though she were pulling fire through her throat. Her vision dis-
torted and her ears rang. The door appeared to undulate, making it
difficult for her to locate the handle to open it. She dropped to one
knee, doing her best to concentrate on the doorknob. She held her
breath and grabbed it. The cold metal seemed to be the only stable

object in the room. She turned it and threw herself past the opening. She lay there, half in and half out, and gasped in another breath of the gas, which seared her throat. She felt her stomach start to dry-heave, and she closed her eyes. Suddenly a hand wrapped around her wrist and someone dragged her on her back across the floor. She opened her eyes. Sumner's face ebbed and flowed in front of her as he pulled her the rest of the way out of the bridge. Blood covered his torso, and she saw that his arm still bled. His face was sheet white, but his eyes shone with determination.

He hauled her to a landing and started upward, pulling her with him. Her spine bumped over each stair, and she was relieved when he reached the highest level. He pulled her into the sunlight and let go. Her arm flopped onto the boards, and she lay there gasping, with her head turned to avoid the sunlight. Spent ordnance was scattered all around her. She watched Sumner crouch down and crab-walk to the edge of the deck. He flattened onto his stomach beside a steel upright, which was all that remained of the railing. Emma crawled next to him and looked down.

A skiff floated directly below them, surrounded by the jellyfish bloom. In it were Abdul, the American soldier, and a man with angry eyes and the attitude of a commander. He spoke, and the others appeared to jump in response. Emma wondered if he was this Mungabe that she'd heard about. Next to him was a pirate holding an RPG with a piece of red-colored cloth attached to it. These three watched as their comrades climbed a ladder attached to the cruise ship.

The blaring of a huge bullhorn overlay the din of gunfire. It bellowed in short blasts. The third held fast, reverberating through the air in one long howl. A massive warship boiled toward them, less than a half mile away. Following the warning blast came the distinctive *chop-chop* sound of helicopter rotors firing up. A copter rose lazily into the air.

"It's the *Redoubtable*," Sumner said.

The pirates who remained on the ladders all leaped away from the

Kaiser Franz. Some fell onto the skiff, but others landed in the water around it. One man whimpered in panic while he splashed at the jellyfish all around him. The man with the angry eyes yelled at them, waving toward the cruise liner, as if exhorting them to return. Abdul, the American soldier, and the pirate with the RPG and the red scarf yelled as well, but the men surrounded the skiff, trying to pull themselves onto it. The one Emma thought of as Mungabe took out a pistol and shot the first two over the side. Their bodies fell backward into the waves.

Sumner shoved the Dragunov at her.

"Shoot it. I can't. My arm isn't functioning." Sumner's voice was thin. "We only have eight bullets left, so keep it on semi."

"I'll miss on semi," Emma said.

"The switch is near the trigger. I'll help you aim."

Emma took the gun and pointed it at Mungabe. She felt Sumner stretch out next to her, leaning onto her side to steady her. He wrapped his right arm around her body but hissed in pain with the motion.

"Aim at the widest part of him. Take a deep breath and then hold it while you depress the trigger."

Emma closed one eye and sighted Mungabe through the scope. He was a continually moving target as he braced himself against the motion of the little boat on the ocean's waves. He glared at the men all around him in the water before looking up.

Emma took a deep breath, held it, and depressed the trigger. The gun bucked, and she watched Mungabe scream in anger. The bullet missed him completely. He raised his own rifle and fired. Sumner moved his entire torso onto her, sheltering her with his body as the bullets rattled into the side of the ship. Two ricocheted off the upright railing.

"Screw it," Emma said. "I'm switching to auto. Help me hold it in place."

She flipped the switch to auto. She didn't bother to hold her breath, didn't bother to sight him—she just pointed in his general direction and squeezed the trigger. The gun rattled in response, bucking and shivering against her as it let loose a volley of bullets. Sumner wrapped his hand around the butt, helping her hold it steady. She moved the weapon back and forth in a sweeping motion. Abdul dropped—if from a bullet, she didn't know—and the American Somali followed. Within seconds the gun was empty.

Mungabe stood on the boat's edge firing back at her, oblivious to the danger. Then, abruptly, he paused and watched. After a moment a grin creased his face. He reached for the rope that attached his skiff to the cruise liner and pulled closer. He placed a hand on the ladder and started his ascent.

"He knows we're out," Sumner said.

Emma could barely hear him, his voice was so weak. She slid out from under his body.

"Don't move. I'll be right back." She crab-walked back to the stairwell entrance, took a deep breath, and stepped inside.

Pirates lay all around, their bodies draped at various locations in the stairwell. Emma picked her way over them, noting that most were breathing, albeit in short, shallow gasps. She pushed the door open to the bridge. Here the pirates were more alert. Some coughed, while others hung their heads outside a window that had been smashed. They'd managed to get enough fresh air circulating to retain consciousness. Still, none paid her any attention as she sidled in and grabbed the bucket's handle. She worked her way back up the stairs and onto the deck. Sumner hadn't moved. She swallowed her fear and focused on inching her way to the edge.

Mungabe had reached the railing on the deck below. His head was down while he concentrated on climbing the ladder. Emma hovered over him.

"Mungabe!" Emma prayed that she was right and the man climbing the ladder was indeed the pirate leader.

He looked up.

She threw the mixture.

The stream hit him slightly off center, landing on his shoulders but still managing to splash onto his face. He let out an ear-piercing howl. He made a grab at his eyes and fell backward, into the ocean. When his head reemerged, Emma saw him desperately splashing the water into his eyes.

She watched the massing jellyfish bloom encircle him. His frantic movements triggered their instincts to sting. His howls reached a fever pitch as the creatures stung him. He thrashed once before disappearing under the water.

The *Redoubtable*'s horn blared again. The pirates who were left in the remaining small craft unwound the ropes that attached them to the cruise liner, tossing them off. They revved their engines and retreated, leaving their remaining crew members in the water to their own fates. Only Mungabe's boat was left. No movement came from it.

Sumner lay on the deck, his eyes closed. The stark look to his skin told her that he was still losing blood from the wound. She inched next to him.

"Sumner?"

He didn't respond. Emma checked for a pulse. She started to cry when she found one, thin but steady. A shadow fell across them. She looked up to see Block standing over her.

"Oh, God, tell me he ain't dead."

Emma shook her head, unable to speak.

Block squatted down next to her. "Marina's bad. Bullet real close to her heart. Cindy's holding a wadded piece of cloth against the wound, but we need to get these two onto that carrier and to a medic."

Emma heard the sound of the first helicopter lowering onto the pool deck. Block shielded his eyes to watch it land.

"Here come the reinforcements," he said.

54

BANNER STOOD NEXT TO THE *REDOUBTABLE'S* MEDIC AS HE
worked on irrigating Sumner's gunshot wound.

"The wound isn't bad, but he's lost a ton of blood and taken a hell
of a hit on his head," the medic said.

Banner nodded. Sumner still hadn't regained consciousness after
they'd boarded the *Kaiser Franz*, and now he wouldn't. The medic
had knocked him out with pain pills. Sumner lay on the gurney, looking like death.

Emma stood on the other side of Sumner, watching. Banner
thought she looked pale but remarkably good, considering her ordeal.

"What will happen to Stark?" she asked.

Banner sighed. "Hard to say. He has an excellent defense, due to
the fact that he notified the authorities about the theft."

"Has he said who the financier was that propped up Price?"

Banner shook his head. "He says he'll take the Fifth if asked. He
seems to think he'll be putting his life in danger if he speaks."

Emma nodded, but Banner thought she didn't look too concerned
about the possibility.

There was a knock at the door. A man stuck his head in. "Ms.
Caldridge? Someone has asked to speak with you."

Emma stepped into the hall.

Stark stood there.

"What do you want?" Emma said.

"I wanted to see if he's okay."

Emma sighed. "The doctor thinks he'll heal."

Stark ran a hand through his hair. "I also wanted to tell you I'm sorry. For everything. I should have spoken up when I realized someone was testing the drug illegally. I was a fool."

Emma didn't reply. People were dead because of him. When she remained quiet, Stark started again.

"I've resigned. I quit."

Emma wasn't impressed, and she let him see that she wasn't.

"I want you to know that I've decided to make some changes."

Emma said nothing.

"May I call you sometime?"

"No."

He heaved a sigh. Emma turned to walk back into the infirmary.

"Emma?"

She stopped.

"I want to be the type of man someone would trust with their life."

Emma went back through the door to two such men.

EMMA STRETCHED AWAKE. She sat in a large armchair placed next to Sumner's bed. She checked her watch by the light of a small reading lamp on the nightstand. It was five o'clock in the morning. She glanced up. Sumner's eyes were open, and he watched her in silence.

"When did you wake up?" Emma spoke in a whisper.

"Ten minutes ago."

"How do you feel?"

He grimaced. "Like a hatchet's been inserted into my brain."

Emma smiled.

"Did everyone make it?"

"Everyone except Herr Schullmann. Hassim's fine. Not a scratch on him. Marina's not so fine. They patched her up as best they could and are flying her to a real hospital. Doctor says she's critical."

"Does she know about her father?"

Emma shook her head. "I don't think so. She wasn't conscious. They'll probably hold that information until she's better. And Block asked me to keep this near you." She bent to the floor and slid the Dragunov out from under the bed. She showed it to him. She was glad to see Sumner smile. "He and Cindy said they'll stop by later."

Sumner shifted. "I'm very, very happy to see you."

"I think you already told me that on the cruise ship."

He nodded. "Well, I'm saying it again."

"We have to stop meeting like this," Emma said, trying to lighten the moment. She was suddenly nervous about the direction the conversation was taking.

He moved to shake his head but hissed in pain. He gave a weak wave of the hand. "I agree. I promise to make it better next time."

She raised an eyebrow. "Oh, really? How?"

"I'm going to teach you how to shoot a rifle."

Emma laughed.

AUTHOR'S NOTE

Little did I know when creating this story that the Somali pirates would explode into the news. Books are written long before they are printed and sold, and this one is no different. When I began with the concept of pirates attacking a cruise ship, no one really thought such an event could occur. The people at Morrow responded with a polite "Pirates? Like Jack Sparrow?," but to their credit, gave me the green light anyway.

Many thanks to Commodore Ronald Warwick, master of the *Queen Mary 2* for more than thirty years. His son, Samuel Warwick, put us in touch, and Commodore Warwick graciously agreed to answer some questions. I appreciated his suggestions about crew size, ship maintenance, and his comment that while turning off the lights and radar to begin "running dark" (my term) is illegal, he doubted anyone would fault the captain in the instance of an attack. Any mistakes are mine.

I also wish to thank Paul Salopek, a Pulitzer Prize–winning journalist who helped me with information about Somalia. Mr. Salopek wrote an article on the subject for the *Chicago Tribune*, though Somalia is only one of the more dangerous places that he has traveled to and reported from. He answered my questions about khat, Somalia, and Somali fishermen as pirates quickly and from God knows where. Wherever you are, Mr. Salopek, be safe.

The jellyfish bloom idea came from my own experience encountering one and the subsequent research that I did regarding the phenomenon. Thanks to Dr. Jennifer E. Purcell, marine scientist and adjunct professor at Western Washington University, for her input, especially regarding the fact that even dried jellyfish tentacles will fire.

Certain types of jellyfish are among the most dangerous creatures on earth, and although box jellyfish are not commonly found in the Indian Ocean, they are migrating more as the pollution in our seas force the blooms to grow and move.

Wilson Vanderlock is a fictional character, but the khat flights from Kenya to Somalia are real and some do take passengers along for a nominal fee. Khat is legal throughout most of Africa, but Somalia's fields were burned during the wars that raged there. They are forced to import it daily as described.

The drug injected into Emma and others in the book is a fictional compound, but I got the idea from two separate drugs that can both increase endurance and create addictions. Neither drug, however, will kill on the second injection.

One drug is called a dopamine agonist and is used for Parkinson's sufferers. Dopamine agonists sometimes have the unfortunate side effect of creating addictions in people who have had none before. I found the idea of turning on an addiction to be fascinating and wanted to explore what would happen to people in positions of power when such a side effect occurred.

The endurance pill also exists, although it's currently investigational. The compound, called AICAR, can increase endurance by a whopping forty-four percent with a single dose. I loved the whole idea of getting such a huge boost while doing nothing—who wouldn't? To my knowledge the endurance drug hasn't been approved for use as yet, so I guess we're all still stuck training to increase ours. I'll be running on Chicago's lakefront and in whatever city or town I travel to, and I look forward to seeing you there!